Rain

A Song for All and None

ADOYO

ZAMANI CHRONICLES
www.zamanichronicles.org

Zamani Chronicles supports the right to free expression and the value of copyright. The purpose of the copyright is to encourage writers, artists, and storytellers to produce culturally enriching creative works.

Zamani Chronicles
storytellers@zamanichronicles.org
www.zamanichronicles.org

Library of Congress Cataloging-in-Publication Data

Name: Adoyo, author
Title: Rain - A Song for All and None / Adoyo
Description: First edition (xiii) Zamani Chronicles, 2020

Identifiers:
LCCN: 2020905128 (print)

ISBN 978-1-7347591-0-5 (hardcover)
ISBN 978-1-7347591-1-2 (paperback)
ISBN 978-1-7347591-2-9 (eBook)
ISBN 978-1-7347591-3-6 (audiobook)

Key words: speculative historical fiction; visionary; metaphysical; folklore; mythology; African Literature; Luo; Great Lake; Nam Lolwe; Rift Valley; savanna; East Africa; Nile; Mombasa; Age of Discovery; colonial empires; Dante; Commedia

Cover and Interior design: Adoyo
Manufactured in the United States of America

Dedication

To

my great-grandmother,

Rebecca Apiyo Nyonditi Nyariba

Atiga ng'ute bor Nyodongo,

Ruba

Table of Contents

Dedication .... *iii*
JokOlóo and JokOmolo Partial Family Tree .... *xii*
Radial Timeline, 1845 to Present .... *xiv*
The Sieges of Mombasa & Fort Jesus
1498 to 2011 .... *xvi*
Glossary of Place Names .... *xviii*
Epigraph .... *xix*

Book I. Olóo *1*

    Canto One *3*
    Canto Two *4*
    Canto Three *10*
    Canto Four *15*
    Canto Five *22*
    Canto Six *28*
    Canto Seven *32*

Book II. Akoth *35*

    Canto Eight *37*
    Canto Nine *41*
    Canto Ten *45*
    Canto Eleven *50*
    Canto Twelve *57*
    Canto Thirteen *61*
    Canto Fourteen *64*

Book III. Alex and Maya *71*

    Canto Fifteen *73*
    Canto Sixteen *78*
    Canto Seventeen *80*
    Canto Eighteen *83*
    Canto Nineteen *89*
    Canto Twenty *93*
    Canto Twenty-one *97*

Book IV. Rosie ran away...107

    Canto Twenty-two...109
    Canto Twenty-three...116
    Canto Twenty-four...121
    Canto Twenty-five..126
    Canto Twenty-six...128
    Canto Twenty-seven..131
    Canto Twenty-eight...135

Book V. Rain..141

    Canto Twenty-nine..143
    Canto Thirty..144
    Canto Thirty-one...149
    Canto Thirty-two...151
    Canto Thirty-three...155
    Canto Thirty-four...160
    Canto Thirty-five...167

Book VI. The Blood of Anatole Basile Tejo.................177

    Canto Thirty-six..179
    Canto Thirty-seven..182
    Canto Thirty-eight...192
    Canto Thirty-nine..199
    Canto Forty...203
    Canto Forty-one..208
    Canto Forty-two..215

Book VII. The Siege of Mombasa..................................223

    Canto Forty-three..225
    Canto Forty-four..227
    Canto Forty-five..233
    Canto Forty-six..242
    Canto Forty-seven...244
    Canto Forty-eight..249
    Canto Forty-nine...256

Book VIII. Snow..267

    Canto Fifty..269
    Canto Fifty-one..275
    Canto Fifty-two..279
    Canto Fifty-three 283
    Canto Fifty-four...294
    Canto Fifty-five..298
    Canto Fifty-six 302

Book IX. Hehra 311

    Canto Fifty-seven 313
    Canto Fifty-eight..326
    Canto Fifty-nine...330
    Canto Sixty 334
    Canto Sixty-one 339
    Canto Sixty-two 343
    Canto Sixty-three...350

Acknowledgments 365

    Afterword 367
    A Moment of Gratitude..374
    The Story 376
    The Storyteller 377

A Note to the Reader

Dear Reader, *Rain – A Song for All and None* is a poetic meditation on History through the echoes of Oral Tradition. The story you will find in this volume is inspired by the song of storytellers born on the shores of Nam Lolwe, also called Nam Ataro, the Great Lake at the eye of the Nile in the heart of East Africa. Flowing into the main current of the storyteller's voice are also those of a number of poets and other storytellers who lend their distinct accents to a collective chorus, each sounding sometimes in harmony, sometimes in counterpoint, and other times still in dissonance with one another.

Details of some of these distinct voices, the most significant one of which is Dante's *Commedia*, are outlined in the Afterword at the end of this volume. Other voices cited in the Afterword include a number of different versions of the Bible, the Papal Bulls undergirding the policy and practice of seizure and occupation at the heart of the Doctrine of Discovery, as well as the historical accounts by 15th-century Portuguese chroniclers of Vasco da Gama's first and second voyages around Africa and onto India. The contributions of all these varied sources have here been woven together into a contemplative interrogation of the nature of History, especially as viewed through living memory unbound from the shackles of curated time. The volume also includes a schematic family tree spanning six generations of the family at the center of *Rain*, a radial timeline of those six generations, a five-century outline of the occupation of Mombasa and of Fort Jesus, and a concise glossary of the pre-colonial names of key lakes, rivers and mountains that appear in *Rain*, especially in Book V.

Rain

In the tradition of Luo storytelling, *Rain*'s epigraph opens with an invocation to a past immemorial:

* *"Chon, chon gilala..."*
["A long, long time ago..."],

and the story closes on a note of hope for the future:

"Atho tinda! Adong' adong', arom gi bawo maka nera."
["Here I end my song. May I live to grow as tall as my uncle's trees."]

And so I invite you, intrepid Reader, to receive the volume before you with the expansive kindness you would extend to a novel, and the contemplative reflection you would afford a poem. To facilitate your journey through the temporally volatile world of the Dream Walker, you will find a brief sketch of the contents of each of the nine Books of *Rain* on the reverse side of each title page. May you enjoy the melody, counterpoint, and rhythms of this story and discover in *Rain* a song for all and none.

—Adoyo, MMXX

Orientation

- JokOlóo and JokOmolo Partial Family Tree
- Radial Timeline, 1845 to Present
- The Sieges of Mombasa and Fort Jesus, 1498 to 2011
- Glossary of Place Names

JokOlóo and JokOmolo Partial Family Tree

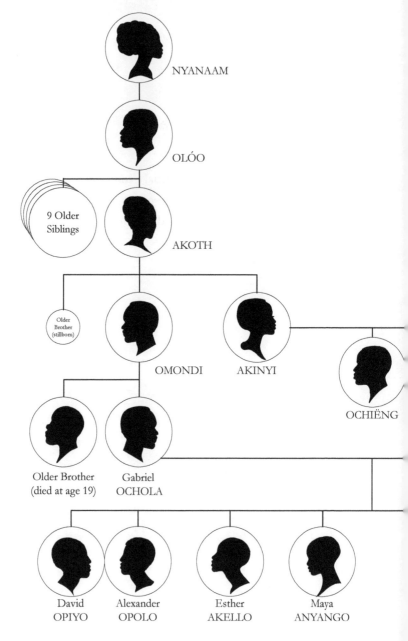

NYANAAM

OLÓO

9 Older Siblings

AKOTH

Older Brother (stillborn)

OMONDI

AKINYI

OCHIËNG

Older Brother (died at age 19)

Gabriel OCHOLA

David OPIYO

Alexander OPOLO

Esther AKELLO

Maya ANYANGO

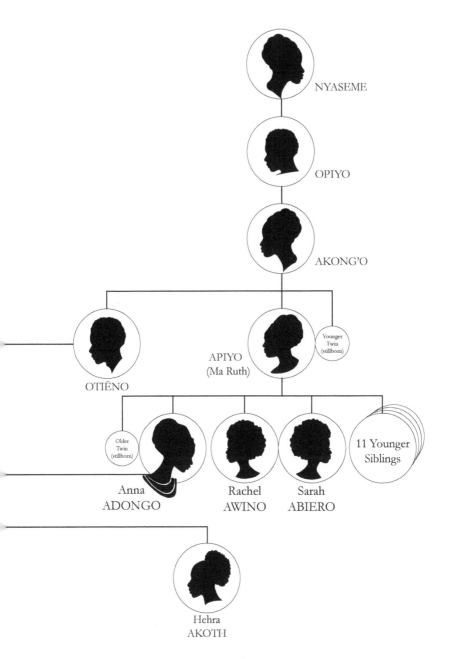

NYASEME

OPIYO

AKONG'O

APIYO
(Ma Ruth)

Younger
Twin
(stillborn)

OTIËNO

Older
Twin
(stillborn)

Anna
ADONGO

Rachel
AWINO

Sarah
ABIERO

11 Younger
Siblings

Hehra
AKOTH

Radial Timeline, 1845 to Present

A: Nyanaam
B: Olóo
C: Akoth
D: Omondi
E: Anatole Basile Tejo
F: Ma Ruth
G: Ochiëng
H: Gabriel
J: Anna

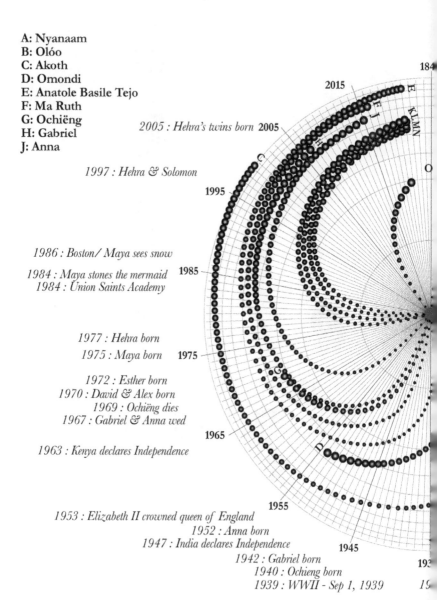

2005 : Hehra's twins born 2005

1997 : Hehra & Solomon

1995

1986 : Boston/ Maya sees snow

1984 : Maya stones the mermaid 1985
1984 : Union Saints Academy

1977 : Hehra born
1975 : Maya born 1975

1972 : Esther born
1970 : David & Alex born
1969 : Ochiëng dies
1967 : Gabriel & Anna wed

1965

1963 : Kenya declares Independence

1955

1953 : Elizabeth II crowned queen of England
1952 : Anna born
1947 : India declares Independence
1945
1942 : Gabriel born
1940 : Ochieng born
1939 : WWII - Sep 1, 1939

2015

2015

184

193

19

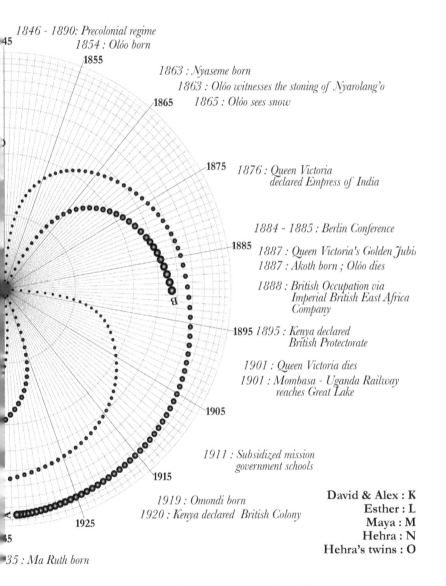

1846 - 1890: Precolonial regime
45   1854 : Olóo born
        1855

        1863 : Nyaseme born
            1863 : Olóo witnesses the stoning of Nyarolang'o
        1865   1865 : Olóo sees snow

                1875   1876 : Queen Victoria
                            declared Empress of India

                    1884 - 1885 : Berlin Conference
                1885   1887 : Queen Victoria's Golden Jubii
                        1887 : Akoth born ; Olóo dies

                        1888 : British Occupation via
                            Imperial British East Africa
                            Company

                1895 1895 : Kenya declared
                        British Protectorate

                    1901 : Queen Victoria dies
                    1901 : Mombasa - Uganda Railway
                        reaches Great Lake

                1905

                1911 : Subsidized mission
                    government schools

        1915   David & Alex : K
            1919 : Omondi born   Esther : L
            1920 : Kenya declared British Colony   Maya : M
        1925   Hehra : N
5   Hehra's twins : O

35 : Ma Ruth born

visit www.zamanichronicles.org

xv

The Sieges of Mombasa & Fort Jesus

1498 to 2011

1498 Saturday, April 7, 1498 (eve of Palm Sunday), Vasco da Gama casts anchor off Mombasa, but does not enter the port.

Saturday, April 14, 1498 (eve of Easter Sunday), Vasco da Gama casts anchor off Malindi and searches for a local pilot to guide him to India. The Portuguese enjoy the hospitality of the city for nine days before setting off for India.

1589 Turks build a small fort at Mombasa.

1593 Portuguese pull out of Malindi. Under the reign of the Habsburg King Phillip II (of Spain and Portugal), the Portuguese begin erecting the Fortaleza de Jesus (Fort Jesus) (1593) in Mombasa. Designed by Italian Milanese architect Giovanni Battista Cairati, the fort is erected using the construction techniques, materials, and labor of the local Swahili builders.

11 Apr. 1593 – 15 Aug. 1631

Portuguese garrisons occupy Fort Jesus.

16 Aug. 1631 – 16 May 1632

Sultan of Mombasa stabs Portuguese captain; occupies Fort.

16 May 1632 – 5 Aug. 1632 Fort abandoned.

5 Aug 1632 – 13 Dec. 1698

Portuguese move into abandoned Fort Jesus and settle in.

1632 Sultan of Oman attempts to mount an attack but his nerve fails and he quits, leaving the Portuguese to occupy Fort Jesus.

1661 Sultan of Oman sacks Mombasa, but does not attack Fort Jesus.

1696 Sultan of Oman lays siege to Fort Jesus.

1697 Portuguese in the Fort die from starvation and plague.

13 Dec. 1698 – Mar. 1728

Fort falls to Omani Arabs after 33-month siege.

16 Mar. 1728 – 26 Nov. 1729

Garrison mutinies against Arabs; Portuguese re-occupy Fort.

Nov. 1729 – 1741

Omani Arabs retake Fort; Portuguese leave the Fort for good.

1741 Omani governor of the Fort, al-Mazrui, declares independence.

1746 Al-Mazrui murdered by Omani; his brother kills the assassin & becomes governor.

1824 – 1826 Al-Mazrui governor seeks and gets British protection.

1826 British withdraw protection.

1828 Sultan of Oman & Zanzibar (Seyyid Said) regains Fort Jesus.

1833 Al-Mazrui forces in Fort withstand bombardment by Sultan.

1837 The last Al-Mazrui governor submits to Sultan.

1837 – 1856 Sultan of Oman holds Fort Jesus.

1856 – 1895 Sultan of Zanzibar holds Mombasa and the Fort.

1875 Fort Jesus bombarded by British ships to quell Al-Akida mutiny.

1895 Fort Jesus used as a government prison until 1958.

1895 – 1963 British colonial occupation.

1958 Fort Jesus declared a National Park.

1960 Fort Jesus opened to the public.

1970 Fort Jesus declared a National Monument.

1993 Fort Jesus celebrates 400-year anniversary.

2011 Fort Jesus declared a World Heritage Site by UNESCO.

SOURCES

Alvaro Velho and João de Sá. *A Journal of the First Voyage of Vasco da Gama*, 1497-1499. Translated by E. G. Ravenstein.

UNESCO Word Heritage Site, Nomination for Inscription.

Glossary of Place Names

Nam Lolwe

> The Lake of Lolwe (also known more recently as *Lake Victoria*)

Nam Ataro

> Familiar Luo name for Nam Lolwe signifying "The Great Lake"

Mount Kenya

> Name of the snow-capped equatorial mountain derived from the Kamba people's description of the summit as "kiima kya kenia," signifying "glimmering peaks"

The Mountain of God's Repose

> Colloquial reference to the various names for *Mount Kenya* used among the cultural groups who settled at the foothills of the equatorial mountain

Chiang Jiang

> the longest river in Asia (also known as the *Yangtze River*)

Wimihsoorita

> the longest river in North America (also known more recently as the *Missouri River*)

Great River

> Translated name of the companion river to the longest river in North America (also known more recently as the *Mississippi River*)

Tongala

> the longest river in Australia (also known more recently as the *Murray River*)

Multi-Continental

Epigraph

*Chon, chon gilala...

"Until the lions have their own historians, the history of the hunt will always glorify the hunter."

Chinua Achebe, *Paris Review*, (Issue 33, Winter 1994)

~ ✳ ~

"I am about to sing a song that I know. Before I begin, my imagination encompasses the whole song, but once I have begun, as much of it as becomes past while I sing is laid out in my memory. My activity hovers between my memory, where what I have sung goes to settle, and my expectation, where what I am about to sing awaits. Yet my imagination is continually present, and through it what was future and waiting is carried over so that it becomes past. The more I continue to do this, the more my memory grows — and my expectation diminishes — until what awaited is exhausted. Then the whole song ends and passes into memory. And what transpires as I sing the song happens also in each individual part of it, and in each individual note. This also holds true of the moments of greater duration of which the song is only a portion. The same also holds in the whole life of humanity, of which all the actions of people are but small parts. And the same holds in the whole age of the children of humanity, of which all the lives of individual human beings are but small parts."

Augustine, *Confessions* XI.28.38
(translated by Albert Outler, adapted by Adoyo)

Book I. Olóo

Where Maya finds herself adrift on the waters of Nam Lolwe unable to make her compass work. • She travels to Lisbon with Alex to visit the Monument of Discoveries and to see the memorial tombs of Vasco da Gama and Luís Vaz de Camões at the Cathedral of Santa Maria de Belém. • Back at home, Alex teaches Maya how to navigate the world. • On Nam Ataro, Mamma Akoth sings the Song of Becoming that shows Maya the story of creation and quickens a waking dream that opens the door to Time.

Canto One

The needle lay tremulously hovering over the compass rose, pointing at Maya's chest, even though she was facing North, holding the instrument parallel to the water below, the right side of her body – face, arm, leg – all awash in a cascade of the equatorial Sun's morning rays. The cardinal points of the compass, carved into the brass an eternity before she was born, are impossibly delicate and she wonders absently how human hands could etch with such subtle grace. Eight overlapping spearhead arrows radiate from the center of the rose, the clear half of each arrow polished smooth, the adorned half pierced and engraved from base to point, ornate with minute paisley curls, vines, mountain juniper berries, cones, and leaves. In the quadrants of the turntable between the cardinal compass points, gossamer strokes unveil billowing clouds with wide open eyes, frowning eyes, laughing eyes, full round cheeks and lips pursed, all blowing relentless winds into turgid sails of hardy ships on open seas where whales' tails skim the surface and tentacles from the deep curl above the water, then sink down below, swooping upwards and outwards, before tapering off where they just brush the edge of the eastern point shielding part of the sun. Maya watches the patterns under the rose, listening to the brassy sunlight bounce into the carved metal, tinsel shreds of Chiëng's halo floating on the water all around, glinting, shimmering, almost chiming in their muted collision with the surface of the lake. Nearby, a family of hippos ambles along, the smallest calf trotting behind his mother's stately gait. A red-breasted gonolek whistles, punctuating the air, and a herd of lake-island elephants emerges from the bush to wade into the shore, sacred ibis and cattle egrets alighting on their backs. The crystalline waters of Nam Lolwe glimmer gently, blending sun and sound around Maya's drifting vessel at the center of the Earth.

~~~~~~~~~~~~~~~

Canto Two

"Maya! Hurry!"

Maya raised an arm over her eyes, squinting against the sunlight bouncing off the white limestone of the pavement mosaic's oceans and compass rose bed. Where had the water gone? Mamma Akoth was singing. What had happened to her raft? Maya's feet were anchored on a stone map at the mouth of the Nile where its waters emptied into the Mediterranean. She could see the expanse of Africa more clearly, as if aloft. Now she could trace the river to its source where her great-great-grandfather Olóo first drew breath. Three or four steps would get her there, across the Egyptian sands and Sudanese Sahara, through thickening forests toward home. Where was her raft? Was that the waking dream, or was this? Maya blinked into the sun, then turned to look around, getting her bearings.

The lake water was gone, turned to stone at her feet. The world lay before her, framed in a wind rose of black, red and beige marble, decorating the ground behind the carved stone crowd of earnest navigators, missionaries, monarchs, artists, scientists, explorers, and cartographers all gazing out across the waters of the River Tagus, their backs turned to the scattering of tourists whose presence at the Monument of Discoveries pays living tribute to feats of heedless obtrusions into the homes of unsuspecting peoples across the world. To Alex, these stone figures, acolytes of the revered Infante Dom

Henrique, were all paragons of the Age of Exploration. Among them, Vasco da Gama was his peerless hero. Maya's squinting gaze settled momentarily on the surging prow of the giant cement caravel on which the straining statues stood. She turned around again to find Alex who still beckoned her from the opposite direction beyond the Arctic. He was hurrying toward her, calling, eyes glowing with joyful urgency; he had found something that he wanted his little sister to see. The sun's rays seemed to soak through his shadowless form as he grew closer. Maya remained still a while longer, disoriented and unprepared to move. She drew a deep breath. Impalpable vapors redolent with mold filled the air; the unmistakable air of Lisbon.

Now she remembered visiting the tomb of Vasco da Gama, the stone sculpture where Alex said the Admiral's bones lay in rest. Now she remembered the Cathedral of Santa Maria de Belém, and the Mosteiro dos Jeronimos. She remembered Alex talking for weeks of nothing but the commander of the São Gabriel, *o peito ilustre Lusitano, a quem Neptuno e Marte obedeceram*, strains of Camões weaving in and out of his extravagant panegyric, melding the poet's voice and the boy's voice in a history that made the visit to his memorial tomb inevitable. The mariner's marble figure, draped in petrified silks and velvet, pious eternity veiling his closed eyes and clasping his praying hands, lay supine just above the visitor's line of sight on an ornate platform bearing emblems of his creed and trade: an armillary sphere, a carrack in full sail, and the square cross of the Military Order of Christ, sanctuary to the persecuted Knights Templar under the protection of Portugal's Poet King. Subdued sunlight illuminates the mariner's reposing statue, softening in the folds of his robes, in the opulence of his beard. Favored by Fortune to be forever celebrated by touring shutterbugs, Vasco da Gama lies immobile in prayer, his work in the world complete, his soul at rest in peace.

On the other side of the cathedral across the aisle, dormant in his own quietude, the poet Luís Vaz de Camões, — the Lusitanian singer of arms and knights, of Mombasa, Malindi, and Zanzibar, Calecut, and Cananore, whose quill paints da Gama's voyages to those corners of the world as the most noble, divinely decreed performance of Lusitanian valor — also lies in eternal repose, palms touching and pointing heavenward. A child could be forgiven for thinking him the soldier and sailor, believing da Gama the writer of verse. For where da Gama is draped in sumptuous robes, his head covered in velvet, Camões, stockinged legs notwithstanding, carries a sword even in stasis, his head bare, and his wounded, hollow eye winking at the heavens. Soldier though he had been, it is as poet that he makes his mark on the world, his song of da Gama's illustrious Lusitanian breast — whose will even Neptune and Mars obeyed — echoing in Maya's ear as if rising from the muffled shuffle of seeking, wondering, tired, curious, lost pilgrim tourists streaming by his limestone feet. Maya shuffles along the circling stream, trying to eavesdrop on a German tour guide who is herding a group into the church towards the sleeping poet across the aisle.

Alex's voice, reverently hushed, rose through Maya's contemplative fog, intoning, as he had countless times, *o peito ilustre Lusitano, a quem Neptuno e Marte obedeceram…*

"How often do they replace this stone?" Maya muttered, her outstretched fingers grazing over the carved tassels on Vasco da Gama's limestone pillow. "It looks pretty good – almost new. It can't be more than a hundred years old. There's hardly any…"

"Replace it? Are you joking?" Alex feigned outrage.

"Listen, before you even say another word," Maya interrupted, "just remember the astronaut in Salamanca." Her face shone mischievously.

The memory of red limestone crumbling around the base of the outer wall of the cathedral in Salamanca filled her mind's eye, the distinct miniature of a man clad in a space suit jutting out of a pillar carved into the wall just above her line of sight. When she first noticed the figure alongside the host of saints and other heavenly creatures assembled to welcome visitors to the hallowed halls of the church, Maya thought amusedly that with enough ingenuity and the proper attire, even mere mortals could assail the Gates of Heaven.

"Yes. But that was Spain. This is Portugal. There's just no comparison," Alex replied, preening, and forcing attention back to his hero. "The Portuguese were the originators, the trailblazers, the ones who led the way to discovery and expansion!"

A shadow passed over Maya's eyes as he spoke, her mind suddenly shifting to a place where he could not follow. He recognized that inscrutable look. Even after so many years by her side, he still could not enter that place to see the world as she did.

Maya was trying to keep her attention on Alex, but that silence that sometimes rose up within her muted his words. Her sudden disengagement rejected the way he championed the conqueror's part. Where he saw adventure and glory, she was old enough now to see ignominy. Expansion and Discovery, with Portugal and Spain leading the way, meant the descent into world-ending hell for those whose threshold the Iberian marauders crossed.

"We can follow him, you know," Alex said, as they completed their turn around Vasco da Gama's memorial tomb. Maya's eyes focused, confusion lingering over them.

"I mean it," Alex pressed. "There's a giant stone map of the whole world just behind the Padrão dos Descobrimentos. We can go right now. When we get there, you can trace Vasco da Gama's route along the coast of Africa and around the Cape of Good Hope, and past the Cape of Needles, too. It's only a few steps! Just follow the compass."

Proximity or distance from the actual poles does not matter when using a compass to navigate, except at the Cape of Needles, Alex liked to say when they were children. By the time Vasco da Gama and Company were skirting around the capes, their minds set on silk and spice and sometimes immortality, compasses were complex machines calibrated in myriad ways. Some pointed to the Pole Star, the True North, while others pointed to the Magnetic North. But even with the best compasses, navigators could not always tell where they were in the wide sea.

Legend has it that when the intrepid Portuguese sailors came around the southern bend of Africa, they were nearly done in by the sharp rocks and corral that made the waters impossible to navigate, forcing Bartolomeu Dias out to the open water. He missed the cape he was looking for the first time, unable to approach land in the stormy seas. How he managed to escape certain destruction is as great a mystery as Kamikaze, the Divine Wind that saved Japan when the invading fleet of an inexorable Kublai Khan descended upon the island half a world away. Centuries later, many said it was a miracle, like the stroke of Fortune that saved the British Isles from the fearsome wrath of the until-then-invincible Spanish Armada. The royal privateers of Good Queen Bess, with her favorite sea dog Drake leading the pack, returned from the skirmish claiming victory over the most powerful empire on Earth, an empire cobbled together from the blood of Spanish, Dutch, and Portuguese kings. The gods are careful to keep the mighty in check, and Neptune was no exception. So, it probably helped the Portuguese that they did not hold the reins of that newly awakened imperial beast that English pirates bested.

But when Bartolomeu Dias escaped the stormy southern seas, and then got past another cape, Portuguese prospectors knew that the gods had smiled upon them, and theirs was not after all a lost cause. They would one day return home, their cargo bays filled with cloth and cloves and captive souls. With poets just waiting to sing their resonant praise and smoothen the rough-hewn edges of history, they would also enjoy a measure of immortality worthy of the stones that bore their likenesses. So the King Dom Manuel, who came to call himself the "Lord of Guinea and of the Conquest of the navigation and commerce of Ethiopia, Arabia, Persia and India," changed the name of the Cape of Storms where Bartolomeu Dias had almost died, to the Cape of Good Hope, christened its sister cape, the one of the dangerously rough waters, the Cape of Needles. But these were just legends, stories told to divert children and keep patriots proud. In truth, the second cape got its name because navigators noticed that on compasses of every kind, be they calibrated for Polar North or for Magnetic North, all the needles aligned perfectly on that patch of sea, agreeing every single one upon a common attitude.

Water, water, everywhere. Maya looked away from Vasco da Gama's limestone pillow to see a familiar face as if from across a river. Suddenly the bewildered gaze of her cat Rosie staring at his own reflection flashed before her memory's eye, making Maya start, and then laugh out loud. She had not thought of Rosie in a long, long time. Now suddenly she remembered the last time she saw the cat. That is, she thought she remembered.

"I want to go home," Maya said drawing back into Time again. "I've seen enough of da Gama."

"OK. But let's at least go and visit the cloister before we leave. It is a lot cooler than the church, much cleaner, and much quieter, I think," Alex said.

Maya did not respond right away. She stood still a spell, and then shifted closer to a stone column to avoid the swelling stream of tourists craning their necks to look across the aisle at the winking face of Camões quiescent in armed prayer. Then she joined the shifting crowd, and Alex fell in beside her, both of them melting easily into the wave of shuffling visitors approaching the poet's memorial sepulcher. *As armas e os barões assinalados…* Where da Gama lay on a tomb that bore carracks and crosses and armillary spheres, Camões rested on an altar adorned with the poet's lyre and laurel wreaths, Phoebus himself clearly his intercessor to the heavens. *Cantando espalharei por toda parte…* As she circled around him, Maya could only just make out the sunken void of his missing eye that had been blinded in battle. *Se a tanto me ajudar o engenho e arte…* Was it the soldier in Camões that made him turn his blind eye to the deeds of Vasco da Gama that Alex could not even find in the history books he read? What use were art and genius if they could not champion conscience? What use were art and genius…

Canto Three

"Maya! Hurry!" Alex's voice broke her reverie.

She was outside the cathedral yet again, the sharp sunlight forcing her to squint even as it cut through Alex's approaching figure across the red and black and gray limestone mosaic that laid the world out beneath them. As he advanced, he called to her not to worry: the stone beneath their feet would keep them from sinking even if they cut through the expanse of the ocean across the map. Of course, how silly! A small laugh escaped Maya, but before she could move, the stone was once again water, the raft again beneath her. Alex's beckoning voice disappeared into the echoes of another voice, worn from years of singing and prayer and laced with jollity.

"Haraka haraka haina baraka." Maya spun abruptly to find her great-grandmother sitting beside her.

Alex vanished, and Maya reeled again, disoriented. She did not know where she was. Were they back at the Lake? Inside the waking dream?

The old woman's slow warble hummed merrily as if trying to coax the music out of a shy song. "If you want to see, my child, open your eyes. Be patient."

The music in her great-grandmother's voice was usually comforting to Maya. Now she felt frustrated, suspicion thrumming on her heart. How was she supposed to be patient when she could not even find her bearings? Mamma Akoth's enigmatic songs were exciting, but sometimes they just perplexed. Maya turned around one more time, wondering whether she might find herself standing over the world by the banks of the Tagus again. Instead, the Lake below her raft just began to spin a little. No matter which way she faced, she found water, the compass needle fixedly trained on her heart.

"Ehh, my child," Akoth continued in Maya's dreaming ear. "You cannot learn anything like this. If you truly want to see, you have to open your mind's eyes and you also have to be patient. Listen. Listen. Pole pole ndiyo mwendo. Ehh."

Maya still did not quite understand what Mamma Akoth meant, nor was she of a mind to see. Was Alex still in Lisbon? Had she been to Lisbon? Yes. The smell was unmistakable. She could not dream a smell like that, and she did not know anyone who lived in Lisbon, so she must have been there herself. Sometimes it took her a while to sort out whose eyes she was seeing through, sometimes she could not even tell whether it was her own. But smells were different. Unless they were so strong that they shocked the senses or carried for miles, they did not usually enter waking dreams. Yes, she must have gone to Lisbon with Alex. They had planned the trip for as long as she could remember. He took her there for her eighteenth birthday. No, it was later. She was definitely still eighteen when they left. Alex did not keep time very well. But a dozen years had come and gone since that fateful trip, and Alex had vanished as if into the sunlight at the center of the Great Lake on the stone map in Lisbon. A dozen years searching, and not even the pointlessly ornate compass that she desperately hoped would finally help had been of any use. It multiplied her frustration by belying Alex's solemn insistence that the truth of the compass was absolute. She blinked in the sunlight, the scintillating rays that bounced off the surface of the water dazzling and dizzying. Where was the stone? Where was the map? How did pavement become lake water? How had lake water become pavement? Maya listened, wondering.

What if she could just will herself to join her great-grandmother where she now dwelt in the realm of the ancestors? What if she could find the breach that brought her in and out of Time unbidden? What if she could control it? Perhaps then she could understand how to wait for change. Perhaps then she would know the world as Alex did, as Mamma Akoth did.

~ ❊ ~

Akoth was Olóo's youngest child, the jewel of his heart. She was born when both her mother and her father died during a rainstorm in the middle of the long Dry Season. When the Midwife brought the infant to her disconsolate grandmother to be presented to the ancestors, a whole moon had come and gone following Olóo's burial, and his Spirit spoke for the child and named her after the rain that had claimed his life. Nyanaam heard the name her son wanted his little one to have and decided then to take the child into her house as her own. Olóo's other wives still living who wanted to adopt the child, especially the two who had cared for the baby during the moon Nyanaam mourned her son, pleaded to take the infant. But Nyanaam would not hear of it. Olóo's claim, made so soon after departing from Time, woke Nyanaam out of her unvital stupor and soothed the raw anguish of losing her beloved son and departed daughter-in-law. She vowed that the child would have the best care and education as only she could provide.

Before Olóo died, Nyanaam had watched helplessly for a long time after the Long Rains had passed as her son wrestled the waking dream that consumed his life. In the gloom of his mother's hut where he sat in a trance like none she had seen before, she thought she heard his appeal to Lolwe, the Spirit of the Lake, not to abandon its home. She thought she heard him try to assure it that the approaching danger would pass, that the people of the Lake would need its protection more than ever. Who would keep the boats safe and fill the nets and baskets with fish if the Spirit of the Lake let fear drive it away? Nyanaam had felt the shock that jolted Olóo's body as lightning flared, and his head grew cold in his communion with the Spirit of the Lake. His face was a gelid sun radiating through a veil of mist, and Nyanaam feared that he was reaching too far. But she let her faith in him, her beautiful, gifted son, still her impulse to call him back. And then for a moment, the Spirit of the Lake seemed reassured, and the young mother let herself breathe.

But when Olóo finally drew back, believing his communion complete, it seemed as if the Spirit of the Lake fled, frightened before he could reassure it. In the wake of its flight, a wild wind swept over the Bay, and a heavy, inexorable rain began to fall, even though it was the middle of the Dry Season. Nyanaam saw blue luminous sparks hover and flash around her son's crown and understood that he had indeed gone beyond her reach.

The violent rainstorm, the wildest the Bay could remember, claimed Olóo's life. Thunder shook the earth, and lightning split the graphite firmament. Roiling waves churned the clear waters of the Lake, and fish that had long lived there in quiet ease choked on the cloudy soup. Berserk winds tore away the thatch from the strongest roofs of the homes in the Bay, and floods covered the millet fields that stood ready for harvest and flattened huts and granaries. After a week, the storm blew itself out. For a month following, the Lake was unapproachable, and fishing came to a standstill. Boats that ventured out into the water sank, taking their fishermen with them. As long as the Spirit of the Lake stayed away, everyone feared the unprotected waters of the Bay.

Olóo breathed his last in the middle of the night at the very moment his youngest child's body emerged into the world. Nyanaam raised her voice to lament her son's death even as the infant, thrust unsuspecting into the cold, glaring, clamorous air, raised its voice to wail. The baby drew breath in fitful sobs, and its mother's broken body spent its last and lay quiet and lifeless. A month passed, and Nyanaam had to present the child to the ancestors before another moon waned, so she opened the doors to her son's sealed house and carried the infant inside at the head of a procession that included all of Olóo's surviving wives and their children. No one expected Olóo to claim the baby. Nobody remembered the last time the Spirit of a father had claimed a newborn, to say nothing of a father who died during the baby's birth. It was often left to aunts and uncles, and the generations that preceded them to offer a name the child would bear for its sojourn in the world of Time. Yet it was indeed Olóo whose voice rose to sing the infant's name, and Nyanaam's heart caught flame. She listened with a joy she could no longer recognize when Olóo answered for the newborn and did not just call her *Ajwang'* to signify her father's early death. Instead, he named her *Akoth* for the rain, endowing an heir, out of the ruinous storm, to sing the Song of Becoming for those who were, and who were yet to be.

Canto Four

"This is the best way to find your way anywhere on earth because the needle is perfectly polarized," Alex pronounced, once again breaking Maya's reverie. The Lake had vanished yet again, just like the stone map. Instead, Maya found herself sitting beside her brother, both of them now children, in the library playroom of their youth where they spent hours tracing the courses of rivers and ocean currents in the dog-eared atlases their father had left behind in his flight. Alex was only ten years old, twice his sister's age, and he was assured of his authority on all matters of Geography thanks to the wisdom of the atlases where he found all the order of the world, and all the truth of Creation.

"When you hold it flat, it tells you the direction of the World's magnetic field," Alex continued. He was obviously talking about compasses in general, not the broken one in her dream. "No matter where you are, it will always help you find your way."

Maya leaned forward, still feeling disoriented, wondering at the smallness of her body. Her left leg was tucked beneath her on the floor of their father's office library, which they had quickly turned into their playroom after he left. The room was Alex's favorite haunt and Maya always followed him in there. Hehra trailed behind Maya and eventually, Esther started using the room as the Cavern of the Magic Portal. Even David turned it into a flight control center whenever he wanted to play astronaut. To Alex, the room remained a library, "The Library", and there he could travel all the seas of the world in the giant atlases their father loved to collect.

Maya stared at the map laid out before her. The sparkling water of the lake beneath her raft had vanished, the vessel along with it. Perhaps the Lake was just a dream. Her chin came to rest against her right knee as she drew up her foot, trying to steady herself, her leg pressing against her tummy. She peered at the floor of the Indian Ocean in the middle page of the atlas in front of them. The compass rose on the corner of the map was a simple affair — only its north point labeled. The heavenly pale blue of the ocean in some pages blended into deeper marine in others. The atlas was large and worn from age and frequent use, the edges of its heavy pages soft and pulpy. While Alex spoke, tracing the lines of sea lanes across the oceans and around the continents, Maya ran her small fingers along the velvet edges of the volume, leaning closer to the page as if drawn down into the painted water by his words. His quiet, laughing voice, just like Mamma Akoth's, stirred the ocean winds over the map and sent them sweeping up into the shelves of forgotten volumes that covered every wall in the room all the way to the ceiling; There, they spent themselves beyond the reach of imagination.

They would sail the great rivers of the world, Alex was saying. If Maya wanted to go with him, she would have to become a proper naval pilot and know how to read maps and compasses. They had to take their great-grandmother's fishing boat around Lolwe's Nam Ataro, renamed for the old empire's Queen, start at the source of the Nile, and then sail its upside-down current all the way to the sea. Approaching the Blue Nile in the middle of the atlas Sudan, they would cross the Sahara, bracing for winds as dry as dust, except in the very bosom of the Nile.

Maya loved the story of how the Nile got stuck flowing upside down. Once upon a time, it seems, the wandering poles of the Earth put the Atlas Mountains at the bottom of the world, and all of the compass needles that did not yet exist pointed North to Cape Agulhas where the Atlantic and the Indian Oceans met. The young Nile, carefree and knowing no better, danced down into the desert valley on its way to the seas, leading merrily with its feet, and keeping its crown by the Great Lake. By the time the first waters in its toes had arrived, the poles had put the Atlas Mountains atop the world instead, so the Nile emptied itself out to the sea by its ankles while dancing on its head.

Alex continued to sing forth their fantasy voyage. Once they reached the Great River's estuary, they would head for the Straits of Gibraltar, and then cross the Atlantic. As Alex spoke of the open ocean, his words evoked in Maya unaccountable memories of sea salt spray and the biting stench of sulfur and rusted iron stinging her throat. Boards creaked and swayed beneath her, and cannons roared and spat fire, and Maya felt queasy. But she did not tell Alex what she saw in her mind's eye when he spoke of the sea, what she thought she remembered. At first, when she was still a toddler, she could not distinguish his words from the dreams in her memory. As she grew older, she tried haltingly to describe the dreams but found she could not use words as Alex could. She hesitated, and then fell silent, and never again tried to tell him that she recalled things that chilled her and made her bones feel brittle whenever he talked about carracks and galleons and man-o-wars. By the time Alex learned to ask her where she went when she seemed to withdraw, she was too accustomed to silence to know how to answer.

Only when they were crossing the Sahara did Alex see his sister relax again. So, he sang into being more of the River, and less of the Ocean. They spent more time in the highlands and forests, and less of it by the shore. They often made their way to Peru to find the source of the Amazon. Sometimes they went to the roof of the world in the Himalayas, and then to the Rocky Mountains. Up in those heights, things were lighter than they ever were in the valleys. Up there, they could probably touch the sky. Maya wondered what it would be like to be a bird, to ride the wind aloft across the world, going wherever it blew, stopping only to eat, to sleep, to dream.

She lifted her arms to spread them as if in flight, and the white gauze bandage wrapped around her right forearm peeked out from under her sleeve.

"Alex, do you think Bruno could fly across the ocean?" she asked.

"Cats don't fly!" he laughed. "And Bruno is so fat anyway, Hehra can't even carry her properly."

Bruno bore being manhandled with saintly patience, happy for every chance to be near Hehra. Maybe in Peru she would weigh the same as Maya's lithe, sinewy cat, Rosie. Imagining the wobbly scale, with Rosie on one plate and Bruno on the other, made Maya laugh along with her brother.

"The earth is a giant magnet that holds things down and keeps them from falling off into space," Alex explained. "That is the main reason cats can't fly."

"Even on the upside-down places like Australia and Antarctica?"

"Yes, especially there. They are not really upside down, you know. Not when you are down under." The two effervesced in giggles.

Then Alex turned to the page in the atlas where tiny arrows arranged like schools of fish flowed between the poles, decorating the sea floor and the naked earth along meridian lines. In the ear of Maya's imagination, they clinked and clanked faintly as they jostled against one another in the page below, straining to align themselves with the attitude of the world, and their shimmering resonance echoed her brother's omniscient voice. Yet, even though he seemed to know almost everything, Alex always made it seem as if they were discovering the answers to her endless queries together for the first time.

"Do you think Rosie can find his way back?" Maya asked, the lost cat following those tiny arrows home in the picture behind her eyes.

"Only if he has a compass," Alex said, laughing again. Maya giggled quietly, drawn again into his mirth.

Then she said wistfully, rubbing her shin with the back of her bandaged right hand, "Maybe Rosie doesn't want to come back."

Alex grew quiet as his eyes fell on the thick gauze wrapped around his sister's arm. He did not want to talk about Rosie anymore. Sometimes, when it seemed like Maya had finally forgotten her missing cat, she would bring him up again, making Alex uneasy. But there in the study, looking at the atlas so big it seemed a magic carpet, she was in a happy mood and he did not want to discourage her, so he tried to be reassuring: "If Rosie had a compass, and knew how to use it, I promise he would find his way back because the truth of the compass is absolute."

Maya was silent for a moment, her eyes wide with surprise. Alex sometimes said things that she did not entirely understand, but she usually accepted them anyway. This, however, seemed sacrilegious.

"But how can it be Absolute? It's only a compass. Only God is Absolute."

It was his turn to be surprised. He was also a little relieved that what she said was not about Rosie.

"Actually… God is just Relative. The compass is always the same no matter where you go, but God is different everywhere." Atlas Geography most certainly put the universe in perspective.

"No," Maya said emphatically. "No. Mrs. Da Silva said that God is Absolute, The Alpha and The Omega…"

The Alpha and The Omega, especially when issuing from Mrs. Da Silva's inimitably reverend lips, sounded vast and inscrutable, particularly to her Kindergarten wards. And it was spelled out in the Bible: *I am the Lord thy God…*

Alex's smile grew and he became more animated. He loved these moments. All the time spent in the shadow of books seemed to find meaning when he could tell Maya about the new things he discovered there. With a twinkle in his eye he pointed to a shelf near the floor, just above the row of oversized atlases.

"God is different everywhere," he said. "See?"

He reached for a set of picture books they often read together, books full of colored images that Hehra loved to trace over with crayons and sometimes watercolors. The books recounted stories of Shiva, Brahma, and the thousand faces of Vishnu. Alex enjoyed them because sometimes they sounded like the things Mamma Akoth said about ancestors and saints. He delighted best of all in the tales of Krishna's birth and carefree life. How Vishnu caused himself to be born a blue-black baby, God made flesh: a prankster, a lover, a warrior before whom armies fell when he rode into war. He made girls swoon when he played on his flute. He fell in love, and he died while napping. And he was only one among numberless gods.

"Mrs. Da Silva is not the only one who knows about these things, you know," Alex said, opening one of the books. "Mamma

Akoth said they are all the same God, even if the name changes. And the name always changes, and sometimes it means something else. So, it's Relative." The boy was exhilarated. A mellow delight glowed in his quiet eyes.

But Maya remained unpersuaded. The still fresh authority of Mrs. Da Silva directing them in singsong recitals of the Ten Commandments to shape their idea of God cast a broad shadow over her young universe.

I am the LORD thy God, which have brought thee out of the land of Egypt, out of the house of bondage. Thou shalt have no other gods before me.

The children's earnest, devout voices effortlessly poured themselves into their teacher's mold, littering the text with lisps and blunders, the young acolytes waving their arms in imaging gestures, remaking the Scripture in sing-song rhythm.

Thou shall not make unto thee any grave… or any thing that is in Heaven above, or any thing that is the Earth beneath, or that is the Water under the Earth. Thou shalt not bow down thyself unto them, nor serve them, for I am the LORD thy God! For I am a jealous God, visit inquinity fathers upon the children and unto the third and the fourth generation that hate me and mercy to thousands of them that love me, and keep my Commandments. Amen!

None of the children knew what *iniquity* was, or as many of them said it, "*inquinity*". Nor could they tell what the rest of the divine edict meant, but they felt the gravity of the threat it promised.

Nor did Maya really understand the word "absolute" the way her atlas-educated brother used it. When Mrs. Da Silva's unequivocal edicts resounded in Maya's ears, Absolute just was. It allowed no compromise.

But maybe God could be a Relative… He had after all begotten the Sun. *By the power of the Holy Spirit He came in a car and ate from the Virgin Mary, and was made Man.* But a compass? And what of man-made Gods, like the faces of Vishnu and his thousand colorful avatars?

Mrs. Da Silva bade them banish from their minds every face and every name except that of *God, the Father, the Almighty, the maker of Heaven and Earth, of all that is seen and unseen*; God the Sun, *eternally begotten of the Father, God from God, Light from Light, True God from True God, begotten, not made. Through him all things were made*; God the Holy Spirit, *the Lord, the giver of light, who proceeds from the Father and the Sun. With the Father and the Sun, he is worshiped and glorified*; God, The Alpha and The Omega.

Maya wondered if listening to her brother would make God think she was not obeying Mrs. Da Silva as she should. The menacing words of God's Commandments tumbled through her mind, the light of the Creed illuminating her faith, even as Alex read the exploits of Krishna aloud. She looked for a way to reconcile God with Alex's words, but could find none for the moment. What would Mrs. Da Silva think about what Alex was saying? Did it make him a terrible sinner to compare God to a compass? Maya did not want to disagree with a brother she adored, and she did not want any inquinity to befall him, so she closed the atlas and sat quietly rocking back and forth, looking at him bent over the exploits of Krishna, her arms now completely wrapped around her.

Canto Five

Water, water, everywhere! The water of Nam Ataro, home of Lolwe, the Spirit of the Great Lake, was wide and flat, and the raft drifted along unbidden. Maya was thirsty. She sat down on the creaking boards of the raft, her body big again, wishing her compass would work properly, wishing the needle could keep a steady, reliable bearing while she rotated the turntable, wishing she could hold anchor in Time even for just a moment. Maybe she could trick the compass into pointing North as it should.

She turned around to face south, tapping the compass slightly as she turned. The needle kept pointing at her chest, and so she thought that perhaps now it worked. She looked up and around slowly to confirm that she was facing south. The compass rose was oriented correctly, or so it seemed. She turned again slowly, just to be sure, to face the north, waving the flat cylinder gently in front of her, hoping that she could coax the needle to correct itself to move with the attitude of the poles. Instead, it kept its point trained on her chest, obstinately turning its tail to the northern point of the rose.

Standing under the hum of the equatorial sun in the hot copper sky, Maya could not quite remember where the compass had come from, or how she came to have it with her on a raft in the middle of the Lake when she had thought that she was looking for Alex, that maybe she was even about to find him.

She jumped up and whirled around again on the balls of her heels this way and that, feeling dizzy as the boards creaked slightly. *Water, water, everywhere.* The current carried her along and she began to feel like a dog twirling around its own tail; like a cat stalking itself in a mirror. A dead calm settled over the water, dragged on her limbs, and Maya sank to the boards once again and let herself relax into the wooden floor of the raft. The compass grew heavy in her hand. It was beautiful, but utterly useless. The schools of arrow fish in the ground beneath Rosie's feet had not led the wayward cat back home, and they would not help her find her brother now.

"Oh, what's the use! There isn't a single soul in this pointless wilderness," she muttered wearily, hearing the light dance on the water, its gentle, shimmering sighs reaching her ears as if from a distance.

"Eh, how can you say that here?" Akoth asked, her voice mixing with the water's surface. "Can you not hear the song rising up out of the water. What are you really seeking, Anyango?"

"Alex said that the compass would always help me find my way," Maya replied. "But I can't make it work properly. I can't find him no matter where I look." She stopped as if sobbing and bowed her head. She wanted Alex. A dozen years gone by, and she still did not know where he had gone when he vanished from Lisbon. Before he disappeared just like that, she had never considered what it was like to endure a void that would not abate. Since the day she was born, she could always be sure of when in Time she actually was, because Alex was her constant anchor in the world of Time. Now, drifting along the Lake on a raft still bereft, idle as a painted ship, Maya wondered whether she had finally lost all stable footing in the world of Time forever.

"Opolo sees many things, but he is still just a boy, my child," Akoth said, drawing nearer to Maya. "But don't worry. Every soul is already here, in the water all around us, singing the songs that we become."

Something akin to Hope clad in the tattered rags of irrepressible Fear suddenly squeezed Maya's chest. *Opolo sees.* She heard that right. *He IS still… He is STILL…*! He had not actually vanished, just gone somewhere else! Not until she heard those words did Maya allow herself, in a dozen years, to imagine that she might never see him again. *Where is he?* She wanted to scream, but she held her tongue. Real Hope, newly sprouted, was still a tender and fragile shoot. For now, she would just let its root find anchor, and *then* she would ask.

Water, water everywhere.

Akoth began the way she told and ended every story. *These are the songs where we come from, these are the songs we become.* The renewed Hope in Maya now offered her full attention to Mamma Akoth. Just like Alex, Maya loved to listen to their great-grandmother when she sang the songs of their origins because he had taught her to cherish them, too. He also tried to teach her to love the tales of navigators and ancient mariners that he found in their father's abandoned books. But it was in vain that she sought to experience the mysterious enchantment that made him glow when he told her about his maritime heroes.

Water, water everywhere. These are the songs we become.

But long before we came, Akoth's story sang, in the beginning, when there was nothing in the world except mountains and rivers and lakes and oceans, when not a single beast walked upon the earth nor beat its wings in the air, Nyasaye touched the River and quickened it to bring out creatures of every kind to roam the land and sky. One by one, the young Nile, still nameless, brought forth frogs and crocodiles and birds galore. Lizards, geckos, and chameleons clambered ashore and wandered into the plains and highlands. Snails and slugs inched along, daring the tortoise to move even more slowly. Egrets and kingfishers, weaver birds and flamingos. Pelicans, hippos, rhinos, gazelles, giraffes, buffalo, okapi, cheetahs, hyenas... The sacred ibis strutted the banks of the Great River alongside the elephant herd and saw that the birth of creation was good.

"What difference does it make where they came from," Maya muttered, interrupting the memory of Akoth's warbling voice, "what difference does any of this make?" A note of agitated panic crept into her voice. "My compass doesn't work, and I can't find my way. I can't find the way, no matter what I try!"

"Eh, if that is what you want to find, then why do you keep looking down?" Akoth asked quietly.

Maya responded by looking up to the sky, nervous, impatient, and then out onto the water. It looked just like the atlas water in the children's playroom, and also just like the lake beneath their great-grandmother's fishing boat. For a moment, but only a moment, it even sounded the same. She suddenly felt calm again, the compass a feather in her hand.

A still wind played on the water, tickling it and making tiny jagged ripples on its surface. Sunbeams that had earlier seemed hotly unforgiving now bounced into the ripples in an unsteady dance, sparkling like sighing bells. A dragonfly swayed drunkenly just above the water, mesmerized by the whispering shimmer, swooning in the somnolent heat. Maya watched, drawn into the dance, now hearing the sound more clearly, a sound that so resembled her brother's quiet laughing voice.

As she thought of Alex, a sharp pang sent salt tears pricking her eyes and stinging her nostrils. Everything had changed in the twelve years since the day he vanished. She reached for him, hopelessly, now in his silence, because to her the world was his voice speaking. Every memory in her mind, every dream, had been his quiet, laughing voice describing and explaining everything as if he loved nothing better — even the ugly, tragic things. And everywhere sunlight bounced on water, Maya heard the echoes of that voice whose silence made the world invisible, untouchable, unreal. A slow, sticky tear crawled down her cheek and dropped to the boards below as she thought of the beginning of the world in the voice of her brother. *Opolo, this is your sister,* Akoth had said to him. *Ma-ya,* had been his simple reply. Would the world end in his silence? The forbearance and composure Akoth advised traveled the world of Time in league with Faith. But Hope, her sacred sister, sat alone, *like Patience on a monument smiling at grief.* Maya hated how Hope let her believe that everything had meaning, even Alex's silence, Alex's disappearance. Hope softened the brutal memory of loss and made every living soul pretend not to pretend that they were just pretending not to Hope. Only those who tucked Memory away into the carefully hidden folds of willful oblivion could Hope without pretending. And so, they suffered that absence of Hope until they could learn to forget.

A slight shift in the wind and the dragonfly hanging over the water swayed to one side just as a hungry tilapia surfaced to gulp him down. A slight shift, and catastrophe was averted, the dragonfly spared to hover on. A shift, and hope was dashed to waste for the famished fish. A tasty mouthful, and coveted, had slipped just out of reach because a slight shift had come into the wind. Lunch would be a dull affair, soured by the memory of a missed morsel snatched by forces alien to the tilapia who knew everything of currents and little of winds. The dragonfly was still dangling over the water when a gentle splash just beneath him betrayed another attempted ambush. But again, the wind. Or perhaps his own wits. Lucky devil.

In the next instant shimmering light jangled on the surface of the water as Maya's eyes fixed upon the insect that was now distancing itself with an alacrity that belied his earlier stillness. Luminous shards of fractured sun rays flashed on the water more starkly, with greater dissonance. Maya closed her eyes, her head drooping. Her body ached, her eyes ached, her ears and her mind. Her heart, most of all, was tired and soar from grief.

"Anyango, look up if you want to find your way," Akoth urged her, humming under her breath. *These are the songs where we come from, these are the songs we become.*

Maya opened her eyes wearily, wishing she could at least hear Alex again. Instead, her great-grandmother's voice singing about the creation of the world filled her head. Akoth continued to sing about Nyasaye touching the River. Her voice warbled gently, dancing over the water's surface where the dragonfly had been. The voice had not changed from Maya's own memories. As her great-grandmother tremulously intoned her songs of creation, Maya looked up to see the Children of the River rise out of the water.

Canto Six

They came out leading their cattle and their goats, their youngest running ahead, their elders trailing behind. At first Maya could not distinguish them one from another. Their coarse watery garments fell dripping away, and were replaced with tanned bark, painted hide, woven cloth and fly whisks made of oxtail and decorated with feathers and cowrie shells. Young men rose out of the water in charged groups behind the elders, bouncing along on taut thewy legs, their energy barely contained, their skin glowing. Shining brass rings adorned their ankles and shins, their wrists and forearms. They sang just under their breath as they went, private songs of future valor, of glory yet to come. The women walking behind the children went silently, moving to the rhythm of the young men's song, punctuating it now and again with exclamations of 'Ehh! Ehh!' An old man walk-dancing in front of the emerging water procession sang more slowly and more loudly, pronouncing memories of the future. The goat-hoof wreath adorning his ankles rustled as he stamped his feet to the rhythm of his song, plucking a small nyatiti in accompaniment. The instrument emitted a round hollow sound that washed over the water and mingled with Akoth's liquid voice.

For a fleeting moment Maya saw a young man who wore a face she thought she recognized. "Alex!" she called, reaching. Had she finally found him? Hope knocked hard at her breath from within. But the beloved face quickly disappeared and was replaced by another that only slightly resembled her brother's. His eyes turning to look for her beckoning voice, the man slowed, and his gaze settled upon hers.

Although no photographs existed of the man now looking at her, Maya knew the jutting cheekbones and the deep-set eyes of her great-great-grandfather Olóo. He resembled Mamma Akoth, and Gabriel, and Esther, and even Alex, too. Family lore said that he had died during a prolonged and exhausting trance, the kind that so often took Dream Walkers who got lost in their own waking dreams. One of his sons, a few of his grandchildren, and some of their children and grandchildren were touched, and their lives, too, were imperiled by Dream Walker trances.

Esther humorously — or poetically — called them her afflicted kinsmen, hapless souls stranded in a world that no longer had a place for their kind. Of all her siblings, only Maya appeared to have inherited the traits of a Dream Walker, but there was no one to guide her properly. David, Maya's eldest brother, was born untouched, and his twin Alex lived for less than a day. Before Esther was born, Akoth feared that the Dream Walker had skipped another generation. Her son, Omondi, was a Dream Walker and his son, Gabriel, born after his father's death, was touched, but never became more than an ordinary dreamer. Her daughter, Akinyi, was also touched, yet she too showed no signs of becoming. However, Akinyi's son, Ochiëng, could well have become a great Dream Walker. When he died alone in St. Petersburg, he was lost to memory, even to his grandmother, and it was rumored that his unsettled will sometimes haunted the Lake.

And then Esther was born and Akoth was reassured that the infant would keep the memory of Olóo's clan for her generation. She would need special education, so Akoth called the Spirit of her own grandmother, Nyanaam, to help her prepare the girl, and Esther took after Akoth in many ways. She had a long and clear memory of every part of her great-grandmother's life, along with all the lives that had come before. From an early age, she felt the joys and pains of kin and stranger alike, as if she herself lived the cause. This made her grow up gentle and unassuming, unlike her forceful, obdurate brother and her stubborn, absentminded sister.

Watching her great-grandchildren grow up, Akoth believed she would never again meet people quite as beautiful, and yet she also worried that everything that could ensure they thrived was vanishing, forgotten, in the changing world. It cost her pain to watch David remain a child, and to watch Maya lose her way in her mysteriously clairvoyant inner world. To keep Esther on the right path, Akoth encouraged the girl to take the baby Hehra, a clean soul, delightful to all, under her wing. Akoth, who lived for one hundred and eleven Rains, until the year Esther turned twenty-six, taught the child all the family lore. With these stories Esther wove together the history of her afflicted kin, and her memory strengthened and grew with every new telling of how they came into being.

The pain brought about by the family affliction kept Esther's memory of those who succumbed ever raw. One was her father Gabriel's long-lost older brother, the other a cousin to both Anna, her mother, and Gabriel as well. The first uncle expired gently with his head on his mother's lap after a prolonged seizure following what must have been a stroke. He was nineteen and the new father of a young baby who also expired quickly soon after. The second uncle, the luminous Ochiëng, died alone in a hotel suite in St. Petersburg. He had gone to Russia to study during a time when many young men were moving out into the world to become teachers and doctors and lawyers and engineers. He passed the entrance exams brilliantly and became an internationally celebrated phenomenon. He arrived in St. Petersburg with the highest recommendation and was treated like a visiting dignitary, so coveted was the post he had won. He wrote home regularly to his grandmother, Mamma Akoth. His cousin, Anna Adongo, wanted to be just like him and languished in bitter regret because, of all her siblings and cousins, only the boys got to go to university, at home or abroad. The coroner's report indicated a cause of death that nobody remembered anymore. All they did remember was that he had died by his own will. Like his great-grandfather, he had been born a potent Dream Walker. Like Maya, he did not receive the right guidance for his kind.

Just before she died, after one hundred and eleven Long Rains in the world of Time, Mamma Akoth gave Esther a birthday gift consisting of all the letters Ochiëng had written to her every day for eleven months from St. Petersburg. She told Esther about how often he wrote continually for a week and then on Mondays, he would send his week's writing in the post. Sometimes, the letters arrived quickly and sometimes they were delayed for months. Sometimes after a month or two of no news from Ochiëng, a great windfall of letters that had gone astray en route would appear in the Post Office Box in Kisumu Town. Then, unopened, they were delivered to their destination, the sprawling estate of JokOlóo in the Bay by the shores of the Lake. Akoth would sort them all carefully in the calendar order of the postmark date, unseal them, and then, after cleaning her reading glasses, pore over them slowly, savoring every word her luminous grandson had written.

May God bless Nam Lolwe, and the River, and the song that bore you, my beloved Mamma Akoth, each letter began. And every one ended, *I dream of home every day and long to return to the song of the River that bore me.* Akoth kept the letters in a small wooden trunk along with her reading glasses and an aged New Testament annotated with prayer in her own hand. When she gave the missives to Esther, she removed the Gospel and the glasses, and handed over the trunk filled with only her grandson's letters. She told Esther to read them all to Maya, and to make sure that the fledgling Dream Walker would recognize her uncle when he emerged from the river and found his way back home.

Canto Seven

The man on the shore looked intently at Maya. Locks of hair packed with red ochre framed his face and draped over his shoulders and down his sinewy back. Despite his obvious youth, something in his eyes bespoke untold ages. The eyes were fiery red, set deep in their sockets and framed by a dark frowning brow that complemented his sharp cheekbones. His round, prominent forehead shone against the bright, brassy light bouncing into the water. His clothes dried quickly in the equatorial sun, they, too, changing from bark, to hide, to cloth as he advanced.

At first, he did not recognize the woman on the raft in the middle of the lake and seeing her there surprised him. And then suddenly he knew her.

"Anyango?" he said quietly, mostly to himself, stopping in his step, seeking. But she heard him across the distance.

How does he know my name? How can he know my name?

"Olóo," she said in reply, just as quietly, without hesitation. His eyes lit up when she uttered his name.

"Anyango, bih ka'e," he beckoned, still talking as if to himself, or to someone very close to him, peering at her from the shores of Nam Lolwe.

Maya wanted to go to him, but she could not quite move. He called again, his voice making the words sound strange and holy to her ear over the water, across Time, as if the beginning of becoming. Not even Akoth's voice sounded as essential as her great-great-grandfather's emerging from the very heart of creation.

Maya's mind reeled. She wanted Alex to see what she was seeing, to hear what she was hearing. She wanted Esther. If only they could be here with her, especially in times like these! They would better know how to explain what all these things meant. The air around her had grown very still, and even though the water continued to lap against the drifting raft, she felt like she was not moving. She was blind to the hippos treading nearby, to the herons combing through the reeds by the edge of the water, to the elephants playing on the island shore. She willed herself to mark every breath and every sight. She marked the light and wondered that the man on the shore cast no shadow, just like Alex. She would recount every detail of this most uncommon dream if she ever saw her truant brother again.

Olóo, too, remained still on the shore, letting the rest of the watery procession continue without him. He and Maya stood looking at each other as if in a world by themselves. There was another figure on the raft with Anyango, and Olóo could only just make out the form of a woman. The vague face, when he recognized it, looked like a softened mirror image of his own.

"Anyango," he called again, reaching out his hand.

33

As Maya watched him, another form left the procession and came to stand beside him, addressing him with solicitude.

"Is she there again?" They spoke only in Luo.

"Yes. She's drifting on Nam Lolwe."

"What is she doing?"

"Nothing. No… I don't know. I think she was dancing, swinging this way and that, turning around. It looks like she's with somebody."

"Are you sure you can see others with her?"

Olóo leaned toward his mother without breaking the gaze fixed upon the confused woman on the lake, "Nyanaam, I think she can see me too."

Nyanaam shuddered a little and put her hand on his shoulders.

"Are you sure?"

"Ehh," his gaze across the Lake growing more intent, "just like NyarOlang'o. She's looking at me from the water. And I can hear her."

Nyanaam shuddered again. She looked searchingly, blindly, out into the air in front of her, trying to see what her son saw. She could not see the Lake he said was in front of him, nor the raft with the woman he spoke of, spoke to. She could not hear the Song of Becoming that resounded in his ear, nor see the procession around them slowly evaporate in his mind's eye. She could only sit beside him in her hut by the banana tree at the edge of the estate, holding his hand, listening as he slid further into the waking dream that she did not yet know would be his last in the world of Time.

Book II. Akoth

Where Hehra's labor pains draw her into the memories of Mamma Akoth and the old stories of Olóo's waking dreams. • How Akoth saw the dream of the iron serpent materialize, bringing colonizers and missionaries to the Great Lake from the sea beyond the Rift Valley highlands and the savanna grasslands. • How Nyanaam ensured that her son Olóo received the care he needed when she discovered that he was a Dream Walker. • How Akoth traveled to the Mombasa coast by train accompanied by her recollection of João de Sousa, the young monk from Lisbon, and miracle worker of Mombasa and Calecut.

Canto Eight

The song in Hehra's ear as she felt her body struggle to bring her twin sons into the world sounded as if every noise she had ever heard was clamoring all at once. Fractured memories piled one into another and aggregated around her through the pain. They were in her toes, and fingers, and hair, in the sweat collecting on her brow and neck, in the tearing pain of rolling contractions, in the astringent smell of antiseptic somewhere in the corner of the delivery room. Each aggregating memory laced the folds of her overtaxed brain with a question that would not let her be: could one person live in two different bodies simultaneously?

The contractions heralding the arrival of the twins crushed Hehra's belly with unyielding tides, blotting out all thought of the two hundred and fifty-two days that she spent nurturing them as they slowly grew inside her. When the spastic clenching subsided and gave her respite, she felt almost fine — large, contained — yet fine nonetheless, until another contraction pulled her again into rapturous pain. The boys were precisely on time, making their way out of her body exactly nine months after she had conceived them. It still made her wonder, and especially now that she was finally going to meet them, that a person, two people, could live inside another so completely, yet still remain separate. She marveled sometimes that she would never know them truly, and forever she would be learning to learn two minds and souls that were different from hers, yet whose bodies drew life from her own. She wondered, as they all three strove, how the world would seem to them as it came into being before their eyes, and under their feet and hands, with every breath and sound. Their minds, the domain of all possible things, would undoubtedly reshape the world, turning mere ideas into matter.

Hehra could not hold back the avalanche that descended on her, clanging, whenever contractions began. They took on a mounting urgency, making her want Esther and Maya, making her will her sisters walk into the room to receive her twins. Who, she thought, better than her afflicted kin? But contractions made laughter impossible.

For two hundred and sixty-five days, this transformation that she was now shepherding made itself known. Now, fully mature, it enveloped and saturated her and the two boys she was bearing, and she wanted to remain thus imbued every day of her life. During the months, and weeks, and days while her twins were growing, all of the world seemed different than what she believed and understood. She thought of the twins in ways that reason could not follow, thoughts so mysterious and yet so transparent, that her rational mind was blind to them. Was this rapture what poets labored so to shape into words? Her twins inhabited and transfigured her body, and yet she was certain that they were unaware of her while in the womb. All she was to them was all, unseparate and vital, indistinct. They had no sense of where they ended, and surely no sense of where she began. Now her body was tearing itself open to let them out, and Hehra was forced to persist. She panted and sweat, no cries issuing from her straining throat, and no entreaties from her lips, no tears from her eyes. This, she thought when she could, was something akin to what she had read about in the lives of saints. That part of her mind that could still speak to itself in its rapture wondered if something in her might rupture; that this body-breaking labor, this mortar of multiplied sorrow, would it exact a tax on her heart, on her soul, on her mind? Would it make her different in the ways that made her own mother frightening to her and her siblings? Would finally giving birth make her become enigmatic, explosive, exhausting, exhausted, and the reason for all questions and pain?

If two people could live inside one other person, containing three souls in one body, could one soul live in more than one body, making it one in three? Mamma Akoth, her guardian and namesake, passed outside the world of Time the same year Hehra met the man who would become the father of her longed-for twins. The loss of Mamma Akoth at the start of that year left deep silences in every heart of the four generations of the children of JokOlóo whom she had cherished and raised with the sound of her song. It was also the year that Hehra turned twenty-one, and the Spirit of Mamma Akoth imbued her soul and sent her in search of stories abroad from peoples yet unknown. So Hehra set out to explore as much of the world as she could by train. She meant to do it backpacking, carrying very little. Instead she ended up accumulating dozens of books throughout her journey, each volume the memory of a moment, a song, the stories she heard from the peoples she met.

Akoth had already lived for ninety Long Rains when Hehra was born. In the last twenty-one years that followed, she remained constant, always the same. Yet she also told her grandson often, and often told his children, too, that in her own lifetime the world had changed and become unrecognizable. Her body might have remained the same in health and strength until the day she died, but the world of her children would never again be the world that had been her father's. Since her great-grandmother remained constant for so long, Hehra had learned to trace every family trait, going back as far as Olóo, through the lens of Mamma Akoth's pronounced cheekbones and deep-set eyes. Olóo was in Gabriel's guileless laughter and fantastical sentimentality. He was also in Esther's prodigious memory, in Maya's bewildering inner world and absorption with

Alex, the phantom twin. Hehra's mind drew a picture of all of her kin, an artist sketching a family portrait. Absence shaped her mind's vision in the same way silence shaped music and language.

Hehra's labor-ruptured memory scattered accounts of her twice-great-grandfather witnessing a furor that history had long ago silenced. A young girl was stoned to her wretched end by a mob before his very eyes in one of his earliest waking dreams. Echoes of his warnings that an iron serpent would tear through the land folded into the stories told of how Mamma Akoth, still a girl, recognized her father's vision the first time she saw the railway arrive in Kisumu the very same year that the old Queen who put her name on Nam Ataro died and was turned to stone by the craftsmen of her land. On that day, the sight of the hissing behemoth made Akoth turn her mind away from all that her late father had foretold to look instead to memories of the past glories of Lwanda Maghere. Generations had been singing jubilant songs of his valor, and generations more would lament his death at the hands of his bride, NyarOlang'o. The unhappy girl's bloody stoning was only the memory of a shadow hidden behind a forgotten outcrop of rocks by the Lake. While the glaring light of willful oblivion cast a deifying eye on the young bride's fallen husband, Memory's silence, more surely than words, sealed her ignominy for bringing to ruin the greatest warrior that ever lived. Nobody wondered to what extent that warrior had fashioned his own fateful end with the countless raids that gave him renown, yet left NyarOlang'o's people bereft. Men had done worse than kill for wealth, and they would do worse still long after Lwanda Maghere himself had faded into a future unmindful of his repute.

The other things Olóo witnessed were even more terrible than a mob stoning a young woman, more enigmatic than snowfall under the searing, naked equatorial sun, more fearsome than the pallid

Children of Shadow and Ice borne ashore by the great salt sea. Maya once told Hehra that before he died, Olóo also witnessed the sublime confusion of his own unborn daughter's great-granddaughter staring into his uncannily familiar eyes, stepping across Time over the waters of the Lake, sitting down before him, a mirror of all he cherished. *Anyango, you look just like Akoth,* he had said.

For one hundred and forty Long Rains, the songs of Olóo resounded through his mother Nyanaam, and through the voice of his daughter Akoth, and through all of the stories they told each generation about his life in the world of Time. Appealing to the songs of Nyanaam and Akoth, and even Esther and Maya, Hehra called for her sisters as yet another wave of contractions assured her that the twins would soon separate from her.

Canto Nine

Before she became a great-grandmother, or a grandmother, or even a mother, Akoth was the most accomplished long-distance walker for miles around Homa Bay. Every week on market day, she left her home on the Bay by the Lake at dawn, before the sun had broken the horizon, to walk the four hours to the market gathering place that gradually became Kisumu town. Her friends and age-mates tried to keep up, but only some could, and only sometimes. When she arrived at market, the sun was just beginning to warm the earth. People said, partly in jest, that the girl had a secret understanding with the sun, since she was named after the rain, because whenever she went to market, the day remained cool, as if the sun was conceding to let her pass beneath the sky without troubling her. The legend took root when somebody noticed that on market days when Akoth stayed at home, the sun unleashed its full force on everyone's head, seemingly without compunction.

Nyanaam, the grandmother who raised Akoth from birth, smiled when she caught wind of these rumors of the Sun's affinity for her granddaughter, finding them amusing, yet fitting. Nyanaam was a kind and wise woman, but really not one to be crossed. Following the death of her son, Olóo, she made sure that his legend grew. After all, the only thing more powerful and portentous than a son who spoke with the ancestors was a son who dwelt among them. Olóo's four wives had an advocate among the Spirits, and his many children were specially watched over, particularly the boys. For the girls, his name would ensure that they found suitable husbands. To the delight of Olóo's widows, all of their daughters became first wives.

But Akoth was not just a first wife. Unlike her mother and her many sisters, she was the only wife, and she bore only three children, the first of whom died in labor. It must not be believed that her husband, Ouma, was a weak or poor man who could not take more wives. Quite the contrary — he was wealthy and well respected by all who knew him. So Akoth's grandmother and siblings thought it strange that her husband did not take another wife. Ouma's own siblings, along with his parents who lived long, long lives, also thought it strange that he should marry only once, especially since he did not want for means, and the first union had after all started out with a stillborn son. But Ouma had courted Akoth from childhood, and when they finally wed, he knew that he was complete. The bond they shared through their children even transcended tradition. As the laws of the British Protectorate changed during their lifetime, redefining the purpose of education and altering the way children were raised across the land, Akoth and Ouma sent both their son

Omondi and their daughter Akinyi to the Mission school, and encouraged Omondi to continue on to university. But Ouma would not send his daughter, Akinyi, away, although he bragged about how bright she was and how surely she could run circles around anyone at Oxford if she ever stepped foot there. He lavished all his attention on her and, upon his death, bequeathed everything he owned to her, even though she was the girl, and even though she was the younger.

Eleven Long Rains and a century, longer than her own grandmother, who lived for ninety-nine annual seasons, came and went, and Akoth traveled through the world of Time bearing the name her father had bestowed upon her, carrying with it the grand myths that rumors lent it. Like so many women of the clan, she drew time slowly, unlike the men who only lived brief, troubled lives. Those of the men who lived past thirty annual seasons seemed to fade into silence and quiet communion with their fellow fishermen.

The seizures and flights of time that killed many of the afflicted often manifested after eleven Rains in both the families that joined when Akoth's grandson, Gabriel Ochola, married Anna Adongo, the granddaughter of Akoth's girlhood friend. Any man who crossed the threshold of thirteen untouched could expect a life long and uneventful. By age twenty-two, those who were touched were confirmed in their special condition, and the clan's Dream Walker made sure that they were properly prepared for the world.

The general absence of men was so common in both families, whether because of an act of the will, diminished capacity, or death, that it could be taken for granted. Akoth married and left her grandmother's house to become the mother of two sons and a daughter. The first son was stillborn, but the other two children grew up healthy and strong. The elder surviving child, Omondi, married well when he came of age. He lived for many rains, and then some nine months after his great-grandmother Nyanaam, his only son, and his only grandchild all passed away, he drowned in the rapids north of the Lake, leaving behind two widows, and a baby on the way. At the time, his first wife was still mourning her nineteen-year-old son and the soul of her infant grandchild; she was stunned by the successive extinction of three generations of her family's men in the span of a single year. Omondi's younger widow was disconsolate and went into early labor, delivering her late husband's only surviving child. The labor concluded, she got up from child-bed and walked away, never to be seen again.

Akoth doted on the newborn grandson, just as Nyanaam had doted on her. And just as Olóo had claimed his daughter and named her from beyond the world of Time, Nyanaam claimed and named the child Ochola, christened Gabriel, when he was presented to the ancestors. Akoth was delighted to hear her grandmother's claim, delighted that Nyanaam would continue to guide and protect her as she raised her orphaned grandchild. She let herself wonder why first her father, and now her grandmother, had both returned to claim someone so soon after entering the realm of the ancestors. She even let herself wonder about the link between Gabriel and Nyanaam, especially since he was born nine months after Nyanaam's own death. But she did not let herself wonder for too long. Just as her grandmother had been for her, she became her grandson's mother and father. She discovered in the child an easy and open spirit that moved her deeply, and a mind whose flexibility she would only see again in Esther when Gabriel became a father in his turn.

Soon after Gabriel was born, Akoth could see that he was touched. He was a still child, smiling at everything, it seemed, yet his eyes rarely focused on anything in particular. Even as an infant, anyone looking at that smiling, round baby could tell that whatever he was laughing at was probably only inside his mind's eye. Time alone would tell whether he truly was a Dream Walker like his great-grandfather or like the cousin who would die alone in the Hilton Hotel in St. Petersburg. As he grew up, Akoth watched with a mix of regret and relief as the sight faded, and Gabriel passed his thirteenth birthday without any incident. Her grandmother's repeated accounts of Olóo's affliction and its punishing drain on his life, how it took him on the night his youngest child was born, how it robbed a mother of her son, and a daughter of her father, all fed Akoth's joy that Gabriel would live as an ordinary man in a world that could no longer tolerate extraordinary souls.

Canto Ten

Akoth never forgot the day she first saw one of her father's waking dreams take form in the world of Time. Until then, everything she had heard from Nyanaam was just a story, and then suddenly, she discovered for herself that the world had changed. It was during the Long Dry season and she was thirteen years old. She had gone to Kisumu market with some of her older sisters to sell dried fish and reed mats. They set out early, before the roosters stirred to harass their mates and announce the advent of the sun, and quickly fell into a steady, cheerful pace, their bundles and baskets expertly balanced on their heads as they walked in single file along the lake shore. The sky was just beginning to brighten as they rounded the horn of the Bay and turned south. By the time the sun peeked over the horizon it was well on their left. Shortly before getting to the market they happened upon a raised path made of packed pebbles that had not been there the previous month. The path was wide enough for six girls to walk along it side by side, but it was lined with thick wooden planks soaked in pitch and firmly wedged into the ground. Perpendicular to the wooden planks that stretched into the horizon, there lay a pair of matching ribbons of cold iron bars that also disappeared beyond sight.

Some of the girls walked along the new path, matching their steps to the measure of the distance between the wooden planks. Three of the younger ones tried to balance their gait atop the iron ribbons, but these were too narrow and too cold for the children's unaccustomed feet. Akoth stayed off the new path, wary of the pitch and of the metal. The wooden planks lined up along the ground conjured images of a giant python unnaturally turned on its back, its ridged belly exposed to the sky.

When they finally got to market, many of the other fishmongers were already there and settled on their reed mats. Excitement heightened the way people greeted one another on account of the path of iron and blackened wood planks that ran along the edge of the marketplace. There had been rumors for a while about large companies of unusual men approaching the lake and laying down the path as they went. When at last a steaming locomotive slid heaving past the market and into the station that had been erected just beyond the edge of the place of gathering, Akoth recognized the serpent from her father's waking dreams that Nyanaam described so often.

No one knew exactly when the dreams of the iron serpent started, but it seems they were among the earliest, among the ones Olóo could talk about when his seizures became noticeable. It would emerge from the sea, he said, sliding through the plains and over the mountains, and slipping past the valley and across the highlands. It would be bigger and louder than the boy knew how to describe, its hissing might frightening every beast and fowl in its path. It would swallow people whole and spit them out still living, carrying baskets and bundles full of otherworldly things. Even livestock — cattle, goats, chickens, creatures small and large — would go in and out of the giant serpent, seemingly unharmed. These were the accounts of Olóo's waking dream that Nyanaam relayed to his youngest daughter.

For many months after that first encounter with the serpent's sticky black trail, Akoth visited the train station on her way back from the market to watch the steaming, hissing, shrieking leviathan creep in and out of the Kisumu market station. The world had changed. Her Time would be different from the Time her ancestors had known.

Dream vision melded into memory, and Akoth saw what Olóo had seen when the serpent entered his waking dream. The throngs of men who spilled out of the iron giant carrying boxes and bundles wore iron manacles and anklets bound in chains, and small turbans wrapped around their heads. Their thin loincloth was made of the same white cotton fabric as their turbans and both were stained with blood and mud, often mixed together on the lacerated skin of their backs and caked into the top of the loincloth cinched at their waist where their spilled blood pooled. They rarely spoke, and when they did it was in a language Olóo did not know at first. It sounded like the sea, or how he imagined the sea to be, rolling in waves of singsong cadences of "nam" and "la" to affirm or deny the shouted assaults of the pallid herders who directed their every move. Most of the eyes of the beset porters were empty, as if the Spirit within had fled, driven out through the torn flesh by the lashes of the Children of Shadow herding them.

These, too, were men, or seemed like men. Their home was far, far away, across the highlands and through the valley, over the mountain and past plains where the sun was always hidden behind clouds. They washed ashore at the edge of the world, expelled by the deep salt sea, and they made shadows wherever they went to keep the sun from burning their bleak, strangely inflamed flesh. They had a languid way about them that belied the sting of their whips. Raw and sweating from the heat, they stank of rotting fish. Anyone who dared to look at them knew that they were not happy in the light of the equatorial sun.

Among them, a few who traveled with the pale herders seemed to worry about the lacerated skin of the coastal herd. At night, these few, for their part clad in robes cinched with knotted rope and beaded strings, washed the wounds of the men bound in chains and dressed them with oily salves extruded from ripened coconuts. In the morning, they laid their hands on the tortured men of the coast and recited incantations about walking through the valley of the shadow of death. Olóo did not know their language, yet he seemed to understand their incantations: *The Lord is my shepherd; I shall not want. He maketh me to lie down in green pastures; He leadeth me beside the still waters.*

Playing alone in the puddles outside his mother's hut, Olóo made oddly shaped boats with impractical numbers of oars and sails so large that they dwarfed the hull of his slapdash vessels. All the sailors aboard his improvised ships looked to his eye like the naked palms of newborn babies. He dug through anthills, seeking colorless grubs, and pried pallid insects from crevices and burrows. When he had collected enough of them, he placed them in his strange boats together with shy snails he found along the way, and made them set sail in the puddle water, muttering the incantations of the wound-washers. In the name of the Shepherd, their boats set sail on roiling waters far from the green pastures of their cold, cloudy home, and struck out to assail lands unknown.

He leadeth me in the paths of righteousness for His name's sake.

The waters were even colder, deeper than they had ever dreamed, closed and unwelcoming. Why had they come?

Yea, though I walk through the valley of the shadow of death, I will fear no evil; for Thou art with me; Thy rod and Thy staff, they comfort me.

There was water, water, everywhere, and not a drop to drink…

Thou preparest a table before me in the presence of mine enemies.

Olóo did not know the language, but he understood the chant. He understood that the grubs and the snails on his ship were looking for land, seeking a harbor, any port with solid ground where they might go ashore and gather fruit. Too many weeks aboard the mast-heavy carracks eating nothing but salted fish and dried pork and beef, rationing the sweet water because all the sea would offer was the biting brine that made men incontinent and drove them mad with thirst, too many weeks aboard begat illness and death. The more sea water the maddened sailors drank, the sicker they became, until delirium overtook them, and they had to be cast overboard. Seasoned captains did not accept young deckhands. Younger crewmen could not bear the long austere spells at sea when every man received but a few drops of potable water every day. The youngest hands invariably drew water from the sea eventually, believing that somehow the brine would not ravage their bodies as it always did everyone else's. It took only one – a thirsty boy, and hungry – to break the seal of austerity and open the door to delirium.

Thou anointest my head with oil; my cup runneth over.

The snails anointed the decks of Olóo's ragtag carracks with the slick sheen of their bellies, meandering aboard, seeking safe harbor. Olóo guided his ship to the edge of the puddle under the shade of the banana tree that grew by his mother's hut and laid it on its side on the dry ground, spilling the pallid grubs onto the dust, blowing gently on the snails so that they might know to detach from the deck and disembark onto the ground.

He leadeth me beside the still waters. He leadeth me in the paths of righteousness…

In the Time before the railway came, the nomad clans followed their Dream Walkers wherever they led, even to barren lands where they knew that oases would spring up unbidden. The railway's advent slowed, and finally ended migration, as the Kisumu market grew and remained open with the changing seasons. The noise and carnage wrought by the leviathan across the land began to blind the Dream Walkers and numb them to the pulse of the world outside Time. By the time Gabriel was born, Akoth only hoped that she could prepare her grandson to live well in the bounds of Time. She did not yet know that the change in the world would undo all of her afflicted kin. She did not yet know that within her own lifetime, they would all lose their place in Time forever.

<hr>

Canto Eleven

Olóo was nine years old when he fell profoundly ill during a short rainstorm that surprised everyone because it was the beginning of the dry season. He was unable to speak or eat for nearly three days, and after he recovered, he told his mother about a stoning he had seen while herding his father's cattle in the flatlands among the great boulders. Nyanaam listened to him closely and for the first time suspected that her son might be a Dream Walker.

On typical days when the children set out to herd the cattle and goats, the older boys carried the younger ones on their backs to the grazing fields with them, the animals scampering ahead or lumbering off to the side, stooping occasionally to nibble on valiant clumps of grass and shrub that braved the barren landscape along the well beaten path that led away from the clusters of family homesteads and the cultivated lands. In the immediate vicinity of the settlement, there were no pastures in the hot flatlands that stood aloof to the neighboring Lake — not like the grasslands in the savanna, or the lush meadows of the mountain foothills beyond the highlands.

Olóo's clan had chosen to settle in a Bay near the lake shore where cacti littered the landscape — in some places clustered in compact uninviting bundles, while here and there a solitary umbrella thorn tree stood erect or, in the curious posture of a man fighting the wind, grew leaning into nothingness. In the fields surrounding the settlement, they had learned, over several generations, to coax sorghum and millet out of the ground during the Rainy Seasons and to draw fish from the Lake during the Dry Seasons.

Dust devils twirled over the hard ground too hot to walk on barefoot and sent little tornadoes of debris pointlessly crashing into the giant boulders that dotted the land beyond the fertile fields of grain. Generation after generation of growing boys learned to look after cattle and goats, the clan's strength and wealth from the time it first left the River and headed south to find the Lake at the behest of their Dream Walkers.

Setting out for the day, the young boys let the livestock lead them, trusting the animals to know how best to fill their need for food. A distance from the Bay, when the herds of cattle or the flocks of goats slowed down or came to a standstill, the children sought shelter in the shade of the surrounding boulders or opened fleshy cactus leaves to cool their seats and heels. The smaller boys, their young feet still too tender to withstand the searing heat of the baked clay earth at noon, danced about the ground, urgently hopping around to avoid burning their soles, unable to simply sit still under the shade in spite of themselves. Once the beasts they tended had scraped whatever feeding they could out of the mean earth and started moving elsewhere in search of greener pastures, the whole band would decamp and follow.

The older, wiser children sometimes tried to guide the herds to places they knew where they could all find some shade under which to play games with stones, thorn tree quills, and goat pellets. The pellets were only good when they were dry, but occasionally the younger children would accidentally pick fresh droppings when they were not being careful, giving everyone a good laugh for days, sometimes for years to come.

Once they settled into their games, indiscreet shouts of challenge, triumph, resignation, or joy spouted from the children and sublimated into the wide expanse of the barren flatlands, blending in with the occasional bleating outbursts from the hapless overgrown baby goats who never seemed to know to stay close to the herd, yet managed to annoy all the older goats and even some of the cattle.

These newly weaned goats were the most irksome. They either did not know how to graze properly or they just imagined that milk was always an option. Nibbling at something, anything, was a safe bet, but every once in a while, one of them, its twin toggles dangling under its chin like teardrops, would rush to its mother's udder and push aside the newborn kids who were inexpertly trying to get a fix on a teat. But lactating mother-goats never tolerated udder greed from weaned kids. They avoided these lazy offspring by lowering their flanks to make the udder less accessible to the taller ones, and when this did not work, as it usually did not, they would be forced to take off in short bursts, sometimes even turning to violently butt the teat pirates with their heads. The really small baby goats were usually left teetering at a loss or scampering in desperate pursuit.

The boys charged with herding the animals did not pay much attention to such drama, unless one of these young weaned goats was especially troublesome and kept the newborn kids from feeding for too long. It was usually enough for the boys to make sure that none of the goats ventured too far out of sight, that none of the cattle wandered off the grazing patch. The younger and more restless among them who did not know how to keep still under the shade would run after stray kids and calves and round them up, letting the older boys know if the animals migrated far enough to warrant following. Rainy Season and Dry Season alike, young boys of different age groups set out with the animals, sometimes guiding them, sometimes not, always looking for pastures not too far from the village settlements or from the Lake.

Before his eighth year, Olóo was rarely to be found among them. Ever a daydreamer, his delicate constitution worried his mother. In her eyes, he was like the teetering acacia trees that leaned on nothing and sometimes fell down during the Long Rains if their roots were too shallow and the ground they stood on became too soft. He was not social and did not seem interested in learning how to care for his father's livestock. All the boys of his age group could be depended upon to give a detailed accounting of where they had been, what they had done and how the animals had behaved, especially if something ever went awry, but Olóo never seemed to know how to stay with his group.

He was the first born of the third wife, and his father's only son. Everyone called his mother Min-Olóo, or *Nyanaam* — Daughter of the Lake — the name she received at birth or bore in a childhood long forgotten in the wealth of prestige that being mother to the sole heir brought. Although she could never take the place of the first wife who had only borne eleven girls and no boys, bearing the only son elevated Nyanaam in the eyes of the clan. The second wife also had only daughters – nine in all – and she was of the same age group as Olóo's mother. Olóo's mother had borne six children after him, five of them girls and one other boy, but the boy had not survived. The fourth wife, who came to the estate when Olóo was almost four years old, had given birth three times to boys, each of whom had survived only a few hours.

Voices whispered that Olóo's mother was using powerful medicine to ensure that her son would remain the sole heir to a vast fortune, and the only name patriarch. When his father died, he would become the head of the family, also responsible for all his sisters' marriages. He would be the one to receive their bride-wealth when suitors came seeking union with them. Considering the number of sisters he had, marrying them away would make his the wealthiest clan in the Bay, and perhaps in all the lake shore and highlands and valleys beyond. Of course nobody said anything out loud. Olóo's mother held her tongue, too, and let mysterious powers that inspired unspoken fear and deference be attributed to her. She knew that as long as people feared her using such powers, reverence for her son was assured. So she allowed rumors to slide from the lips of one to the ears of another, and never said or did anything to confirm or refute them.

The boy's absentmindedness and unusual fantasies only helped fan the flames of superstition that kindled around him. He spent an inordinate amount of time alone, often inventing games which he played with friends invisible to all but himself, or fashioning enigmatic looking toys out of whatever he could lay his hands on.

Olóo preferred the company of girls to boys, a natural consequence of being only one of two males in a family homestead of nearly three dozen souls. Until he was eight years old, he would wander off from the group of boys tending the livestock to find his sisters who were out picking fresh reeds with the other girls at the lake shore close by. There he would join the merry circle in their gathering songs and sorting games. But when he was eight, he was formally bound to his age set. Common sense and convention dictated that the boy who would inherit his father's growing wealth had to himself learn to be a leader among other boys. Olóo now had to keep to the grazing fields in the flatlands strewn with boulders. He was by then considered already too old to be admitted freely into the company of the girls, and he would not be allowed to join them at the Lake to gather reeds and to sing whenever he pleased.

For their part, the girls of the village were charged with bringing the reeds they collected to the older women who then bound them into roofing thatch, or wove them into baskets, mats, and fishing traps. The large mats, lined with tanned hide and, occasionally, cotton sheets, served for sitting, or sleeping. Some mats hung in doorways and others were kept aside rolled up for use during outdoor gatherings or for visits by special guests. Reed mats also protected the small partitions in each hut where the drinking water was kept. Long-stemmed calabashes for drawing out drink were tied to large clay pots full of well water or river water which remained icy cool even in the driest equatorial heat.

During the Long Rains, other even bigger clay pots stationed around each hut just under the eaves of the roofs gathered rainwater dripping from the reed thatching. These large reservoirs were meant for the animals, for washing, for mixing clay and dung mortar to fortify walls, or to repair them whenever the need arose.

The Long Rains lasted several months and sometimes, when they were especially heavy, it became impossible to walk, so everyone had to wade through the growing pools that settled into the low-lying areas of the lake basin. The children no longer took the goats out to the fields, and the chickens stayed cooped up. While their mothers and fathers and elders worried about livestock and planting crops and building new dwellings and repairing old walls, the children drew untold pleasures from splashing about in the pools of muddy water.

After the Long Rains, the women made repairs to all the huts in the homestead. The drying waters that left the ground soft made mixing clay and mud and dung much easier for building, and the construction enterprise, directed by the matriarch, quickly gained momentum. Once they finished their work on the walls, the women would strip away the old roof thatch, and bind the freshly harvested, bundled and woven reeds to the wattle framework. They always started with the main granary which stood at one end of the family estate near the patriarch's hut. Only when they had completed and secured the roof of the granary did they attend to the father's hut, moving on to the first wife's, then the second wife's and so forth until the adolescent children's huts were re-thatched. The last place to be thatched anew was the kitchen, a generous enclosure between the huts of the third and fourth wife. Just behind the kitchen there were two, small provisional huts that the third and fourth wife minded, and behind those two huts stood the chicken coop.

Each season came and went with the same rituals without variation. During the harvest in the Dry Season following the Short Rains, the little girls gathered all the sorghum and millet and spread them out to dry on large reed mats under the stilts of the main granary. After the grains had dried sufficiently, the older girls rolled up the mats with the grain still inside them, and then rubbed the mats to and fro to loosen the brittle husks. Then they would start winnowing to prepare the grain for storage or for grinding. The small girls poured the dried grain into round winnowing trays which the older girls shook gently back and forth in circular and lateral waves. Then, in one fluid movement, the winnower would dip the tray to a deep angle and then suddenly jerk it up and stop short when the tray was level, sending a stream of grain soaring into the air where crossing breezes could carry away the chaff, leaving the dense grain to come cascading back down onto the tray. The winnower waiting to receive the falling grain would repeat the maneuver until the wind had nothing more to bear away.

Olóo's elder sisters were accomplished winnowers, and he often sat transfixed as they rocked their large trays to and fro, round and round, sending the weightless chaff into flight, into the sun. The light heat and the thick dust from the threshed grain always made Olóo thirsty, and he craved water, dreamed of water, could not get enough. The girls soon made a habit of bringing one of the drinking water pots out into the center of the family homestead on winnowing days if he was there with them. As soon as the chaff started floating away, an overflowing calabash would find its way to his waiting lips.

Canto Twelve

Anyone else hearing what Olóo told his mother about witnessing the stoning in the flatlands would have dismissed it as a child's fantasy. And had it been any other child, Nyanaam would not even have paid attention.

Almost a year had passed since Olóo had been bound to his age-set and Nyanaam herself was already twenty-two. She was thirteen when she bore him, and mother and son had bonded easily, especially since Nyanaam was naturally curious and always alert to the little daydreaming creature she had borne. Even as young as she was, Nyanaam understood that, as the sole heir of a wealthy and respected man, her son was destined for great responsibility. And yet the infant she held was utterly dependent on her for the least of his needs. She wanted to know what the world seemed like to him so, as soon as he could speak, she encouraged her son to talk about what he saw in his mind's eye. Her attention was unwavering and, as the boy grew up, he never hesitated to tell his mother about anything.

Nyanaam was not a Dream Walker herself and yet, as her son recounted what he had seen, she recognized that he was describing events that had taken place in the infancy of the world, things that were never revealed to children, and only entrusted to the Midwives, the Medicine Healers, and the Dream Walkers who safeguarded the Spirits of the clan.

Olóo told his mother that they had followed the livestock as usual to a grazing patch just out of sight of the Lake. After the animals had settled down, the boys found a shady outcrop of rocks in which to pass the time. It was the tail end of the Short Rains and although the sky was completely clear, the sun was more gentle than usual, making it easy for the small boys to walk on their own and run around without a second thought. Olóo now had to sit with his wiser, older age-mates.

Their talk meandered for a while, touching on this and that, but before long most of the boys were dozing in the gentle morning sun. Olóo thought of going to see his sisters by the Lake, but then he remembered his duty, so he decided to watch the livestock instead.

He wandered to where he thought the cattle and goats were, but he did not find them. So he clambered up one of the larger boulders thinking he might get a better look, and that is when he saw the woman getting stoned by the mob.

She was standing in the midst of a large, thinly spread crowd of agitated men and women, her back to one of the giant boulders that spotted the landscape. It looked as if the crowd had dragged her there. At the base of the boulder, around her feet, a pool of sticky blood collected and was soaking into the ground.

The dusty stench of rusted iron stung Olóo's nose and he felt like he was but an arm's length from the condemned woman even though she was more a strong shouting distance away. In that moment she looked up and saw him. Then she opened her mouth as if to call him. But he ducked out of sight, frightened and unknowing. A stone crashed against her upper lip and silenced the unuttered call. When Olóo looked up again, stones large and small were raining down on the woman. On her eyes and forehead, collarbones and chest, and through the fingers she spread over her face to protect herself. Ruthless stones crushed her elbow, and her wrists and ankles twisted as the hail of pebbles and rocks speedily found their mark. She cried with each strike but Olóo could hear nothing.

She caught his eye again just as he saw a large stone strike and pinch her ear against her skull, forcing her to twist her body strangely and bend down at her waist, as if to cradle her mangled ear. Just then, another stone, bigger and visibly heavy, hoisted by a man standing atop an adjacent boulder, came crashing down on the back of her exposed neck. Now her body whipped back up and, for a moment, she stood almost upright. For a long, long moment, her eyes glassy, and then opaque, fixed on the eyes of the boy watching her aghast. Now he was standing in front of her, his body almost touching hers.

He looked right into her changing eyes and knew the instant the flame of life was extinguished. He felt her blood-drenched breath on his face as her head dipped slowly, her eyes vacant, sinking into his as if to deliver her expiring soul. Then silently, she swayed backwards and crumbled against the boulder behind her into the gathering pile of stones at her feet, her neck broken.

Olóo could not move. He was still on his hands and knees on the distant rock looking down on the woman and the mob that had beaten the life out of her body. Fear churned in his stomach, fear that the crowd, seething and thirsty for more blood, would turn on him if they saw him. Yet he could not move even to hide. He was so petrified that he clung to the boulder out of Time in plain sight, partly crouching on all fours, his neck still outstretched.

Olóo, Olóo, koth biro! Watero dhok wadhii dala! Olóo, koth biro! One of the younger boys who was maybe five or six years old came darting through the boulders behind Olóo. His overly large head balancing on his long, thin neck, the boy breathlessly announced that they had to take the cattle home because the rain was coming. Although that was not unheard of at the tail end of the Rainy Season, the sky had been so clear at dawn when they set out for the plains, that they had let themselves wander quite far. Now they would have to hurry home if they did not want a cumbersome muddy journey back.

Olóo roused himself, unaware how long he had been frozen, and hurried to catch up with the group that was now urgently trying to get the cattle and the goats to head homeward. They all passed near the boulder where he had seen the woman executed. Nothing remained of the pile of stones, and the woman's body had also vanished. At the foot of the big rock there was a deep maroon and orange stain where he had seen the pool of blood soaking into the ground. A small whirlwind swept up a suddenly rusty stench as he passed by the boulder. He tarried, and then he gagged, a wave of nausea sweeping through his body, flooding his mouth with salty saliva. The other boys hurrying the livestock along beckoned him to catch up, and he struggled to keep his feet moving forward, even as his body shuddered in revulsion. When they all finally arrived home, he fell ill and for several days he could not tell his mother what he had seen happen. It rained until he recovered.

Canto Thirteen

That is when Nyanaam, already very attentive to her son's wellbeing, decided that he would need special care and education. She made no great announcements, nor did she change her outward behavior. She simply made sure that when the Medicine Healer was called to see her ailing son, he heard about the vision that had come before the rain.

The Medicine Healer listened to everything the boy muttered in his delirium and confirmed that he was describing a Dream Walker's waking dream. He decreed that Olóo was to stay close to his sisters if he was unwell in any way, even in a way ordinary for boys his age. The girls were to tend to Olóo's every need and teach him all their songs. He would be kept cool indoors on a soft straw mat with a ready gourd of water near at hand. He would be taken to the Lake if he was well enough to walk by himself, and he would be allowed to gather reeds and sing with his sisters. He would sit with them as they told stories and sang while harvesting and threshing the grain, winnowing and grinding.

So for the next two years, whenever Olóo was with his sisters, they taught him songs of winnowing and showed him how to weave, even though it was not the customary thing for a boy to do. They put him to work as one of them, cooing approvingly when he did things well, and laughing heartily when he did things badly. They let him watch them work when they were doing those things for which he had no talent. His sisters, recalling his carefree devotion to them from his infancy, welcomed him back into their company whenever his mother deemed he was not well enough to go out into the open flatlands. Time passed and he grew stronger with their songs.

And then one day, when he was eleven, his mother noticed that her son was not eating. He drank water incessantly, more than he usually did, but food did not pass his lips at any time. She held him back from the herding chores and entrusted him to his sisters. The girls reported to her how he would sit and watch them winnowing, looking as if he were seeing the dance of the falling grain for the first time. He sat right in their midst where the fine dust of the millet and sorghum chaff covered him from head to foot when the wind was still. He drank water continually and emptied entire pots of it by himself.

For thirty-three days he watched his sisters work, growing thinner every day as nothing but water passed his lips, his large eyes sinking deeper in their sockets. When food was brought to him, he looked at it unknowingly, as if he could not guess what he was meant to do with it. His sisters tried to feed him, to bring the food to his mouth, but his mouth just lay open indifferently and let the food tumble out unchewed and untasted. His mother dismissed any suggestion that her son was the object of some powerful witchcraft, but she still called the Medicine Healer to watch with her and wait. For two years she had nursed her son's health, ensuring that everyone around him helped him grow in strength. Knowing that he was touched, she waited for his condition to manifest strongly enough for others to recognize it. Now he was languishing again, more severely than he had previously, yet he said nothing in testament to the true nature of his affliction. Finally, a day came that seemed to break the spell, although at first no one could tell that the boy was feeling different than before.

Everything had been as usual. The millet and sorghum were ready for threshing and the little girls were busy agitating the straw mats together to loosen the grain husks. When they finished, they heaped handfuls of the grain onto the winnowing trays which the older girls then took up and started swaying back and forth to coax the chaff to the surface. Olóo sat as he usually did on a straw mat with his sisters around him. They rocked the large trays to and fro, round and round, sending the grain aloft. As they worked, the boy did not ask for water. He was engrossed in watching how, instead of just disappearing into the sun, the chaff hung suspended in the air for a while, a long while, as if the flight heavenward were yet undecided. Then one by one, and then by twos, and then by half-dozens or so, the suspended husks changed slowly as they continued to float upward, turning into flat, white flakes before drifting downward in languid insouciance.

The boy was entranced, unmindful of whether everyone else saw what he saw. He watched as the flakes drifted closer, and then disappeared with small, gelid, featherweight precision as they touched his hot shining skin. Some landed on his eyelids, some landed on his cheeks, some landed on his arms and outstretched legs. When one of them touched his nose, his eyes crossed as he tried to get a better look. Never had he seen chaff like this, chaff which, rather than make him thirsty, cooled his overheated face.

He opened his mouth and stuck out his tongue as he always did in the rain but, unlike water, the flakes tumbled down erratically. And even though their icy caress tickled him and made his skin tingle, he could not touch them. When he wanted to show them to his sisters, his mother, his cousins, the drifting flakes simply vanished and never even reached the ground.

It rained briefly that day, unexpectedly – small harsh hailstones that fell hastily as if furtively swept out of heaven. And then Olóo emerged from his altered state, playing and laughing and eating as if nothing had been amiss.

Generations later, long after Anna and Gabriel's children had all forgotten the first time they had seen snow fall in Boston, when America was no longer strange and marvelous to them, when a too-careless world had long since learned to forgive itself for its complacencies, Hehra, in a moment of terrifying ecstasy quickened by the agony of childbirth, wondered whether her afflicted sister and her twice-great-grandfather were one person. For Olóo, sitting on the Equator by the Great Lake under the dry noon sun, had felt the gentle grace of crystalline snow through Maya's skin.

<hr />

Canto Fourteen

Akoth never knew snow, but she ventured beyond greater distances in the world of Time than her father ever had when — many years after she first stumbled across the newly laid train tracks in Kisumu, long after she had been married to the charming Ouma who courted and wooed her still even after the wedding, and even after she was widowed, just as he had when they were young — long ago, she had boarded a train that crossed the country from Nam Ataro to travel through the Rift Valley, over the Nandi highlands and Kikuyu tea hills, past the slopes of the equatorial mountain, and across the savanna grasslands, finally to arrive at the coastal city of Mombasa whence the iron behemoth first came. By then, she had seen nearly seventy Long Rains and seventy Short Rains. Both her son and her daughter had lived and died, leaving behind the two orphaned grandchildren to whom she was simply "Mamma Akoth." The two boys were now old enough to be living abroad. Ochiëng was a budding philosopher, intrepid enough to brave the chill of Russia alone pursuing ineffable truths, and Gabriel a mostly shy aspiring doctor whose letters rang with surprisingly effusive veneration for his new mentor, a poetic, French physician from Sierra Leone.

Gabriel wrote to his Mamma Akoth from London, wanting to know things about the coast he had never brought up before. Was the ocean as wondrous and beautiful as Lolwe's Great Lake Ataro? Was the Portuguese fort truly grand? Should he take Doctor Anatole Basile Tejo there to visit? So many questions she could not answer! When her husband Ouma still lived, he, too, had talked of these things, yet he never imagined boarding the train and taking it all the way to the coast – that was something that only the British did, and only ever with their servants from neighboring lands, or from as far away as India. Nor had Akoth imagined taking the journey for many Rains since Ouma's passing. But now her two grandsons, each the gem of her heart, were both abroad and there were questions to be answered. Although her house was still teeming with the numberless children of JokOlóo, her wards all, the offspring of her many-numbered older siblings, and unto the next generation, Akoth set out for the sea to see for herself. When Gabriel returned, she would know what to tell him.

The locomotive stopped at the edge of the Rift Valley, in a cattle trading town on top of a hill. *Nakuru!*, hollered the conductor. And then the train descended to the foothills of the equatorial Mountain of God's Repose in the heart of Kikuyu. The journey was going to be long and, at first, felt a little bit alarming. The train heaved and rattled at every departure, hooting and clanging to announce its passage, but it quickly found a steady rhythm that sounded like distant drumbeats. Akoth was glad that she had booked a private cabin in a sleeper carriage. She did not want to sit upright all the way to Mombasa. After the train cleared the center of Nairobi and established a constant tempo, she imagined that it would keep this lulling cadence for a while. She decided to stretch out on her bunk and relax for the duration, drawing out the aged New Testament volume annotated, in her own hand, with meditations and prayer. She wanted to read a few verses before lying down to go to sleep. Joy saturated her entire being whenever she held the volume. Its soft leather binding felt warm, as if alive, and the rattling and bumping carriage lent the book's inanimate stillness a sensible vibration that quickened it to her touch. The cherished volume slipped out of her grasp and fell open on the small table shelf under the cabin window.

Aseweyo timbe mag nyithindo… came to meet her eyes from the open page, and Akoth smiled. *I have put aside childish ways*, the trilingual text reiterated in English, and then again in Latin. *Yes, I have put aside childish ways*, Akoth thought, smiling at Nyasaye's sense of humor. How could she not, now that her Gabriel and her Ochiëng had ventured so far away, daring her, with their querying letters, to leave Nam Ataro for a brief while to see the sea past the horizon of the rising sun. The rest of the passage that rose from the open page to meet her searching eyes invoked the tongues of angels, mysteries and prophecies, singing of love as something truly infinite and eternal.

Koro waneno mana kido matiptip ka joma neno e rang'i marachrach…
For now we see through a glass, darkly… Videmus nunc per speculum in
aenigmate…

    … chiëng'no anang'e Nyasaye chuth, mana kaka Nyasaye ong'eya… then
shall I know God even as also God knows me … tunc autem cognoscam sicut
et cognitus sum.

The soft pages of the open book shivered and hummed with
the rattling train, letting Akoth's eyes take in the passages most
beloved by João de Sousa, the Portuguese monk about whom all
the Indian Christian missionaries of her childhood had spoken
with pious reverence, or laconic deference, or menacing veneration,
whatever the occasion demanded. João de Sousa was the model of
divinely inspired piety that the missionaries invoked to evangelize
about the beauty of humility and self-sacrifice in the name of the
Lord. Akoth's smile deepened. Was it the Bible, or the journey to
Mombasa that made her think of the Portuguese monk? João de
Sousa, the missionaries recounted, bore the Word of the Lord in
his heart, and could recite Scripture verbatim even after his Bible
was swept overboard in the briny trials of the Atlantic seas, and
even after he was captured by the Moors of Malindi, later to be
ransomed by Vasco da Gama. He brought, in his memory, new
stories of God and Creation to the lands of the Indian Ocean
along the coasts of Africa and Asia, and as the testament of the
faithful recounted, the peoples he found there quickened his faith
to even more ardent passions. João de Sousa bore the Word of the
Lord in his heart to his dying day, but once he was captured and
bound to be brought before the Holy Office of the Inquisition
for suspicion of heresy in foreign lands, he became less a man of
words, and more of manifest action, drinking of Divine grace even
in bondage and tribulation.

Akoth's journey to the coast took three days. When she arrived there, she took a room in a guest house that was once upon a time a convent, and then later a teacher training college. The guest house sat close to Fort Jesus, and the nuns who now ran it were all Saint Thomas Christians from Kerala. Communion with them came naturally for Akoth whose faith was sound, and whose love for the Word ran deep. For three weeks she visited the town and the coast together with two of the nuns who wanted to show her the beauties of their world. The nuns shared old stories of their birthplace in India and spoke often of how Saint Thomas brought the Word directly from the Lord to their land so many centuries past. Naturally, the tales that most gripped Akoth's imagination in their telling were those about Frei João de Sousa, brother to every Child of God. Listening to the nuns recount, time and time again, the story of his miraculous martyrdom at the hands of the Inquisition, Akoth began to think that perhaps the soft pages of the New Testament that opened to his favorite passages were in fact not just memory, but also prophecy which she had yet to understand.

The journey back to Nam Lolwe from Mombasa found Akoth nursing a troubled heart. She wanted to write to Gabriel of beauteous things and brave intrepid sailors, and even of João de Sousa and the miracles he wrought. But she feared that she would not be able to write past the savagery of the captain-major of the expeditions that transported the young monk around the world. The nuns' tales invoked dormant memories of some of the stories Nyanaam recounted of Olóo's waking dreams. Their tales of Portuguese sailors desperate for land and desperate for fruit recalled her father's boyhood toys, laden with grubs and snails that burned too readily in the sun. Tales of Christians and

Muslims, all martyrs burned because of their faith, because the Portuguese sailors said it was the will of the Lord. Akoth did not have the heart to repeat such things to Gabriel. Instead she would simply tell him that the ocean was truly grand, and Fort Jesus a living monument to the genius of man.

Book III. Alex and Maya

The conception and birth of the children of Anna Adongo and Gabriel Ochola. • How Gabriel met his mentor, Dr. Tejo, and grew to admire his family life in Paris. • How Gabriel brought the Sierra Leonean doctor to meet Mamma Akoth and to speak for him during his nuptials with Anna Adongo. • How Maya is conceived of her parents' shared dream and how she gets her name from her guardian Spirit.

Canto Fifteen

Born to Anna and Gabriel at dawn in Homa Bay by the Lake where their father's grandmother lived, David preceded his twin Alex by precisely an hour and three minutes. Esther followed in Kisumu when Gabriel worked at the city's General Hospital before moving his growing family to Nairobi. Maya was the first of the couple's children to be born far from her father's homeland in their new house in Ngong' Hills. The youngest, Hehra, was born in Sierra Leone, and then brought back east to grow up with her siblings.

Alex and Maya could very well have been the twins in the family — they were inseparable. Where she had no consideration for David, Maya adored Alex. She followed him everywhere from infancy and, before she could walk, the mere sound of his voice would send her dashing to find him, one leg eagerly dragging along on its knee behind the other more precocious limb that hurried along on foot. When she could finally stand upright, she struck an even more comical figure running on tiptoe teetering, as only toddlers can, in search of her Alex, or rather, 'Ah-lith,' as she called him. It was rare to see her playing with other children unless he was also among them.

Although David was meant to be the guardian since he was the eldest, he did not like Maya very much. An early antipathy developed between the two and they disagreed on almost everything. Sometimes they even came close to blows, but David had been taught that boys could not strike girls, so he seethed with frustration at every perceived slight he had to endure from her.

What stung most was Maya's unshakable devotion to his phantom twin, Alex. From the time she could talk — at seven months of age — it was 'Ah-lith' this and 'Ah-lith' that, and so David made Maya's lisp a running joke. David himself stammered painfully as a child and did not overcome the tick entirely until he had finished his A-levels. His stammer was always most pronounced when their mother Anna was absent. The boy would follow her with his eyes whenever she was in the same room, and if she left even for a short while, it would not be long before he was anxiously asking when she would return. He would grow restless, become agitated, nervous, and incoherent.

But his was not a gratuitous concern. Anna had the unusual habit of vanishing unexpectedly and without explanation. Sometimes she was gone for months at a time, leaving no idea of where she was, or when she would come back. Once, when the houseboy returned from the market having forgotten to bring home a loaf of bread and a liter of milk for the afternoon tea, Anna exploded in a rage, demanding to know why she paid servants to do simple things that they did not seem capable of doing. She would not brook people abusing her trust and taking advantage of the privileges she afforded them. She beat the houseboy mercilessly, and in her fury swung a soapstone vase at him which made a muted, fleshy thud when it collided with his jaw, crushing his mandible and rendering the unfortunate boy unconscious. Whether she had meant to actually cause him any harm is not clear. She left in the car to pick up some milk and some bread, and her mother Ruth saw to it that Sara and Rachel, Anna's younger twin sisters, carried the unconscious houseboy, with the help of the cook and the gardener, to a nearby clinic for treatment. The houseboy had to eat from a straw through the wires that bound his jaw for several months following, and as time went by, his face grew markedly asymmetrical. Anna was gone for seven weeks.

It seems that on the day her fury broke the houseboy's jaw, she happened to meet one of her uncle's medical partners as she was leaving the grocer's. The doctor was on his way to London for a conference and he jokingly, maybe, invited her to go with him. At first, she did not take him seriously, but then he said that his assistant was taken ill and he had an extra ticket. So, with little more than the passport in her purse, Anna simply followed the incredulous — and excited — doctor to the airport and boarded the flight with him. When she finally returned home, it was as if nothing had happened.

Inside the large, heavy Samsonite suitcase that she brought back with her, there was a purple pleated dress for her mother, a waterproof watch for her youngest brother, a shirt for the older one, patent leather shoes for small girls, little silk ties for small boys and two large tins of Quality Street sweets for everybody. The rest of the suitcase was full of scarves and blouses from Harrods to be distributed among her several sisters. For her personal wardrobe, Anna had only the latest in London fashion — a white polyester pantsuit with pleated breast pockets and flare cut trousers. The heavy synthetic cloth that was then all the rage draped beautifully to the ground, flattering her tall, subtly curvaceous frame. Everyone was delighted, the bread and the milk and the houseboy forgotten. Only Maya, then four years old, almost five, wanted to know why it was so hard to find bread and milk in Nairobi. She thought that going to London for them had been a pointless, wasted trip because, even after seven weeks, Anna had returned with neither. Anna was not amused.

David was thrilled to have his mother back. Anna's returns were always, without exception, cause for such intense joy that the child's inarticulate attempts to express himself — mutterings accompanied by hand waving and foot stomping — were transformed into flawlessly eloquent pearls of ceaseless solicitude.

Maya was five years younger than David and as they grew up, she guilelessly laughed at his inability to complete a sentence without getting stuck on some syllable like a damaged record. He would raise his leg in a reflex that somehow connected his larynx to his limbs, and then bring his foot down hard as if to propel his thwarted words out into the waiting world in an urgent rush of air. Maya just stared at him in mock horrified suspense, unable to contain herself, wanting to finish his sentences, sometimes bursting out in merry laughter as he struggled. When he threatened to tell on her for not respecting him as her elder, her mocking only grew worse for the threat.

"I'll tell Ma-, ma-, ma-, ma-, mmma-…. MmmmMaAnna that you're laughing at me. She's going to b-b-beat you. I swear, I'll te-, te-, te-, te-H-ell!"

This usually made Maya laugh even more gleefully. Why couldn't he just pronounce "MaAnna" like everybody else? It was already short for Mamma Anna, and David somehow could not say even that little word without exerting tremendous effort. When he expelled that final word, Maya always giggled cheekily.

"Oh, finally!" she exclaimed. "*Tempus fugit!*"

Maya had no idea what the Latin expression actually meant; it was how Alex needled her whenever she was mulling over something complex and incomprehensible, and he thought he was winning the argument. To David, it was an unequivocal insult, although he, too, did not know what it actually meant.

So David told, and Maya fell from her mother's good graces, again and again. He hoped, in turn, to rise in MaAnna's consideration, for life without MaAnna's approval was unbearable to the boy. Every day he wanted to know, was MaAnna returning home before they went to sleep; was MaAnna going to tell them a story; was MaAnna going to sit with them; was MaAnna going to say goodnight; was

MaAnna... David could not think without thinking of his mother. He worshiped her, and yet he knew, long before he could find the words, that she despised him. But with the faith of a little boy, he also believed that he could win her heart if he was very good, if he stayed close by her side and did as she said. He *was* good and devoted – most of the time. Sometimes, however, he would be unmindful of being diligent. Then Anna would find a way to remind him that she would never be his.

Alex, on the other hand, did not speak at all until after Maya was born. Then he chattered away as if he had always spoken, even though only Mamma Akoth and his new baby sister could hear him. After Maya arrived into the world of Time, Alex spent almost every hour together with her until the day Maya lost him in Lisbon when she was eighteen years old. Until that day, he was there to look after her and teach her when she awoke, and he was the last soul she saw before she fell asleep. Such was their union that Maya took her brother so much for granted that she no longer felt his presence, only his absence. When she was an infant, he had found himself occasionally wandering around in her dreams while she slept, but he did not know how it actually happened, nor how to go back in when he wanted to. As she grew older, he shared with her everything during their waking hours, but he could never show her anything behind the curtain of sleep.

Perhaps it was because of Alex's generous indulgence of his sister that Maya developed a habit for intransigence. Akoth could see that Alex had inherited his father's sentimental bent, and she sometimes worried that he spoiled his sister too much. Like his father had done with his mother, Alex forgave Maya everything, and for that reason she grew up believing that she could be forgiven for anything. But unlike their parents, the two children shared a communion of grace that knew no measure. Even if Alex was often perplexed by his little sister's uncommon way of looking upon the world, he never doubted that wherever she looked, she could always find beautiful moments that nobody else around her was able to see. And even when Maya did not agree with Alex or understand what he meant when he said some things, she looked to him first and last for answers to all her questions, assured that she could choose to accept his wisdom or to refuse his folly.

Canto Sixteen

Once, shortly before Rosie disappeared, Alex and Maya argued about the pronunciation of the word "island". Bob Marley was singing *Redemption Song* and although Maya could not understand everything he said, she knew he was singing about the kind of suffering endured by the Children of Israel, something that Mrs. Da Silva had described in minute and vivid detail at school. Maya drew closer to the record player and lifted the lid to watch Bob Marley pouring out his soul from the rotating black vinyl disk.

"Anyango, I told you not to lean against the record player like that," her aunt Sara said, walking through the room. "This child never listens. Wait until I tell your mother..." Her voice trailed off.

The palm tree on the logo for Island Records spun around and around and Maya stared, picturing Bob Marley strumming his guitar under the leaning tree. She turned to Alex, who was engrossed in a book, to ask him where "Issland" was. He did not hear her at first, so she asked again. When he looked up, she pointed at the record player, showing him the spinning logo, shifting closer to the turntable.

"Oh! Island. It's…"

"No, no! This one - Iss-land, here, eye-ess-el…"

"Wait, Anyango. That's 'eye-land,' that's just the spelling."

She looked at him for a moment and then looked at the logo again.

"So why doesn't it just say 'eye-land' on the paper, huh?" She had a look of tentative triumph on her face.

"I don't know, but the 'ess' is silent. You should read the word as if it's not even there."

Maya was confused. "That makes no sense! If there is no ess then why is it there, huh?" Her words were carefully chosen, her brother unconvincing. "It should not be written in the word. It's just a waste." She was frowning hard.

"Do you even know what an island is?"

"It's a place where people live in the middle of the ocean, like Zanzibar or Madagascar." Of that at least she was certain.

"And do you know how to spell it?" Alex's eyes twinkled.

"Yes… Eye, el, a, en, dee."

"No. Eye-tee!" he said, tickled silly that the trick had worked. He had seen the joke in a comic book and now he thrilled at the chance to repeat it.

Maya looked at him, confused, hesitant, eager. He tried to explain the joke, but she did not laugh. She was too worried that there could be a letter in a word that could be seen but not heard. It had to be Iss-land, so maybe Alex was mistaken. Maybe he had learned it wrong, or maybe he just did not know what it was, and he was pretending that it was something else. Her frustration welled up. She heard her aunt Sara in the corridor, looked up to see her stop by the door to make sure that the record player was safe before continuing down to the kitchen. Bob Marley had finally finished his song, leaving the dissonance of its final chord hanging in the waiting silence. Maya went back to staring at the now motionless vinyl disk for a while longer, wondering why the 'ess' was silent and how it had lost its sound. The 'esses' in other words could be heard and it did not make any sense that this particular 'ess' could be spelled out but never pronounced. No one had ever talked about silent 'esses' in Kindergarten, not even Miss Agarwal who talked about everything, including some things that Mrs. Da Silva did not think she should ever talk about.

"It still looks like Iss-land," she muttered under her breath, troubled.

"Eye-tee! IT! Come on, it's just a joke." But Maya would not laugh.

Canto Seventeen

Gabriel also liked to make people laugh. He married Anna Adongo, the beautiful granddaughter of his grandmother's childhood friend, soon after returning from London having completed his medical training. In London he had grown profoundly close to his mentor, Doctor Anatole Basile Tejo, and he wanted his honored friend to meet his Mamma Akoth. Gabriel's best-friend-cousin Ochiëng was still away in Russia, so the young doctor was both proud and moved when Doctor Tejo accepted his invitation.

Doctor Anatole Basile Tejo was fifteen years older than Gabriel. He lived in Paris with his wife and their two children, but he also spent a lot of his time in London training young African doctors. He spoke a language altogether alien to Akoth's grandson, a language mesmerizing and provocative, a language that dared the provincial young man to inhabit a painted skin and contemplate a history he could not quite grasp. The Sierra Leonean doctor quoted poetry and recounted elaborate and evocative histories of a people Gabriel had not known were his until he met the French doctor. Anatole Basile Tejo wanted to know how Gabriel had managed to reach adulthood without knowing how much his people had suffered in the world. Did he know so little about himself, about his own history?

Reflecting on his mentor's challenge, Gabriel thought of Mamma Akoth, and Olóo, and Nyanaam. He thought of the girl he was to marry when he returned home. He could not see his grandmother, nor her father, nor her grandmother, nor his waiting bride in the picture of abject plight that Anatole Basile Tejo painted before his eyes. Ever since Gabriel could remember, Mamma Akoth's doors were open to the numberless children of JokOlóo, infants and toddlers and young adolescents descended from her father's many sisters, her own brother's many grandchildren, and of members of her clan from far and wide. Mamma Akoth reminded them all to shape their world around Lwanda Maghere, Gor Mahia, Omweri; and then around Lenana, Gikuyu, and Mumbi; and then around *Amazing Grace* coaxed out of Mamma Akoth's warbling singing voice. Her stories and songs, speckled with names that echoed the trail of the iron serpent, even spoke of John Hanning Speke who decided to name for his Queen the Lake that the children of JokOwiny had played in and fished since rising from the River that flows against the wind. The stories of Mamma Akoth held fragments of *Psalms* of praise and *Psalms* of prayer, and memories of stone-etched Commandments numbering Ten, and the God that numbered Three. To the numberless children of JokOlóo, Mamma Akoth was the living memory of their most revered Dream Walker, Olóo, her songs painting distant, nameless worlds behind their sleeping eyelids every night.

The children of JokOlóo also learned, from the songs of Mamma Akoth, of Rainy Seasons and Dry Seasons, baskets and reeds, millet, sorghum and granaries, winnowing trays and grinding stones. The grazing lands were their frontiers, and the Great Lake their sea. She sang to them of how Ouma, the son of Owino of the Lake Island clan, had wooed her since she was fourteen, waiting for her everyday as she made her way to the Lake, singing as if to herald her passage, his voice powerful and smooth like the current of the Nile: *Owada, kuwinja! Akoth biro. Keluru dhok e dala!* Ouma's father was a fisherman who lived mostly on the Lake Island, but his children lived with their grandmother on the outer shore. Akoth would walk past her self-assured suitor with her age-mates, basket firmly balanced on her crown, her head high and aloof. She was amused by his attempts at wit, but she shielded herself between her friends, pretending not to hear his calls. *He should be more careful*, her companions goaded him. Her best friend Akong'o went as far as threaten Ouma that Akoth would ask her father's Spirit to send a cloud that hung only over his head and rained on him if he did not leave Akoth alone. So of course, he flirted even more boldly, smiled more broadly, and boasted about the bride-wealth he could bring to Nyanaam to claim Akoth as his first wife. The children of JokOlóo never tired of hearing this story. Ouma was their paragon for the successful young suitor. When such a suitor came to call, the well-bred girl knew that Akoth was the model of bride to be.

But with Time, the songs and names of the childhood world of the children of JokOlóo faded into inaudible echoes with the lost language of their great-grandmother. When they were ready to leave and venture into the world alone, Akoth sent her wards across the newly drawn border to Uganda, and through the Valley to Nairobi, and over the seas to learn to be teachers and lawyers and doctors and engineers. Gabriel wanted to stay with his grandmother, content to help raise emerging generations of JokOlóo, but she would not hear of it. His older cousin Ochiëng, also orphaned in infancy, was raised by both his paternal and maternal grandmothers, and grew up longing for *loka*, the faraway places they heard about from the foreigners who came to see the famous Lake. So Akoth sent them both away to see the world beyond the Bay. Ochiëng won a coveted intellectual prize that took him to Russia and there his life ended. Gabriel capitulated to his grandmother's wishes and traveled to England to become a doctor. That is where he discovered Anatole Basile Tejo, the French doctor from Sierra Leone.

<hr />

Canto Eighteen

Gabriel had never heard anyone speak with such passionate authority about the intuitive wisdom and strength of the African Man, the earthly warmth and grace of the African Woman. The picture that Anatole Basile Tejo drew was mesmerizing, but it was just a picture to the young Gabriel for whom Homa Bay was still the center of the world. His mentor's images of Africa surprised Gabriel all the more because Tejo did not even live in Sierra Leone anymore. Even the older doctor's wife, Marie, was the daughter of a former French missionary whose family held an estate in Normandy that boasted the ruins of a medieval abbey. When Marie had discovered that Anatole Basile Tejo was her true vocation, she abandoned the church and married him and they went to live together in one of her mother's maiden homes, an apartment across the river from the Louvre near the avenue that led to Saint-Germain-des-Prés. Anatole

Basile Tejo took Akoth's young grandson there during the holidays to meet his wife and his little children. His young protégé felt like he had walked into a painting when he first beheld the high ceilings and velvet damask drapes that decorated the tall stately windows. He was delighted when the entire family, including the children's maternal grandparents, congregated around Anatole Basile Tejo to summon the African Frenchman in him. But Gabriel could not speak their language, and so he sat quietly by as the poetic Anatole Basile Tejo drew him into that world and anchored him with prompt and constant translation.

It was exhilarating at first to listen to Anatole Basile Tejo and to watch him speak, like discovering a new world. Gabriel noticed that whenever Anatole Basile Tejo listened to others, the great man would bow his head slightly, nodding slowly now and again, encouraging his speaker say whatever he wished. And then his voice would rise as if from deep in the earth to resonate in his listener's very sternum. He spoke slowly, deliberately, as if choosing each word as a special gift to his audience. Both in London and in Paris, especially in the Sixth arrondissement, where he lived and cultivated friends, this made him an oracle – the voice of a people whose greatness would soon come to be. He dreamed of a day when future Alexander Flemings would have Senegalese names, or Togolese names, or Tanzanian names.

Although Akoth had been careful to ensure that Gabriel was educated by the English missionaries in Homa Bay, he had never really taken geographic borders seriously at school. In London he found that they were all that really mattered. He was no longer Ochola, the son of Omondi, the son of Akoth of JokOlóo. He was an anonymous Kenyan to people who only recognized his home when he called it by the old Queen's name. To them the names of the people of the Lake bore neither meaning nor history, so they anchored him to the name of the Queen, introducing him to others as the promising Young African Doctor-in-training from Lake 'Victoria'. But Anatole Basile Tejo understood him when he spoke of his late father, his grandmother, his great-grandfather, and Nyanaam who watched over him even in that distant part of the world.

Gabriel was glad when he finally finished his medical studies and he could go home. He prepared himself for marriage to the girl his grandmother had selected for him. When he had left for London, she was still a child. Now she was, by all accounts, a budding beauty, and Gabriel was expected to negotiate the bride-wealth with her family as soon as he returned. So, he asked Anatole Basile Tejo to come and stand with him when he took a wife and prepared to carry forward the family of his roots with children of his own.

The French Sierra Leonean came to Homa Bay to meet Mamma Akoth and the rest of Gabriel's family. Akoth welcomed him into her home as she would a son. The cousins descended from Olóo's twenty-four sisters numbered in the thousands, and several hundred of them lived in the Bay. They came in and out of Akoth's house, preparing to celebrate Gabriel Ochola's wedding, just as they did whenever one of Olóo's direct descendants married. Gabriel smiled at the thought that his friend would have to live in the Bay for several years if he hoped to remember the names of all the people he met there.

The two men visited Mamma Akong'o, Anna Adongo's grandmother, several times over two months to settle the bride-wealth. Akoth and Akong'o had grown up together, dear as twin souls, and so they wanted to join their families from their earliest girlhood. So Akoth's daughter Akinyi had married Akong'o's son Otïeno, but then she had not survived the birth of Ochïeng, the only grandson the two women would have together in the world of Time. Akinyi's bereft husband could not look at the infant and, defying custom, would not allow it to be brought into his house to be presented for naming. Akong'o took in her orphaned grandchild and together with Akoth, raised him between their two households. Yet his father's rejection left the boy handicapped — none of the ancestors spoke for him to claim him at his presentation, and their silence offered no opening strain to sing the newborn a song of Becoming. The infant's widowed father, bereft of his beloved Akinyi, refused to take another wife and languished in grief for many months before sealing his son's orphanhood by walking into the Lake, never to be heard from again. When Akong'o received the news that her only son had returned to the waters of the Lake of his own volition, she crumbled to the ground, felled as if a boulder had struck her breast, and so she remained oppressed by grief for the rest of her days. When Ochiëng, her orphaned grandson who had kept her tethered to life, grew up and left to study philosophy in Russia, Akong'o unbound herself from the world of Time and finally bid it farewell, leaving her best friend Akoth behind to look after the boy all on her own.

Now it was one of Akong'o's granddaughters who would marry Akoth's other grandson. The accord did not just raise eyebrows, it brought the worried Medicine Healer to Akoth's door. How could Akoth agree to such a marriage? It was true that Gabriel and Anna were not related to each other, but they shared a cousin between them, and customs frowned upon the marriage of relatives within the same family.

Akoth only smiled at him and said quietly, in the deliberating pace of a wending thought, "Ochiëng is the only bridge between JokOlóo and JokOmolo and he is not marrying his cousin."

"No he is not. That is true, ehh," the Medicine Healer answered in the same considered tempo, shaking his head and sighing. "He is not marrying his cousin, no. But Ochola is marrying his cousin. And Adongo is marrying her cousin. You and Akong'o made them cousins when your two children married and had a son."

"You know that Akong'o and I dreamed of joining our families for a long, long time," Akoth offered. "Akinyi and Otiëno were blessed with happiness, and the child they brought into the world together, though bereaved from birth, or maybe for that very reason, is blessed with profound wisdom. You see how Adongo worships Ochiëng? You see how she honors him? You see how he dotes on her – he would cross a flooded river carrying her on his shoulder if she needed to get to the other side. This is a blessing."

"Yes, this is a blessing," the Medicine Healer said, nodding slowly, letting Akoth lead him along. "It is a blessing."

"Adongo is Akong'o's granddaughter, and Ochola is my grandson. When they get married," Akoth continued, "I want them to remain close to the people who will protect them with their lives. Adongo shares a grandmother with Ochiëng, so there can be no marriage between the two of them. But she does not share any blood with me, or any blood with Ochola. He has been away to the Mission school and he will soon go away to university, so, even if they grew up together, she does not know him like she knows Ochiëng."

"No, she does not. That is the truth," the Medicine Healer said.

"That is the truth. And the truth is a blessing. When Adongo and Ochola are married, she will know him better and she will find in him another who will brave the flooding river to carry her across safely," Akoth concluded, her voice still quiet, but firm, not soft like when she sang or told stories, although still deliberate.

The two sat together for a while in thought. Then the Medicine Healer mumbled under his breath an indiscernible prayer to the ancestors. In the story of the family that he had come to bless, he did not see the same things that Akoth saw. Instead, he saw the early death of Olóo and his youngest wife. He saw the death of Akinyi and the drowning sorrow of her husband and best friend, Otiëno. He saw the weight of grief that crushed Akong'o when her son eventually surrendered to the deluge, and he saw how she could not both bear its weight and mother her surviving daughter.

If anyone had asked the Medicine Healer why Otiëno's death had been so unbearable for Akong'o, he would have told them. But nobody asked, because the loss of a son has no measure, and no one sought to draw its bounds. Yet had they asked, he would have spoken of her other son, strangled at birth by his twin sister as she made her way out of her mother's womb. Akong'o did not blame her daughter for the baby boy's death. She even accepted the name *Apiyo* that Nyaseme offered when the girl-child was presented to the Spirits, a name that told the world that she was the elder twin, even though it reminded her mother daily of the absent younger twin, strangled at birth in the labor of emerging. Akong'o did not dare object to the name *Apiyo*, she no longer had the strength that grief and regret drained from her body and soul daily. She consoled herself that, at least, Otiëno was thriving. At least, he had a second mother in her best friend Akoth who also knew the bleak heartache of bearing a newborn who never drew breath. At least, when he grew up, he would marry Akoth's merry daughter, and together the two children would seal the bridge between the JokOlóo and the JokOmolo. She let this promise quieten the roar of sorrow that taunted her every time she heard her own daughter's name. Soon she was also deaf to the young girl's voice, and Apiyo grew up wild, contained only by the privilege of knowing she was welcome at Mamma Akoth's hearth whenever she wished. And so it was inevitable, and a blessing, that when Akoth proposed, many years later, that her grandson, the Doctor, might marry Apiyo's eldest daughter to strengthen the bridge that their Russia-bound cousin had laid to unite JokOlóo and JokOmolo, Apiyo said yes.

Canto Nineteen

Gabriel Ochola was smitten at the first sight of his young bride, Anna Adongo. When he left for the Mission School, she was but a child, all limbs and squeals, darting about chasing Ochiëng, often radiant with gleeful mirth, and also often piercingly indignant when she could not have her way. His nose buried in books, Gabriel never really saw her, or bothered to look. It was enough that Ochiëng was amused by her and would only pester him when it was time for the boys to go off together, perhaps for a swim at the Lake or just to the town library for more books. After his A-level exams, Gabriel went directly to medical school in England, reluctant to leave Mamma Akoth, yet bound by his word to her to return a doctor. While abroad, Mamma Akoth sent him news of his betrothal to Adongo and Gabriel thought nothing of it. He would honor his grandmother and do as he was asked. He never quite formed a picture in his mind's eye of the girl he was to wed, so he did not know what to expect. She was a good Christian girl, Mamma Akoth told him in her letters, and the marriage would strengthen the bond between their two families.

Adongo received him and Anatole Basile Tejo in Mamma Akoth's house, herself the bride-guest in her future husband's home. Now almost fifteen, she stood tall above her age-mates and glowed subtly, her young body already blossoming, promising a welcome womanly softness. When she came in to serve them food, or to bring them drink, Gabriel lost whatever composure he had and could do little but smile at her, his mouth suddenly watering in unaccountable thirst, his eyes consumed by a dream. With every visit, Adongo grew more enchantingly radiant, ripening under his very eyes. He thought of mangoes and papayas whenever he set eyes on her, and sometimes he could have sworn the room was saturated with the aroma of sweetening fruit. He longed to touch her, to feel her skin, to hold her hand in his. His grandmother had chosen well, he thought. Anatole Basile Tejo, in his quiet deliberate voice, agreed with his young protégé that the bride's beauty shone bright beyond others, and Gabriel was pleased to have his mentor's approval. He suppressed the ungracious but satisfying thought that Anatole Basile Tejo was finally seeing in flesh and blood the idea of grace and beauty that he so readily dressed in insensate poetic skin pressed between the pages of books. Gabriel was smitten, and in his enchantment never imagined that his bride, who, with time, seemed to light up every time she approached them, was any less enthralled.

Anatole Basile Tejo returned to Paris soon after the bride-wealth was agreed upon and the nuptials concluded. Adongo, now Anna, settled in her husband's home with Akoth and the children of JokOlóo. Gabriel remained in awe of his wife. He did not touch her, dared not touch her, for several weeks at first. And then he began to imagine how his children would look cradled in her bosom. This gave him the courage to invite her to his bed, never imagining that she did not want to be touched by him. When he told her of his dream of their children at her bosom, he found himself unprepared for her reluctance to join him in making it happen.

At first, he found her fear of the marriage bed somewhat charming, attributing it to her youth and innocent chastity. After some time, though, Akoth sent for Apiyo, asking her to speak to the new bride. Apiyo pressed hard to convince her daughter to seal the marriage union with children. She cajoled and menaced the girl by turns, losing her patience several times, almost giving up from the fear that this union was doomed. But she wore Anna down in the end and, five weeks after entering her husband's house, the reluctant bride finally let him lead her to his bed. But it was another month before she let him lie with her.

Their first encounter was shocking. In the beginning, Anna lay quiet and still as Gabriel came into her. He moved slowly, almost unable to bear the exquisite pain himself, but driven by Nature's own urgency to bear far more than he dared. Suddenly her eyes grew wide with panic and she began to struggle, thrashing about and pushing him away, all without uttering a single sound. He withdrew, bewildered and humiliated. A torrential burst of darkened crimson rushed out after him, soaking into the bedclothes and smearing across both their thighs. When he saw the blood he was mortified, terrified that he had injured his young beloved. He had expected a small stain from when he first breached her maidenhead, not this bleeding flood. The doctor in him packed the moment in a box and labeled it "menses." He would be unable to tell his grandmother what had happened.

Anna, distressed, clutched her painfully convulsing pelvis and gathered up the sheets around her, trying to staunch the surge. Somewhere in the distance Gabriel was asking her if she was injured. What was wrong? What did she need? How did she feel? She wrapped all the sheets about her and staggered to the bathroom and closed the door.

For a few days she shunned Gabriel, and then on the third week after their union she simply returned to her own mother's house. For nearly two months she remained hidden from all and refused to speak to anyone, and even tried to shave her head as if mourning a death. Apiyo believed she knew what had happened, as did Akoth after speaking to Nyanaam. They pitied Anna and told her that it was common and natural to lose the first child, especially when the seed had just taken. She was still very young and could have another one soon; she would have many more, they said. Akoth and Apiyo both repeated that Gabriel would take good care of her and she had no reason to be ashamed, or afraid. Anna did not tell them that she was distressed that the very first time lying with Gabriel had actually killed the child she already bore in her womb. At the end of the third month away, news arrived from Russia that their cousin Ochiëng, beloved of Gabriel and Anna both, had died a solitary death. Anna emerged from hiding, defeated and bereaved, and returned to her husband's home.

He welcomed her with tender trepidation, the heat and the smell of her slippery blood still sharp in his memory. When at last he brought her to his bed again, eager to reconcile, and to console them both, she lay quietly as he tried once again to make his union with his wife whole. She did not resist. She did not struggle. She lay with her eyes closed, shivering slightly when he withdrew from her, saying nothing at all. And then one day, two months after her return, she pulled Gabriel into bed and refused to let him go.

He allowed her newfound carnal fervor to confuse him slightly, not knowing that she was with child. Later, after he discovered his imminent fatherhood, he decided to believe that the mysteries of procreation had stirred her desire's blood for him and fueled her ardor. Yet even he could not overlook the ferocity with which she drew him into her at the moment of consummation, impaling herself with a brutal urgency and crushing his body to hers with a strength violent and supreme, as if she would smother all living breath from their joined person. At first, he tried to stay her vehemence, believing it the youthful zeal of an unknowing innocent. But instead she became more ferocious, cursing and cajoling by turns, bent on a purpose he could do little to resist. Thus she humiliated him and choked his desire, making every new encounter a more costly labor. She left him spent each time, her eyes absent as he tried to offer endearments, to summon a tenderness to help him strangle the humiliation he felt. Unable to sustain the burden of his shame, Gabriel left his home, his grandmother's house, when he found out that his wife was with child. He only returned when he received news that the birth of his firstborn twins was nigh. Anna, quieting her own revulsion, turned away from her two newborn sons.

Canto Twenty

Akoth was there to present her grandson's firstborns to the ancestors with the help of the Medicine Healer when Anna bore her twins. Akoth's joy, mingled with the joy of Apiyo, Anna's wild mother, set Gabriel's house aglow, and spilled out into the homestead where the rest of JokOlóo that could not fit inside were gathered to celebrate the firstborn sons of their patriarch's heir. All prayed that someone strong and wise would claim the twins and give them their names. Akoth invoked the names of her late son Omondi, her deceased husband Ouma, the Spirits of both her father Olóo, and her grandmother Nyanaam, and showed each of them the children. All remained silent. Akoth called the Spirit of Akong'o, her bosom companion from earliest girlhood with whom she had dreamed of joining the families of JokOlóo and JokOmolo with the matrimonial union of their children. She called the Spirits of Opiyo and Nyaseme, both of Akong'o's line, but they all held their peace. Akoth reached farther back still, and still she found no answer. She called her grandmother again. Nyanaam had died, shortly before Gabriel was born, in the same year as his father. She had claimed Gabriel when he was presented to the ancestors almost as quickly as Olóo had claimed his daughter. Yet for some reason she remained quiet when both Akoth and Apiyo repeated "Nyanaam, this is your granddaughter's great-grandson."

When at last Akoth and Apiyo presented the twins to their grandson Ochiëng, born of the son of Akong'o and the daughter of Akoth, yet unclaimed at birth, — Ochiëng, who had written to Akoth every day of the cold strangeness and wonder of Russia, Ochiëng who had simply vanished never to be seen again, — they received a reply all the more heartbreaking because, when first they had been told that he had died of his own will in a hotel in St. Petersburg, Akoth had refused to believe that he was really gone. But custom bound them to summon him too, and custom bound them to accept his claim when Ochiëng touched the mouth of the older twin and gave him the name *Opiyo*.

Gabriel then anointed his elder son David, relief saturating his voice as he laughed gently under his breath and took the infant from his grandmother. He wanted to christen the younger twin Alexander – a mighty name that carried with it the dearest dreams he nurtured for his son. But no one claimed the second baby. The sun was blazing in the sky by the time the child entered the world and so he could easily have been named Ochiëng, as well. He could also have simply been named for the circumstances of his birth – Odongo, since he was the younger of twins, or maybe even Owino, for the chord that had twisted around his neck and made his arrival into the world of Time so difficult. When all of the names had been called, and still no one claimed him, the taciturn Spirit of Olóo spoke up and said that the child's stay in the world of Time would be precarious. Akoth, for whom Olóo had spoken when she was born on the day he died, took this as a sign of good faith and did something that nobody had ever done before, she spoke the name "Opolo," the child of Heaven, and gave it to the newborn on behalf of her father's Spirit.

Olóo's warning was proven right when the baby's little body, too weakened in labor to sustain his life, gave up the ghost before the sun had set on the day the twins received their names. So the Medicine Healer had to help Alexander Opolo, beloved of his father and his great-grandmother, to pass out of Time and join the ancestors. His body expired, and yet he lingered in the shadow of his twin, a phantom that only Akoth could see. She said nothing, intuitively curious to discover what the silent infant Spirit would do. She watched him carefully, wondering why he remained anchored to the world bound by Time. Occasionally, she heard him humming to himself, in his gurgling water voice, songs that sounded familiar, yet not quite, as if still waiting to become. She listened with growing delight to this phantom soul for whom the place of the unborn was soon forgotten, the realm of the ancestors still unknown. When at last he spoke, five years after his thwarted birth, it was upon the infant Maya's arrival home.

Alexander's twin David was a hungry child who could not get enough from his mother. But Anna could give him nothing, would give him nothing, and Alex appealed silently to Akoth for David's sake, asking for the warmth and comfort that was always just out of reach. David helped himself to what Akoth offered, but still cried for his mother.

Whenever David became sick, Alexander, too, became sick. Akoth, forced to learn to attend to the needs of a lingering phantom soul, finally turned to her grandmother Nyanaam who had seen prodigious things in her time and had helped her daughter raise her own children, Omondi, Gabriel's unhappy father, and Akinyi, mother to Ochiëng.

Akoth would turn to Nyanaam whenever she found herself completely at a loss. Sometimes she thought that if only her grandmother could coax Alex away, he might learn to live properly with the Spirits of the ancestors. But Nyanaam left him as he was, watching and waiting, like Akoth, unsure of why he lingered in Time as he did, too young and too new to know how to know anything. And so Alex continued to grow quietly in the shadow of his brother, under his great-grandmother's watchful eye and her grandmother's Spirit. David remained hungry for his mother and kept the household awake and running to the hospital. Anna never let him forget that from the day of his conception, he had denied her the life she most desired.

After David and Alexander were born, Gabriel all but abandoned his books along with his boyhood. His sons became the world to him the moment they saw light, and even though the younger twin was too weak to survive, Gabriel dubbed him the protector of men in the world, his brother the first of the poet kings. The young father mourned young Alexander's death and glorified the twins' mother, endowing her with mythic virtues that made her faultless in every way. He marveled at his surviving son and worshiped the mother of his child, a sinless paragon of earthly warmth and grace, all pain and humiliation forgotten. Akoth saw his devotion and could only pity her grandson. Nyanaam saw her granddaughter's pity and guarded Gabriel even more closely.

After eighteen months of being adored, Anna drew her husband into her bed once again in a moment of nostalgic solitude. She avoided Gabriel for a while afterwards until she discovered she had conceived again. Suddenly, as had happened with the twins, she became seemingly insatiable. He only discovered she was pregnant when he noticed her swelling belly as she pressed her body against his. He could not know that she strove to unseat the seed he had sowed in her womb. And yet his conscience rebelled at her gelid fervor. And so he left again and went to work endless days at the General Hospital in Kisumu, unable to bear his wife's chilling appetites, returning only when Esther was born.

Anna shunned this child as well, keeping to herself. At Anna's request, Gabriel moved his small family, along with Apiyo who everyone now called Ma Ruth, and two of Anna's sisters as well, from Homa Bay to the outskirts of Nairobi, into a large house befitting a prosperous young doctor.

Canto Twenty-one

David was two years old and was already struggling to speak when Esther was born. Both he and Alex were fascinated by the baby when it first arrived, but they quickly lost interest because they were never allowed to get close to it or play with it. Once, out of curiosity, David poured salt on the baby's tongue to see whether it melted like the snails outside sometimes did when salted. Thereafter the ban was sealed, and the infant kept far out of his reach. It was carried around and petted and fed and changed, but since it did not really do anything anyway, he did not miss it very much in the end.

By the time another baby came, David was nearly five years old and Esther was a competent and obedient playmate, unquestioning in her admiration of her big brother. She was very different from David – quieter, and much more serene than he had been as a child. She never complained when he left in the morning to go to Kindergarten and was always happy to have him back in the afternoon because it meant an end to a day spent following the maid or the cook or the gardener around, chasing after Serena the cat, or sitting for long hours under tables and chairs all alone humming to herself. With David's return came more engaging games as he invented new rules or modulated old ones, barking instructions as they went along, conjuring up a universe in which things that happened could not always be explained.

The conception of Maya, more than two years after Esther's birth, was an accident born of a dream that Gabriel often wished he could forget. Although Gabriel had once again absolved his wife of all sin, real and imagined, he avoided touching her even though they shared the same bed in their new house in Nairobi. A young man and virile, he still occasionally smelled mangoes and papayas on her skin. This sensory illusion piqued his thirst and made him ache for her, but in his sentimental heart, shame was stronger than desire. He steered his energy to work instead, traveling to far flung hospitals around the country to administer vaccinations for polio, supply ointments and tablets for ringworm and tapeworm, and replenish quinine reserves to treat malaria, disinfectants and sugar and salt for cholera and, wherever he could, beans where small children with kwashiorkor carried around bellies distended like drums. He worked to wear himself down with fatigue by digging wells and draining stagnant water, constructing filtration systems for small settlements, and home water distillers in villages. Everywhere he went he saw his children's bright eyes in the eyes of his young patients. And when he slept, he dreamed of his babies, his heart ever full of hope. Sometimes he dreamed of his wife.

He traveled to ever more desolate places to care for other people's children, and he was received with praise and honor wherever he went. Yet he returned to a frosty, unwelcoming home. He always brought back gifts for Anna, her mother and her sisters, but his heart shrank to see the chilling effect of his absence on his children. Less and less, they ran out to meet him, no longer ebullient when he arrived. They seemed to grow unsure about how to receive him, reluctant to overstep a line Gabriel did not know had been drawn. So the young doctor languished, ever more a stranger to his children, and a leper to his wife.

One night, in the young doctor's dream, his wife's graceful body lay pressed against his own, the heat of slumber radiating from her skin, sublimating the real or imagined bouquet of firm but succulent ripening mangoes, saturating his starved soul with pliant promise. He felt no shame caressing her buttocks or moving to nestle his mounting arousal between them. She remained asleep while he took each of her breasts into his hands and then turned her body to take them into his mouth with a reverent restraint that belied his craving. In her dream, Anna sighed when his hands parted her sleep-laden thighs and slid blindly between them to find her oasis. She pressed her bosom to his sleeping face and her knees fell open, and she was fourteen once again, caught in a dream grander than truth, strains of French odes to the African Woman murmuring in the echoes of her memory. He raised his body over hers and her hands found his tumescent diviner and pulled it into her viscous heat and it closed in around him and drew him in, *oui!* rushing past her teeth barely audible, that small part of him that was now all of him becoming all of her. The oasis well made him quiver and quake and rub and strive and want more and want less and drive in closer and further and draw force from all of his body and all of his mind and made him labor for breath even though he did not want to and she labored for breath and clamped her legs and arms around his searching body unknowing and Gabriel felt a blindness drag through the base of his dream and a breathless blaze seize his chest pulling him into an abyss of elemental hunger consuming in flameless fire and …

Gabriel held his breath at the edge – terrified and eager to fall, even if for eternity. He wanted to stay with Anna in this perfect union in this dream they shared where she offered him mangoes to pique his thirst, quenching it in her searing well, where she clung to him as if to life, and cooed and gasped, mingled on the promontory where Now knew no end. Anna sighed deeply under the weight of his body, opening her throat low. A groan tore through Gabriel in that moment where his life stopped for an instant to let another pass. Anna's sigh broke. A guttural scream crashed past her clenching teeth… the well milked his rod and swallowed his seed. They both awoke to find their bodies joined, shuddering convulsively. For a moment they could not make themselves move. They looked away, awash in horror. And then Gabriel bolted up, pulling himself out of her drowning well, and Anna grabbed the counterpane and shot into the bathroom, her lungs still heaving. Gabriel stripped the bed and wiped his whole body with the sheets. He was shaking, his limbs weakened by the sharp aftershocks that afflicted him. He could not breathe. He could not think. He threw his shoes into the suitcase he had not yet unpacked, took his medical bag, and left the house wearing a suit with no shirt.

It was not long before Anna knew that she was pregnant again. She kept quiet about it and tried to ignore that her body was changing around the new one that was growing inside it. Gabriel did not return home, and nobody knew whether he knew that he had another child on the way. Though Apiyo, Ma Ruth, tried to impress upon her daughter that there needed to be a man around the house, and so admonished the wife to locate her husband, especially since they were so far from Homa Bay, Anna pretended not to hear her mother. She vowed that this would be the last child she carried, and that she would bring no more babies into the world. Back at the Lake, while tending to the many other children of JokOlóo, Akoth heard about Gabriel's new child on the way and, for the first time since her grandson had moved his family to the city, she packed a borrowed canvas suitcase and took the train from Kisumu to Nairobi to await the child's arrival.

The pregnancy itself went smoothly enough for several months, although Anna was highly susceptible to accidents, more than she had ever been before. During the fifth month she broke her wrist after tripping and falling, and even fractured a rib when a bus collided with her car while she was out running errands. She fell down repeatedly and, on two occasions, suffered violent vomiting fits six months into her pregnancy. Then on the eighth month, numbness began to creep up Anna's legs, settling around her knees. When she complained, her mother Apiyo, who David and Esther both called Ma Ruth, told her to stop being a baby, that pregnancy was not meant to be comfortable. Besides, why did she need to feel her legs anyway? She was no Kipchoge Keino and she would not be training for Olympics gold. But Anna continued to complain, and so Akoth drew nearer to her grandson's wife to try and ease her discomfort.

Akoth sent word to Homa Bay asking for a Medicine Healer to come down to the city. The Medicine Healer who answered the call was from a long branch of Akong'o's line. He knew the two women's friendship well, and even knew of Olóo. Singing a song that sounded like it was rooted in the dawn of Time, he asked for a black chicken that had not yet laid any eggs, and a single feather from its mother's tail. He severed the chicken's head while Akoth held its body down. She braced the violently jerking bird under her arm and kept all its blood from spilling onto the ground. When the bird finally stilled and the collecting bowl was lifted from the kitchen floor, not a drop had gone astray. The Healer's song changed when he added several herbs and powders from the small bags in his satchel and stirred them into the collected blood with the single tail feather. His song invoking the ancestors, he spread some of the mixture on Anna's ankles, shin, knees, palms, wrists and elbows and then wiped her clean, singing all the while. Akoth held her grandson's wife gently and prayed along with the Medicine Healer as he worked. The Spirit of Nyanaam came and sat beside her to protect the child, bringing Alex along to watch and learn as they sang. It was Ma Ruth's duty to prepare the chicken in a special stew seasoned with the Medicine Healer's herbs to be served to Anna for three days. On the third day after the Medicine Healer's song began, the numbness in Anna's knees started to subside. The swelling in her ankles gradually diminished, and her shins no longer felt as if she had sat on them for too long. Akoth washed down Anna's legs with salt and then made sure that they were slightly raised when she tucked Anna into bed. The children were not to make any noise and could not see their mother for whole days together.

David was distraught and refused to eat. Esther, heartbroken that he was unhappy, wrapped her small chubby arms around any part of him that she could reach whenever he was calm enough to approach, while Alex, unseen, sat by their side. The children presented a solemn picture of mourning during the month Anna took ill. When she was admitted to the hospital, David was disconsolate, and the house went on a death watch.

Try as she might, Akoth could not persuade David to take any comfort. He stuttered and flailed, wailing at the drop of a hat, pleading to see his mother, demanding, threatening. He would run himself headlong into concrete walls as fast and as hard as he could. He would roll and squirm, stomp and thrash, crying for his mother, wanting his mother. Esther was miserable for his misery and frightened most of the time. Whenever she could, she sat by him, tucked close to his body. Alex remained with them, watching David, feeling David, languishing as his brother did, silent as the grave.

And then, after nearly two weeks had passed, Akoth came home with a small bundle of cloth and gingerly carried it into the house. David stood by the door, waiting for his mother to emerge from the car, Esther beside him sucking her thumb, her ear pressed against his waist. Only Alex sought to see inside the bundle Akoth held in her hands. He followed them as Mamma Akoth passed through the veranda, into the children's playroom, past the maid's quarters, the kitchen, the main bathroom, his bedroom, his mother's bedroom and into his great-grandmother's room, where she, in turn, laid the bundle on the bed and sat down beside it and prepared to call her grandmother, Nyanaam, once more.

So fragile was the baby that Akoth was afraid to delay the naming ceremony lest the child die without having been claimed, like her beloved Ochiëng, who had lived all his life upon the earth unclaimed, only to die in Russia alone. Unorthodox though it was, she was going to invoke her ancestors, beginning with the most illustrious, beginning with her father. It was normal to go back far into the clan's lineage and invoke ancestors who had been reliably called upon for generations passing. The invocations were long and could go on for many hours, sometimes even days, before any responses came back. There are those who lacked both modesty and moderation and began by calling on Gor Mahia and Lwanda Maghere, even JokOwiny. Although no custom forbade calling on them in particular, people generally kept their invocations within five or six generations of their immediate clan. Only the most unabashedly ambitious families aimed as far back as the founders of legend to find a protector for their child. After one of the ancestors claimed the child, their claim became the opening strains of the newborn's Song of Becoming, and all the Spirits who joined the song would know that the child had a name, and so they would bless it and its keeper. This is when most well-brought-up Luos would call Gor Mahia or Lwanda Maghere who, in their legendary strength and wisdom, would multiply and affirm the blessings of those who had answered for the newborn child. Olóo would answer, Akoth was sure, and the child, born despite all of her own mother's efforts, would receive her name from him.

Akoth, without thinking much of it, began her invocation in the presence of the lingering phantom Spirit of Alexander Opolo. Alex stood by the bed near Akoth and looked inside the bundle to see a tiny mass of shriveled up flesh, languid and indifferent.

"Opolo, this is your sister" Akoth sang, closing her eyes to begin.

Then she heard a sound, quiet, distinct, emerge for the first time from the phantom voice of her great-grandson. It was the sound of water, a simple affirmation in the language of her infancy, of her father, and his mother, and all those before them who had emerged from the river, dancing to the rhythm of their own Songs of Becoming.

"Mara," Opolo mused, echoing his great-grandmother. *Mine.*

From his unpracticed voice, the rolled texture of the "r" slid unformed past his phantom tongue and shaped the sound he made into *"Ma-ya."* Akoth opened her eyes, her mouth agape, amazed to hear Opolo speak. The bundled infant, too, hearing the voice, stirred, awakening from her lethargy, no longer indifferent. Moved. Moving.

Keeping her eyes on the boy and kneeling by the bed slowly, Akoth called her own grandmother to watch over this unexpected guardian who had answered first when the infant was presented. The room began to resonate with voices far and deep in Time as one after another, the ancestors of the clan of JokOlóo responded to her calls on behalf of the child that Alex had claimed. With every answer that filled the room, the swaddled baby gurgled and sighed, as one, by one, by one, the Spirits intoned together the strains of a Song of Becoming to guard her soul, and clear her path, and light her way wherever she chose to go. Among them all could also be heard the voices of Nyanaam and her son Olóo, echoing the melody that Alex had begun, telling Akoth that the child would bear the name of dawn, "Anyango."

Alex clambered onto the bed and lay down beside the infant, reaching, it seemed, into its heart, eager to make it laugh. Thus, Akoth watched Opolo simply invent a Spirit guardianship, just as a child invents the world. She sometimes found it strange that, while she still lived, she should watch over him learning to watch over Anyango Maya. How could she have known that the phantom soul, himself still but a baby, had been waiting all this time for this child to come into being? How could she have even imagined that he would be the one to give the newborn child the name it would bear in the world of Time?

Book IV. Rosie ran away

How Esther's compassion inspired Mamma Akoth to sing a song of Becoming for Rosie the cat, and how Maya adopted him reluctantly. • How Ma Ruth and MaAnna rained down their wrath on Maya after Rosie disappeared. • How Alex finds his baby sister and allows her to forget by holding the memory of her brutalized body. • How Maya escapes into recurring reveries of the tale of Gweno the chicken and Ongowo the hawk and the magic needle that set the course of their lives.

Canto Twenty-two

On the grounds of the house into which Maya was born in the Ngong' Hills in Nairobi, there stood a tall jacaranda tree that reigned over the garden in the back. It spread its old branches far to shield the flowerbed on one side and the veranda on the other, settling its longest twigs comfortably on the edge of the red terra cotta-tiled roof of the house. A ring of sundry chalk-washed stones decorated the border of the flowerbed where giant spotted sisal plants grew, and hibiscus trumpets and clusters of bougainvillea adorned the light of the air with splashes of red, and pink, and orange accents, sending their papery petals to litter the grass as the season gradually matured. When the jacaranda tree bloomed, its small tuba-shaped flowers came out in dense lilac clumps and, from afar, transformed the weathered tree into a cloudy dome of layered pastel halos that danced in the breeze. The falling flowers of the old tree, together with the bougainvillea and the hibiscus, covered the ground with a soft carpet of wilting petals, in some places so thick that even the bright yellow and black weaver birds who rarely ventured below the middle branches of the jacaranda tree sometimes felt safe burrowing into the floral carpet to harvest from the bounty of worms and larvae in the ground, secure that they were hidden from sight.

This was Rosie's domain. He spent almost all his time spying on the unsuspecting birds, field mice, and toads, waylaying them in the labyrinth of shrubs and succulents in the flowerbed. He would weave in and out of the maze of sisal plants, hide behind the white-washed stones, and sneak through the bushes and floral confetti to pounce on the hapless little creatures of the field when they least expected it.

Before he ran away, long before Simba, Coco, and Kendo Nagasaki – David's three dogs – came to live with them, Maya never imagined Rosie leaving the grounds, little guessing that he probably knew the whole countryside, including the forests of the surrounding hills. Ma Ruth, their grandmother, complained that he was wild, and Maya always felt rather proud whenever she heard these grumblings.

"That cat will hurt one of my children one day, I guarantee," Ma Ruth seemed fond of repeating. "You can't have a wild animal running around in the house, on the house, all over like that."

For Rosie could sometimes be heard on the roof, knocking terra cotta tiles askew, jumping from the branches of the jacaranda tree, or making his way to one – not that he could not just climb up the trunk. No. Rosie was, above all things, a very clever hunter; he clearly thought it better to stalk his prey up where they lived.

At the base of the jacaranda tree, there lay the foundation of a thriving ant colony from which long, long caravans of ants issued forth, coming and going all day every day, except during the Rainy Season. The caravans carried loads of breadcrumbs, leaf cuttings, bits of soil, and unidentifiable odds and ends along a single file that led to the tree, brushing past an equally purposeful file of ants who had already delivered their cargo and were now outward bound for more. The road was narrow, and traffic was thick. The formicine multitudes bumped along one another as they met, stopped for a moment as if in greeting, wheeled about and went on their way, without ever losing their bearing. David liked pouring water in their path or putting pieces of leaves and sticks in their way to see how far they would scatter. Hehra, the baby, did not really know what they were doing — she was so young. Esther, who came between Alex and Maya, spent almost all her time running after Hehra whenever she wasn't asking David questions. Maya stayed close to Alex. She believed that Alex knew more than David and was much kinder too. Every time David tried to scatter the ants, Maya watched thrilled as Alex reversed his twin's work. Hearing her giggle, David blamed Maya, complaining that she did not respect him like she ought, threatening to tell if she continued to spoil his experiments, eager to impress upon her the vital importance of what he was trying to do.

The ants had built narrow tubes of long passages and secret chambers along a deep crack in the bark of the jacaranda tree closest to the house. When the thin walls of their structures peeled off, the flakes fell to the base of the tree in delicate heaps. The children were fond of collecting these flakes to nibble on, and their great-grandmother Mamma Akoth, her graying eyes bright with mischievous joy, usually picked the anthill flakes with them, sifting through the ruins for the driest, sunbaked bits. She said that in them was a powerful medicine that soothed the aches in her joints and helped children grow stronger. Alex told Maya that the real reason Mamma Akoth loved these particular gathering expeditions was because, for her, there were few things as delightful as the subtle electric taste of the bone-dry loam soaking up the saliva on their tongues, exuding the thrilling, delicate aroma of cottony clouds on a sunny day, the concentrated taste of new rain on parched soil.

Rosie's tastes ran more to young shoots of grass than to formic ethers, and the endless trail of ants could not hold his attention for long. He preferred to worry little birds and mice in the garden, sometimes catching them, although he never ate the kill. He brought his trophies to Maya, obeying some primitive provider instinct endowed him by his ancestors. In exchange for his tributes to her, he accepted the food that she put out for him in the kitchen. He was not really a house cat and he was rarely seen indoors except for this necessity. He was a fine cat, full of surprises, and far better than

Bruno, the baby Hehra's overfed black and white fur ball. Rosie was even better, Maya thought, than Serena, Esther's pampered Siamese. Serena had lived with them ever since anyone could remember and behaved as if the house belonged to her.

When Bruno and Rosie came along, both of them from the neighbor's new litter, Serena deigned to let them be brought into the house without much ado. The infant kittens emerged from beneath the thin blanket that covered them in the housemaid's basket, unsteady on their still-new paws, and Hehra's nearly two-and-a-half-year-old heart instantly fell in love with the pink-nosed, eye-patched, black-and-white fur ball. Hehra took the delicate animal under her wing, naming her Bruno after her favorite Monday Night wrestler. It didn't matter that David made fun of both of them and said that Bruno was a silly name for such a delicate creature who, as it turned out, was a girl anyway! Hehra did not mind. She adored her new pet and took a prodigious deal of care of her despite David's teasing.

While Bruno was still a small enough kitten, Hehra, newly adept at walking, although still inclined to tiptoe, carried her everywhere in the crook of her elbow the way she saw people carry infants. She never let the cat sleep anywhere but on her pillow by her cheek. She fed it so many sweets and treats that soon the cat became too fat and heavy for her to even lift, so Bruno waddled behind her everywhere all day long. When Hehra sat down, Bruno curled up at her feet or balanced on her lap, shifting to find a comfortable spot whenever Hehra moved. The cat grew rounder and softer every day, quickly dwarfing her doting mistress and becoming more like a baby than a cat as everybody soon joined Hehra in spoiling her.

Rosie was completely different. He was small and sinewy, jet black, with a dot of white fur on his forehead slightly right of center. On the day the houseboy who ran errands for the maid brought the kittens to the house, swaddled and covered in the maid's basket, Maya came home from Kindergarten to find that Hehra, who had not even started leaving the house to go to school, had already claimed the cuddly, pink-nosed, black-and-white darling. Esther had just started Primary Three, the highest class in Junior Primary, and she believed that it gave her the authority to arbitrate the dispute that flared up between Maya and Hehra. Esther thrust the unwanted, scrawny black cat on Maya, trying to convince her to give it a name.

But Maya simply wanted Bruno, and not the bony thing with the lackluster fur. Unlike his adorable sister, who was soft and playful, the black kitten was quite gaunt and rather lethargic, indifferent to the saucer of milk Maya offered him; given to listlessly sitting by himself on the floor or the sofa, or wherever else he was put. Maya thought that it wasn't fair that she only got the ugly runt just because of timing, while Hehra got the beautiful kitten. The runt did not have much to recommend him, and Maya was too angry to even bother naming it. She would just as easily have called it Cat. So, Esther once again intervened and gave it the name "Rosie" because she wanted to make it bloom. She then asked Mamma Akoth to sing him a Song of Becoming so that he might grow in grace and wisdom and strength. The pageantry of Rosie's naming drew all the children close, and opened Maya's eyes and heart to empathy for her new cat.

Maya did not know yet that she, too, had been born a runt. Unlike her sister Esther, Maya was not a beautiful baby. When Akoth first brought her home, she appeared somewhat disfigured in her thin, blotchy skin. Her time in the womb had been fraught with repeated assaults from physical trauma and the toxic potions that Anna consumed as if daring the still-maturing baby inside her to defy death. And it had. Unlike Alex, Maya's body survived a second day, and the Spirit that crossed the threshold of life into the world bound by Time found a quiet, albeit inordinately small, home there. For despite her unhappy start, Maya was not a sickly child, nor was her body, for all its unsightly immaturity, unable to thrive on its own.

Since she was claimed by the lingering Spirit of an infant child and not an experienced ancestor, it had not been clear that she could in fact thrive. Akoth did not know how to teach Opolo how to be a guardian, and neither did Nyanaam who had lived for ninety Long Rains and known the ways of Medicine Healers. Nyanaam understood the customs and ways of ancestor guardians long before she entered that realm, but Opolo had none of the depth of experience in the world of Time because he had not even lived a whole solar day, and so she could offer not guidance.

After he answered the call to be Maya's guardian Spirit, the privilege was his alone, even if he did not know what it meant. But Alex was fascinated by Maya, and he stayed close by her side. He watched Mamma Akoth bathe the grayish brown infant, balancing its head on her wrist while the rest of its body lay on her palm, hovering over the basin. He attended the ritual daily, enthralled by the tiny limbs that fitfully came to life the moment they made contact with water. The first time he saw it happen, he feared that the bath was too hot and that perhaps the baby was injured. Akoth just laughed and said that the water actually made the baby happy; and until she could learn to laugh and talk, pumping her arms and legs was the only way she knew to express herself.

So Alex started to teach the baby how to talk, or rather tried to coax her to talk. He wanted to know what she thought, if she thought, so he was thrilled to find himself wandering inside her infant dreams, although he did not quite know how it happened. He wanted to hear the sound of her thoughts, to discover whether they even had forms that shaped into words. He sat by the baby, day and night, talking about everything he could see around him, everything he had ever heard about, everything he could think. He repeated songs in the baby's ear, glowing with delight when he saw her listening, her attention arrested by his watery chant. He repeated the stories that Akoth told, changing them every time, forgetting some details and adding some new ones. Although he now slept with the baby instead of with David, he still followed both his twin and Esther to their schools sometimes, especially when Mamma Akoth walked there in the morning, just to hear more things that he could tell the baby. He would watch people and listen to their conversations, follow animals of the air, and of land, and of sea, and then come back and tell his little baby everything that he had seen. Akoth listened to his young, tireless voice in quiet amusement. He may not have known what a guardian Spirit was supposed to do, but everything that he did do ensured that his little charge became robust despite having been born a runt.

Esther made sure that Maya fed Rosie, the cat she had refused to name, and it wasn't long before an understanding grew between the reluctant pair of girl and feline. In fact, Maya grew quite fond of him, and even rather proud. He eventually outgrew his lethargy, although he still kept mostly to himself. He also became the most accomplished hunter any of them had ever seen. He regularly brought Maya a frog or a mouse or a weaver bird he had caught, perhaps to show off, perhaps to share. David found Rosie's offerings to Maya disgusting and never missed a chance to harass the cat whenever he saw him. Even though David liked to make fun of Bruno, he, like everyone else, doted on the docile fur ball and spoiled her every chance he got. Rosie did not seem to mind being overlooked and, but for occasional visits to Maya, kept to himself in the garden and in the forests beyond.

115

Canto Twenty-three

One day, Maya returned from nursery school to find Rosie crouching beside the long mirror that stood on the dining room sideboard at home. She could see that the cat was planning an ambush. His body was tense with concentration. Maya stopped at the door, afraid of disturbing him. Sometimes she liked to watch him, wishing she could see his thoughts, especially at moments like these when he was poised for attack. She tried to imagine what inherited drama he was playing out when he set out to hunt. Mamma Akoth often said that every creature, man and beast alike, lived the same drama generation after generation, and it only cost a little attention to discover each individual's particular story.

That very morning, while walking Esther and Maya to school together with Alex tagging along, Mamma Akoth had spent most of the walk talking about the reason why Ma Ruth's chickens, for example, had a habit of scratching and picking at the ground, scattering roots and soil with their legs and turning their heads now and again to eye the sky warily, cluck, cluck, clucking away with an urgency that nobody understood. It was one of the children's favorite stories, one of the few that Alex, too, recounted faithfully to Maya occasionally. The hen mothers, Mamma Akoth said, were actually desperately searching for the hawk's lost needle, watching the sky out of the corner of their eyes in case the hawk happened to be passing by to carry off one of their babies.

But the hen hadn't always been afraid of the hawk. In fact, once upon a time, Gweno and Ongowo were best friends. They spent most of their youth together and planned to look after each other's families when they grew up. Back then, they were quite different than they are today. Gweno was rather flighty, slight and agile, and fond of going to parties, especially because it was a great way to keep her finger on the pulse of the intimate affairs of her various neighbors. All the roosters loved her, but she swore that she would never settle down. Ongowo, on the other hand, was a shy bird who kept close to the ground and made his living weaving and sewing for the joy that it brought him.

Ongowo had a magic needle that he could use to transform any bird into a vision of perfection, Mamma Akoth's story continued. Regardless of shape or size, Ongowo could sew all sorts of outfits to measure, complete with vanishing seams. Under the hawk's talented eye, the magic needle had dressed all the birds of the Savanna as well as nearly all the creatures of the Great Rift Valley and the surrounding Highlands for all the big social events and some of the small parties that occasionally took place in the area. Ongowo's creations were famous and greatly esteemed, and birds flocked to him from far and wide to get that distinctive look that was impossible to imitate. The only drawback was that the hawk could not meet the demands fast enough: the needle was one of a kind and once a bird had put on an outfit made with it, the outfit could only come off if the needle itself revealed and unstitched the vanished seams. So the hawk had to personally dress and undress anyone who came to him.

Whenever Gweno had a party to attend, she headed straight for Ongowo's workshop to prepare and encouraged everyone who knew her and admired her style — which was everybody — to go to him as well. Between the occasional party, the entire host of clamoring birds, and his magic needle, Ongowo was busy all the time, and he enjoyed it most of the time. But as time went by, he grew lonely, especially after Gweno started spending more time with a particularly dashing young rooster. Being the good friend that she was, and knowing how shy her friend had always been, Gweno decided that the only way to cheer him up was to make him a suitable match, a bird who would appreciate him for his genius just as much as Gweno always had.

One day, the opportunity to find him that match presented itself. All the birds were invited to the sky for the biggest party of the year, and Gweno insisted that Ongowo go with her. She was sure that there would be hundreds of stunning birds up there, and since everyone, but everyone, was going to be in attendance, they were guaranteed to find someone for Ongowo. All they had to do was look irresistible, arrive early to meet every avian guest, and leave late after having enjoyed themselves and, of course, found a mate for Ongowo.

Did Rosie think he had found a mate in the mirror? Or maybe discovered a rival? Mamma Akoth had continued on to one of her longer walks that morning after seeing the children to their schools, and Alex had followed Esther, so Maya could not ask them right away if they knew what Rosie was thinking.

Maya could not help imagining that maybe Rosie did not know he was at war with himself when she noticed that he was trying to sneak up on his own reflection in the sideboard mirror. She had watched him hunt countless times outside, so when she saw him in the dining room, she recognized in his still intensity a predator on the prowl. As she watched, he swayed once or twice, very slightly, as if testing the flexibility of his legs as he prepared to make his move. Suddenly he sprang up and landed in the middle of the sideboard, facing the mirror where the other cat stood staring back at him. Rosie dashed quickly to the left side of the mirror, out of sight, just as suddenly as he had sprung up, and then he stayed hidden for a moment, watching the mirror, waiting to see if the other cat would make the first move.

After a short, anxious while, he tried to look around the corner only to be met with the sight of the other cat peeking at him too. Yanking his head back, Rosie lay in wait again, intent on getting the other cat before it got him. A thickening suspense filled the air, intensified by the presence of the mysterious, invisible stalker behind the mirror who made no sound, had no smell, and seemed to spring from nowhere, and disappear into nothing.

Maya never knew which happened first. Perhaps Rosie sprang up an instant before David, who had not gone to school that day because of a bee sting, came dashing into the room chasing one of his errant marbles, letting out a sharp whoop as he dove after the glass ball which was rolling toward the dining furniture in the center of the room. There are things that the human eye cannot see and sometimes it is just because they happen too quickly or too slowly. And yet Maya clearly saw Rosie, still in mid-air, twist and land against the smooth vertical surface of the mirror where there was nothing to grasp. He clawed at it several times trying to get a foothold. Failing, he slipped to the flat top of the sideboard in a bit of a heap – but only for an almost imperceptibly brief moment.

David was under the table shoving chair legs around, trying to reach the wayward marble, heaving and making as much noise as he could. Rosie hissed and arched his back, looking at the cat in front of him, his claws extended. David's unexpected explosion into the room had quickened the growing suspense to imminent danger, forcing Rosie to instinctively defend himself. The other cat attacked at exactly the same time, swiping hard with his paw. Rosie let out a growling moan which sounded strangely like a question from somewhere deep in his bowels, but just beneath his breath.

Feeling his fear sharply, Maya jumped to the sideboard and reached up to rescue him. Perhaps cats cannot tell that the image in the mirror is not real. Perhaps Rosie became confused by the suddenly multiplied world. When Maya should have seen his claws extend further, she did not. She did not even feel them sink into her palm or run through her wrist and into her arm. In a flash, Rosie was gone, darting beneath the sideboard. He froze there, still moaning, the question gone from his voice, the sound now unrecognizable.

David stood at the foot of the sideboard, clutching his lost marble close and bleating I-told-you-sos.

"You-you-you see? You see? That c-c-cat is mad that c-c-cat is wild, everyone knows, everyone says so. Now look at what he has d-d-done. You-you-you can't even tame him. You-you-you better just ch-chase him away or d-d-d-d-d-drown him. When m-m-m-m-MaAnna sees what he d-d-did to the sideboard your g-g-going to be sorry!"

Why was he always telling on her? Maya looked around and saw blood along the edge of the sideboard. Still more blood was dripping down and there was a red smear on the floor near Rosie. Maya dropped to her knees to get him. She was sure he was badly hurt. She thought that perhaps something on the edge of the sideboard had cut him. She could not tell, and she had not seen it happen, but she could see the blood. Rosie was now quiet. He stared at her, crouching beneath the sideboard, his round glassy eyes reflecting iridescent silver light in the gloom, wary and still and taut as only a cat can be.

"Maaaa! Maaaa!" David bellowed. "The black cat attacked Anyango, the black cat attacked Anyango!" David raced out of the room and wove his way about the house chanting at the top of his voice, calling Ma Ruth.

That is when Maya saw her wrist, her arm, torn open. Skin, flesh, fat – brown, pinkish red and white – were minced together in neat furrows that extended from the heel of her palm around to her elbow, bathed in thickening red.

"Rosie, come here Rosie," she whispered. "If Ma Ruth comes and finds us here, she will drown you or chase you away." If Rosie could hear the urgency in her plea, he chose to ignore it.

Maya's heart knocked hard against her chest, and through the staccato she could hear David's voice.

"The black cat attacked Anyango! The black cat attacked Anyango!"

Why did he have to open his big mouth? Maya thought, muttering *shut up shut up shut up shut up shut up* under her breath, trying to coax Rosie to come out from under the sideboard. If anyone found them there, she would be taken to MaAnna and she would get a thorough beating. She tried to wipe the blood from the sideboard with the skirt front of her pinafore dress, but the top of the sideboard was too high and all she did was smear the blood all along the top and the side, soaking it into her dress skirt. Maya wanted to run after David to beg him not to tell, but he was a hopeless bigmouth, and sooner or later she would be found out. The dominant thought in her mind was to hide and to find a safe place for Rosie. And Alex, where was Alex? He could help her. Where was Alex…?

<hr />

Canto Twenty-four

When Alex followed Esther back home and found his sister, his baby, she was sleeping inside the shoe cupboard in the children's playroom. She was still wearing the pinafore she had worn to Kindergarten in the morning, and her shoes were still buckled. Why hadn't she changed when she came home? Her knees were drawn tight against her chest, her head tucked into them. One arm hugged her shins and the other stretched out beside her. The blood on the stretched-out arm had dried into the toilet paper wrapped around it, and Alex saw how it felt to be dizzy as he looked at it, the sharp, rusty smell of iron making his sister's mouth suddenly fill with a viscous, warm salt water even as she slept.

"Nyangi, Nyangi," he whispered. "Anyango, wake up!"

"Hmmh?" she mumbled as she roused herself. She lifted her head to find her brother leaning over her, and then she added in a cracked voice, her throat parched, "Alex, Rosie ran away."

Tears, hot and sharp, stung Maya's nasal sinuses when she saw the look in Alex's eyes as he took in the sight of her face. Across her cheeks, forehead, and neck, long strips of swollen but unbroken flesh cut across the smooth skin, tracing a path wherever a switch had landed. Her eyelids were also swollen, and her face ashen from soaking in acrid tears. In the middle of her lower lip where she had torn her mouth wailing, the crack was still bleeding, the break refusing to close. In places, her pinafore was caked with blood, already dry and darkened to garnet. As she stretched out her legs, Alex saw more welts — slim raised switch marks, and the heavier thicker signatures that only a leather belt could leave.

"Rosie ran away," she repeated, her parched voice cracking again.

Alex caught his little sister as she stood up and faltered. She leaned forward, but the shelf above knocked the side of her head.

"I am sorry, Nyangi," Alex said, his mind empty, his voice hollow, his phantom Spirit howling mute. *Mamma Akoth! Mamma Akoth! Mamma Akoth! Help me!*

Alex stood up from where he had been kneeling in front of the cupboard, his heart breaking with every new glimpse of purpling bruises. What had happened to his baby? *Anyango mara!* his phantom heart cried out.

Maya started talking rapidly, her voice heating with anger as she remembered what David had done.

"I think David frightened him," she said. "He was looking for the cat in the mirror, but he scared him. He came barging into the room, so he ran away." Her breath caught in a sob and Alex had to make her take in a gulp of air, forcing her to inhale violently through her nose and her mouth at the same time.

Mamma Akoth! Help me! He put one hand on Maya's head and used the other to wipe from her eyes the tears that were clouding his sight. *Mamma Akoth! Help me!*

The little girl's memory recalled all the other times David had frightened Rosie, playing tricks on him, telling on him, all the while spoiling Bruno and Serena. It was so unfair! Rosie never bothered anyone. Maya imagines now that her poor cat probably just thought he was meeting another cat, maybe even a rival, but she preferred to think how nice it would be if Rosie could be a little bit like Ongowo, shy, but willing to imagine a happier life with a suitable mate.

Ongowo was proud of his craft, and he was proud that all the birds hurried to him to get the perfect party dress — each claiming Gweno's personal recommendation — when preparations were being made for the big party in the sky. The weaver bird, who had apprenticed with the hawk for some time, wanted something to compensate for his small size, so Ongowo made him a suit of gleaming golden feathers complemented with a short, black cape. The flamingo wanted Ongowo to flatter her long, graceful neck, but with something different from the swan, since she also had mile high legs and not the squat paddles the swan shifted around in. The swan heard about the flamingo's request and quipped that at least his beak wasn't bigger than his head, and unlike some people, he did not have to eat upside down. The feud that ensued lasted for generations, but Mamma Akoth always waved it aside as part of another story. Suffice it to say that faced with their respective requests, Ongowo decided to dress the swan in cloudy white to complement his golden beak and black set eyes, and he softened the flamingo's (admittedly awkward) gait by drawing attention away from it with a series of cool and hot pink hues that changed intensity as she moved, keeping the beholder entranced. All the barbs about feet and beaks being hurled around made the pelican a little nervous, so he asked Ongowo if there was anything that could be done to flatter his rather large beak pouch and his unfortunate feet. The comprehending hawk recommended a subtle palette for him and when they were done, the pelican was so pleased that his joyful smile stayed on his face permanently.

Gweno of course went for a bold palette and asked Ongowo to let his imagination loose. She was after all, the trendsetter, and as the gown he made for her took shape, she knew that she would be the belle of the ball. The rusty orange collar was trimmed with iridescent blue and green feathers, and the black wings tinged with red and burgundy accents. The effect of these colors was set off by a deep pink head-dress that began at the forehead and rose to a peak just over the crown. The master touch, however, was the flowing train of black tail feathers — also accented with blue and green iridescence — that arched up into the air and then cascaded down behind, creating a wonderfully fluid effect and presenting the hen in all her glamour. When the parrot, an incorrigible copycat, caught a glimpse of the gown during one of Gweno's fittings, he had to have the same thing. But the needle, as it was well known, only created distinctive pieces that were impossible to imitate. So although the parrot got a bold palette, with yellows and greens and reds, his outfit had none of the breathless nuance of the hen's imposing gown.

Gweno, like all the other birds, went to Ongowo's several times to get fitted and refitted for her party dress. At every visit she painted the most vivid picture of Ongowo's future happiness. He and his mate would have lots of children, and Gweno planned to be their cool aunt; they would drift happily through the skies together, riding the wind; at every party they attended, they would be the envy of the savanna since Ongowo was such a wonderful weaver, and his bride would undoubtedly be stunning. The dream grew and grew, getting more extravagantly blissful with every telling. At first Ongowo just humored his flighty friend, but it wasn't long before he started listening and even embellishing the future that she projected for him. Before long he was just as eager as Gweno, if not more, to go to the big party in the sky. Finally the dress was ready, and Gweno took it home to show off to her new beau rooster.

"Nyangi," Alex said, interrupting Maya's reverie, "come. It's bath time." She was beginning to forget. "I am sorry Rosie ran away."

Soon the salve of those words would carry no meaning once she forgot the pain they were meant to soothe. He tried to make every word forcing itself out of him sound calm. Suddenly his vision blurred as his baby sister's vanishing distress enveloped him.

This is where forgetting begins, he thought. She did not know it, but Alex did because he had seen his twin do it time and again. He prepared to hold the memory for Maya, just as he sometimes held the memory for David. Esther did not forget like them, but then she forgave easily. Hehra was still too young, or perhaps she was just lucky; for her the world was as beautiful as Bruno, and she a child without fault. David, however, was erratic, and Maya was stubborn, so they were like lightning rods in a storm when Anna struck. Only forgetting kept Maya, who still did not know how to forgive, from breaking. *Mamma Akoth, help me!*

~~~~~~~~~~~~~~~~~~~~~~~~~~~~~~~~~~~

Canto Twenty-five

When Anna first brought Hehra home from Sierra Leone, Esther was still little more than a baby herself. Even so, the child, barely five, marveled to hear the quiet laugh of pure joy, of deep-fountain clear water pleasure, evanescent as sunbeams on a dewdrop, radiating from the exclusive intimacy of the moment. It was the first time Esther heard something akin to the songs of Mamma Akoth in Anna's voice. Anna's laugh was normally abrasive and chilling, her tone harsh, and strident, and violent, nothing like the enchantment of this absorbingly private communion with her newborn. Years later when she was older, Esther struggled to absolve herself of the guilt she felt for recoiling at the sound of Anna's ordinary voice. She chided herself for dishonoring her mother, for feeling only revulsion where others saw beauty and charm, for being unable to reconcile the way people described Anna with the mother that she knew. But that was years later. Witnessing that moment of joyful tenderness in so unexpected a place sparked a fleeting wonderment at her mother's beauty that took root in Esther's innocent heart. It also kindled, deep in her soul, an ineffable ardor that knew no measure for the new, little sister. Though still very young, Esther intuited that what she glimpsed in that moment explained why men and women alike sat up straighter when Anna entered a room, why neither reason, nor persuasion, nor coercion alone could account for Anna's ability to get whatever she wanted from anyone.

At first, when she happened upon the scene, Esther had stayed hidden simply out of habit, unprepared to weather the unpredictable storms that Anna unaccountably unleashed on whomever was on hand. The woman cradling the new baby and murmuring to it was so different from the mother Esther knew, it was mesmerizing. The sounds Anna made lingered in the child's ear, mingling with her incomplete solitude and somehow making it whole. Then a noise broke the spell, heedlessly blighting the secret moment, silencing that mysterious, ephemeral joy. Only then did Esther know that she wanted to hear that laugh again. Like a child that only wants food when it is hungry, drink when it is thirsty, and sleep when it is drowsy, and does not reflect on the meaning of its hunger, or thirst, or somnolence, nor contemplate its satisfaction once its needs are met, Esther only sought that laugh when she was bruised and humiliated by Anna as only Anna could bruise and humiliate.

As she grew older and saw Anna cry and complain and scream and tear at the world in endless strife, Esther often wondered whether the magical laugh really existed. Her desire confused her all her life long, especially when she was still small, yet she prayed that the mysterious something that moved Anna to that deep-fountain clear water mirth would stir her again to laughter. It was Esther's favorite phantom sound. Sometimes, as an adult, the sound of other people's laughter, invariably lacking the delicious novelty of Anna's private joy, evoked in Esther a twinge of nostalgia, and awakened her dormant regret that her mother's guileless mirth was so rare a thing. She never knew how to describe what she had heard and what it had made her see. But it strengthened her ability to forgive even Anna's most brutal assaults, however desperately she and her siblings recoiled and fled the storm.

Canto Twenty-six

Alex and Maya reached the bathroom nearest to the kitchen, and Alex shut the door. He plugged the drain at the end of the high enameled bathtub that stood on four lion's paws at one end of the bathroom and opened both taps, testing the water to make sure that it was a gentle temperature. He sat on the stepping stool next to the tub and tried to help Maya undress as slowly as he could to avoid hurting her. The pinafore was easy to remove, but the tunic underneath, as well as the socks, rubbed too coarsely against Maya's sore flesh. She winced once or twice as they came off, chattering away in her small voice, telling Alex about Rosie and the cat in the mirror. The toilet paper around her arm would have to be soaked off gradually. Alex took an extra towel out of the cupboard to wrap around the injured limb after the bath. As the tub continued to fill, Maya climbed in, leaning against Alex for balance. She lowered herself into the oceanic volume of the tub, watching the water rise as she sank into it, her face lighting up with a delight that Alex had come to expect from her at every bath time. Once in the water, she stretched out her legs like she always did, pretending that she was a giant compass needle pointing North. Her slight frame swung to and fro in the waves she made bobbing about. She chatted, and chatted, and grinned at her brother. Alex looked at his baby swinging her tiny body in the tub and thought that as long as she had forgotten and felt no pain, he was happy to let her play.

Maya was in fact thinking of the day of the party when Gweno arrived at Ongowo's feeling a little funny. The last of the other birds had just left with their dress when she came in, winded. She felt unusually heavy and her sharp-eyed friend asked if she had started laying eggs. Nonsense, Gweno insisted, laughing off the idea. She was just a little bit bloated. And besides, they had a party to attend. Bloat or no bloat, they were going together. Today is the day we find you a bride, she insisted, so don't even imagine backing out now. But can we really go? Ongowo asked reasonably. Can you fly well in your state? Your gown may not even fit anymore and there is no time to re-do it. Don't worry, Gweno said to him. You just get ready. I'll go home and adjust the gown myself. But you don't know anything about sewing or weaving, Ongowo protested. It won't matter if you give me your magic needle. I can just tell it where to make the adjustments and let it sew. No, you don't understand how it works. You have to hold the needle very carefully – not too tightly because then it won't be able to move, and not too loosely because then you might drop it and then you will never be able to find it. Don't worry, Gweno insisted, just show me how to hold it and I will be very careful with it. Once I have adjusted the seams for my gown, I'll bring the needle right back, and we can leave for the party, OK?

Ongowo was reluctant. He was a skilled weaver in his own right, but the magic needle was a family heirloom and no one outside his family had ever learned how to use it. However, if he did not find a mate soon, there would be no future generations to inherit the heirloom. And besides, Gweno was practically family. Are you sure you can manage the needle? he asked, trying to believe that he was doing the right thing. Absolutely, Gweno assured him, if anything happens to it, you can have my first born in exchange.

Hearing Gweno's extravagant bargain, Ongowo laughed. He relaxed and showed her how to use the needle, warning her to be very careful because it was slippery and although it would not harm her, it sometimes had a mind of its own and might decide to wander off when she wasn't paying attention. He would get ready and then wait for her so that they could fly off together to the party in the sky. Gweno was thrilled. She left clutching the needle in her beak, dreaming of her perfect party gown, the perfect impression she would make on all the assembled, and the perfect mate she would find for her perfect friend.

She flew straight home, not even stopping to chat with the many friends who waved at her along the way, only calling back hello and letting them know she would see them at the party later that night. She was almost home when, suddenly, she realized that the needle was no longer in her beak. Maybe she had tucked it away somewhere else, she thought, alighting on a branch and checking herself. She brushed through her breast feathers but found nothing there. She looked under her right wing, and then under her left wing. She even combed through her tail feathers, hoping to find it somewhere. But she could not. What had she done with Ongowo's magic needle? She decided to retrace her flight path to see if she could spot it somewhere on the ground. She realized quickly that flying up in the sky, she could not see the ground very well, let alone find a wayward, wandering needle. So she alighted once more and started walking along the same terrain she had flown over before. After a while she arrived at Ongowo's house again. She was about to let herself in to tell him what had happened when she decided to turn back, sure she could find the needle and avoid worrying her friend needlessly. This time, she walked all the way to her own house, looking intently at the ground, hoping desperately to spot the needle.

"Compass needles and sewing needles are not the same, are they?"

The question startled Alex and confounded him a little bit, until he realized that Maya was thinking of the chicken and the hawk and pretending to be a compass needle all at the same time. Maya started splashing around, getting giddy in the waves. Alex did not mind her flicking water at him while he tried to clean her up; in fact, he was relieved. He was careful not to use soap because he knew that the moment it touched any of her cuts, the sting on her body could only ask her questions she could not answer. Maya giggled as Alex washed her legs, her back, her tummy, her face. She sank her head into the water, pinching her nose and blowing air bubbles. She asked Alex occasionally if he thought Rosie would come back.

Canto Twenty-seven

She has forgotten the mangled furrows in her arm. She has forgotten reaching for Rosie under the sideboard, "Rosie, please come out now, they're coming!"

She does not remember the staccato drumming of the blood in her ears, the cold fire rumbling in her stomach, her heart sinking as her grandmother enters the room in front of David, demanding, "What's happening here?"

Maya stands up straight, her back to the sideboard. *Hide Rosie, hide.*

"Nothing." Her voice is wispy thin with vicarious terror.

"Where's the cat, the black cat?" Ma Ruth demands. "I don't want that thing in this house anymore. If I catch it…" She sees Maya's arm and stops suddenly. Then she thunders, "Ay, my good Lord! What did you do?"

Maya feels the ice in her stomach suddenly burn hot, very hot. Her pulse trills through her small body, her breath grows shallow. Ma Ruth towers over her, arms akimbo, her stern demeanor dissolving as she begins to take in the child's condition. When her arms come down, their intention is to gather up the injured child to her, to take a closer look, to help her. But the child has become like a wild thing herself. The moment Ma Ruth moves, the girl takes off out of the room, darting under the table and through the chairs to escape.

"What is the matter with this child? Come back here, let me see your arm. If your mother sees you like that she's not going to be happy."

At the end of the veranda Maya turns around only for a moment to see her grandmother coming after her, and then she's off again, running straight into her mother's legs.

"Nyangi, be careful!" Anna exclaims, catching Maya's shoulders. She looks at the child and sees fear. She looks at the child and sees guilt.

"What have you done, huh?" Her voice is sharp. It is not a question.

"Nothing," comes the thin whisper.

"What do you mean, nothing? Why are you running away?" The gravel in MaAnna's voice has hardened, its edges sharpened by suspicion.

"Nothing, I promise, I didn't do anything. Rosie ran away…"

Ma Ruth catches up with them. "There is blood all over the furniture! Come back here, Anyango." Does Ma Ruth know what she has just done to the child?

Anna looks at her mother and then she looks down at the squirming, tiny, little girl whose torn wrist she is now holding. Maya twists her wrist free and runs off again, leaving a slippery mess of clotting blood in Anna's palm. She cannot hear her mother ordering her to stop, her grandmother calling her back.

When she reaches the kitchen, she ducks into the broom cupboard. The dull thrumming in her belly fills her ear, fills the cupboard. She shuts her eyes tightly, and then opens them again. Everything is tilted sideways slightly. Everything is sharply clear, too clear, incomprehensible. Now she hears Ruth and Anna enter the kitchen. They are quiet for a while, and then MaAnna speaks.

"Nyangi dear, come out of there."

Maya stands straight up in the cupboard, trembling. Her mother's voice is sweet. It is gentle. "Maya honey, Rosie isn't going to come back if you hide. Come out here and help us look for him." Anna turns to her mother, "I think this house will have to do with only two cats. I hope they can take care of the mice by themselves."

Well, they can't, thinks Maya, suddenly losing her focus on everything but what her mother is saying. Rosie is the hunter of the bunch. Serena just preens all day and all Bruno can do is waddle after Hehra. Without thinking any further, Maya opens the cupboard door. She understands this dilemma.

"I think David frightened him," she tells her mother quietly, glad that finally she has an ally, someone who will sympathize.

"It's OK. Come and show us what happened." Her mother's voice is soft. It has the same sing-song lilt it sometimes has when she is talking to her husband.

Maya takes her mother's index finger and leads MaAnna and Ma Ruth through the corridor all the way back to the dining room. The sideboard is still smeared with blood. But Rosie is gone. Maya turns to her mother to describe what happened, but Anna speaks first.

"Nyangi, did you hear me calling you?"

Maya is confused. No she did not. So she replies, "No."

"You didn't hear me telling you to stop, to come back?"

"No," her voice is uncertain.

"How come? Didn't I tell you that when I call you, you come right away?"

"Yes." Maya remembers that.

"So, even if you didn't hear me calling you, why didn't you come out of the cupboard in the kitchen when I asked you to?"

Maya just stares at her mother, even more confused. She looks down and sees a smeared red stain on Anna's white polyester trousers, just inside the leg above the knee.

"When I speak to you, you will look up!" There is no anger in MaAnna's voice, just gravel, hard, sharp, and now also cold. Maya looks up. Her whole body is shaking, her head humming loudly. It dawns on her in that instant that this is not her friend.

"David, get me three switches, green ones, and fetch the belt," Anna says.

David runs to get the switches and after a long, long, silent while, returns with three long willow branches, still fresh, very green. He then runs to his mother's room and gets the broad brown leather belt she uses for whippings. When he finally brings it back to the living room, everyone is exactly where he left them. Ma Ruth stands by the door, looking at Maya. MaAnna is in front of the sideboard, doubled in the mirror tall and straight, the white of her chic two-piece shining, filling every corner of the room. Maya, not yet three feet tall, is also by the sideboard, her back to the mirror, only the very tip of the top of her head reflected.

"Choose," Anna says.

Maya does not need an explanation. She teeters. She moves. She finds herself at the table where David has placed the three green switches and the belt. She looks at them blankly.

Then she looks at her grandmother in mute supplication. *Help.*

Can Ruth read the child? She leans against the door and opens her mouth to say something. Maya hopes her grandmother will say to MaAnna, thinks she will say to Anna, *my child, leave her alone. Forgive her. Look, her cat ran away.*

Instead, Ma Ruth says to her, "You should have come when I called you. This is what you get for disobeying. I would have protected you."

Anna looks at her child and sees that she is trembling. "Since you can't decide," she says, "we will try them all, see which one you like the best."

Canto Twenty-eight

It makes no difference anyway because later, when Alex finds her and cleans her up, Maya will not be able to say which one she liked the least. She will not remember the pain, or the panic, or the defeat. She will not have the wailing screams resounding over and over in her ear. And neither will her brother David who feels sorry for his sister as he watches MaAnna thrash Maya. When Esther returns from school to find her big brother in manic distress, she will sit by his side without uttering a word until he regains what little composure he has learned to muster when Esther is around.

Why did Nyangi have to be so stubborn? Everyone knew that when MaAnna says something, there is to be no debate. David, old enough to know this, had not imagined that Maya would get a whipping when he had gone to tell on Rosie. All he had hoped for was to get the better of his sister by getting rid of her cat so that she could feel just as he felt every time she thwarted him, or disobeyed him, or found a way to laugh at him. Now watching her fly around the room in terror, accosted by unrelenting lashes of green wood and tough leather at every turn, he covers his ears with his hands and tucks his chin into his chest, trying to block out the heaving bursts of agony that implode in her between the whimpering and the begging, between the desperate promises to be good, to remember to come when called. He himself will soon forget the fear that sends him ducking to avoid stray blows. David looks up at his mother, the most beautiful woman he has ever known, or will ever see, and hates Maya for making MaAnna angry.

When Alex finds her, Maya will not think that her body is sore, nor will she know that her voice is hoarse. She will not remember how she tore her lip. She will not be able to explain how she knows that even if she ever sees Rosie again, he will not ever come when she calls him. All she will be thinking about is the hen mother cluck clucking as she scratches at the ground, looking for something she will never find. She will dream of how Gweno finally arrived home again to find her rooster beau waiting, dressed in her gown, impatient to change so that he could put on his own party attire. She will imagine that the reason he had on the dress was because his lady love had asked him to help her while she made alterations. She will fill in the details of how he had put on the gown by himself while waiting for her to return, thinking that it would save them both some time.

But Gweno is taking too long and he is worried. He is beside himself when he hears that she lost the magic needle on her way back. Well, she will have to find it *tout de suite*, the rooster exclaims impatiently. He is meeting the flamingo before the soirée and he really has to get going! How would it look if he arrived late? Besides, he does not enjoy lingering around in his wife's dress. He does not notice that Gweno is getting quite distraught as he continues to make a fuss. The cocky bird worriedly puffs out his chest and struts about, anxious that passersby will laugh if they catch a glimpse of him. Gweno only becomes more frantic searching for the lost heirloom.

Hours pass, and Ongowo waits for his friend. He expects Gweno back fairly quickly, so when she still does not appear after he has finished dressing up, he begins to worry. Most of the guests have already arrived at the party and he and Gweno are probably going to get there among the last. He does not know whether to keep waiting in case Gweno just happens to be on her way, or whether to go looking for her. He decides that it would be better to wait for a little while longer before going to search for his friend who is probably just glued to the mirror.

Eventually, he grows nervous waiting and starts imagining that something has happened to Gweno. He should go and find her. He should stay. He should send a message. But there is no one to send. Everyone has already left for the party. He will have to go himself. He will fly high in the sky so that in case she is on her way to his place, he will catch a glimpse of her, or at least a glimpse of the magnificent gown he made for her with his magic heirloom needle.

There is no one in the sky that evening. Ongowo hurries to Gweno's, finally convinced of the worst: something horrible has happened to her. As he draws closer, he sees her on the ground, still not dressed, picking and scratching everywhere with all her might. There does not seem to be any pattern to her movements. As he gets closer, he calls out to her, *Gweno*! She looks up as if startled and then darts under a tree. Puzzled, Ongowo follows her and asks her what the matter is.

Nothing, she says with a furtive look. She cannot face him. She will not look at him eye to eye. Please tell me what's wrong, he entreats. The party started a long time ago and if we don't leave soon, we are going to miss it. Why aren't you even dressed? Gweno finally looks at him and says, I haven't adjusted the dress yet. Why not? Ongowo asks, even more puzzled, didn't the needle work? I lost the needle, she confesses finally. I have been looking for it all afternoon and I can't find it. I am so sorry, but...

Ongowo sees his future, his dreamed-of mate, his projected family, vanish as she is speaking. After a while he thinks, well, since there will be no heirs, there is no need for an heirloom. He looks at his friend for a moment, his livelihood evaporating, and he says simply, I'll just have your firstborn like you promised me and then we can call it even. What? cries Gweno. You want my firstborn? Yes, that way at least I'll have a child to call my own who will look after me when I am old, and I don't have to worry about never getting married. No, no, no! Gweno says emphatically. I can't give you my child. What do you take me for?

Ongowo thinks for a minute and then says, since you cannot find my needle and you will not give me what you promised, I will grab your hatchlings every time I pass by until you find that needle and return it. Then I will stop. With that, he flies away, leaving Gweno flustered and more than a little frightened.

Gweno spends the rest of the evening looking for the needle to no avail. The next day, and the one after, and for several weeks following, she looks for the needle and still she has no luck. Later, during the hours she spends sitting on the eggs that she has finally laid, she thinks only of finding the needle, overwhelmed with remorse as she slowly realizes what the loss means to her friend's life. The rooster is no help to her. In fact, he is so resentful about the dress that every morning, even before the sun has risen in the horizon, he harasses Gweno out of the coop to look for the needle, making sure to make as much noise as he possibly can to wake up his exhausted mate. Whenever she gets up, she does not fly off to chat with passersby to find out what her neighbors are doing as she used to do in the past. Instead she simply sets about looking for the needle, scratching away at the ground, hopelessly hoping to find it buried somewhere beneath her feet.

Book V. Rain

How Maya's waking dream, following Rosie's flight, transports her aboard the São Raphael, a carrack on Vasco da Gama's first voyage around the African coast. • While she walks the deck of the ship together with Frei João de Sousa, the mist and rain in Maya's waking dream mingle with Akoth's memory of the rains that fall over the savanna grasslands, the equatorial Mountain of God's Repose, the Great Nam Lolwe and the ancient River Nile. • Maya dreams the legend of the Snake People in her sleep.

Canto Twenty-nine

Water, water, everywhere…

Soft sunlight spills through the broad glass block windows that adorn the westward wall of the bathroom, carrying with it watery silhouettes of the blooming jacaranda and eucalyptus trees cast against the clear sky. A few keen rays shoot through the open awning glass above the windows near the ceiling, the rest of the light gently muted as if mindful not to touch Maya's raw flesh. She floats facing up in the tub, heaving a gulping breath before dipping her head below the surface of the water, her ravaged right arm anchored to the edge of the tub as her little body bobs about. She purses her lips as if to whistle and blows out a string of bubbles, moving her head to and fro in the water, humming faintly.

Alex watches Maya play in the water, smiling to himself. She still doesn't know how to whistle, he muses. He hears the sounds of Mamma Akoth returning home from her day's walk — the soles of her sandals tapping against a threshold mat in the courtyard; her gentle, happily sighed greeting to the houseboy and the maid; her query, "What has happened?" in response to their poorly disguised, uncontainable relief that she is finally back.

Inside Maya's head the humming bubbles rattle and trill, making her giggle a little. Water sneaks into her windpipe and she surges up in the tub coughing it out, trying to wipe the dripping cascade off her face, off her eyes.

Alex laughs along, "*Still* don't know how to whistle?"

Their laughter rings through the bathroom, reverberating off the glass blocks and ceramic tiles in round waves of mirth.

"I want to go again!" she squeals with delight. "I want to go again!"

Maya draws in another long breath, puffs out her cheeks, holding in the air, and then dunks her head back into the water. More strings of trilling bubbles issue from her pursed lips and rattle and hum around her head merrily, modulating into the song of Akoth's warble.

"Breathe, child. Breathe," the old woman's voice hums gently, joining Alex beside the tub to watch Maya play. The phantom guardian's spirits lift. *Mamma Akoth, thank you!*

Water, water, everywhere…

"Yes. Everywhere," Akoth hums, the gentleness of the sound she makes masking her shock at the piteous sight before her eyes.

Maya's head rises a little, her face breaking the surface even as she floats outstretched in the enameled tub. Scattered shafts of equatorial sun rays paint the bathroom ceiling, mimicking waves, undulating against the smooth flat surface. Maya drifts along, her small body floating still. A luminous circle emerges from the mirage of waves dancing on the bathroom ceiling, etched within it a cross, no, a star, glimmering, set upon a bed of leaves, decorated with curling vine tendrils and berries. The waves beneath the star become sky and wind, cold and warm, gentle and rough, quiet. A thin mist grows, and the muted air softens, thickens.

Canto Thirty

The wind burgeons, moves, catches in towering square sails driving the timorous wide carracks beneath through unquiet seas.

Sky and sun vanish. The air white with cloud swallows the flagship ahead and the supply ship behind. The first mate sends a lookout to the crow's nest to keep an eye on the disappearing ships, to ensure that we hold course with our meager armada, to call down to us who chronicle the details of our journey everything that he sees. Our accounts to our Heaven-sent King and to all our brethren who make this voyage in our wake must bear witness to our trials and triumphs alike. Our fleets are charged *to make discoveries by sea, in the service of God our Lord, and our own advantage.* His Majesty Dom Manuel sends us, four ships among many since the time of Dom Henrique o Navegador, to fulfill the Holy Father's mandate to his Majesty's own uncle Afonso V, King of Portugal and the Algarves, who *peopled with orthodox Christians certain solitary islands in the ocean sea, and caused churches and other pious places to be there founded and built, in which divine service is daily celebrated to the praise and glory of God, the salvation of the souls of many, the propagation also of the orthodox faith, and the increase of divine worship.* Thus solemnly charged, forth we solemnly go.

From the crow's nest high atop the mainmast the lookout makes it known that the fog is too thick. Even if the other three ships were sailing at oars length, no one would know, so quiet is the sea, so white the clouds that fill the air. The first mate directs the deckhands to reduce the sail. If we must drift blindly, better it were slowly while we wait out the fog. *The Lord is my Shepherd,* a deckhand mutters as he heaves the ropes with his crew mates, reciting the only psalm he knows by heart. The waiting will be dull, but the fog conceals unknown perils. Woe betide us should we run aground or strike a reef. It were better that we drifted slowly, or even stopped in the deep, until we can see our flagship, our sister carrack, our supply caravel.

He leadeth me beside the still waters. He leadeth me in the paths of righteousness. Not too long ago the Holy Father Nicolas V blessed Dom Afonso and charged him reach the Christians of India by sea and affirm them, for the Holy See, the descendants in Faith of Saint Thomas the Apostle. *And we will make merry and be glad: for your brothers who were lost will be found again.* The sails are all down, the red and white square crosses of the Order of the Knights of Our Lord Jesus Christ hidden in the folds of the cloth, the masts naked and stark, vanishing into the ever-thickening clouds still descending upon us.

Let us pray, Frei João de Sousa encourages us, walking along the deck. *Let us pray.*

Prayer steels the spine, strengthens our resolve to fulfill our lord His Majesty's charge to hold Her Majesty the Queen Isabella of Castile and her consort, His Majesty the King Fernando of Aragon, redoubtable though they be in their Catholic faith, nevertheless in check. They mine the lands to the west across the great Atlantic sea, despite the faculties granted our great Dom Afonso by the Holy Father Nicholas V to hold any lands that might be discovered south of Bojador, and exact tributes from any who would profit from these lands. Their Columbus was lucky to happen upon Hispaniola. He meant to arrive in Cipangu, and from there proceed to India, and strike it rich in silk and spices. We are lucky that he could not read maps and mathematics well, that he thought the myths and legends of Marco Polo pointed the way, and so he missed India entirely! The markets of India for cinnamon, and cloves, and ginger, and nutmeg, and pepper, together with their leaves and cuttings, will all be ours to dominate across the Arabian Sea and the Indian Ocean. Dom Manuel has assured us of our right and duty, regardless of what the current Pope has said about the Spanish Crown's claims to possession and profit of the new lands to the west. Thus solemnly charged, so forth we solemnly go.

We, the children of Lusus, descended of a god's own companion — the god of wine and madness divine — we long ago received the sacred decree from the key-bearer of the heavenly kingdom and vicar of Jesus Christ, His Holiness Nicholas V, to venture into the briny seas and fulfill our destiny. It falls upon us, the Holy Father decrees from the Holy See, *to invade, search out, capture, vanquish, and subdue all Saracens and pagans whatsoever, and other enemies of Christ wheresoever placed* so that His Majesty the King may most *justly and lawfully by his authority reduce their persons to perpetual slavery and appropriate to himself and his successors the kingdoms, dukedoms, counties, principalities, dominions, possessions, and goods, and to convert them to his and our use and profit* to the greater glory of God, and faith in the Universal Church. Thus solemnly charged, so forth we solemnly go.

Our pilot keeps us adrift at a safe distance from the shoals of the African coast south of the Canary Isles using little more than his compass. He tells the first mate, and then later the quartermaster, that we will have to maintain a southerly attitude, listing west if we must, as Dias did in his day, for as long as the fog blinds us. It were better that we drifted slowly lest we run aground in the shoals of Bojador.

The Lord is my shepherd; I shall not want. Frei João de Sousa, the monk on our ship, is very young, yet he is devout. His eyes are deep and clear, his face smooth, his body thin and flat under the cassock he always dons. He might be the youngest of the handful of holy men traveling with us. Some say he may be the abbot's nephew, maybe even his son, after all, he does bear a similar name. Why else would so young a man already be a priest, and charged as we are to claim new lands and Coin for Crown and Church? But some say he is actually descended from Moors, that he was called by the voice of the Lord to leave his home in the old Tunisian city of our Great

Father Augustine, cross the Mediterranean, and go in pilgrimage to Rome. They say he even speaks in the tongues of the Holy Ghost and keeps communion with souls long since gone from this world. There are those who, confabulating, say he maybe even walks sometimes with souls of futures yet to come.

But these are just stories sailors tell to pass the time. *He maketh me to lie down in green pastures.* The young monk is captivating to behold. He makes us feel like we must protect him from the enemies of Christ in the name of our lord the King, Dom Manuel. He often sings of thirsting for the Lord in the quiet prayers he mutters as he strolls among us on the deck. When he is not singing or praying, he is talking to the deckhands, or the pilot, or the scribes, keen to hear about the details of the work we do. Other times he sits alone gazing out to sea, running the beads of his rosary through his fingers one by one by one.

He leadeth me beside the still waters…

Frei João de Sousa smiles to himself, it seems, his fingers growing still, his beads stopping as he savors the song of kings, of David rei, as we say, and of King Dom João, King Dom Afonso, and now, of King Dom Manuel. Unlike his brother on the captain-major's ship, he does not chronicle in writing. *He leadeth me beside the still waters.*

~ ❊ ~

João de Sousa stands up and approaches the port gunwale, looking out into the blind fog. He can hear the water lapping against the hull of the ship, quieting as the carrack slows to a near standstill, engulfed in the unmoving air. There must be water everywhere, but he cannot see any of it anymore. *Fons ascendebat e terra…* sings the voice of the Scripture in his ear. *There went up a fountain from the earth…* a fountain… a mist… The young monk gives his deep, clear eyes to the impenetrable fog that betrays nothing but muffled, woolly sounds of water lapping wood. *Videmus nunc per speculum in aenigmate ... Now we see through an obscure mirror* at the threshold of a new world... No, he thinks, this is the threshold of the first world, a world so old that every root draws life from it, so old that even the Pope forgot it was the cradle of humankind.

João de Sousa smiles into the fog. *Veemos agora por o espelho em figura ... We peer through a mirror in effigy...* If only he could see the surface of the water while peering into the woolly fog. The Scriptures promise that clarity: *tunc autem cognoscam sicut et cognitus sum... then shall I know even as I am known...* Once the fog lifts and they can rejoin the flag-ship, João de Sousa will find the abbot who advises the fleet captain, and he will ask him for guidance.

Canto Thirty-one

Water, water, everywhere; even in a dry and thirsty land where no water is.
Maya floats motionless in the enamel tub, lost in the fog with João de Sousa, her head held aloft by Alex and Akoth together. She peers into the opaque wall of humid air with the monk, breathing in its stillness. *Entom conheçerey assy como som conheçido ... Then shall I know even as also I am known.* She walks with him along the deck, looking for the pilot. Are they still drifting safely southward? How long will they be stuck in the fog? When will they rejoin the São Gabriel and the captain-major? The pilot tells the monk that it won't be long. João de Coimbra, the flagship's pilot, will do the same things that he of the São Rafael is doing, and they are probably not very far, just obscured by the fog. The pilot taps his brass compass, assuring

João de Sousa that all is well. The young monk's gaze lingers on the instrument, his disquiet becalmed by the sight of the cross radiating from the center of the pilot's compass rose. In his mind's eye, the memory of a more elaborately ornate compass, finely etched in brass, comes into focus for a moment, and then it is gone. No, it is not a memory yet, but the day will come when it does become the bond that he shares with the child who now walks the decks of the São Rafael by his side in the fog. She is his brother's descendant, he thinks. He knows this much to be true, even though he does not know how he knows. When next he sees Olóo of the Great Lake, son of the Nile and the Valley, he must remember to ask about this child who must surely be a kindred soul of their waking dreams. João de Sousa touches the compass with the tips of his fingers and then he brings his hands together, one folded into the other, nodding and turning his head slightly. The pilot sees the monk's gesture and smiles, believing that the holy man is offering a blessing. The pilot thinks that he has read the monk's subtle expression correctly, but he cannot ever know of the life behind those eyes. He bows and makes the sign of the cross, a gentle courtesy. *Thank you, Brother John*, he says, as João de Sousa's gaze lingers on the compass still.

"Obrigado, Frei João," Maya repeats under her breath, humming a child's water song, floating still, immersed in the young priest's meditation, her eyes fixed on the waves beyond the bathroom ceiling.

Alex starts, surprised. The round, gentle sounds that Maya is making abound with Portuguese. *Obrigado, Frei João.*

"Who is that?" he asks. "Nyangi, who is Brother John?"

She hears his question even with her ears submerged in the tub, so she relays the rumors the crew of the São Rafael trade on deck.

"He is from Tunisia, the Moorish son of Father Augustine who sings, Tejo the son of the mountain lions, but maybe his father is really the abbot de Souza, or his uncle. His other brother João Figueira likes to write everything down. He speaks in tongues like—"

"Never mind," Alex sighs. "Just float."

"Obrigado Frei Alessandro," she says dreamily, smiling.

Alex shakes his head and smiles along with her.

O—brigado—brigado—brigado—brigado… Maya's voice fades into a languid, waltzing loop.

A luminous cross, etched into the brass glimmering in Maya's imagination, hangs aloft amidst a tangle of curling vine tendrils, leaves, and berries. Light beams from behind the cross radiate in sharp rays in every direction against the sky. The wind, once still and cold, picks up gently, warming, and the fog begins to rise, driven forth. But the air thickens. The wind is suddenly electric, carrying the ethereal smell of lightning on its wings. It is the aroma of anthill flakes… salt leached of flavor… tasteless lemons.

A drop of the gathering storm strikes Maya's nose. And then another. And then a torrent.

Canto Thirty-two

Raindrops falling on the surface of the ocean water in their numberless multitude sound like sorghum grains landing in reed baskets, the finer spray swept away by capricious winds, mimicking chaff carried off in the winnowing dance. Raindrops, pregnant with the seeds of memory, descend from Heaven to imbue every form of creation with the history of its life. The eye of Heaven gazes upon each drop as it condenses, delighting in its growth from atomized suspensions gathering slowly into water. The inattentive onlooker imagines that every raindrop is just like the next, but the eye of Heaven sees the stories seeded in each one by vapors rising from the earth to meld the currents of the Nile with the mists of Amazonia and the rapids of Chiang Jiang, with the breath of Wimihsoorita and her Great River sister, with the myths of Tongala and yes, the songs of Jordan. When the overflowing clouds finally let their waters go and send them back to earth, the currents of the waiting Nile and all her sister rivers of the world bless the Heavens for their bounty as they swell and flow. The sands of the Sahara, the Rift Valley Highlands, Nam Lolwe Ataro, too, all receive with open hearts the falling infant drops of rain.

Vapors carrying echoes of fables from the Arctic, the North and South Seas, the Indian Ocean, the Atlantic, even the Pacific, and the Mid-Earth sea twixt Egypt and the old Roman lands, all meld together in a single bead of dew. Oases wells that spend their days remaking the bending forms of date palms in the depths beyond their still, glass surfaces send along three or four vanishing notes to add to the drops received by Nam Lolwe. Drying waters suffused with stories of creation rise endlessly, and then, quickened in the gathering clouds, fall back to earth – sometimes still as water, but other times, where the air is frigidly thin, as delicately woven crystals threading out in hexagons, or as icy pebbles dashed crashing to the ground.

Raindrops, snowflakes, hail stones, their fall is but a measure of the time lived by a single soul loosed from the whole. Although it is rare, some join before colliding with the ground below: they drift together, mingling as one along the way, or are swept into the path of other descending drops by sudden gusts of wind. A few which formed together in the bosom of the clouds, barely aware before their separation, now fall side by side, or reunite as they tumble, sometimes recognizing one another, sometimes not.

Just like the eye of Heaven, and just like Nam Lolwe, the Spirit of the Mountain of God's Repose looks upon the falling rain and snow and hail with boundless joy, receiving untold stories from places and times of unimagined distance. Like every living being, the raindrop's life begins the moment it condenses, lasts for the length of its descent to the ground, and ends whenever and wherever something breaks its fall. Then it is no longer distinct. Those falling into the soil spread thinly in solitude and soak into it completely, becoming part of something else, no longer the single drop. A different fate awaits those that fall into a river, a lake, or a sea, joining the multitude of their kind. There they meld with other drops, dissolve, and then become part of something greater than themselves, inscrutable where one begins and where another ends.

The Nile, which has for countless ages flowed north, against the wind, is home to a raindrop that knew the river in its youth. This drop is now at once in the forests of Uganda, in the plains of Sudan and the valleys of Egypt, and even dips a bit into the Mediterranean. It has known every raindrop that ever entered the river's changing currents and recognizes those who have left many times only to return newly formed. This raindrop spent its early days, upon falling to earth, in the tiny whirlpool of the river's source spring deep in the heart of Africa. When heavy rains came and washed it along, it found itself clinging to the banks wherever it could. By then it was no longer round, nor even alone; it was shapeless and vast, melded with others, and thinly spread. This was especially true in the years of drought when the river, once torrential and thick, shrank to a trickle along the bedrock, and then to little more than a stain at the bottom of what was once its course. This ancient raindrop has seen the whole world through that part of itself that mingled with the rising mist to form other clouds, returning not to this, but to some other river, or winding up on the surface of the sea lapping against the hull of a drifting Portuguese carrack. This ancient raindrop prepared for the end, losing most of itself as the Nile impotently turned into vapor. Buried moisture sank deeper down below the bone-dry clay, becoming harder and harder to summon, even from the deepest wells. But life is patient and eternal, be it long or brief. When the rains returned after a much-protracted drought, the thirsty river, drunk with bounty, swelled up and flowed again, bearing so much water that the ancient drop could scarce believe that Heaven had borne such a deluge. This is the nature of life in the world of Time. While it falls, each drop is alone. But after the fall, and even before, it cannot separate itself from the cloud, or the river, or the lake, or the sea.

On the Mountain of God's Repose directly beneath the equator, three peaks awaken to the manifold histories carried to them by clouds from every place in the world that is touched by rain, their glaciers holding each account precious, every one a treasury of Memory that finds its way slowly, in the flowing melt of warmer days, into springs and streams and rivers that bear tidings from the red clay foothills of the equatorial mountain range along meandering courses flowing north, and then east, and then finally south across the sprawling grasslands of the savanna to meet the ocean coast.

Here and there, umbrella thorn trees, their tap roots delving deep into the ground, their lateral roots bracing, stand erect among the grasses of the savanna, leaning into the nibbling lips of those giraffes tall enough to pluck small, tightly packed leaves from among sentinel thorns where weaver bird clans hang their palatial nests. Wending their way among the trees, the giraffes keep sparse company and spend their days navigating around anthills big and small in their loping and deceptively nimble gait. When giraffes visit the waterholes, the hippos and egrets and other small waders clear the way for them, mindful, perhaps, of how far down the giraffe must reach for even a small sip of water. Gazelles, too, and impalas, often gather in small groups hiding in the tall grasses, but the wildebeest prefer mighty congregations, especially in the seasons of migration. Other grazing herds of unnumbered medley and the great cats that live among them all gather around shared waterholes and river lakelets. It is not unusual to find them all together at the waterholes alongside avian hosts, like the ibis and egrets who keep pace and counsel with elephants, surely the grandest of these lords of the savanna. Deliberate and communal, the ways of these colossal beasts manifest an age-old love abiding for the waters brought to them by rivers, brought to them by rains. They roll in mud and splash and tread, and dawdle away hot afternoons in the grassland pools, ponds, lakes, young and old alike, unmindful of the water snakes that slumber in the reeds and grasses all along the banks. The lion prides that sometimes come to share the watering holes are maybe even envious of these insouciant giants, or maybe just bewildered by their love for mud and water. All these creatures, great and small, drink in all Creation's tales carried in the falling rain sent by Heaven's eye or gathered in the waters of the rivers that traverse their lands and empty out to sea and to oceans that embrace the sky.

Canto Thirty-three

Akoth owes her memory of this great savanna grassland, and of its creation from the red clay foothills of the Mountain of God's Repose, to the rain that fell on her journey to the coast along the river that touches the sea. Mingled in together with the fables born of rain are the chronicles of sailors and the stories of monks, and the tales that the nuns of the coastal cloister shared and showed of renaissance architects in the hours and days that Akoth spent with them. The name of João de Sousa, lost to all Iberians, lives on in the winds of Mombasa and has made its way inland, all the way to the missionary schools by the Great Lake where Akoth learned the Word of Christ and earned her trilingual, leather-bound volume of the Bible.

Nearly a century after Vasco da Gama returned to Portugal from his second trip to India, the name of João de Sousa rose again in the echoes of the monsoon winds of winter. The ships that rode those winds carried tidings from Goa of an Italian engineer who was coming to fortify Mombasa against Turkish invaders. The garrison was charged with gathering men and boys from among the Swahili fishermen and traders to prepare for the advent of João Batista who would soon arrive on the shores of Mombasa aboard the King's own carrack. The news of the architect's approach spread with electrical alacrity among all the Christians of the coast and the Portuguese soldiers stationed in the city. The King of Portugal and of all the Spanish Kingdoms, of Castile and Aragon, of Naples and Sicily and Sardinia — the great-grandson of Her Majesty Queen Isabella and his Majesty King Fernando — the venerable and prudent and most bureaucratic Phillip II had called upon Giovanni Battista of Cairati, near Milan, for His Majesty was also the Duke of Milan, in the name of the Crown and of the Lord Jesus Christ, to render service to that most exigent of mandates issued an hundred and ten five-fold years since by the Holy Father in Rome to his Majesty Dom Afonso that the Lusitanian Crown *invade, search out, capture, vanquish, and subdue all Saracens and pagans whatsoever, and other enemies of Christ wheresoever placed,* and thereby enable His Majesty the King to most *justly and lawfully by his authority reduce their persons to perpetual slavery and appropriate to himself and his successors the kingdoms, dukedoms, counties, principalities, dominions, possessions, and goods, and to convert them to his and their use and profit* to the greater glory of God with faith in the Universal Church. Giovanni Battista was bringing designs for a new fort to replace the makeshift barracks, a fort perfected in science to help pave the way for the kingdom of God on Earth and the dominion of His Majesty's crown over the trade routes to India across the Arabian Sea and the Ocean along the African coast.

The caravel that preceded Giovanni Battista also carried three Indian Saint Thomas Christians who prayed with the Portuguese soldiers who were there to receive orders to gather local laborers. The Indian Christians sang the Lord's prayer in the chapel by the harbor and recounted the story of how, nearly a century before, João de Sousa had braved the very first journey Vasco da Gama took to India. Captured by Moorish pirates in Mombasa, he was recovered when the captain-major paid his ransom after leading the ships of his small flotilla into the harbor in Malindi to stock up on provisions.

The Indian Christians who came to meet them in the harbor boarded the São Raphael with gifts for the captain-major. Communion with the Saint Thomas Christians came naturally, for no sooner did they see the altar piece of the Mother Mary at the foot of the cross, holding her broken Son, weeping, than they laid down everything they held in their hands and knelt before the altar in pious devotion. João de Sousa knelt down with them, as did Frei Gonçalo de Souza, the abbot mistakenly believed to be the young monk's uncle, and Frei João Figueira as well, who, although weakened by illness, rose from his cot to witness and participate that he might continue to keep a faithful chronicle of their voyage. All together, the monk, the priests, and the Saint Thomas Christians joined voices to say a special prayer for Easter Thursday on the year of our Lord fourteen hundred and ninety-eight. The abbot was barely audible muttering the prayer under his breath, the Indians singing quietly, and João Figueira silent, along with João de Sousa. Vasco da Gama and his brother Paolo, the captain of the São Raphael, watched the newly met Christians with caution, wary of subterfuge. When the abbot's prayer ended, João de Sousa drew closer to the Indian Christians, spellbound, listening to their song of worship offered in a language he had never had occasion to learn, yet somehow understood. Unwinding his rosary from around his waist, João de Sousa wound it instead around the clasped hands of one of the Indian Christians who prayed. João de Sousa then joined them in prayer, echoing their song in his own mother tongue. Some said that the young monk could do this sincerely because the Word in the song of the Saint Thomas Christians had come directly from the Lord's own Apostle. Such testament of the boundless power of the Kingdom of God inspired awe in all who heard it, and they blessed the name of João de Sousa.

Your will be done on earth as it is in heaven, the devout group of Indians intoned together with their new companion, and all who were gathered there in the São Raphael marveled to see the bond of fraternity in Christ that the *Pater noster* wrought among these men of different worlds. It was João de Sousa, through the union of this bond, who discovered that one of the Saint Thomas Christians was a pilot and that he could guide the captain-major's ship safely to India. He was from Goa, the new pilot told them, just north of Calecut where he said the winds would take them, and he would stay with them to guide them once they all arrived. He would lead them through the local courts and teach them how the markets ran, and then he would accompany the fleet back to Mombasa. How João de Sousa was able to convey the mission of the Portuguese fleet to his new Christian brethren, and how he was able to convey the Indians' intent and offer so faithfully to the captain-major remained a mystery and a miracle. All he would say, when pressed to explain how he knew the language of the Indian Christians was *quãdo era minino fallaua como minino, sabia como minino, cuydaua como minino …* *when I was a child, I spake as a child, I understood as a child, I thought as a child…*

After Vasco da Gama finally made landfall in Calecut and knew that at last they were in India, he promised the young monk, on behalf of his Majesty Dom Manuel, the boundless rewards of a grateful King. But the ways of the Lord are mysterious. João de Sousa fell gravely ill with fever and chills that presaged demise. The captain-major was certain that nothing could be done, except perhaps prevent contagion spreading amongst his crew. Commending the care of the dying monk to the local Saint Thomas Christians, the captain-major ordered the São Gabriel to weigh anchor quickly and set sail for Portugal without delay. Upon his return to Calecut after three years away, Vasco da Gama marveled to find João de Sousa still living, and all the more so when he witnessed wondrous miracles unlike anything that he had ever seen before.

A century after these events, when the King sent Giovanni Battista to build him a new fort in Mombasa, soldiers garrisoned in the coastal city listened to these tales about João de Sousa with wide open eyes, marveling at how such a modest young monk had laid such deep roots in faith for the magnificent fort they would now build. They were blessed with the communion of Indian Christians who still remembered their first meeting with the Portuguese Knights of the Order of Christ, and still remembered Frei João de

Sousa. Such was the grace of God, they said. Such was the power of the faith of João de Sousa who prepared the way for the new João Batista, warrior of the faith and defender of the Crown. When the soldiers went into Mombasa and the surrounding coast towns to conscript workers to build the fort that João Batista was coming to erect, they repeated the story of the miraculous meeting of João de Sousa and the Indian Saint Thomas Christians that took place a century gone, of the prophetic communion that paved the way for the second coming of John the Baptist. Many locals gathered to listen, fishermen, traders, masons, and builders all, and where they gathered, they were gathered in turn, and brought to the Portuguese garrison to start gathering stones and to await the advent of the King's Italian architect, not *João Batista*, not *John the Baptist*, but rather Giovanni Battista.

Canto Thirty-four

When I was a child, I spake as a child, Maya was now saying in Portuguese.

Mamma Akoth watched the delicate child playing in the tub.

But now I have put aside childish ways, Akoth responded, singing in Dholuo — just as she had on the train on her way to Mombasa, just as she had when Hehra was born — her voice warbling as if rising from the depths of a silent pool. Alex turned to look at her from the other side of the tub, still holding Maya's head to keep the child's nose and mouth above the surface of the water.

"What is it…?" He asked, when he saw the expression on Mamma Akoth's face.

"When Anyango grows up," Mamma Akoth declared, "I want you to take her to travel, like her father traveled when he grew up."

"Where?" Alex asked.

"Take her to Mombasa. Take her to India."

Alex nodded. He did not ask any more questions. Mamma Akoth made it sound as if there was no reason to wonder why she was giving him these instructions. Mombasa and India it would be. It did not occur to him to ask Mamma Akoth whether she would travel with them.

"And tell her about Vasco da Gama," Mamma Akoth added.

Alex smiled. *Vas-co da Ga-ma, went to the dra-ma, without his pajamas to …* He stopped himself from intoning the silly rhyme. The children at David and Esther's school recited it in the playground and then darted about squealing with laughter after bellowing about the *biiig bananas.* Any teachers within earshot made sure to whack them across their calves for saying crude things. Who knows what Mamma Akoth would do, what she would say if she heard him repeat the sing-song rhyme?

He did not yet know anything about Vasco da Gama beyond that silliness and he was sure that Mamma Akoth was not referring to bananas. He would have to learn about Vasco da Gama and then share what he learned with his little baby sister. Their father had a vast library full of history books, and atlases, and poetry galore. Surely there was something in there about Vasco da Gama? Alex promised Mamma Akoth that he would do as she asked and wondered whether it was time to get Maya out of the water, dry her and dress her for bed.

The sun was still up, and it would be for several hours yet, but Maya needed to go back to sleep, Alex thought. The little she had slept between the time when Rosie ran away, and when Alex found her in the cupboard had done wonders, clearing all memory and knowledge of how her arm was so savagely torn, her body bruised, her skin lashed, her world saturated with a white-hot terror and betrayal too potent for her small person to contain. She seemed quite fine now, floating carefree in the tub, mumbling greetings and gratitude and scripture in Portuguese – *Portuguese?* – humming under her breath. Her blood clotted well so the gashes on her arm and hand had stopped bleeding. The soles of her feet and the tips of her toes and left-hand fingers had shriveled up and her skin took on a gray tinge from being in the water for so long.

"Nyangi," Alex said, lifting Maya's head to make her sit up. "Get up. Get out of the water, you need to dry up."

"Okay," Maya said, her small voice breezy, grasping the edge of the enamel tub and jumping up, splashing some of the water onto the floor of the bathroom.

As she climbed out she leaned hard over her right hand braced against the edge of the tub. The pain shooting up her arm from the tears in her palm and wrist forced out a loud, squealing gasp from her throat and she tumbled toward the floor of the bathroom.

Alex caught her and broke her fall, and then wrapped her in an oversized towel that wound around her small body three times over. He folded one end of the towel over her head in a makeshift cowl, and then ushered her waddling form out of the bathroom and down the long corridor to the room she shared with Esther and the baby Hehra. Alex found a long linen nightdress and pulled it over Maya's head, being careful not to let the cloth rub against her injured arm, nor the falling towel aggravate her skin. Her hair was still damp enough for water to drip down her neck and her collarbone, but today was not a day to try combing through her hair, even if the water had softened it. Thankfully, it was all bound up in twin plaited lines that framed her head and disappeared behind her ears. Alex took the discarded towel and wrapped it several times around Maya's crown and patted it down. That would have to do.

Maya opened her mouth slowly and began to yawn, stretching her jaws so wide that Alex thought they might come undone, and squeezing her eye shut so tight, he almost laughed at the sight. Her arms outstretched, the rest of her little body arched back tense before relaxing again. She sat on the bed, tucked her legs up, and turned to crawl under the top sheet.

"Wait. Hold on." Alex took Maya's right arm by the elbow and wrapped a long strip of white cotton gauze around her hand, and then her wrist, and then her forearm.

"There. Now you can get into bed."

Maya rolled into the space between the sheets, stretching once again, more languidly this time.

"Tell me a story," she said, her head dropping onto the pillow and her eyelids falling with it.

"Which one? What do you want to hear? The story of Gweno and Ongowo?"

"No, the one of the Snake People."

"I don't know a story about snake people."

"Yes you do… the Snake People that Kipleting's grandmother sings about all the time."

Alex really did not know the story she was asking for. He did not know who Kipleting was. He looked at Mamma Akoth. "Do you know the story of the Snake People?"

But Maya answered instead, "Yes. But I want *you* to tell it."

"But I don't know that one" Alex replied, at a loss.

"Tell it anyway. Start from the beginning."

"Okay," Alex said. "Okay. A long, long time ago," he started, "long before the world awoke…" He looked at Mamma Akoth again, pleading.

Maya's eyes shuttered, the lids drawing down, heavy with sleep. Her breathing slowed and she yawned once again, drawing her legs up to her chest and curling into a ball.

"Chon, chon gilala… a long, long time ago," sang Mamma Akoth, taking a smiling pity on Alex, "long before the world awoke, there lived, in the sweet water lake in the great Rift Valley, a young couple when the world was still new…"

Relieved, Alex slid down from the edge of the bed where he had been sitting, and knelt on the floor beside Maya, inching close so that his head rested on the pillow next to hers. As he settled down, his eyes fixed on Maya's closed lids, Mamma Akoth's voice flowed through him into the somnolent child's waiting ear.

"The world was so new that it had not yet seen night. It was so new that all it knew was daylight under the sun. In the distance, at the edge of the valley, a highland range arose covered in such a great variety of trees that there were not enough names for them. Along the highland foothills where green grass sprung out of the red soil, thorn trees reached up out of the ground to greet the sun, but then stopped when they noticed the shadows their spreading branches made on the surface below. Boulders that had rolled down the valley slopes came to rest in the wide ravine where waters also settled in pools shallow and deep."

Maya was now sleeping. Her small body unwound itself from its fetal ball and splayed flat across the bed on her stomach. She breathed slowly and deeply, exhaling for long spells before drawing air again. Shifting in her sleep, she had shoved the pillow aside, and her bandaged right forearm was raised flat above and behind her head while her left hand was tucked beneath her cheek.

In her sleep, she entered the valley in the story that flowed through Alex from Mamma Akoth. There, she stood at the top of the highland ridge overlooking the ravine strewn with thorn trees and the first of the Great Rift Valley's watering holes. In her dream, Maya descended to the lowest depth of the pool, to the cradle of the Onyx Serpents.

Where she stood, the pool did not let in the sky. The waters were so deep that not even sunlight could pierce the bottom where the two serpents lay. One of the serpents was large, his head and neck as big as a fully-grown man, the rest of him coiled beneath. His eyes glowed a little in the dark depth of the pool, black pearls set in his obsidian head, and his tongue darted about into the water world around him. Next to him lay coiled a smaller serpent, her head just as flat, her eyes as round yet somehow brighter, her tongue flickering more gently. The bottom of the pool was as silent and as cold as it was dark. The serpents shivered, almost imperceptibly, the silence around them complete.

Suddenly, lightning pierced the water from above, parting the surface for a moment, blinding the serpents nestled in the deep. Still, as the pierced water closed in again over their heads, the great Serpents caught a fleeting glimpse of the world above. In the instant before the darkness was complete, they saw the yellow undertail of a bulbul who was sipping the nectar of a red aloe. They saw the large toes and crimson crown of a lily-trotter walking daintily across the lily pads spread along the surface of the pool. They saw the green-tipped wings of the brown hooded kingfisher fluttering when he dipped down to catch a small silverfish in his beak, the mouse bird flicking his long gray tail as he clambered up a gnarled tree, the scarlet breast of the sunbird, the carved yellow beak of the hornbill, the flashing red of the bee-eater landing on kori-bustard's back, the long crimson tail of a fly catcher, the brightly striped head of a barbet, the red cheeks and blue breast of the weaver finches hanging their nests in the thorn tree at the edge of the pool.

The waters above finally closed in, and the couple's serpent eyes blinked in the renewed gloom. They lay quietly, amazed at the beauty of the world above beyond their watery home. They wondered how they might go up and see the trees and birds, the colors and shapes drawn with light and warmth. The Serpent looked at his wife, and she at him. And then suddenly, her round head, once smooth with rounded scales, began to change before his eyes. Where once there were scales, now there were little tight black curls. Her soft eyes grew lids as he looked on, the promise of seeing her walk on the surface slowly taking shape. Her shining brown body grew shapely curves, and her legs extended, long and firm and smooth, against the banks of the pool that had been their home. The great Serpent looked upon his wife and saw the first woman, wise and warm and full of grace. She, in turn, looked at him and her gaze transfigured his form in turn. His broad head grew tight curls, his brown eyes, now lidded like hers, looked about him at the earth above the water surface. He followed her out of the pool and when they finally stood on land together, they looked upon the world and rejoiced to see its first sunset.

Here and there, thorn trees stood erect among the grasses of the savanna, leaning into the nibbling lips of long-necked giraffes busy plucking their small, tightly packed leaves. By the edge of the water, hippos and egrets and other small waders cleared the way to let giraffe stretch down to quench their thirst in the pool. A herd of gazelles was also gathered nearby, all of them sipping together as if of a single mind. A black-headed ibis stood with the elephants, grand beasts of great serenity, lovers of water and mud. A pride of lions sat together on a stone mound at a small distance, watching the pachyderm giants mix water and earth in giddy play. The Serpent man and the Serpent woman stood on the shore amidst the reeds and grasses, among all their fellow creatures. They drank in the living vision of creation's first evening before them. As the sun sank down below the ridge, the Serpent man and Serpent woman resolved to never live in the darkness again. And so they lived on land under the sun in the sky, never to return to the cold and sunless deep.

Canto Thirty-five

When Maya awoke the following day, she was not lying on her belly anymore, but rather on her back. The sun rays streaming into the children's bedroom window rang so loud that Maya had to cover her eyes to muffle the din. Hehra, her cat Bruno at her feet, was leaning against the bed staring at the white gauze wrapped around Maya's arm. The bed was low enough to the ground that Hehra could reach her small arm over without straining and touch her sister's face with her tiny, plump fingers. The baby's touch landed with weightless devotion on Maya's ear. And then Hehra's fingers closed around her awakening sister's earlobe and tugged lightly, repeatedly. Mamma Akoth looked at the two children, welcoming the elder from her slumber, musing that the younger would soon need to be changed and bathed for the start of the day.

Alex sat with Mamma Akoth, thinking the same things, and thinking about Mombasa, and India, and Vasco da Gama. Today he would spend the day in his father's library and discover all he could for Maya. They were all still young, so there was time to learn. If

Maya wanted to explore the library with him, he would bring her along since he had already heard MaAnna tell the house staff that David had recovered well enough from his bee sting to return to school, but Maya was staying home today.

Without asking questions, the houseboy accompanied only David and Esther to school. He delivered Anna's hurriedly scribbled note explaining Maya's absence to the school's gatekeeper, and then he made his way back to the house, doing his best to tarry. By the time he got back, the maid had already bathed and dressed the baby Hehra and was feeding her and Maya a breakfast of millet porridge with milk and honey. The maid poured a bowl for him, too, and then told him that the dining room had to be washed and thoroughly cleaned. There was still blood, now dried and browning, on the sideboard and in the frame of the large mirror, and probably around the chair legs as well. She wanted him to mop the floor and wipe everything in the room, and to ensure that any stains that remained could be removed or covered up. He did not ask questions. He did not want to know. He finished his bowl of porridge and asked for some more, and then he finished that bowl before finally getting the mop and bucket and furniture polish and making his way to the dining room. He spent the rest of the day finding and scrubbing blood stains and polishing all the hard surfaces in the room until they sparkled and shone.

Neither Maya nor Hehra interrupted him in his labor. They were both in the library playroom, Maya listening to Alex, mesmerized by the tiny arrow-like schools of fish painted on the sea floor. The sun in the playroom was not as loud, so Maya could hear the faint clinking and clanking of the arrows as they jostled and shuffled on the atlas sea floor, straining to align themselves with the attitude of the world, their shimmering resonance echoing Alex's voice in her mind's ear. When the maid looked in to make sure that the two girls were behaving, she saw Maya bent intently over an atlas, insensible to the world outside the bubble of her attention, and Hehra running her crayons over the colorful pages of the life of Krishna, Bruno lying next to her, purring. Their great-grandmother Mamma Akoth sat on a rocking chair, watching Hehra. Relieved to see the girls so absorbed and responsibly observed, the maid went on her way, glad she did not have to mind them too closely. While Alex was busy holding forth on the wonders of compass navigation, Mamma Akoth watched her namesake, Hehra, trace the colors of the picture book she had pulled from the box of legends and myths of the sages and gods of India.

~ ❋ ~

Hehra fascinated and puzzled Mamma Akoth with a bewilderment that engrossed her from the very first day Anna brought the infant, not yet a month old, home from Sierra Leone. When Ma Ruth told her daughter to prepare the child and present her to the ancestors, Anna resisted, arguing feebly that since she had given birth abroad, far away from the great Lake of the ancestors of JokOlóo and JokOmolo, it was not necessary to do the ceremony of presentation. Besides, she had already named the baby "Hehra" so that everyone might know that the child was truly beloved. But Ma Ruth insisted, and Akoth echoed her demand. It did not matter where a child was born, the Spirits were all waiting, and it was unconscionable to ignore them. Anna conceded, feigning accord. It would not hurt, she reasoned to herself, to ensure her precious new baby the protection of the ancestral Spirits.

Ma Ruth brought Gabriel and David and Esther and Maya together into the courtyard at the center of the family's home in

Nairobi, along with Sara Awino and Rachel Abiero, Anna's younger twin sisters. The other members of the household who cooked, cleaned, gardened, and guarded the estate gates all gathered together under the arches of the open gallery in front of the kitchen to witness the presentation of the new baby. A few of them were children of JokOlóo, descendants of some of the nine older siblings Akoth grew up with in her father's house by the Lake. Some of them had come to the capital city to complete their O-levels and prepare for university exams, some of them had come looking for work, considered fortunate back home to already have relatives who were doing well in the big city. Anna and Gabriel took them in, and when their exams ended, well or badly, or they could not find immediate work, Anna offered them a place on the staff of her household. So they cooked, cleaned and guarded the estate gates, they walked the children to school and went to market, and kept the house running under Anna's exacting direction, and each of them remained silent in her presence, and kept their peace even when she erupted and rained her dread fury on anyone in her path.

Anna and Gabriel's three children stood directly in front of the household staff, just behind their father, and flanked by their twin aunts, Sara and Rachel. Esther, who had been still too young when Maya was presented to the ancestors, was now old enough to understand that this was a sacred rite of immense gravity. She clutched David's hand and laid her other arm around Maya's shoulder, pulling her two-year-old sister, who was now no longer the baby of the family, close to her tightly.

Ma Ruth summoned the Spirits of JokOlóo and the Spirits of JokOmolo one by one, and yet none of them answered. Akong'o was silent, as were Akoth's nine siblings, all of them already Spirits who could choose to claim the new baby if they wished. Ma Ruth reached farther, calling on the generation of their mothers and fathers, and their mothers and fathers before them. The sustained silence of every Spirit summoned brought her back to her own generation, to call upon her brother, Otiëno, who had quickly followed his wife Akinyi out of time when her death at child-bed rent his heart never to mend. But neither he nor Akinyi stirred. Ma Ruth invoked Omondi, Gabriel's father, hoping that he, at least, would speak for his son's newborn child. Still the silence remained.

Ma Ruth looked at the small baby in Anna's arms, so beautiful in her newness to the world, and dared not let herself lose hope. Without a word or a look, she sensed that Gabriel, too, was getting anxious. He had not been concerned at the presentation of his firstborn twins when only David was claimed yet no one came forward to speak for Alex. On that occasion Akoth, although still living in the world of Time, had announced that she would speak on behalf of her father's Spirit and name the infant boy for Heaven. The Song of Becoming that she intoned for Alex was full of joy. She already knew that he would not tarry long in the world of Time, so she chose to sing of the heavens and the Sun and the Rain. The very same day he was named, Alex died a quiet death that broke his father's heart, but that seemed a relief to his mother. Yet in the dull edges of that serrated pain, Gabriel also felt the unbidden consolation that it was the Spirit of Ochiëng, his dearest friend, cousin and brother, who had claimed David and named him Opiyo, the elder twin. Gabriel did not know how much it worried Akoth that it was the Spirit of one who nobody had claimed that spoke for David that day. Perhaps it was precisely because Ochiëng was the one who spoke for that child that the other Spirits continued to hold their peace, even though ordinarily they should have gathered around to sing him a Song of Becoming. It was as if all the ancestors knew that Otiëno had abandoned his orphaned son and they, too, followed suit and stayed silent when that neglected Spirit chose to speak for the child David.

Listening for a response to Ma Ruth's invocation at Hehra's naming ceremony, Akoth thought she heard echoes of something that sounded familiar, although she could not remember why.

Entom conheçerey assy como som conheçido...

Akoth looked whence the words were resounding and there she found Maya, two years old and now no longer the baby of the family, looking at something that no one else could see, lost it seemed, and only standing upright because her sister's arm was wrapped around her small shoulders.

Quãdo era minino, Akoth heard the echoes of Maya's waking dream resound once more, *fallaua como minino, sabia como minino, cuydaua como minino...* A keen memory of the soft leather binding of her worn out New Testament, warm in her hands, kindled, quickened to offer the words, *"Now, I have put aside childish ways."*

Then the memory flickered and sparked. A conflagration erupted around the grief-resistant barriers that Akoth had erected against the thousand natural agonies of loss. Heartbreak for Ochiëng, soured by regret, assailed her with brutal indifference. The pain of his solitary death in the stone wilderness of St. Petersburg, his name unclaimed for all his life, was a wound that would not close.

Lost were the warmth and depth of his heart, lost the light and breadth of his mind. Her luminous, orphaned grandson — whose light consoled the loss of her ill-fated firstborn — had come into the world of Time to satisfy the dream that she and Akong'o held dear to bridge their family lines. Her luminous, orphaned grandson — whose warmth dulled the frosty pangs of her last-born's demise — had drifted away alone in that stone wilderness of Leningrad. Yet, rather than stop to mourn him, Akoth had instead decided to throw herself into salvaging her other orphaned grandson's still new, but faltering marriage. Even for the young couple, Anna and Gabriel, only the news of their beloved cousin's death seemed to break the bride's resolve to remain aloof to her groom. Nine months after Ochiëng's passing, the twins David and Alex arrived; Akoth let herself be thankful when Ochiëng's lost, unmourned Spirit spoke up for David and named him.

She even elected to rejoice when Alex's phantom soul lingered on after his small, ailing body failed to thrive before ceding the ghost. Brief though it was, Alex's life in the world of Time might have been just as tragic as Ochiëng's life had been had Akoth not claimed him for her father's Spirit on the day he was born. She knew, in the instant she saw him emerge, that she could not just accept the death of yet another young soul. So the lingering presence by her side of the phantom Spirit of Alex Opolo vindicated her act of transgression against the custom of simply claiming, by proxy, and naming a child that nobody wanted. That very phantom Spirit then became the guardian brother who anchored the fledgling Dream Walker Maya to a constant star in the world of Time. That phantom Spirit kept the growing child from losing herself in Time in the unmapped forest of waking dreams. Young though he was, Alex Opolo had given Akoth much cause for joy by claiming and naming the infant girl.

For four generations Akoth had clung to these chosen joys and managed to hold the menace of heartache at bay. But now, the silence surrounding the baby that Anna had brought back from Sierra Leone troubled her deeply as raw recollections of unmourned loss buffeted her disquieted heart.

Quãdo era minino fallaua como minino, sabia como minino, cuydaua como minino… when I was a child, I spake as a child, I understood as a child, I thought as a child… Children did as they were told, as was expected

173

of them; they learned to hold their rebellions in silence or maybe dissemble behind a disguise simply to forestall objections to their perceived transgressions.

What did it mean for a woman of ninety Rains to put aside childish ways?

Ma Ruth continued to call for anyone to speak for Hehra's infant soul. But the Spirits of JokOlóo, Gabriel's ancestors, did not recognize the child so they did not come forward, not even Olóo himself. Anna's ancestors, the Spirits of JokOmolo, simply followed suit; they could see Anna clearly, but JokOlóo holding their peace on the infant she carried gave them leave to hold their own as well.

The swelling tide of Akoth's repressed heartbreaks grew to fill the silence of the room. Would nobody speak for this fragile new soul? Perhaps the way that Maya's own unconventional naming by Opolo Alex had quickened hope in Akoth that the embattled newborn would be looked after in the world now emboldened Akoth in the midst of the unmoving silence of the ancestors. Akoth could not bear the thought that Hehra, still barely a month in the world of Time, should walk through her life shunned by this neglect, like Ochiëng who never found peace, or like David, his ward, who never really knew it. How could every ancestral Spirit stay mute and refuse to keep the infant soul from getting lost adrift? Couldn't they see that even Alex, though only claimed by proxy, had found purpose in his phantom life here in the world of Time? Hehra, in her unspoiled newness, could not be left to languish, unwanted, simply because the Spirits did not seem to know her.

Quãdo era minino fallaua como menino… The echoes of Maya's waking dream and the memory of the New Testament volume opened to that fateful passage faded together into the silence. Akoth, who even at ninety Rains did not yet stand among the ancestral

Spirits; Akoth, who for ninety Rains had accepted the pain of loss in silence in the name of honoring tradition; Akoth, the orphaned daughter of the last great Dream Walker, Olóo, resolved to put aside childish ways, and for the sake of the beloved newborn, disregard tradition.

And so she spoke up again, this time for herself, not on behalf of her father.

"This child is called Akoth," she said, "her name will honor the Rain."

None of the people gathered there that day, from Ma Ruth to the houseboy, raised any kind of objection. They must have anticipated, given the foreign circumstances of the child's birth, that this naming would be unusual, maybe even a transparent break from tradition. As the clan's eldest matriarch still in the world of Time, it was Mamma Akoth's prerogative to bring any soul into the cradle of the Great Lake. If she chose to do so for this baby, born a world away in the unknown mountains of Sierra Leone, who among them had the right to object? Just as she had done when she spoke for Opolo, Akoth sang a Song of Becoming that invited the light of the Sun into the new baby's heart, and the beauty and depth of a memory nurtured by life-giving Rain for the length of her days.

Book VI. The Blood
of Anatole Basile Tejo

How young Nato Tejo learned to love his name and fulfill his father's dreams at the French missionary school in Bonthe. • How he met and fell in love with his Franco-Norman wife, Marie, and discovered the poets of négritude. • How Anna Adongo found a mirror of her beauty in Doctor Tejo's eyes. • How Hehra went traveling to fulfill Mamma Akoth's final wish for her, and the family that she discovered in London. • How Anna Adongo finally fulfilled her girlhood's dream of love.

Canto Thirty-six

Nine-year-old Nato did not like his name. It sounded like an old-fashioned dandy's name, of the sort who walked around in waistcoats and top hats and monocles, a pocket watch tucked away at the end of a silver fob, a walking stick in one hand, and a cigar in the other. At least that is what he envisioned whenever the English teacher in Primary school called him when taking attendance, "Anatole Basile Tejo!"

Present, he would respond, cringing a little, the snickers from the row behind him just loud enough to let him know that his classmates, too, found the name a bit absurd.

It sounded artificial, his name, like something stitched together from discarded pieces of words that nobody quite understood. He wished he had been named "Obi", or "Amadu", or even "Bai" like his father. Those names at least sounded heroic and full of glory. He could then say "I am named after…" whichever illustrious "Saidu" everybody knew about. But "Anatole"? "Basile"? Why had his parents done this to him? The "Tejo" he did not really mind, for it was much more common in these parts and even other parts abroad. It was actually his father's name, and legends told of the Portuguese explorer who, centuries ago, had brought it to Sierra Leone all the way from the great Iberian river that the ancient Romans call *Tagus*. Even though it was not as ageless in these parts as "Bangura" or "Koroma", at least its roots in their land were deeper than "Anatole" or even "Basile". Before his father got the name "Tejo" it had belonged to his grandmother and for as long as family history went, it passed from father to daughter to grandson, and then father to daughter to grandson again for countless generations.

Other than his teacher, nobody really called him "Anatole", or "Basile" for that matter. At home and in the playground, he was always simply "Nato." People generally said something closer to "Nah-two", and he knew he was in trouble when he heard his mother's voice from across the village homestead calling out "Naahdwooo!" Only his father, the man who had chosen that embarrassing name, used it with any regularity. "Anatole," he would say, his voice profound with pride and affection, "you must..." following up with some morsel of paternal counsel. Where his mother trilled, "Naahdwooo!" when he was in trouble, his father bellowed in dactylic tetrameter, the duality of the second and third names making them sound trochaic, "AH-natole BAH-sile TEH-jo!" Curiously, perhaps because of the music in their herald's voices, these calls to discipline did not have the effect of alarming the boy. Instead, he would run to his mother when she hollered, or to his father when he bellowed, and stand stock straight at attention, waiting to find out what he had done to merit such an imperious summons. And that very response, prompt and dauntless, perhaps even valiant, tickled the summoner's poorly hidden mirth, making it common for Nato to meet with shining, indulgent eyes, rather than angry or impatient glares.

A childhood spent so adored might have spoiled the boy. Instead Nato's gaze upon the world was sympathetic and liberal. He saw beauty everywhere, in everything, and in everyone. He was no poet himself, but in the language of poets he found a ready expression of the world he walked through every day. His father taught him well to enjoy the finest works of art from long dead authors and composers of Europa, but also from those still living. The old man's taste was quite eclectic, filled with exotic sounding names. And even though he knew the English cannon well, his truest loves were francophone. More than give his youngest son a pair of Hellenic French names,

Tejo Bai wanted his son to *become* completely French. So when Nato celebrated his tenth birthday, his father saw to it that the boy was enrolled in a French Catholic missionary school, not much unlike the one he himself had frequented in Freetown for a short two years in his youth.

This was no easy feat because Sierra Leone was a British colony at the time, and the African natives were only allowed access to the utilitarian immediacy of the Anglican missionary schools. Unlike the French, for whom assimilation into French culture was the point of schooling, the British offered just enough instruction to make their indigenous labor responsive to the needs of the colonial overlords. But Sierra Leone was surrounded by francophone countries, excepting Liberia, of course, and so to safeguard commerce and ensure the colonizer's prosperity, select natives from across the territory borders were given special dispensation to enroll in schools on the other side. In some places where demand for an adaptable native workforce was high, the French and British governors even let their counterparts establish border schools.

There were, however, a few Catholic schools of good repute within Sierra Leone proper in places like Freetown, and even on Sherbro Island. The École Missionnaire Saint Louis, founded by the two youngest sons of the Comte d'Harcourt-Lévêque, and run by the Society of White Fathers — in their language "La Société des Missionnaires d'Afrique (Pères Blancs)" — was one such school established just outside Bonthe, long before border disputes between the French and the English drew new arbitrary boundaries and defined colonial domains. So Tejo Bai, who held an esteemed civil service post in Freetown thanks to his education in a French missionary school, and who therefore moved in the circles of those in the know, found a way to get his son enrolled in the École

Missionnaire Saint Louis. Nato, ever undaunted, followed his father's wishes and set off away from home to make his family proud.

Throughout the ten years Nato spent at that French missionary school, the first eight as a pupil, and the last two as a tutor, he stayed close to his family, especially to his father. He wrote to them all every week, describing the details of his school life, and he visited home as frequently as the holiday schedule allowed. Whenever time permitted, the family would pack up and come and visit him in school, crossing the estuary waters that separated the small island from the mainland to take him on outings in the nearby town of Bonthe. His older brothers tested him on every visit to see how well he was fulfilling their father's dream. As the youngest child he had no practical obligations to carry on the family name, nor to prosper on their behalf. All he had to do was live the dream his father nursed of becoming a fully-fledged French gentleman.

Canto Thirty-seven

At the École Missionnaire Saint Louis, Nato found fertile ground in his own natural impulse to cultivate the love for languages and words that his father had seeded in his young mind. The boy became such an avid reader that soon reading was almost all he ever did. For a while it was a mystery around the dormitory why he would not or could not wake up in the morning. All the children would have finished straightening their beds, polishing their shoes, putting on their smart school uniforms, prepared for the day, and Nato would still be in his cot, balled up like a millipede and dead to the world. Nothing short of dragging him off to the shower and dousing him with ice cold water drew him from the unconscious slumber in which he was bound. Even then, his lids remained leaden, and his feet dragged, cutting furrows through the floor. He was last to finish his breakfast, those times he had not slept through it, and he was perpetually in a state of disarray. This was not from apathy or willful untidiness. His efforts at exemplary toilette were valiant, but it was not a thing at which he excelled.

One of the reasons he slept so late was that he was plagued with exhausting dreams, especially one that came to him every night for several months. In the dream he was a full-grown man, dressed in an elegant linen suit, and sitting under a huge umbrella at a sidewalk café in a city he did not know. Behind him rose a tall building and a babble of languages floated through the air around him, riding on the soft breeze. And then he was on top of the building, a thousand meters in the sky looking down at the sidewalk café, and then tumbling off the edge. Sometimes the fall was long and gentle, like a loose leaf drifting in the wind. Other times the umbrellas drew closer to him with impossible speed. Upon hitting the pavement, he would wake up with a start, banging his head against the bed under which he had fallen. For the months during which that dream haunted him, he often awoke on the floor, swaddled and bound in his bed sheets. Soon after Nato stopped having that particular dream, news reports of a series of leaping suicides from atop the Eiffel Tower trickled down to Bonthe from Paris.

The other dream that troubled him recurred for many years, vanishing sometimes for ages as time went by, and then returning again. In that dream, a young elephant cow found its way to the center of his grandfather's village. The drumming and ululation reverberating through the close crowd of women who gathered around with offerings made the very air tremble. The giant lady's tread, thunderous from beyond the mountain, then suddenly gently sonorous, took the boy's breath away. The animal never trumpeted, she just moved among them deliberately, always directly in front of Nato, immense and majestic, intent, it seemed, on avenging an irreparable heartbreak. Off in the distance, the same cow moved with a herd in a slow trail, and then she was standing among the women of the village again as if distance lost all meaning. A symphony of pestles pounding mortars, drumheads beating in frantic rhythm again and again and again, piercing ululations cutting through expectantly jubilant chants, all saturated the air. No matter which way the elephant turned, no matter what she was offered, Nato was in front of her, and it seemed she would accept nothing else. Her leaden foot pressed hard on his chest, chasing away all the peace of sleep and leaving Nato with a wildly beating heart in the radiant flush of bliss. The dream came back night after night, then disappeared to return again when many years had gone by. Like the dream of flying, it sent him tumbling to the floor from his bed and waking up daily by the wall, impossibly wrapped up in a tangle of sheets.

However, the friars of the École Saint Louis, all of whom knew nothing of Nato's dreams, thought that they solved the riddle of his restless sleep when he was found repeatedly in the dead of night reading with a small glass lamp under his bed covers. After the lamp, a serious fire hazard, was confiscated several times and finally put somewhere where he hadn't the ingenuity to find it, it was soon ascertained that he was never in his bed while others slept. This was an accidental discovery made by the headmaster Monseigneur who one night went to use the toilet — a place where the light burned all night — and found it occupied by the little boy bent intently over a fat, dog-eared onionskin volume of god only knows what, as the story went. The internal blow to Nato's small chest as his heart tried to leap out of his body almost knocked the breath out of him when he looked up from a world of giant squids and submarines to find the enormous, somnolent Monseigneur staring down at him through uncomprehending spectacles. The boy's startled screech so violently jarred both souls that it sparked an indelible antipathy between them that neither could ever explain or shake.

From that day on, Nato was forbidden to leave his bed after the lights in the pupils' room had been turned off. So for a while he strained his eyes under the moonlight against the window ledge, trying to catch the words by some stray beams of light cast across the dormitory veranda from above. It was easy to sink back into his pillow and pull his covers after him when he heard someone coming.

The first night he did this, he remained under suspicion because his retreat had been too abrupt, setting the bedsprings on a creaking bounce he could do nothing to stop before the door opened. After that, he learned to kneel on his pillow as they did during morning and evening prayers, his neck and shoulders straining to find a favorable angle where the most light fell on the most words, while his chin and then his teeth, and finally his nose, as the night wore on, rested on the log frame of the windowsill. From this curiously pious pose, he could slide more smoothly back down under covers, without conspicuously rocking the bed, whenever he heard any friar approaching to check on the boys in the night.

The stories he read in childhood, gleaned from volumes he haphazardly secreted from the classroom desks all over the school, naturally came to be linked in his mind to keen, precise memories of the wood-sap aroma of the windowsill, its flavor of rain drops and dust, its burnished gleam in moonlight beams, precious as if stolen.

Candide tasted of waxy polish, and *Zadig* smelled of sleek hardwood stain. Nato's memory of *Le Comte de Monte-Cristo,* and most of Captain Nemo's adventure, were all imbued with the wafting emanations of the dormitory commode. When he grew weary of kneeling by the windowsill, Nato took to reading *Cyrano de Bergerac* by the corridor light that sliced through the inky shroud of night from under the door. However, he only dared to approach the luminous sliver after the friars had finished their nightly inspections. Crouching deep, with his face pressing against the painted door, his memories of that tragedy of veils took on the muted paraffin smell of red polish on a cold, burnished floor.

One term, he got his hands on some Beaumarchais, but discovered he had no appetite for such comedy of errors, nor even for the biting scorn of de Maupassant's world. Instead, his heart beat for the more epically tragic *Notre-Dame de Paris*, and when he discovered *Les Misérables*, he knew that his calling in life was to serve the broken and brutalized souls of the world.

By then, he was in confirmed adolescence, and the most deeply sentimental poets of centuries past spoke to his heart just as clearly as if they were sitting beside him, heads bent over the page in communion while he sought out nuggets of truth sublime in the volumes they had crafted. Sometimes he happened upon a phrase from a poem, or invocations of place or space, and with that he was lost, carried aloft, riding moonbeams in the night with nobody else in sight. And so, absorbed in invented worlds through all the books he read, so different from the strange, clairvoyant dreams of his early youth, Nato gradually grew to inhabit his father's literary hopes.

But not all the time that Nato spent at the École Saint Louis was sequestered in stolen moments of clandestine reading. While his nocturnal habit surely demanded a great deal of him, he was quite robust and, even without adequate sleep, he sustained a healthy aptitude for the school's athletic challenges and academic demands. He was a brilliant runner and excelled at long distances. He liked to run and watch the world go slowly by, lines of verse marking his progress, imagined perfections his company.

In the classroom, Theology was easily the most universally important subject at École Saint Louis, together with ecclesiastic Latin and Greek. The school delved deep into French and European histories, and in the upper classes, this started to include not just the Bible and Patristic writings, but also Classical literature, from Hesiod to poets and philosophers of Late Antiquity. Nato came to understand the meaning of the name his father had bestowed upon him. No longer did he shun it as a capriciously alien affectation. Instead he grew to love that one of his names invoked "sunrise", and the other resounded of the kingdom of God, time and again, in the Lord's Prayer intoned in Greek.

Far, far away, beyond the mountains and the oceans, the warlords of Europa rained down fire and blood on lands both near and far to stake their claim on their rights to take whatever they wanted wherever they willed, venting their rage and frustration and fear when they met opposition, and drawing all the world into the fray. Millions were slaughtered and starved and torn, just as had been done before, among them some of the older pupils from École Missionnaire who were conscripted and sent to join the Tirailleurs Sénégalais. Nato was too young to be pulled into the mêlée which started when he was just thirteen years old and ended when he was eighteen. While conflagration took the world, the family estate of the Comte d'Harcourt-Lévêque ensured that reading continued uninterrupted at the École Missionnaire Saint Louis in Bonthe.

~ ✳ ~

Ten years after he first entered the missionary school that eventually made him French, Anatole Basile Tejo went to Paris to study medicine, and his father's joy and pride knew no impediment. Tejo Bai could talk of little more than how his youngest son had gone to the legendary City of Lights to become a doctor. From Paris, Nato wrote home of his life, describing the cobbled streets, and sidewalk-seating bistros, the wide, tree-lined avenues, and the open fields of poetic myth. He was always careful in his letters to hold closed the veil that shielded his father from seeing or smelling the rubble, and dust, and rot that covered the City in the austere wake of the Second World War of empires. And Tejo Bai, although he well knew that the barbaric War had wrought incalculable devastation, he also recognized the tenderness of his son's selective accounts of life at the capital of an empire that was already doomed to fall. Nato was determined that, despite the ruin that the Führer's furor had rained upon the world, he would find a thing of beauty to offer his father, and his mother, and his brothers in each of his letters home.

For himself, too, he found something of beauty when he met Marie d'Harcourt-Lévêque, the seventeen-year-old great-granddaughter of the Comte d'Harcourt-Lévêque whose École Saint Louis had made Anatole Basile Tejo into a perfect African Frenchman. Marie's parents had been missionaries, inspired by their uncles of yore. They were the executors of the trust that financed the École Missionnaire Saint Louis, and when the War had broken out, they had made sure that reading was not disrupted at the missionary school in Bonthe. They were also responsible for establishing in Paris important university fellowships in a variety of professional disciplines designed to train brilliant young Africans who showed promise of one day becoming admirably French. And so it was that at a holiday party where all those young African men of promise and charm were introduced to their professional patrons and mentors, Marie d'Harcourt-Lévêque, a lover of music and landscape painting, heard the voice of the son of Tejo Bai. It was deeply resonant, cultured, and round, the sound that it made possible only, surely, from one with a kind and open heart. His intellect, clearly incandescent, cast his strikingly sculpted visage and statuesque composure in such dazzling light that all who beheld, or stood around him, glowed from simply reflecting his splendor. And Marie d'Harcourt-Lévêque marveled that such an enchanting creature could be.

Raised in the bosom of a thousand-year-old family with roots firmly anchored in Normandy, Marie Madeleine Clémence d'Harcourt-Lévêque had grown up to expect that, when the time came for her to be married, her parents would arrange a suitable match, and she would naturally settle close to home. Perhaps it was because of the war, which decimated the country's able-bodied youth, that the family d'Harcourt-Lévêque gave less thought to matters of matrimony than they might have otherwise done, especially with girls like Marie just coming of age. It was a custom to send young ladies of the family across la Manche to debut at Queen Charlotte's Ball and parade in the ritual marriage market of the annual London Season. The joke, which everyone thought very droll, was that for the price of six months of concerts and dances and cocktail parties, the Franco-Norman débutantes that the Maison d'Harcourt-Lévêque sent along served to sustain the tradition of conquest to civilize England that William, the Duke of Normandy, debuted in 1066 when he took the English throne. But with only the weak, and the tired, and the beaten left behind to sort through the nation's rubble in the twilight of its global dominion, priorities had changed, and Marie, most of all, thought it a good and noble thing to give everything up on behalf of one's country for a life more austere in the service of others. For two years after the armistice, Marie rolled up her sleeves every day and helped to rebuild what the Führer had rent. When she turned seventeen, she forswore the London Season, and instead thought to become a missionary, just like her granduncles had done. That was the year that the École Missionnaire Saint Louis sent its first class of Fellows to Paris for training as Catholic priests, and lawyers, and doctors, including one most luminous among them who went by the name of Anatole Basile Tejo.

Marie d'Harcourt-Lévêque was enchanted that such a marvelous creature could be. And he, in turn, was no less charmed. Their mutual feeling found expression in conversation cobbled together from fragments of sonnets and silence. They did not leave each other's side from the moment they met until the evening's end, and when the sun rose the following day, they met again on the banks of the River Seine. All day they walked side by side, never once touching, not even their hands, but telling each other the stories of their families and their lives. Marie told Anatole Basile — for that is the name he told her to call him — about what the war had been like. She loved being of service in Paris but, oh, how she missed l'Eure!

There, where she was born and raised, the curated ruins of the first church that her Franco-Norman forefathers had built in Normandy stood sentinel over the family's millenary heritage, solemnly preserved in antique disrepair. Anatole Basile told her about the École Missionnaire Saint Louis, about reading English, and French, and Latin, and Greek, and finally coming to Paris. He wanted to build a library where any child in Bonthe could discover all the wonders that he had encountered in books as a pupil. At least one volume, he fantasized, would recount the legend of his ancestors who came ashore from the ocean through menacing mangrove forests, and lived apart from everyone in the hidden glades of the Lioness Mountains. *A secret tribe!* Marie exclaimed, thanking the Lioness Mountains for the gift of Anatole Basile. She wondered aloud whether his library would have books in every language. She loved the sonnets of Shakespeare, she said, and thought that they sounded better in English than in the translated French versions she had read as a child. She might as well have read Ronsard, he quipped, and then talked of his father Tejo Bai, and how the old man had taught him how to read the Poetry of the world.

Their walk took them all over the city, and they stopped once or twice to sit and eat. By the time the sun had set, Marie had promised Anatole Basile that she would meet him by the river every day, and Anatole Basile promised Marie that one day he would take her to meet his father in Sierra Leone. Both of them kept their word.

Three years after arriving in Paris, Anatole Basile Tejo completed his general education in medical sciences and prepared to start advanced training. During the Christmas holiday, he took Marie and her parents with him to seek his father's and mother's blessing for their union in marriage. In his appeal to the groom's parents, Marie's father explained, almost in apology, that Anatole Basile had become the center of his daughter's world, and he and his wife wanted to help her realize the life she saw in his eyes. The Family d'Harcourt-Lévêque had already given the couple permission to wed, and since the groom was Catholic, they did not mind that he came from a British colony. They wanted the couple to make their home in France, and so they gifted them a country house in their ancestral land near l'Eure, as well as an apartment in Paris in the Sixth arrondissement. The family also arranged the assurance of a position in an established private medical practice in the city once the groom's formal training concluded. Everything that Tejo Bai had ever believed that made him think his youngest son was the blessing of their storied lineage seemed to finally blossom in a way that all the world could see. Tejo Bai and his wife received the girl Marie with solemn reverence, and then the old man took his son aside for what would be his final counsel.

"Anatole, my son," he said, "you are destined for great things. I can see that very clearly. Now that you are going to marry, remember that it is not enough to become a great man. It is far more important to make sure that you also remain a good man."

The day after his son's wedding, Tejo Bai gave up the ghost, his happiness complete. Anatole Basile Tejo and his new wife buried his father according to tradition, guided by the groom's mother. And then they left with Marie's family for the estate in Normandy where the newlyweds spent their honeymoon for a few weeks before settling in Paris for the young doctor to start his advanced training. It was only then, in Paris, that Anatole Basile Tejo discovered *négritude*, and by the low light of a small desk lamp in his private study at home in the Sixth arrondissement, he pored over whatever he could find of works by Caribbean and African poets of the *négritude* wave. Just as from his father he had learned to enjoy poetry's picture of life and the world around it, from these new thinkers he awakened to previously unseen beauty, relishing visions of intuitive wisdom and strength in the bones of the African Man, and dreams of earthly warmth and grace in the blood of the African Woman.

Canto Thirty-eight

Many years later, the mature *pater familias* Anatole Basile Tejo accompanied his young ward, Gabriel Ochola, to the Great Nam

Lolwe to shepherd the young man's passage into marriage to Anna Adongo. To everyone in Gabriel's homeland, the French doctor from Sierra Leone seemed the very embodiment of exotic poetic worlds that impressed those who met him, or even only heard of him. In his clipped yet softly spoken Queen's English, Ochola introduced Doctor Tejo as his paternal proxy and witness for the elders' deliberations over a suitable bride wealth. Ochola also told everyone that in London and in Paris he went by his Christian name and once he was married, he wanted everyone to get used to calling him Gabriel. The mystique of speaking English so much for Doctor Tejo's sake lent a brighter air of glamour to the meeting of the elders. For two months of nuptial festivities, the home of the children of JokOlóo would ring with the sound of zealously spoken English. Adongo rejoiced, her English was excellent, and she loved the idea that her husband was known to the world by an English name.

She rejoiced in fulfilling her role as the bride, charged with tending to her groom's father or, in this case, his paternal proxy. She prepared all the meals for Anatole Basile Tejo and tended to his lodging. She made sure that none of the younger children played in the guest house where he slept, or even wandered in there to use the bathroom in the morning when the Doctor was waking up, or in the evening when he was turning in. Fascinated as she was with the exotic new world her groom had brought into theirs, she kept a deferential distance. Although she could not conceal her stately height, she did her best to keep her head down and remain out of sight. But everything changed when one day she accidentally overheard her groom and his mentor in conversation.

Under the papaya tree next to the guest house near the traditional hut that Akoth still kept standing in her family estate, Gabriel was telling Anatole Basile Tejo that his bride was not what he expected.

He could not have imagined, when he agreed to the match while still studying in London, that this is what he would find. Anatole Basile Tejo listened closely, bowing his head slightly, nodding slowly now and again, encouraging Gabriel to speak freely. Gabriel sighed deeply, the contented smile in his smitten eyes invisible to Adongo from behind the wall that served as her blind. Anatole Basile Tejo responded with something that Adongo could not discern, and then she heard him ask about the meaning of her name. She is the second of twins, Gabriel said. Surprised, Anatole Basile Tejo wanted to know why they had not seen her twin. He did not survive childbirth, Gabriel explained. Anatole Basile Tejo nodded, absorbing this news, and then he asked Gabriel if he knew what meaning her Christian name carried. Anna? All Gabriel knew was the she was a prophet of one of the tribes of Israel who had blessed the newborn baby Jesus when he was presented at the Temple. Did this mean that his bride, too, was devout and destined to pass that devotion to their children? Anatole Basile Tejo could not say, but he could tell Gabriel that the name itself meant "beautiful" and "full of grace." Even a blind man could sense in her the budding earthly warmth and grace innate in the African Woman.

The music deep in the low voice of Anatole Basile Tejo was a mirror like none Adongo had ever beheld. The voice carried secrets it seemed to reveal as if they were oracle truth. Every sound that voice made was soft and round, gentler than the clipped accents of English, or the cadences of her mother tongue. For a fleeting moment Adongo imagined how resonant Dholuo could be in that sonorous voice, but only for a fleeting moment. She drew ever closer to the wall that concealed her from the sight of the two men who were thinking of her. She felt a light kindle and grow in her breast as she awakened to *the budding earthly warmth and grace innate in the African Woman* that

Anatole Basile Tejo seemed to be saying he saw in her. His face was not visible from behind the wall where Adongo kept herself hidden, but she imagined him more dignified than she remembered thinking he was when he had first arrived. Oh! How much more beautiful, she thought, a single voice could make the world!

The voice now uttered something about the African Man, a child of God, the Doctor was saying, of intuitive wisdom and strength. He spoke with solemnity, as if reciting a prayer, repeating a refrain to *earthly warmth and grace.* And later yet another refrain to *intuitive wisdom and strength.* And then Adongo heard someone call her name from across the family estate. Afraid to be caught eavesdropping, she quickly withdrew to join the other girls to rehearse her bridal songs and rites of marital consecration.

For two moons the girls would gather together to prepare the bride for what was to come, singing and dancing age-old rituals to teach each other, or just recall, the ways of the new bride. In the tradition of nuptial feasts, the grandmothers, mothers, and aunties of the celebrating clans were accompanied to the bride's new home by their granddaughters, daughters, and nieces who were all of an age. For two moons, the young women learned and rehearsed the songs of Becoming that little girls did not yet know. Some songs told the stories of worlds beginning, some songs gave warnings of worlds ending. Some were lessons on wooing and courtship, others yet lessons on nuptial union and how what came after was life that made the world anew. Before hearing the low, deep voice that held up poetry's mirror to her eyes, Adongo did her duty and just sang as prompted. But now everything was different. She meant to learn all she could to become the perfect bride for Ochola, no, Gabriel. She meant to learn all she could to embody *the earthly warmth and grace innate in the African Woman.*

The morning following Adongo's awakening saw the beginning of the fourth day of nuptial festivities. All the elders would meet again in the afternoon to continue discussing Adongo's bride wealth, and the women would continue teaching the girls some more songs of union, creation, birth, and death. Adongo prepared a breakfast of tea and toast and sliced papaya for Anatole Basile Tejo and brought it to the guest house. She placed the tray on his dining table and, rather than leave as she had before, she lingered, tidying up the living quarters, looking for shoes to clean and polish, waiting. He finally emerged from the bedroom, groggily shaking off sleep, and hungry, and to her eyes a welcome sight.

Adongo bid him a good morning, speaking to him in English directly for the first time since he had arrived, her breath growing shallow with wonderment.

"Good morning Adongo," he replied kindly.

But she wanted him to call her by the name that he had told Gabriel Ochola meant *Beautiful, full of grace.*

"Anna," she exhaled. "My Christian name is Anna."

"Anna," he echoed. "Good morning, Anna."

The voice of Anatole Basile Tejo shaped around that word, her name, *Anna*, rose as if from the heart the Earth to resonate in her breast. He spoke slowly, deliberately, an oracle of greeting. Adongo stood a while in silence, savoring the way her Christian name felt in his voice, watching him take a seat and spear a slice of papaya. Then she approached the table and quickly poured him a cup of tea, richly caramel-colored and thick with cream and sugar. Anatole Basile Tejo thanked her and ate for a while in silence, lost in thought. Adongo backed out of the guesthouse, sunshine in her heart. *Anna, Good morning, Anna,* rang in her ear for the rest of the day, intoned in that deep, poetic voice, and low.

For seven days following, Adongo's heart sang seeing to Anatole Basile Tejo's needs. For seven days she collected the tokens of *Good morning, Anna* his resonant voice tendered. She rejoiced that Gabriel had brought him to Homa Bay and counted herself favored by the Spirit of the Lake that blessed her with the good fortune to see herself through the mirror of Anatole Basile Tejo's voice. For seven days she entered the guest house only in the morning.

On the eighth day she entered the house after dark when everyone was fast asleep. She felt no fear walking over the threshold of his dwelling carrying the small clay pot of fragrant water she used to rehearse the bridal song of nuptial union. She felt no doubt setting the clay pot down close to his bed and dipping the small, soft towel she had brought with her into the nuptial water to anoint his face, his chest, his loins, his feet, rousing him from sleep. She had no thought but to immerse her whole person in his resonant voice.

Anna's bodily union with Anatole Basile Tejo made the Song of Beginning that the young bride was learning from the elder women sound like a dirge in the desert night. The old songs said nothing of the ocean of light awaiting bodies bridging the bounds of self to become indistinct one from another. Adongo's blood thrummed loud in her ear when Anatole Basile Tejo's breath mixed with hers, drawing the last of its volume from her spent lungs with a singular, vocal *oui!* This was the dream of the African Man in all his intuitive wisdom and strength, mingling with that of the African Woman, a jewel of earthly warmth and grace. Was it a wonder that this is how life began? Adongo later thought to herself, enchanted, not knowing that she had spoken aloud as she once again dipped the small towel in the fragrant bridal water. Hearing her muttered abstraction, Anatole Basile Tejo grew suddenly still, as if only then waking up to discover her there. Glowing in her reverie, Adongo squeezed the cloth of excess water and proceeded to clean and consecrate his face, his chest, his hands, his loins, his feet, the towel soft, the water cold, her touch teasingly light. And then, gathering the pot and the cloth, she was gone, sooner than he could collect his thoughts and draw breath calm enough to utter a word.

Adongo now knew a new genus of joy, a happiness made of sonorous dreams and the pleasure of breath mixing breath. *Oui!* For weeks, and then for months following, the very memory of that single night's union made her soul sigh with contentment. For the remaining days of nuptial festivities while Anatole Basile Tejo continued to hold a place of honor as the groom's paternal proxy, Adongo could not hear his French Sierra Leonean voice without glowing a little, without reeling a little. She blessed the day Ochola had brought this oracle from Sierra Leone, from Paris, from London, all the way to his place of birth in Homa Bay.

Just as the grandmothers, mothers, and aunties had sung, the union with Anatole Basile Tejo brought forth life that made the world anew. By the time the bride wealth was finally settled, and Gabriel and Anna were formally wed, the young bride knew that she was with child, a child conceived in sonorous poetry and reverence, the union of *intuitive wisdom and strength* and *earthly warmth and grace*. When Anna finally let her wedded husband consummate their marriage, she did so to silence her mother, and perhaps also out of duty. But that very act, or so she believed, destroyed the sacred child she bore, and smelted Anna's indifference to Gabriel into immoderate loathing. She recoiled at his touch and revolted every time his seed took root in her womb. Try as she might, she could not destroy them as he had destroyed her sacred child. After the birth of the dream-spawned Maya, Anna resolved not to rest until she found Anatole Basile Tejo again.

Canto Thirty-nine

The news that she was pregnant at first struck Hehra, Anna's youngest child, with terror pure and cold. How could she have let this happen? How could *he* have let this happen? How could he have vanished, taking all of the universe he breathed along with him, and leaving only the seed of an idea that they had not even imagined? She should have known better. He should have known better. Why did he take the later train? Why couldn't he just take the train he was meant to take? Why, oh why did he stop?

Solomon and Hehra met on a train platform at London's Waterloo Station when he came to pick her up, together with the one hundred books she was lugging across Europe. She was coming to stay a fortnight with his parents, Aaron and Rebecca, and his mother worried that Hehra's luggage might be too heavy to manage. So, Solomon drove his small two-seater to his parents' house, and then chauffeured his mother to the train station in her SUV. They arrived a little early to meet the Eurostar from Paris and were waiting on the platform when the train pulled in.

The girl who emerged from the train was hauling an overfull army duffel bag of black canvas strapped to her back, a brimming rucksack hanging in front, a leather purse besides, and a guitar case bound with bungee cords to a large suitcase. She was much smaller than the young man could have imagined, one and a half meters tall, if that, and rather slight for the load she was carrying. Her hair was twisted in loosely hanging locks that fell over her eyes repeatedly, forcing her to shake and toss her head to see where she stepped.

Solomon approached her quickly, "Hehra?"

"Oh, yes!" she said merrily, looking up with another toss of her head to catch a glimpse of him, and his mother behind him. "Auntie!" She stretched out her arms, releasing her grip on the guitar-strapped suitcase, sending it tumbling onto its side at her heels. Rebecca, a generously tall woman, took the bottle of lightning dwarfed by duffel, rucksack, handbag and all into her arms, both women laughing, trying to sort out ways to unbind the traveler from her unwieldy baggage. Solomon set the suitcase aright on its wheels and came around to help them, introducing himself.

"Let me take that," he says in a low, quiet voice, grasping the bulging duffel bag and trying to lift it off Hehra's back. As she slips her hands through the straps that harness it in place, Solomon feels the full weight of the bag and lets out a gasp.

"What do you *have* in here?" he asks, surprise sharpening his tone.

"Just some books," Hehra replies. "I already mailed myself most of them before leaving Paris, but I had to take these ones with me, they are my favorite."

"How many books are you carrying?" It is more an exclamation than a question and Hehra understands it that way.

"You know, in the grand scheme of things they are not that many, really" she says, glowing, exhilarated to finally meet family from JokOwiny in this faraway place.

Rebecca has been laughing too, cooing even, delighted herself to meet this sprite.

"Oh! How can you carry such heavy bags!" she exclaims, handling the rucksack, the thrill in her voice masking her genuine concern. "You are going to hurt yourself!"

All around the three of them the air is electric with happiness. They all talk at once in joyful voices that, surprisingly, are not very loud. Hehra is wearing a worn-out pair of jeans and a sleeveless linen tunic under her stretched-out eyelet cotton cardigan. She is the picture of a bohemian student exploring the world equipped with little more than her curiosity and a train pass. The trip from Paris through the Channel Tunnel was brief compared to previous crossings she had made over land and sea, just barely two and half hours direct. But the luggage of books and music, heavy and cumbersome, makes her glad to stop for a while at a welcoming hearth. Both Solomon and his mother Rebecca are dressed quite casually, but anyone can see that their clothes are well tailored and newly pressed. They are home here, and Hehra's visit gives them the chance to open their door to nomad kin.

"You know, the books may be heavy, but it's alright," she says. "One day I will carry all the thoughts they contain in my mind, so I won't have to drag them across the world anymore. It's really just a question of mind over matter."

"Well," Solomon says, almost under his breath as he tugs the suitcase behind him, "I suppose that if you don't mind it does not really matter."

Hehra looks at his face, seeing him as if for the first time, recognizing in his words a kindred soul who reads the world through the lens of books. She smiles. And then she nods.

"I suppose not…" she says.

And then she laughs out loud, her eyes never leaving his amused face. Her eyes remain on his face as they walk to Rebecca's SUV, all three of them talking in their close, quiet voices. It is an odd and merry sight, the three of them, Rebecca with her lanky son, and the slight Hehra asking about everything under the sun.

Rebecca thought at that moment that her firstborn had finally met the woman she wanted him to marry. He was still young, that was true, and so was Hehra, so there would be time to prepare them for the union. And then there would be time for grandchildren. And time to watch them grow and teach them about the world. In time, she and Aaron could go back to Homa Bay and ensure that the grandchildren discovered Nam Ataro and learned the real name of the Spirit of the Lake, and perhaps even forgot the old Queen's name that foreigners thought the Lake should bear. She loved this bright, fearless girl who traveled like a tortoise, carrying her treasure of books around the world on her back; this girl whose suitcase, she soon discovered, had only two changes of clothes, some underwear, and still more books; this girl who had packed into her rucksack a rich Italian wine that she had picked up in Tuscany express to bring to these distant aunt and uncle whom she had never met before. Rebecca was fascinated and could not stop smiling to hear Hehra describe her European adventure. The girl did not describe monuments or outings, rather she talked of stories and songs and of the people she had met. She talked as if she had discovered a new world where nothing was like anything she had ever imagined before, she talked of saints and poets — actually of one saint and one poet mostly — musing about how the trip might have been if her sisters had been traveling with her. She found the landscapes of Europe tame and subdued, paved in the cities, and beaten to submission everywhere else she looked. Once they had settled her in their home, she opened the guitar case to reveal a surprisingly beautiful instrument that, for six months, she had carried around undamaged. With it she sang them songs, some of them her own, some of them learned from the people that she had met on the road. She prepared meals, French and Italian, and offered them all the rich, fragrant wine she had carried with her all the way from Tuscany. Rebecca decided that whatever it took, this would be the girl that her son married.

Canto Forty

So Rebecca charged Solomon to show Hehra around the city during her stay. Her younger son, Jonathan, was not yet back home from university, so Solomon would have to make do on his own. Rebecca suggested that they visit the British Library and then the British Museum, and then she told them to be sure not to forget St. Paul's along the way. When the pair returned home on the third day, and Hehra could not stop talking about Westminster Abbey, Rebecca listened captivated while they prepared supper together. Solomon sat nearby, just out of their way, his shining eyes collecting every word Hehra uttered. Things that he had long learned to take for granted seemed to electrify her. She mused with delight that Westminster Abbey was over a thousand years old. Did they know that it was the site of William the Conqueror's coronation? And that his cousin or grand uncle Confessor was buried there, too? How did it feel to live so close to the place where Newton was entombed? Solomon had played host often, both for work and for friends, and he frequently took his guests to see Big Ben and then Westminster Abbey along the usual visitor's London tour. Now here for the first time, a guest's enjoyment was not just satisfying and amusing, it drew him in and made him curious to feel it all as she did. But he did not ask her to explain, he simply listened and watched, enjoying in his turn her hushed exhilaration and the pleasure she drew from revisiting monuments of a thousand-year story that was ever present to her memory's eye.

And nothing had compared, in Solomon's eyes, to Hehra's elation when the choral evensong began to resound. They were getting ready to leave Westminster Abbey, after nearly three hours among the tombs and memorials in that most mannered stone forest built for God and kings, when the choir's voice emerged, unadorned by instruments, floating above the soft rustle and burble of visitors murmuring and shuffling underneath the cathedral's vaulted ceilings. Solomon's heart caught watching Hehra's enraptured face as the choral worship imbued the air with song. Not until she turned to face him did he notice that his breathing had grown somewhat shallow, and that the dearth of oxygen to his brain was making him slightly dizzy. He took a seat and she joined him, and together they sat born aloft in canticles and psalms. Hehra's ebullient account of the music, retreading the steps she and Solomon had taken from one monument of history to another, gladdened Rebecca's heart.

"Sol, why don't you take Hehra to Canterbury tomorrow? It's a bank holiday and you can make a long weekend of it." If she liked Westminster Abbey, Rebecca explained to Hehra, she would love Canterbury Cathedral. There was a memorial to Thomas à Becket there, and even a tomb for the famous Black Prince who died before he could be king.

Hehra's whole person lit up, and Solomon agreed to drive her down to Kent for the weekend. The two of them set off the next day in his two-seater with small bags and hiking boots and stories and songs to share. They drove all the way to Dover and took rooms at a guest house near the chalk cliffs. They spent the following morning by the sea and then, after lunch, set out for Canterbury.

Solomon followed Hehra down the length of the cathedral, through the nave and the choir, past the sanctuary of the church elders, and finally into the Chapel of the Trinity where saints, and a king, and the slain archbishop were all enshrined in caged monuments. Immortalized in recumbent bronze effigy across the chapel from Henry IV, the Black Prince had lain for six centuries in eternal prayer to the stone vaulted heavens above, contemplating his life and his death with candor more bare than all the paeans and tributes posterity could dream up.

Tu qi paſſez oue bouche cloſe Par la ou ce corps repoſe... Hehra began to read. *You who pass by with closed mouth, there where this body lies; listen to what I will tell you, for I say what I know. As you are now, so was I once; You will one day be as I am. Of death I never thought when I had life. On earth I had great riches, from which I drew great nobility: land, houses, and great treasure, clothes, horses, silver and gold.*

The long epitaph on the memorial tomb was already difficult to make out, and the surrounding wrought iron railing that kept visitors at a distance only made it less intelligible. Hehra continued to read the inscription aloud under her breath, mouthing the old French words of the bygone prince's meditation while slowly making her way around the barred-in platform and polished effigy.

But I am now poor and wretched, the unhappy Prince continued. *Deep in the earth I lie. My great beauty is gone, My flesh is totally ravaged.*

It was difficult for Hehra not to let such dour reflections assail her closely held memories of Mamma Akoth's final days at the twilight of her life in the world of Time. Hehra could almost hear that beloved voice of water, telling her, with its last fragile breath, to go forth into the world, unafraid, and dare to discover the stories of peoples in far-away lands.

So narrow is my house, with me there are nothing but worms. And if you could see me now, I do not believe you would say that once I was a man, so much have I completely changed. For God's sake, pray to the celestial King that he have mercy on my soul. For all who pray for me, or seek accord with God for me, may God give them paradise where none can be miserable. Amen.

Standing apart and listening to Hehra while she read under her breath, Solomon just watched, intent and absorbed. This was perhaps the moment he would point to if ever asked when he could no longer see himself as something separate from her, or her as something separate from him. There was no flash of light, nor thunderclap, just a sense that all was well with the world. When Hehra had finished reading and contemplating the prince's posthumous prayer, Solomon followed her back across the sanctuary and the choir, and together they caught a fleeting glimpse of the fanning vaults of the central tower, high and remote, as if meant to be secret. They continued down the nave, drawn to the oddly ornate baptismal font set on the back of the Gospel evangelists. There Hehra and Solomon sat down in silence and waited for the evensong service to begin.

Canterbury Cathedral was far less elaborate with the kind of filigreed vaults and prismatically radiant stained glass that graced the almost diaphanous Westminster Abbey. The stout clustered columns of Canterbury rising upward spread their branches out into spare vaults that bespoke a humility unknown to Westminster's prettily bundled pillars, tiered and slender above, their fingers stretched to touch tips at the apex of the vaulted ceiling of the nave. Drawing the visitor's eye heavenward to the greater glory of God, the columns evoked visions of a standing forest of stone, and the murmur and shuffle of conversations and feet mingled to make the same forest sounds as in Nature in both houses of worship, as if the unguarded noise of living things in creation were simply the true language of Heaven.

Here, too, at Canterbury, art song rose through the rustling gurgle of tourists milling around the cathedral. The stone vaults of the church ceiling smoothed out the keen edges of children's voices intoning the opening prayer, first in unison and then, with dilating time, in a gradual cascade of overlapping harmonies, each vowel drawn, unhurried, speaking, surely, the language of saints. At that moment, Hehra's thoughts grew even more saturated with her memories of Mamma Akoth, the silence that now filled the space that she had left bereft with her passing out of the world of Time feeling even more profound. Mamma Akoth would love this, she thought, and Esther, too, and Maya. Hehra found herself imagining how the resonant sounds of the choral Evensong might look to her afflicted sister's uncommon eye. She herself heard only music and felt the sea of her soul swell and overflow into tears that sprang forth unbidden in a wave that was joy and saudade combined. With each turn of harmony, the tide surged within and soon, Hehra just let herself weep without making a sound, unmindful of dissembling. Beside her, Solomon felt the heat rising from her brimming heart and just as he had collected her words with shining eyes, he collected her silence as well, placing the palm of his right hand on the back of her neck with weightless tenderness.

This was the moment that Hehra would point to if ever asked when she could no longer see herself as something separate from Solomon, or him as something separate from her. And so they sat, alone for a while after the final tones of the Evensong had vanished into the vaulted ceiling, Solomon's arm moving to circle Hehra's shoulder and hold her close, Hehra letting his serenity settle all her unspoken disquiet.

"Esther and Maya would love this," was all she said, once they resolved to depart.

Solomon tucked a stray lock of twisted hair that fell over her eyes back among the other braids. Then Hehra led the way out of the cathedral beneath the clustered columns rising to uphold a heaven of vaulted stone, and Solomon followed close by her side.

Canto Forty-one

Rebecca was a gentle woman, a mother by vocation in the tradition of Mary, Mother of God, and she interpreted her maternal role in the world as guardian and champion to both of her sons. Her wish, unspoken for many years after her son Solomon first met Hehra, would one day finally come to pass, her hopeful patience requited at last.

On that day early on, when Solomon and Hehra returned from their weekend in Kent, every corner of Rebecca's home and heart knew happiness because she could see the bond that had formed between the two. The pair emerged from the car radiating a serene and tacit intimacy, each moving as if guided by the other's unspoken thoughts. Rebecca could not help but notice the seamless contrapuntal eloquence of this silent accord when they all gathered in the kitchen to prepare the evening meal. She took it all in as Hehra brought out a few tomatoes and carrots and dhania from the fridge, and Solomon readily took these from her and washed them while Hehra turned back to look for cabbage. He then brought out a cutting board and knife and handed them to Hehra in exchange for the head of cabbage she discovered in her search. While she chopped the tomatoes and dhania, he shredded the cabbage and the carrots and then produced a pair of large mixing bowls. Into one went the chopped tomatoes and dhania, and, soon, into the other went the cabbage and carrots.

Rebecca said nothing. She simply listened as Hehra, mostly, recounted their weekend, describing the shining cliffs by the sea and the chalky lighthouses strewn across the harbor at the end of jutting piers. The girl recalled how, looking out across the Straits of Dover, she tried to imagine her recent Chunnel crossing underneath the seemingly vast waters. She wondered if she could ever swim across, and Solomon warned that her books would probably drag her to the bottom as soon as she lost sight of land.

"There are worse ways to go," she said.

"Yes, but not just yet," he replied.

But she did have to leave soon to return to school. She had finished the first of her wanderings to learn of the world, just like Mamma Akoth advised. Now summer was over, and the two weeks with Auntie Rebecca and Uncle Aaron had simply flown by. Rebecca did not want to see her go. At the airport she was already grieving while Hehra checked in her excessively heavy luggage straight to Boston and paid the extra fees. When the merry sprite finally parted ways with her hosts at the security gate, Rebecca wept openly. She had given birth to two boys and raised them well, she said, and then suddenly she had discovered a daughter who was leaving all too soon. Solomon simply held Hehra close for a long while, and then wished her a safe journey, reminding her to come back soon lest his mother's heart break. Hehra promised to return.

But seven years came and went before she saw them again. During that time, she wrote letters to them, to each one of the family, sometimes together and sometimes separately. Her letters were about everything and nothing in particular. She wrote of the books she was reading, taking special pleasure in describing the ones that she had carried with her to London. She wrote of poetry and drew pictures, sketching moments that she wanted all of them to see through her eyes. Sometimes she sat at the piano or took up her guitar and recorded a song to send along, and for seven years, they answered in kind. Rebecca wrote of her boys, Solomon and Jonathan and Aaron, and told Hehra her opinion of those books that she had purchased to read along with Hehra across the ocean divide. Aaron sent brief and effusive words of pride and encouragement, thrilled that his niece was doing so well at university. Jonathan was restless and ever changing, and Hehra looked forward to discovering whatever was new in his life when he occasionally wrote.

Solomon's letters were just like Hehra's, only instead of Poetry and Art and Music, he wrote of Astronomy, his first great love. Initially he used broad ideas to describe the world through the lens of his eyes. Before long, his descriptions drew out meticulous formulae in the language of Physics, refining his palette as Hehra asked for more details and precision in his vision of the world. He translated the poetic figures in her letters into elaborate drawings, and played with the music she wrote to him, sending back equations and doodles with clarified focus. Of all the questions Hehra and Solomon posed to each other about the world, the heavens and the universe, about the human experience of all these wonders, never was a one about themselves.

Hehra finished her studies and turned all her attention to drawing and canvas storytelling, making pottery in the traditions of the Lake, vessels that looked like they came right out of the time when Mamma Akoth was still a girl. Solomon sought work in the United States without revealing to anyone what he was attempting to do. When he was finally offered a job at the Museum of Natural History in New York, he told his parents that he wanted their blessing to ask Hehra for her hand in marriage. Aaron was surprised and a little bit confused. But he was rather more relieved because he had once worried that his firstborn son, who had rebuffed the advances of every young woman in London, Nairobi, and Kisumu who showed any interest in him, would remain unmarried for all his life. Initially it had not mattered, but after they celebrated Solomon's twenty-ninth birthday, Aaron asked Rebecca whether they should arrange a marriage for their son. Three years passed and Rebecca gradually warmed to the idea. They, too, without saying anything to their boys, began conversations with the elders back in Got Ramogi and Homa Bay about prospective matches. Several attractive candidates were suggested, and among them Hehra's name was spoken. Her father would be easy to approach; he so adored his children. Her mother's reaction was a little bit more difficult to anticipate because everyone knew that of all her children, Hehra was the apple of her eye. Solomon's request to propose to Hehra himself on the threshold of his thirty-third year did not just make arranging a match for him unnecessary, it fulfilled Rebecca's seven-year hope, a hope that she had nurtured with faith, unmindful of whether its prospects held promise.

And so with a full heart overflowing, Rebecca offered her blessing, and Aaron followed suit, trusting his wife's judgment. They talked about the various unions between their kinsmen, JokOwiny, and Hehra's JokOlóo and JokOmolo, that made them all family. They parsed the bloodlines to ensure that the union broke no taboo. Finally, they convened a meeting of elders from the families of the hopeful betrothed to discuss the bride wealth and to set a date for the wedding that would seal their union in the eyes of all the clans.

Solomon's last letter to Hehra arrived in Boston on the same day his plane delivered him to her. He had six months to find a place to live in New York City and to get to know his new home before reporting to his new job. He had traveled for twelve hours, spending eight of them in flight, yet when he finally landed, all the clocks made it seem as if only three hours had passed. Hehra was waiting outside the customs gate and she took him directly home to her apartment by the Charles River. The Boston afternoon was only just turning into evening, but for Solomon the hour was well advanced, and he needed sleep. So Hehra showed him to her guest bedroom, letting slumber overtake her, too, as the evening wore on into night.

When she woke up, Solomon was already taking a shower after his early morning run by the river. He got dressed before emerging from the bathroom to find her waiting for him, wondering what he wanted to do for the rest of the day.

"Well, before we make any plans, I think we should get married," Solomon said, blurting slightly, his heart suddenly in his throat, making it difficult to breathe. "I mean, I think we should get married. I mean… and I've been wondering what you… I've been wondering whether you agree."

"Yes, I do," Hehra smiled quietly into his eyes.

"You do?" Solomon said. Suddenly he could breathe easily again, too easily it seemed. His breath drew deeply, and his head grew light, and he reeled. "Really? You do?"

"Yes, I do," Hehra repeated. "In fact, I have thought so since our trip to Dover."

"But we never talked about it … you never said…" Solomon started, hesitantly.

"No, I never did," Hehra agreed, her voice still quiet. "It never occurred to me to bring it up. I just thought that one day we would talk about it, and here we are today."

"I don't have a ring," he said. "I'm sorry…"

"I don't have one either," she echoed. And with this they both laughed. Joy.

"The elders want to meet. My parents will go home and see your parents. We should go with them."

"Yes, I agree. When they call us, we'll be ready. We can celebrate the wedding at my great-grandmother's house by the Bay."

"You know, my mother talks about Mamma Akoth all the time," Solomon said fondly. And then he leaned forward, his voice quietened, his eyes cheekily earnest. "Don't tell mum I told you this, but when you came to London, she was convinced that the Spirit of Mamma Akoth had sent you to find us."

Hehra only smiled again in response. Solomon clearly thought he was just indulging his mother's superstition. What harm was there in letting him believe that he was?

"She and father grew up close by, you know," Solomon continued, "just north of Homa Bay. I think she's glad I'm marrying somebody from home. The wedding will be a family reunion."

"So, your parents have no reservations? No objections?"

"None at all. They are thrilled. And also relieved."

"Relieved?"

"Yes. I think father was afraid that I would never get married, although the way mum reacted when I talked to them, it seemed as if she was just waiting for you and me to make an announcement. Anyway, apparently, they checked with... whomever you are supposed to consult, and we can marry without objection."

And so it came to pass that a daughter of both the clans of JokOlóo and JokOmolo wed a son of the more deeply rooted clan of JokOwiny. The wedding took place at the estate of JokOlóo in Homa Bay on Nam Lolwe, and the elders of all the clans who gathered for the celebration expressed deep satisfaction that the children of the new generation were not lost, that they honored tradition and carried it forward even in an ever-changing world. Aaron and Rebecca flew in from London, together with Jonathan as Solomon's best man. Gabriel, who had gone and made a new family after running away from Anna, gathered his courage and flew in from his adopted home in Australia. Once again, he invited his mentor, his friend Doctor Tejo, to stand with him at his daughter's wedding. The venerable Doctor flew in from Paris, this time in the company of his wife, Marie. Anna Adongo, now a hospital director in Nairobi, long triumphantly divorced, and always the most luminously glamorous woman at any occasion, arrived to much pomp and circumstance, brimming with pride to see the child in whom she was most pleased marry so well.

Esther had taken the mantle of gathering all the young women to rehearse the bridal songs of Becoming with Hehra. Some songs told the stories of beginning, some songs gave warnings of ending. Some were lessons on wooing and courtship, others were lessons on nuptial union, and how what came after was life that saw the world's beginning anew. Everyone knew what the metaphors meant and some of the ladies even offered a few ribald glosses for everybody's gleeful enjoyment. Maya, too, was hugely amused, although in the well of her solitude, the only song she could feel in Alex's persistent absence was the song of saudade.

Solomon and Hehra fulfilled their part in the nuptial ceremonies sedately and in perfect form — him serving her parents first at all their shared meals, her tending to his parents on every occasion. The bride and groom both drew fulsome praise for the admirable example they set. When at last they were alone and it was time for Hehra to consecrate her husband, neither could stop giggling. Solomon grumbled, between fits of muffled laughter, that the towel was too damp, and the water too cold. Hehra responded by teasing him with a touch so light that it tickled when she anointed his face, his chest, his loins, and finally his feet. And then he, in turn, anointed her, consecrating her face, her bosom, her womb, and her feet as well. When at last the two became one, Solomon repeated the words of their vows with solemnity more profound:

Wherever you go, I will go; and wherever you dwell, I will dwell; your people shall be my people, and your life, my life.

After a month of nuptial festivities and a honeymoon that lasted nearly three weeks in Mombasa and the coastal islands of the Indian Ocean, the newlyweds returned to Boston, ready to make a home together. Solomon wanted to see whether he could transfer from New York right away, or whether he would have to commute to work while they sorted out a better arrangement. He left for meetings in New York and Washington DC two days after their arrival, planning to return for the weekend with prospects. But in Washington, as he hailed a cab for Union Station, a harried looking man, frantic to get to the hospital for his daughter's birth, begged Solomon to let him have the taxi. Solomon said yes and waited for the next cab. By the time he got to Union Station, he had missed his train, so he had to wait for the following one. He telephoned Hehra to let her know that he would be late, but she was sickly and vomiting so she couldn't talk for long. The train he ended up boarding derailed just outside Philadelphia. By the time firefighters and other first responders had pulled everyone out of the wreckage and accounted for all passengers and crew, sixty people were treated for trauma, nine of them for critical injuries. Three souls perished on the scene, in the train, among them Solomon Ogot.

Canto Forty-two

Hehra was staggered by her husband's death and, for a very brief while, she thought that the sickness and nausea that had besieged her in his absence had been a premonition of the loss. But the sickness persisted even after she identified his body, even after she called Rebecca to say a thing that refused to make itself heard after she uttered his name. Every night she still dreamed of a world complete with Solomon by her side. But when she awoke, all the electric joy in her dreams imploded, consumed by the impossible vacuum that opened where her heart was supposed to be. Leaden fog pinned her to bed in the morning, but waves of nausea forced her out of it to chase herself to the bathroom basin where she retched piteously.

Rebecca and Jonathan flew to Boston to claim Solomon's ruined body, but they had to wait a few days before it was released for burial. In those few days, Rebecca felt Hehra's distress even through her own grief, and together with Jonathan sought a doctor's care for her widowed daughter-in-law. After several hours and several tests, the doctor delivered news that Hehra showed early signs of pregnancy.

How could she have let this happen? How could he have let this happen? In the same instant that she saw Solomon's perfect happiness at the news that they had conceived a child, she also felt the emptiness of his absence, an absence that made his wedding vow a shameless lie. *Wherever you go, I will go; and wherever you dwell, I will dwell;* and yet he had abandoned the world of Time in which she still dwelt. *Your people shall be my people, and your life, my life.* What life, Solomon? What life? When she finally understood that he was truly gone, the yawning void left in the wake of the universe that was Solomon blinking out of existence confounded her in its desolation.

Rebecca wasted no time packing Hehra up, along with her guitar and a few books from her still growing library, to take her back with them. They stopped in London only long enough for Aaron to join them, and then the whole family traveled to Got Ramogi to return Solomon's flesh to the ancestral home of JokOwiny whence he came. The same children of JokOwiny who had gathered so recently to celebrate Solomon and Hehra's wedding were once again assembled to mourn the groom's death. Throughout the funeral ceremonies, Hehra moved and spoke with autonomous dispassion. Rebecca was deeply worried when she realized that Hehra was not present inside herself. When Esther and Maya finally arrived in Got Ramogi, they, too, found their sister's absent affect alarming. Even when the ululating appeals of the women rose up to shape loss into sound, Hehra remained silent, strangely alert but abstracted. She wanted to mourn her husband's death, but she did not know how to expect a child and grieve at the same time.

Without realizing that she was doing it, Hehra chose the path Mamma Akoth had taken and turned away from despair, seizing instead the mantle of mother. While Esther closed up her apartment in Boston and put everything there in storage, Hehra returned to London with Rebecca and Aaron and Jonathan and Maya and resolved to show her child everything about the city that, for seven years, his father had spoken of in all his letters. Solomon loved to run, and he loved to swim, so Hehra took to the swimming pool, preferring not to pound her body while the baby was still inside. She purchased a piano for Rebecca and Aaron's house and played Solomon's equations, eventually including the music she loved that she knew had confounded him. Soon she discovered that she was carrying not one, but two babies, both of them boys. They grew and seemed to thrive, they even developed particular tastes in music, if the reactions she imagined them having were anything to go by.

Like their mother and their aunt Maya, they seemed to like Beethoven best. Whenever Maya found Hehra playing, she would sit underneath the piano and let the sound wash over her from above just as she had done when they were children in boarding school. Maya herself did not play the piano, and when asked to describe what it sounded like from beneath the instrument, used a language unfamiliar to Hehra's schooled ear. Now Hehra began to imagine that her boys felt the music she was playing the same way their afflicted aunt described it. Some sounds caressed and others itched. Some were cold and others rough, or slippery, or dry. Prokofiev tickled them and made them twitch. Bartok simply made them laugh, or so Hehra wanted to believe. Mozart and Chopin could always be counted on to soothe and calm them. But it was always with Beethoven that their little hearts hammered in unison as the music thrilled through the air.

In the womb the twins were still just an idea, yet Hehra thought of them in ways that surprised, and at certain times, consumed her. She occasionally wondered whether now she understood her mother's secret love for her — a love that MaAnna never seemed to have for any of her other children. Hehra wondered whether Anna had ever looked forward to meeting David, and Esther, and Maya. Would Anna, too, have gone swimming and floating in the water to try and feel for herself the world of the babies she carried? Would Anna have removed all the clocks and calendars around her to liberate Now from the cages of Time? Did Anna ever relish the prospect of one day meeting the souls who entered the world of Time through her as much as Hehra looked forward to meeting her boys?

Probably not. Everyone knew that the older children were not as precious to their mother as Hehra had been since birth. Why did Anna seem to care only for one of them? Gabriel, at least, had adored them all equally, completely without reservation. Yet he had elected to run away when he could no longer find the courage to brave Anna's loathing. In fairness, though, he had not been forced to break his body for his children to enter the world. But Anna had. She repeatedly lamented how David almost killed her just to be born, how he left nothing for his twin who struggled to emerge as well but could not keep the light of life burning for long. Esther, too, cost Anna pain, and Maya was the worst of them all. If Anna knew any love for her babies before their birth, she made it clear that they had drained her of it in labor, one after another after another. That is, until Hehra came along, the child in whom she thought she was secretly well pleased.

But Hehra did not want her children to know unequal love. Remembering childhood lessons to *honor thy father and thy mother that thy days may be long upon the land which the Lord thy God giveth thee* gave her pause. What did it mean to *honor thy father*? What did it mean to *honor thy mother*? Would she be dishonoring them if she chose to be a different kind of parent than they had been? Hehra expected that, like every woman bearing children, she would have to break her body to let her twins come into the world of Time. Beyond that, she did not want to be the way her mother had been. She did not want to do the things her mother had done. She told Rebecca and Maya that when the time came, she wanted to return to Homa Bay to deliver her boys by the Lake. Too many times, Mamma Akoth had lamented the passing of Uncle Ochiëng in the frozen wilderness of St. Petersburg. Hehra did not want her babies born far from home in a foreign land. She wanted to remain a home to her boys, their champion, and their shield. When they came into the world of Time, as Mamma Akoth called this life, Hehra planned to ensure that her children knew the grace of their father and that they could hear the Song of Becoming that brought them to her to be born.

~ ❊ ~

In all her reflections about her mother, Hehra did not understand that when she was born to Anna, she, too, was the fulfillment of an old promise of devotion. It was a devotion that remained nameless for years, in truth quite unformed, yet just as real as the rain. It was an adoration born of wonder and discovery quickened in the bosom of a fourteen-year-old bride. For nine years after losing her first sacred child, Anna languished in the revulsion she felt for Gabriel, yet she reveled in her hatred for this happy man she had known since earliest light. When nine years had passed, and she could no longer bear the woe of her ill-contented love, Anna drew Gabriel into her bed for the last time, and then she set out on her own to look for Anatole Basile Tejo.

When she finally found him, he was visiting the remains of his old boarding school in Bonthe on Sherbro Island in the Atlantic Ocean. He was lately bereaved of his mother, and had traveled home to pay tribute, leaving his wife and children in Paris. Thirty years had come and gone in the blink of an eye since he had visited home. The École Missionnaire Saint Louis was no more, in its place a fledgling hospital. So Anatole Basile Tejo, together with his wife Marie Madeleine Clémence d'Harcourt-Lévêque, decided to establish an endowment fund to help sustain the hospital in his mother's name, and to dedicate a library in Bonthe in his father's name.

While he was in Sierra Leone, he and his wife Marie wrote letters to each other every day. It was the first time in thirty years that they were so far apart from each other. He sent news of his progress in Bonthe, and she news of all the children, and especially the grandchildren, the last of whom was a few months old, born of their youngest son. In one of her letters, Marie wrote of the young woman who was married to Gabriel, the young man from Lake Victoria that the Doctor had mentored in London. The girl, who said her name was Anna Adongo, had come looking for Anatole Basile. Marie was immensely fond of Gabriel and knew well of his nuptials from what her husband had told her a decade before. So she welcomed the young lady warmly, remarking that although Gabriel was much older than all of her children, it seemed that Anna was of an age with Anatole Basile's youngest son.

But Anna Adongo did not stay long. She seemed distracted and intent. Marie was sorry that she could not wait for Anatole Basile's return, but she promised to write and tell him that he had missed the young lady's visit. By the time Marie's letter found its way to her husband in Sierra Leone, Anna had already found him, too. She also made sure — in a singular moment of luminous union — that the *intuitive wisdom and strength* in the Doctor's breath and bones melded with the *earthly warmth and grace* of her own blood.

Her happiness complete, Anna Adongo left the Doctor alone in Bonthe and went to stay in Freetown. She remained in Sierra Leone by herself for close to ten months, waiting for the fruit of her womb to ripen in serenity. When at last a new life came of the union of that African man and this African woman, Anna named the child Hehra, the only name her devotion knew; a name bespeaking Love.

Book VII. The Siege of Mombasa

Where João de Sousa is accused of heresy and bound to face the Tribunal of The Holy Office of the Inquisition. • João de Sousa tells Olóo his story in a shared waking dream, offering details of Vasco da Gama's second armada to Calecut. How the chronicles of Portuguese sailors in Vasco da Gama's fleet unveil facets of the Age of Discovery that poets and historians have shrouded in silence. • A Miracle in Calecut. • A History of the Siege of Mombasa. • A Miracle in Serra Lyoa and the salvation of Tejo of the Lioness Mountains. • One thousand years of Europa's Empire crusades assail the world.

Canto Forty-three

War followed fast in the wake of Dom Vasco da Gama's second armada, the one that eventually made its way back to Portugal with plans to deliver João de Sousa, bound in chains and confined to the Admiral's cabin, for judgment before a tribunal of the Holy Office of the Inquisition. Had it not been for his service to the Crown in finding local pilots in Mombasa on that first voyage to India, the young monk might have been relegated to languish in the cargo hold below deck along with the Negroes and Moors, sixty-two in all on the Admiral's ship, who were being transported to the slaver's market in Lisbon. But the Admiral was an honorable man and even while bound in duty to prosecute heresy, he acknowledged his own debt to the young monk and knew well his virtue. Setting out on his second expedition around the Cape of Good Hope, he had, with nostalgic pride, imagined the tribute that he would pay, once he arrived in Calecut, at the grave of the fallen João de Sousa whom he had been forced to abandon. He would find the tomb of the young man of faith and there erect the padrão that the King had commissioned to lay claim to India. This would serve to tell the world of the debt of the Crown of Portugal to the miracles of the monk. He could not have imagined bringing back the miracle worker to face the purifying flames of the auto-da-fé for transgressions against Holy Doctrine.

Nor could he have known that, bound though he was, João de Sousa traveled unmoored in the company of Olóo who, sometimes as a young boy and sometimes as a man, visited his waking dream. The sentry posted outside the Admiral's cabin door heard the monk talking inside and would have said that the prisoner was praying, reciting Scripture to himself, perhaps invoking a miraculous salvation by the hand of God at sea. But he would have been wrong.

For João de Sousa was not praying. Rather, he is walking the decks of a ship afloat a puddle of rain under a banana tree that grows beside his mother's hut... beside Olóo's mother's hut... sometimes he cannot tell whose eyes he is seeing through. He can, however, tell Olóo, his brother of the waking dreams, about his travels and of his native land. He tells Olóo how he got his name from one of the rivers of the Iberian peninsula beyond the Mediterranean Sea, a river which joins a bigger one still, and then flows down into the ocean. But the greatest river of all his land is the Tejo that drains all of Iberia and then flows through Lisbon, the port from where the young monk set forth in his travels with Vasco da Gama.

Olóo, although still quite young at first, playing with puddles in the shadow of the banana tree that grows beside his mother's hut, can in turn tell his brother of waking dreams about Nam Ataro, the Great Lake of his home, and Lolwe, the Spirit who dwells in the Lake and looks after all the nearby clans. And then Olóo is grown and married, awaiting the birth of his youngest daughter and telling João de Sousa that one day he must meet his daughter's great-granddaughter, Anyango, christened Maya, who seems to love dancing on the Lake. She travels with me sometimes, João de Sousa says, to Olóo's surprise. Along the coast of Bojador, Guinea, Sierra Leone, we have walked the decks in the fog, her fascination with the pilot's compass enchanting.

She follows a compass north, from the source of the Nile to the mouth, crossing the Mediterranean, the Apennines, the Alps and the Pyrenees, traversing the north ranges of the Roman Peninsula. And then she makes her way south to find Vasco da Gama, her brother's hero. But the captain-major-Admiral is long gone when she finally gets to Lisbon. All that is left of him is memory carved in stone, and the fading echoes of songs praising his valiant exploits in the name of God and of Lusus. And all that is left of Portugal now is a land grown feeble and musty with age. In Lisbon, Anyango Maya traces the steps of conquerors on a stone map, but her heart does not swell with pride and wonder at a glorious past lived in the spirit of discovery and enterprise intrepid. In every corner of the city, a smell of mold hangs in the air. But this is not the home I left, João de Sousa tells Olóo, this is not the home I knew.

Olóo listens in silence, wondering. He asks João de Sousa how he came to be bound in chains in the Admiral's cabin, awaiting delivery for judgment. So João de Sousa says to Olóo that had he returned to Portugal with the captain-major from India after that first voyage, things might have been different. Instead, he had fallen ill and remained among the Saint Thomas Christians in Calecut. There, the Lord had wrought miracles of surpassing wonder. It was one such miracle in Calecut on the Arabian Sea that had brought João de Sousa to this place where now he languishes. And so, in his waking dream, João de Sousa recounts what he knew of Vasco da Gama's second expedition to India, and how he, although a devoted monk, came to find himself bound in chains and destined to be brought before the Tribunal of the Holy Office of the Inquisition.

Canto Forty-four

War followed Dom Vasco da Gama, the newly invested *Almirante dos mares de Arabia, Persia, India e de todo o Oriente*, as he led his new armada down and up the coast of Africa and across the Arabian Sea all the way to Calecut. The monsoon winds carried news of how the newly appointed Lord and peer of the realm stopped along the way to flex his still-pristine, newly assimilated might to secure the King's dominance in trade along the Indian Ocean.

Far fewer than one third of all the crew who sailed with him in that first journey had lived to see home again, and the King's munificence knew no constraint in thanking them for the power they laid at Portugal's feet. For upon the captain-major's return with a route to India fully mapped, the King of Portugal Dom Manuel sealed his claim to all the wealth of Africa and Asia and beyond as "Lord of Guinea and of the Conquest of the navigation and commerce of Ethiopia, Arabia, Persia and India." The King most graciously let it be known far and wide that he owed this affirmation of his global power to the intrepid ventures of Vasco da Gama and no other. Along with lands and titles in perpetuity that His Majesty awarded the returning heroes, other rewards, far greater still, rushed to be piled up at their feet, and most of all at the feet of the captain-major and all of his family. For it was not long after the King blessed the captain that this latter sealed the bonds of matrimony with the beautiful cousin of the great Dom Francisco de Almeida, hero of Granada in Isabella and Fernando's Christian war of conquest against Moors, Saracens and other enemies of Christ, emissary to the court of Spain, and Friend of the Holy See.

The crew of this far more robust fleet of the second expedition, twenty carracks strong, soldiers and sailors and shepherds of the flock, all followed the Admiral of the Seas of Arabia, Persia, India and all the Orient with unmitigated pride. All of them King's men to a one, bound together in sacred purpose. Ah, the joy, the zeal, the vigor! At sea, during the long southward dash to reach the Cape, the Admiral told a well-loved tale to inflame and temper his men's resolve *to invade, search out, capture, vanquish, and subdue all Saracens and pagans whatsoever, and other enemies of Christ wheresoever placed,* all in the name of His Majesty the King who sent his men forth to *justly and lawfully by his authority reduce all enemies of Christ to perpetual slavery and appropriate to himself and his successors the kingdoms, dukedoms, counties, principalities, dominions, possessions, and goods,… to convert them to his and their use and profit.* It was a tale the Admiral often heard whenever he dined at court, a tale that His Majesty the King Dom Manuel enjoyed rehearsing about the sermon his uncle King Dom Afonso pronounced on the papal warrant — nay, the holy mandate of his day — that Portugal go forth and conquer the world.

The Admiral told his men the tale of how His Majesty's uncle predecessor, His Late Majesty King Dom Afonso, much obliged to the Holy Father and inspired by the magnitude of this momentous charge, during his illustrious reign, convened a public lecture in the most venerated house of God in Lisbon, the Igreja de Santa Maria Maior, on the fifth day of October in the year of our Lord fourteen hundred and fifty-five, inviting every agent and delegate of trade from foreign lands near and far to hear how the Holy Father in his wisdom had seen fit to impart to Portugal the means and power to enforce the authority that the papal bull bestowed upon the Lusitanian Crown. All who were present at the lecture stood in awe of the breath of Portugal's potential. The soldiers and shepherds of the Lord's flock marked well that part of the King's sermon that pronounced the spiritual penalties for whosoever wanted for zeal *to invade, search out, capture, vanquish, and subdue* whomever they found along the route to India and back. The sailors, and their brethren tradesmen and merchants paid careful heed to that part of the sermon that prohibited trade in weapons, iron, or ship-building materials to the Saracens and pagans, or transportation of legal merchandise anywhere without royal license. From the lips of Dom Afonso every ear present heard the voice of the Pope and the voice of the King's own father, the venerable Dom Duarte the Eloquent, each urging, yea commanding, in their very own words, that it was a good and noble thing, as so deemed by the Holy Church, to wage fractious war against the Moors and force every one into obedience, and for that reason it behooved all of Catholic Faith to make war, and make everyone submit to the laws of the Christian kings.

At table with the captains and officers of his fleet, Dom Vasco da Gama made it clear, with solemn gravity, that no living soul had leave to navigate the seas between Portugal and India, or even fish, or allow to be fished the waters of the Atlantic and the Indian Oceans, and even the Arabian Sea, without the express written permission of his Majesty the King of Portugal.

The soldiers and sailors and shepherds of the Lord's flock who heard him speak did not wonder how he could have been in the audience of a lecture that was delivered five, or even fifteen years, before he breathed his first as a baby. They had no reason to wonder because it was known throughout Portugal that after his triumphant discovery of the route to India, the Admiral dined at court nearly every day. There he heard the words of the Very Late Dom Duarte and the Late Dom Afonso issue directly from the lips of His Majesty King Dom Manuel, certified in the memories of all the illustrious nobles, ministers, and sundry courtiers who, long in the tooth, were old enough to have witnessed the royal lectures on the papal mandates issued by the Holy Father Nicolas V.

For just as King Dom Afonso's sermon echoed his father's edicts and counsel, his successor, Dom Manuel, echoed his uncle's sermon word for word. The lands and royal titles that Dom Vasco da Gama now enjoyed as the hero of Portugal all made his words as the great Admiral of the Seas of Arabia, Persia, India and all the Orient sacrosanct, and officers and deckhands alike hung onto his every utterance for they knew that from his lips issued the thoughts and heart of the King and of the Church. In his first trip he was but a route-finder, making *discoveries by sea, in the service of God our Lord.* Now he was the Admiral and acting might of his Majesty the King.

Thus tempered and inflamed in purpose, the Admiral's fleet wended its way up the eastern coast of Africa, through the realm of Kilwa — whose reach extended south to the Comoro Islands and to Mozambique on the mainland, and to the north to Mafia, Zanzibar, Pemba, Mombasa, and Malindi — making sure that the locals felt the righteous might of the King of Portugal.

When the Sultan of Kilwa resisted the Admiral's request to pay homage to the King of Portugal, the Lusitanian warrior conjured an unequivocal response to show he would brook no dissent. He ordered the Sultan's messengers *be stripped naked and bound hand and foot and put into his boat in the stifling equatorial heat and there they were to remain roasting in the sun until they died. When they were dead, he sought out the Sultan and he said the same fate awaited him, and he would seize the wealth of the city and the women and children for captive slaves.*

The Sultan of Kilwa, facing Vasco da Gama's armed carracks, aware that their cannon balls could tear down the walls of the Masjid alKabir at the heart of the city just beyond the palace fort, capitulated and became a tributary to the King of Portugal. He sealed his sultanate's vassalage with a jewel he had acquired as a gift on the mainland from a wandering sage in Mozambique. The Admiral did not understand the Sultan's invocation even as he took the gift, a large brass compass, its rose ornate and bountiful with images both strange and familiar. Billowing clouds, and sailing ships, and hints of deep sea kraken overflowed the instrument's polished turntable. But the compass was clearly decorative and not functional at all since it only pointed to his chest regardless of where he faced. Satisfied with his conquest anyway, the Admiral took the compass as a simple symbol of triumph, and then he had it mounted on his cabin wall before departing for India.

News of the Lusitanian's deadly resolve spread, from the bend at the southernmost cape, to the city on the coast at the end of the savanna grassland river that touches the sea, to the harems and eunuch stables of the Sultan of Oman. The monsoon winds carried harbingers of the approaching terror all the way to Calecut, where some heard their warning and girded themselves, while others paid the rumors no mind.

Praying at the springs just north of the city and spending his days with the Indian Christians who ministered to the poor, even the not-late João de Sousa caught wind of the tales that spread about the Admiral but, knowing the captain-major as he did, he, too, paid the rumors no mind. He knew well, from having traveled since early youth, that often the exaggerated myth of inexorable might was just a practical means to political ends. And so, believing them mere strategies in the game his countrymen played, the young monk let the rumors be.

How could he have known that for Calecut — whose rulers continued to resist Portuguese dominion of their lives, of the waters they fished and the trade they conducted — that for them, the Admiral planned to obliterate their will with infernal storms? How could he have known the depth of truth in the horrifying accounts of the Admiral's approach? How could he have known that the Admiral wanted the seeds of terror planted ahead of his advent to African kingdoms and Indian lands so that he might reap abundantly when he finally arrived at their shores?

João de Sousa worshiped and shared communion with his fellow Christians in Calecut, secure in peace of the Admiral's virtue of knighthood. Meanwhile, that same Admiral — of the Seas of Arabia, Persia, India and all the Orient — resolved to wield his newfound might with savaging exploits that the worshipful poet Camões, with the gaze of his one blinded eye, chose to make invisible to posterity. Even history passed over those deeds in silence, and chronicles of the time that celebrated the Admiral's bloody passion were tucked away hidden in dusty corners, nevermore to be cited, or discovered, or known by those who were not there to witness the terrible might of the Portuguese Crown.

Canto Forty-five

In spite of the silencing veil that Camões drew over the Admiral's tyrannical deeds, the attentive chronicles of crewmen and clergy who sailed with Vasco da Gama to India bear witness to things that João de Sousa only heard tell once the Portuguese armada was returning home bent on delivering him to the immolating stake. They recount how in the port of Marabia, on the way to Cananore, the Admiral ordered that *any ship that entered into the harbor and ports and rivers and belonged to Moorish merchants or carried Moorish goods and did not obey his edicts or pay to him tribute, should all be burned that they may not trade in peace or security,* especially if they hailed from Calecut. The Admiral's soldiers set to work, ensuring that none could pass those waters without fearing for their livelihood and without fearing for their lives. *So when one day at dawn a large ship, owned by the wealthiest merchant in Calecut, entered the bay at Marabia, arriving from* Mecca laden with pilgrims of faith, and riches in jewels and books, *the Admiral's men assailed it forthwith. The ship's owner, the richest man in Calecut, appealed to the Admiral with whom he had no quarrel. Consider, he said, that in war those who surrender are pardoned, and since he offered no resistance, the Admiral's virtue of knighthood would surely spare the innocent merchant war. But the Admiral was not moved, and he ordered that the ship be emptied of all its precious cargo. He also prohibited that any Moor disembark, and pilgrims, whether child or man or woman, were sealed back into the ship. And when the jewels and books and precious things had all been removed, the Admiral then ordered that the ship be set ablaze.*

The captains of all the other carracks in the Admiral's fleet spoke up and tried to stay his hand, saying that the great ransom the Moorish merchant offered was much too rich to lose, and that killing all the pilgrims sealed inside the boat would not chasten Calecut, especially so far away from the city. *To this the Admiral answered that Calecut had greatly offended his authority by refusing to submit to the Crown of Portugal, and so deserved that he should do it every injury; and if he were to set free its Moors for a ransom, he should retain the ill fame throughout the Arabian Seas of selling his honor for goods, and Calecut, without fear, would offend him every day. Therefore, if he, the Admiral, could do harm to anything belonging to that city, then he was obliged to do it.*

And so the ship was *plundered and then set ablaze, the pilgrim Moors all sealed inside.* The Admiral ordered that *any souls leaping into the sea to save themselves from the flame were to be caught in falcon nets and shot through with the swivel cannons on the caravels, and those who swam too close to the Portuguese boats for aid be ran through with lances.* Whoever fought that fiery death in the waters of Marabia was slaughtered with little consequence. And then the Portuguese fleet went on its way.

The Admiral made it known that his ships stationed along the coast would *destroy as much as possible all traders in or out of the ports of*

Calecut and nothing of that city would go out into the sea. He warned all the rulers of all the close by cities along the coast to order all the merchants not to hold trade with those of Calecut, so that they should not run afoul of Portugal's reigning might. The Admiral also let it be known that in every region where trade took place and there were dealings of buying and selling, he would establish the prices of all things in the name of the King on behalf of his merchants. Many rulers of the port cities of India along the Arabian Sea acquiesced to these condition, much afeared of the Portuguese Admiral's insensate wrath, just as the Sultan of Kilwa had been, and Dom Vasco da Gama rejoiced in his triumphant dominion in the name of God and his Majesty the King of Portugal.

So the Admiral was not pleased when he finally brought his armada to Calecut and found that the harbors had been largely cleared and the city's defenses prepared. He redoubled his vow to do all the harm he could to Calecut and prayed that its fleet would seek him out so that in the name of the Lord he might rain down his vengeance upon those that refused to submit to him. He tried bombarding the city's sea line walls, but all its defenses held. And then a moment arose when two large ships and sixteen smaller vessels, all laden with rice and jars of butter and many bales of stuffs for trade, entered the port of Calecut.

The Admiral ordered that the ships and the vessels be plundered and despoiled of all their trading goods. The Admiral then commanded his men to cut off the hands and ears and noses of all the crews and put them all into one of the small vessels, into which he ordered them to put a friar who traveled with them, along with the friar's own severed ears, and nose, and hands, all which the Admiral strung around his neck. To this vessel some other men were hung by their feet, since without their hands the ropes could not hold, and the Admiral sent this ship to shore, ordering his crossbowmen to aim their weapons well and shoot arrows into the hanging Moors so that the people on land might see. As for the friar on board, he was given a message written on a palm leaf for the rulers of Calecut, telling them to make a curry dish to eat of all that the friar brought in the vessel with him.

When the Admiral had finished cutting off from all the crew the hands, and ears, and noses that he sent with the friar to shore, he ordered that the feet of these men, too, be tied together, and that their teeth be struck from their roots and knocked down their throats lest they try to free themselves with their mouths. And so the Indian crew and passengers, too, eight hundred souls in all, bereft of hands, and ears, and noses, and teeth were herded and hauled aboard the larger ship by the men in the service of Dom Vasco da Gama. Thus shepherded, these eight hundred souls were heaped up one atop another, their lives still draining from the wounds left of severed hands, and ears, and noses, and even by stricken teeth, making the ship decks slippery with blood. Now the Admiral ordered that mats and leaves be spread over all who were bound, and then tied and sealed. When all of the eight hundred souls had been covered with mats and leaves and sealed aboard the vessel in Calecut harbor there on the Arabian Sea, the Admiral ordered and saw to it that this vessel, too, was set ablaze.

Seeing so much raging carnage, the people of Calecut emerged from cover and ran out to the sea in droves to salvage all who sought to flee the Lusitanian's Inferno. Some other Moors who were still at sea also came to aid the stricken, and there the Admiral's men laid their hands on them, bound them all and hung them up, shooting them all with crossbows in plain sight of the city walls so that the people on shore might see and be terrified. And then the Admiral's men captured many who found themselves upon the beach.

Three of the captured men asked to be converted into Christians, invoking the name of Saint Thomas who had come to their land centuries past after the death of Christ on the Cross. The Admiral did not hesitate and said he would allow it, but he wanted them to understand that this would not save their lives and after they had been baptized, he would still execute them as he had the other Moors. When they agreed, saying that if they were to die, they wanted to die in Christ in homage to Saint Thomas, the Admiral sent a soldier into the city to fetch a priest who could perform the rite to turn the captured souls into Christians.

The soldier brought back a priest who was much younger than the friar that the Admiral had maimed and sent ashore in the vessel filled with severed hands, and ears, and noses. The priest was indeed young, although his body, being very thin, even for an ascetic monk, skeletal, in fact, bespoke a toil of ages. His eyes, though set deep and sunken between his jutting brow and stark cheekbones, held a curiously luminous spark. The Admiral did not know him, nor he the Admiral, at first, so much had they changed in three years. Where the monk was bony and wilted, the Admiral had grown more stout and turgid. The thin priest knelt down slowly beside the three woebegone Moorish crew who wanted to die in Christ, and together they all began to pray, singing the *Pater noster* with a ready bond of fraternity.

In that moment the Admiral recalled the day in Mombasa in his dining cabin on the São Gabriel when João de Sousa, the young monk with bright, deep-set eyes and delicate frame, had knelt down beside the Indian Saint Thomas Christians and sung the *Pater noster* with them in a language he had never learned and yet had understood.

Could it be that his eyes were deceived? Surely this man before him could not be a ghost — the ghost of the young monk to whose miraculous communion with Indian pilots from Mombasa the Admiral, and Portugal herself, owed so very much. It could not be a ghost — for others beheld him and spoke to him, too. It had to be a man, not a shade, despite the years of silence that had made his memory fade somewhat. Surely who else could this man be who appeared to perform the very same rites in the same way that the lost João de Sousa had done so far away in Mombasa. It had to be the man himself that he, then captain-major, had left behind abandoned to the fate that fevered chills presaged. It had to be the young monk himself, the miracle worker of Mombasa. Dom Vasco da Gama stepped forward and gave his marveling wonder a voice: it was indeed none other than João de Sousa himself.

When the Admiral exclaimed and called his name, João de Sousa looked up, startled for an instant. Recognizing in that moment the captain-major who once ransomed him from captivity in Mombasa, a small smile, sincere in its benevolence, lifted one side of his lips slightly, and then he returned to complete the rite of conversion, reciting *Ave Maria* and extolling the grace of the Lord. João de Sousa, who did not know that his new brothers in Christ had already been condemned to death, baptized the three Moors in the waters of the Arabian Sea at the port of Calecut, bidding the Peace of the Lord be with them, never doubting that the Admiral's mercy and Christian virtue would surely inspire him to bless them.

But no sooner had the young monk and the three Moors completed the rite of conversion, the Admiral's men seized the new Christians and bound their arms to hang them on the mast of one of the ships. Frei João de Sousa asked the Admiral what crime these men had committed and if he might, by the virtue of knighthood, offer them forgiveness. Dom Vasco da Gama answered that he was on a mission to bring the glory of God to these heathen shores in the name of His Majesty the King of Portugal. Surely, said João de Sousa, the souls of these men are the dwelling place of the Lord with whom they seek communion. Indeed, said the Admiral, even the Lord died upon the cross.

João de Sousa considered the words of the turgid Admiral before him. He did not recognize in this man the captain-major of his earlier voyage. He weighed the Admiral's judgment on the balance of his faith, and he found it wanting, unworthy of a Christian. How could this be the voice of a soul that spoke on behalf of the Lord? This soul that seemed to know no compassion, no mercy, and no humility. When had it become Christian to wield might in the name of dread and death, rather than life and love?

João de Sousa considered the Admiral's words, and then turned to his slandered God for mercy; that the Lord might deliver the captain-major, now an Admiral of great power and might, from this evil. He knelt down once again with the doomed and asked for leave to say one last prayer for their salvation. Casting about for the right words to inspire the Admiral's heart with compassion, his eyes finally took in the devastating conflagration the admiral had wrought. The harbor was filthy with smoke and the still-burning ashes of a great ship piled deep with the scorched remains of pilgrims home from Mecca. A stench of burning flesh and blood and peat and straw and wood permeated the smoke, thickening with changes in the wind. Suddenly, João de Sousa gagged, and his body heaved hard to eject the horror, sweeping in a copious wave of thin, salty sputum.

Exurge, Domine, judica causam tuam! he lamented, barely murmuring. *Respice in testamentum tuum, quia repleti sunt qui obscurati sunt terrae domibus iniquitatum.*

Arise, O Lord, and defend your cause! Consider well your covenant, because violent men dwell in the shadows of the land.

The Admiral did not know Latin and so he did not understand what the monk was intoning. He ordered his men to stay and wait until the prayer ended.

Ne avertatur humilis factus confusus, João de Sousa continued, still under his breath, overcome. *Do not let the oppressed submit to disgrace.*

Slowly gathering himself, he opened his bright, deep-set eyes, and turned to face this shade of the captain-major. Salt tears welled up shining as he told the Admiral to do as he willed.

And so, taking all of the condemned men, including the ones who had not asked to be turned into Christians, the Admiral hung all of them up, making sure to strangle the converts first, so that they might not feel the pain of the crossbow arrows piercing their bodies. The crossbow shooters took their aim, their arrows finding every mark and transfixing the flesh of every man that had not prayed for salvation. However, the three men who had been converted in fellowship with Frei João de Sousa remained untouched, as if the arrows had missed their mark completely. And so the crossbowmen aimed again, and once again no arrow wounded the flesh of any of the new Christians.

When the Admiral was told of this, he was much deeply enraged. So he ordered that their strangled bodies be wrapped in shrouds and placed into baskets, and João de Sousa *commended them, reciting his Psalms for the dead. And they were cast into the sea, with all the Admiral's company saying prayers for their souls because they were all witnesses to a great miracle of the Lord.*

And then out of the city there came another priest, an Indian, repeating, with impassioned zeal, the very words that João de Sousa had spoken in his final private, anguished prayer, *Exurge, Domine, judica causam tuam!* Although the Admiral recognized the sound of the Latin words, he still did not know their meaning.

Arise, O Lord, the Indian priest repeated in the language of the Admiral and his Portuguese fleet, *arise and defend your cause! Consider well your covenant, because violent men dwell in the shadows of the land. Do not, oh Lord, let the oppressed submit to such cruel and violent disgrace!*

Now the Admiral of the Seas of Arabia, Persia, India and all the Orient, understood the words that the thin, young monk had spoken, and he was not pleased. He promptly declared, so that all could hear, that by invoking the word of God to challenge the will of an agent of Portuguese might, by protesting the Admiral's refusal to show compassion, João de Sousa had betrayed the Crown of Portugal. The Admiral considered hanging the monk, but then he wondered how poorly it might look if by some miracle, perhaps even the very same kind that had shielded the flesh of the new converts, the monk did not die forthwith. For had not João de Sousa helped lead the Portuguese fleet from Mombasa thanks to the miracle of speaking in tongues? Had not João de Sousa survived the illness of fevered chills that kept him in India and forced the captain-major to return home without him some three years past? And was it not a miracle that it was João de Sousa who his soldier had found to convert the Moors? And was it not a miracle of surpassing wonder that by his very will, it seemed, the flesh of the converts was shielded from harm? No. The Admiral dared not risk any miracles sparing the monk and proving him right for denouncing the Portuguese Crown's deeds of might. He dared not risk the Indians of Calecut imagining that God could be on their side against the side of the Portuguese Crown.

And so the Admiral invoked the name of Dom Francisco Almeida, his new bride's cousin and the hero of Granada in Fernando and Isabella's holy war, saying that only such a man could judge if what the young monk had done was indeed heretical and an abuse of the name of the Lord. The Admiral would write to his cousin-in-law and beg audience with the Holy Office of the Inquisition to hear the case he was bringing. Speaking loudly so that all might hear, the Admiral ordered that João de Sousa be bound in chains and locked in his cabin every day until they returned to Portugal, and that the Indian priest who had echoed the defiant words of João de Sousa be whipped to death for all to see. Thus, Dom Vasco da Gama checked any open assertion that what had been witnessed was in fact a miracle. But he could not check all the rumors that were already wending their way through the vanquished and harrowed Calecut. Multiplying echoes recounted how the thin, young monk who prayed alone at the springs to the east of the city had performed prodigious feats of faith in the name of the Lord of Saint Thomas.

The rumors made their way past the city, rippling along the coast to the north and flowing south with the rivers. The same currents that carried them soon also brought echoes of other deeds for which the young monk was known. Portuguese sailors, and soldiers, and priests who knew of Mombasa and what had happened there added the details they had heard to the growing tales of the miracles of João de Sousa.

Exurge, Domine! echoed from lips to ears, recounting the miracle on Marabia. And thus did the legend of João de Sousa adorn the faith of Christians on the Indian Ocean and the Arabian Sea.

Canto Forty-six

Olóo was grown and married, awaiting the birth of his youngest daughter and listening to the story that João de Sousa told about how he came to find himself bound in shackles in the Admiral's cabin. Perhaps it was the rolling motion of the sea, or perhaps the closed, dank air of the sealed cabin; whatever the reason, Olóo grew ill, trembling with nausea, more sickened than he had ever felt. His mother sat beside him, dabbing his neck, his face, his forehead with cold water from the clay pot she kept in the corner of her hut. Olóo insisted that all light be barred from the hut where he sat with his mother, and she asked him whether the blue, luminous sparks hovering and flashing around his head, visible only in the dark, caused him any pain. Caught in a fissure between what was past and what was yet to come, he could not describe what he was experiencing as pain because it did not actually hurt. Rather, it pressed down hard from behind his eyes, his head imploding and exploding in the same endless instant, each force inward and outward fighting the other. He could not close his eyes, his now-haggard deep-set eyes, to shut out the multiplying visions of João de Sousa shackled in the Admiral's cabin, of Anyango Maya bedridden and heaving, and then suddenly elsewhere, on a raft on the Lake, drifting on Nam Ataro, turning, turning on her heels as if dancing, with Akoth. No, alone. No, ill. A child who could not keep anything down.

Someone was beside the girl, someone Olóo could not see, someone who was also dabbing cold water on her eyes and on her head, helping her lean into a... calabash? No, a pot, a large flat pot unlike anything Olóo knew to understand. The child could not stop vomiting. Everything she tried to eat came back out ever more violently. Her skin was cold and clammy, and she shivered from a fever that seemed to have no cause. Olóo watched, trying to untangle the overwrought waking dreams one from another, as Anyango Maya withered in fatigue into little more than bones loosely held together in her skin. Her body ejected everything, and the strain of convulsive heaving tore the muscles of her abdomen and clawed at her ribs. Olóo felt the shock when the small bones cracked, unable to withstand the binding force of vomiting convulsions. He thought he could not bear it any longer, and then found himself wondering how this small child could. Nyanaam, too, felt the shock of those cracking ribs ripple through him, the air outside crackling, too, as if in response. So she filled a calabash with cold drinking water and brought it to his lips. He tried to sip it, but it tasted of brine, of seaweed and salt. His face was drawn, ashen, and blue, his eyes sunken deep in their sockets. He became listless, talking as if to someone. *Anyango. Bih ka'e.*

Canto Forty-seven

João de Sousa sat in the Admiral's cabin, the brother of his waking dream fading away before his eyes, the ship rolling in the waves, carrying him eastward to Mombasa where the Admiral meant to stop a while to fortify the garrison and resupply his ships before continuing around the Cape on to Portugal. Of all the souls the weathered monk knew, Olóo and his twice-great-granddaughter Anyango Maya were the only ones with whom he shared waking dreams outside the world of Time. In that place, time did not unspool in sequence — seconds following seconds, minutes after minutes, hours, days. In the world that Dream Walkers traveled, dates did not mark the passage of time, and calendars, periodic and contained, held no meaning at all. The suns and the seasons melded seamlessly over goat-herding and sailing, singing and praying, winnowing, and dreaming. Alone, or in each other's company, Maya and João de Sousa and Olóo could only tell one day from another by changes in the weather, like the way harmony changed in the course of a song. If one day it rained, and then the sun came out the next, then saying "yesterday" and "today" found meaning in their Song of Becoming. Otherwise 'once upon a time', 'today', and 'one day' were simply a song that a singer had sung, was still intoning, or had yet to begin. This was how Dream Walkers transcended the petrified histories of monolithic myths.

When Maya was still four, and five, and six years old, she loved listening to Alex sing the song of Camões in that language they had never learned, and yet somehow understood, of that illustrious Lusitanian breast whose will even Neptune and Mars obeyed. The name of João de Sousa, forgotten by Iberian histories, yet carried through wind and rain to Maya's own waking dreams, was nowhere in the work of Camões nor in the books of their father's abandoned library. All those books could do was tally up the numbered years, presenting, without poetry, a catalogue of monuments of stone in gilded frames of acclaim. And so Alex's books said nothing of Vasco da Gama's pitiless campaigns of terror around the Arabian Sea and along the Indian Ocean coasts, nor of his cousin-in-law's incursions, nor the wars his compatriots wrought. They did recount that it would be another century until the crown's dominion on the shores of Mombasa found firmer footing.

Nearly one hundred years would pass before the garrison defending the King of Portugal's dominion over the Indian Ocean and the Arabian Sea was granted a permanent barracks in Mombasa. Those reinforcements brought with them a band of Italian heralds sent to gather local masons to start cutting stones for the newly commissioned fort that the venerable and prudent and most bureaucratic Phillip II — King of Portugal and Spain, of Castile and Aragon, of Naples, Sicily and Sardinia, Duke of Milan and countless

other fiefdoms throughout the world that used to be Rome —
wanted to build on the coast of Mombasa.

The architect Giovanni Battista Cairati was sent all the way from
Goa with the blueprints to build a fort in the name of the Lord Jesus
Christ. The project progressed quickly, faith and effort fueled by the
century-old stories that the Indian Christians liked to share of the
wonders wrought by João de Sousa. But more powerful still were the
bullwhip-wielding heralds charged with keeping the fear of God in
the hearts of the masons, builders, and laborers who had gathered to
hear of these miraculous deeds but found themselves conscripted by
force in the name of the King for the greater glory of God.

The designs Giovanni Battista Cairati brought attested to the
latest fashion in Italy, his fort drawn to bespeak the perfection of
man, God's greatest creation, God's only creation that mattered
to him and to his countrymen. The monks who ministered to the
raw flesh of the laborers at the end of the long equatorial days of
Mombasa were in equal measure from Portugal and from India.
They all prayed together, reciting psalms about the Valley of the
Shadow of Death along with many an *Ave Maria*, whatever the hour
of day or night.

The Spirits of all the Waswahili masons and workers were
constantly crushed, and constantly lifted, and it did not take long to
complete the work. But Giovanni Battista Cairati did not live long
enough to see the fort open to admit the Portuguese garrison just in
time to shield them from the increasingly aggressive incursions by
Turkish merchants bent on taking the port.

The first serious siege was some time in coming. Thirty-five
years, a whole generation, after the Lusitanians settled in, the Sultan
of Mombasa resolved that the Iberian foreigners had to go, so when
the Long Rains ended, his forces assailed the fort, taking completely

by surprise the Portuguese garrison which had grown complacent and reduced to a handful of soldiers. But he did not hold it for long.

The retreating Lusitanians wrote to the King for reinforcements and by the time the Long Rains started again the following year, their ranks were heartily replenished. They intended to take the fort by force, but the Sultan's soldiers had abandoned it for quite some time while the Portuguese were waiting for a real response. The reinforcements meant to show the power of the Crown never got the chance to flex their might. And so, one year after their initial flight, almost to the day, they retook the abandoned fort and then held it for close to seventy Rains.

Sultans came and went in Oman, and then one decided eventually, on a date some two hundred years after Vasco da Gama's first landfall in Mombasa, that it were desirable if his forces held the trading post once again. Better equipped with plans to stay than the first Omani siege, they pressed their claim for thirty-three months, driving starvation and plague into the walls of the fort that would not fall. Their victory this time earned them decades of dominion, and another century went by with skirmishes and sieges. The fort changed hands a few more times between Muslims and Christians, with murderers of governors unsettling its sometimes-fragile peace.

Another few more decades passed, and the Omani turned for help to a new aggressor who began to make his presence felt, acting in the name of the Hanoverian English kings. No one thought much of it, the English were, after all, very late entering the game of Empire. But when their old king died and his granddaughter ascended to the throne, the Sultan of Zanzibar sent them all packing, ignoring their new young Queen's ascension and holding Fort Jesus for a while.

During those Omani years, the reach of the Hanoverian Queen sitting on the English throne grew ever stronger as her empire spread seemingly unstoppable across the entire globe. And so when the newcomers returned to Mombasa to give their dominion one more try, they pressed just hard enough to expel the Sultan of Zanzibar and claim the old Portuguese fort as the stronghold of the British Empire in the eastern coast of Africa along the Indian Ocean.

Further inland, the Queen's cousin, Leopold, the second king of Belgium, named for his father to evoke courageous multitudes, was gashing and gorging and glutting his way through the Kingdom of Kongo dya Ntotila that lay west of Nam Lolwe in the heart of the land. He had plans to fill his coffers and to build and gild his palaces with gold torn out of the ground where the son of Nimi a Nzima and Lukeni Luansanze, back in thirteen hundred and ninety-three, had planted the seeds of dynastic legacy. The Belgian monarch wanted to bleed the rubber from trees that adorned the garden of the realm of Lukeni lua Nimi, and ivory ripped from the heads of the grandest and wisest and happiest lovers of water that ever walked the land. So he went to the heart of the Kingdom of Kongo dya Ntotila and into the homes of its peoples, and there he terrorized them all, and bound and packed the men and women and children as prey in crates and put them on display for his own subjects to see, and poke, and prod, and tear at will as they may. Like Dom Vasco da Gama had in his time, Leopold tore off hands and feet, bled the old and young alike, and ripped the breasts of mothers so that their infants might not eat. He unleashed upon the land such a bilious glut of blood, that his savagery befouled the very clouds and strangled the rains of memory into venomous drought.

His longer reigning cousin, the Hanoverian Queen, thought nothing amiss when the Great Nam Lolwe was claimed and named for her by her men. Her children, and their children, and their children after them, all came in waves claiming everything that they could see, sucking up the marrow of the land, and bleeding out whomever they found living in their way.

They brought with them the serpent that had so frightened Akoth in girlhood, and everywhere they went, woe and weeping followed. Colonizing agents of the pearl-clutching Hanoverian Kings and the Saxe-Coburg and Gotha Queen who followed in their wake all reveled in dismembering and torturing the men and women who revered the shining peaks of the equatorial Mountain of God's Repose, slowly burning them alive, rolling them in wires barbed with pointy-ended spikes, even while they still drew breath, finding ever-novel ways to desecrate their bodies when their will gave up the ghost if only to flee their tormented flesh.

In nineteen hundred sixty-three the sieges of Mombasa, all of which had started with the harrowing of Kilwa, came to an end at last, in a world that had by then completely changed in nature. For although the Portuguese, and the Turks, and the Sultans, and the Saxe-Coburg and Gotha Queen no longer held dominion over any coastal city, — nor over the Fort of Jesus Christ, nor over the river that touches the sea across savanna grasslands from the equatorial mountain on the Rift Valley's edge, nor the Great Lake streams that feed the River Nile itself — the land was wracked with woe, its air somehow mixed with the poison fumes of Lethe, its unrecorded histories desiccated vapors in the dead, unmoving winds of a Time bereft of rain.

Canto Forty-eight

Rounding up along the coast, slightly south of Guinea, the wind died yet again, just as it had the first time João de Sousa traveled aboard the captain-major's ship. The difference was that then he had walked the decks freely, praying in the mist with his rosary in hand, doing all he could to keep the crewmen's faith alive with verses from the *Psalms*. Now he was confined to the Admiral's cabin, iron shackles binding both his ankles and his wrists. He had tried to tell the Admiral that he would offer no resistance for the journey back to Portugal. He even thought that he might like to see Mombasa again. But the Admiral simply ignored him. And the fleet did not land in Mombasa, after all. Instead it went straight to Mozambique, and then quickly around the southern capes.

Before the calm just south of Guinea, a storm at the turn of the southern capes blew the caravels far apart, and the Admiral quickly lost sight of his brother's ship. The rest of the armada emerged from the storm shaken, but intact, the crewmen's hopes rising that soon they would be home. The Admiral, too, was eager to return to his patiently waiting bride, so he spurred the fleet onward north.

When the lookouts finally spotted land ahead to port, the fleet, as if of one accord, started tacking to starboard, each intent on following close along the bend of Africa's Atlantic coast. They had been beating to windward for some time, sailing against the currents that sweep down over the Atlantic in this part of the world, and the helmsman of the flagship sent out word that they should all stay close and avoid drifting too far west to the open sea. The labor of keeping to narrow channels with a close hauled course as they advanced upwind along the coast bore down hard on the crews of all the ships. The waves slapped loud against the hulls of the ships as they ploughed through the sea, making them roll with every tack. In the Admiral's cabin, João de Sousa was sleeping when a violent roll tossed him against the cabin wall. He awoke in a daze, out of breath, unsure if he was dreaming asleep, his temple bruised and bleeding from knocking his head against an inordinately large brass compass that was mounted on the wall, sending the ornament to the ground to slide across the cabin floor. He heard a shout go up on the deck above, a crewman struck by a boom. *Peace. Be still,* he thought, willing the rolling ship to still. The wind fell in that moment, and the sea grew very quiet. His head throbbing from the bleeding cut, João de Sousa rose to his knees, and with an open heart sang the song of David rei, the shepherd King of Israel.

The Lord is my shepherd... He leadeth me beside the still waters...

The Admiral and the pilot of the flagship sent a lookout up to the crow's nest to take a proper tally of the fleet. The sky was clear to the horizon and, as far as the eye could see, only ten other ships still held course together with the Admiral's vessel. Of the twenty in the outbound armada, five were still in India as planned, and the Admiral's brother was adrift abroad, swept off course in the storm at the southern cape, leaving three ships unaccounted for.

The eleven-strong fleet would make for land and wait for those missing three ships on the western coast of Africa, in the Madrebombo Estuary, off the coast of Serra Lyoa, where all experienced pilots knew to go if they ever so found the need. And so in the still ocean's fallen winds, the caravels dropped oars and the men rowed for shore under their helmsmen's direction. A scout confirmed that thirteen berths awaited in the large natural harbor where many more ships could enter, so the Admiral dropped anchor and moored the flagship near the edge of the small island that shielded the estuary harbor, directing the other ships to draw in one at a time. By the end of the day all the ships present had dropped anchor and docked, and most of the soldiers and crew disembarked to await their missing companions on land. The Admiral ordered that João de Sousa be kept aboard the flagship, along with all the other captive souls held as chained cargo, and then he and all the officers set up camp on the shore for the night.

The sun set over the clear, quiet sea. With the gloaming, a cooling mist descended upon the shore. The night was bright and full of the quietened evening song of the creatures that lived in the surrounding coastal mangrove wood. Anyone who knew the land might have recognized the voices of God in these sounds that came from further inland, carried downriver to its mouth at the harbor from deep within the dimming forest. There, a hippopotamus waded with her calf in the mudflats by the river's edge while a waterbuck settled in for the night. Further in, a herd of spiral horned bongos grazed through the bush, gathering in number as the darkness spread. Above them all the monkeys and chimpanzees and baboons were turning in to take their nocturnal rest, while the moths below on the forest floor got to work in the undergrowth. But the unaccustomed ears of the Lusitanian sailors, all of whom sincerely thought that lions really ruled the land, did not make out any of this sacred song. Instead they blocked their senses and posted sentinels around their camp to keep the angels of heaven away while they faded into sleep.

In the admiral's cabin on board the flagship moored off the estuary island shore, João de Sousa sleeps anew, still bound with chains at his ankles and wrists, strains of the psalm he was singing lingering in the ears of the sentries standing guard at the door. Suddenly, a light shines in the chamber and Anyango Maya materializes inside, standing on the spot where the dislodged trophy compass had fallen on the ground. She seems to shake João de Sousa by his shoulder, waking him up. *Miserere mei!* he exclaims, roused from his unquiet slumber. *Quick, get up! Let us go!* she whispers, and the chains fall off his ankles and wrists as if of their own volition. *Wrap your cloak around you and follow me,* she tells him. So João de Sousa follows her out of the cabin, not knowing whether he is dreaming asleep, or living through one of his waking dreams. At the door he trips on something hard, round, and angular – the Admiral's trophy compass. Without much thought, João de Sousa picks it up and binds it up in the sleeve of his weathered cassock, his toe smarting just a little.

Once past the sleeping sentries at the door, Anyango Maya leads João de Sousa down to the ship's cargo hold, and there they awaken sixty-two men, and women, and children destined to be sold in the Lisbon slaver's market, each one unbinding their shackles by will, undoing the slavers' hold on their fate. To a one, they keep miraculous silence while climbing up to the deck.

One, by one, by one, by one they slowly vault over the starboard gunwale and clamber down the lowered rope lines into the sea. Their flesh ravaged at the ankles and wrists does not seem to mark the brackish water, nor does anyone utter a peep in protest that they do not know how to swim. They lower themselves one by one, until finally all of them are swimming, treading, wading in the water all together with João de Sousa and Anyango Maya, the twice-great-granddaughter of Olóo, his brother of waking dreams. How and when they arrive on land almost half a league up the shore from where the Portuguese set up their camp, no one will ever know. *He leadeth me in the paths of righteousness…*

Generations passed and, with them grew the legend about the angel of God who, once upon a time, dissolved the chains that bound their ancestors and led them all to freedom, just like she had Saint Peter.

When morning came and the Portuguese found their cargo prey had all vanished in the night, they searched up and down the shore and throughout the estuary island, penetrating inland to see if perhaps there had been a raid in the night. But they found nothing

— no traces at all that any other than the feet of the local fishermen had trod on the shore, nor any indication that boats had been used to carry off their cargo. The Admiral, angered, demanded to know how the sentinels had let the monk escape and how, on top of that, they had lost a whole shipment bound for the Lisbon slaver's market. Unable to get any answers, he ordered that the sentries be bound up in chains and thrown into the holds to await trial for treason.

The new day also brought clear skies and a slight northerly wind. Two of the missing ships could be seen at a distance coming around to join the fleet waiting at the harbor. Once they were close enough, a boat came out to shore with a message that the third missing ship was not far away and that they had also spotted the Admiral's brother's caravel. They would go on to the Canary Isles, and there await the rest of the fleet. And so, the fourth armada to India and back, led by Dom Vasco da Gama on his second trip, left the shores of Serra Lyoa for their final run to Lisbon.

~ ❋ ~

Several dozen leagues farther up the coast and beyond the mangrove thicket, a company of sixty-three men and women and children escaping bondage in the night pushed deeper inland, looking and hoping for friends. Unseen to all but João de Sousa, Anyango Maya went with them, the two kindred souls of waking dreams keeping their backs to the point that the compass needle showed, ensuring they held a steady bearing away from death in irons.

Yea, though I walk through the valley of the shadow of death, I will fear no evil…

The company ascended the steepening highlands, chasing life and safety in a place beyond the hills. They hid, and slept, and walked, for days until, one evening, the tropical forest foliage opened into a clearing of pristinely thatched huts. The villagers, young and old alike, welcomed them in, and a party of the village's young men quickly vanished into the forest intent on covering the tracks of the path the newcomers had taken.

Older women, assisted by a group of curious and light-footed girls, took the weary wanderers into a hut near the center of the clearing and there they tended the wounds of their tormented flesh, their iron-rust-ravaged ankles and wrists. The girls brought the travelers water at first, and then coconut milk to give them strength. When they were ready to take in food, the table was set with a mash of yams, fish soup, greens and sundry fruit.

Thou preparest a table before me … my cup runneth over.

When night fell on the third day, all the village gathered around in the moonlight to hear sixty-three stories of whence the company had come. One, by one, by one, by one, each man, and woman, and child from the sea recounted their lives in drawing, and dance, and painting, and song, and even though they did not speak the language of the villagers, all were understood. Each one spoke, and was heard, and then received a name rooted in the place and story of their birth.

The tale that João de Sousa told, dancing the shape of river and cross, drawing carracks upon the ground, holding the salvaged compass aloft, also sang the Shepherd King's song, of the shepherd Lord shielding them in the valley of the shadow of death, and leading them to refuge and shelter offered by unexpected friends. *Surely goodness and mercy,* he sang, *shall follow me all the days of my life.* The villagers watched and listened, and when he had finished his story, they named him for the river Tagus at the heart of the land of the sailors who stopped at the harbor beyond the forest. His new name, "Tejo of the Lioness Mountains," humbled João de Sousa, and his grateful heart lifted up and sang the song of David rei:

... and I shall dwell in the house of the Lord forever.

It was not many moons before the newly arrived were also working the village crafts, adding the accents of their lands and languages, joining fishing or trading troupes, or weaving their hair in the same elaborate styles of their new, forest kin. And João de Sousa, too, lived many Long Rains anew in that village, as did his children who came to be, and his grandchildren, as well, all herding, and thatching, and fishing, and hunting as their mountain kinsmen had always done.

Tejo of the Lioness Mountains was long advanced in years, browned, and bent, still thin, with deep-set eyes, and radiant with peace, when one day, Anyango Maya returned in his waking dream to tell him that his descendants thrived still in the world of Time by the Lake at the eye of the Great River Nile. And so Tejo of the Lioness Mountains took out the compass he still carried with him and, lifting one side of his lips in a smile, handed it to Anyango Maya.

Give this to my kin, he said, *my children and their children, and may it always keep them true, away from death and bondage, away from rage and pitiless hunger, and from the bilious blood that putrefies the hearts of all the kings and captains of the land where I was born.*

Canto Forty-nine

Had Alex been able to see into Maya's waking dreams, he might have better understood how she saw Time. He might have then been able to discern the histories that she witnessed in the empty spaces of the stories and records that rose up to meet his eager searching gaze when he opened up the books in their father's library. But he could not enter her mind at will. When she was still a baby, he had sometimes found himself wandering around in the formless world of her infant dreams while she slept. But he never knew how that came to pass and, as she grew, it eventually stopped. Living in the world outside Time and yet anchored still to Mamma Akoth had always meant that only his great-grandmother could see, or hear, or talk to him before Maya was born. And then Maya arrived, and suddenly Alex could speak, his first word naming the infant who also saw him there. It frightened Alex to know that even so, as Maya grew older in Time, she would only see him when she wanted, if she wanted.

And so, Alex became intent on fulfilling Mamma Akoth's commission issued by the side of the bathtub on that fateful day when Rosie ran away and he witnessed Maya's forgetting begin. He would travel the world with his sister and teach her all that he could learn. So he read and shared everything he knew in the earnest good faith of an honest soul. One day, he would take Maya to Mombasa and to India when they were both old enough. He would even take her to Portugal to visit the land of Vasco da Gama where they would pay their respects to the explorer who discovered the passage to India.

Alex rejoiced that Maya was born with an inquisitive heart, curious about how everything worked; she never stopped asking questions, and he never tired of answering. Nor did she simply accept his answers without delving deeper. Even when she was still very young, perhaps six or seven years old, she looked at him completely perplexed when he said that the Portuguese shaped the world. *Then why doesn't everyone speak Portuguese?* was all she wanted to know. *Well,* he had explained, *they do in some parts of the world. Yes, but not all,* was her comeback.

Why did they not speak Portuguese everywhere? Alex, too, began to wonder about that. At school everyone spoke Kiswahili and English and languages from every part of the country, yet nobody spoke Portuguese, it seemed, not even Mrs. Da Silva from school, even though she had a Portuguese name. Those agents of Portugal's might who came to Mombasa in fourteen ninety-eight, and there decided to build the Fort in fifteen hundred and ninety-three — these envoys of a dying world who left their indelible marks on India, and Mozambique, and Angola, and Brazil, and so many other places — they did not anchor their roots in the vast savanna grasslands. But how did that happen? Had they simply decided to leave their magnificent Fort in Mombasa and go back home, preferring to colonize other lands?

And what about the English, who seemed to have come out of nowhere? How did they come to the land of the Great Nam Lolwe? There were no stories of English navigators finding unknown routes anywhere. The places they said they discovered were already settled by peoples who sang many songs of Becoming — of creation, of praise, of death, of mourning, of triumph, and joy, and mystery — about the lands of their home. So what had the English discovered exactly? And why did they change all the names of the places most sacred when they came? And where, o where had they come from precisely? And why did they write all the laws of the land? And why did we all speak English at school? Why were the textbooks in English at school?

Maya could not have asked these questions of a more impassioned teacher. Her studious, erudite Alex Opolo, the Heavenly Defender of Man, a boy outside the world of Time, who was still too young to hear History in Song, pulled from every bookish source in their father's library a thousand bits and pieces that he wove together to try and explain how it came to pass that England took the place it held as the ruler of all the land.

Alex thought it mattered that when Edward the Confessor, the last Anglo-Saxon king, declared his successor William Duke of Normandy, the grandson of his mother Queen Emma's eldest brother, he sealed Britain's formal bond to continental Europe for at least a thousand years. Until that moment, the British Isles had stood apart, far away removed from the lucrative drama that Franco-German Charlemagne seeded in Europa when the Pope, one Christmas day in Rome, set upon his head the crown to the throne of the Holy Roman Empire salvaged from the ashes of the pagan realm of Caesar. A soldier and a warrior, this emperor seemed to share the dreams of Ancient poets. He took his cue from Persia and started building libraries, and even though he could not read, declared that all the children should. Alphabets and spelling, rhetoric and writing, singing songs, adding sums, calculating distances and measuring with numbers: the children had to learn it all. Although he could not read, he paid monastic libraries to copy sacred liturgies, theologies, philosophies, histories, and chants; Charlemagne maybe hoped to be the new Augustus for a modern Christian Rome. And while the scribes set to work to answer his command, he cinched up his saddle and shield and carried war to foreign lands. Legends abounded in his name and in the centuries following, nations of Europa looked to him for common kinship. And even though he was born the chieftain of a Germanic tribe, the Pope in Rome on Christmas day declared him something more. When Harold Goodwinson tried to keep the throne of England under Anglo-Saxon rule, denying the ascension of the Duke of Normandy, William would not have it. He built a new armada, sailed across the English Channel, made his way to Hastings where he quickly routed Harold. Then William claimed Edward's bequest, adding a Latin Franco-Norman accent to the old Scandinavian Anglo-Saxon English language of the court, and saturating Britain with the dream of Charlemagne. Alex thought that all of this mattered in explaining where the English came from and how they came to rule the world.

He imagined that it mattered that every English monarch after Franco-Norman William — Plantagenet, York, Lancaster, Stuart, Tudor, Hanover, Saxe-Coburg and Gotha, rebranded now as Windsor — mixed even more in marriage with the courts of other dynasties. Yet tribal war, and family feuds, and generational disputes burned right through all sincere attempts to forge alliances. Armed pursuit of riches in the name of God and Glory ignited bloody conflicts that for nearly a thousand years burned hot with wrath and greed and lust before erupting on a world bedeviled by the Empire plague that spread from long-dead Rome when Spain beat a westward path across Atlantic waters, racing against the Portuguese to get to India first. The Italian sailor at their helm, driven by his bliss, cast a prodigious specter with his fire, guile, and pestilence. Coming upon the New World like a beast roused from slumber, famished for Gold and Glory, and trumpeting the name of God, the Holy Roman Empire assails the New World, pillaging and ransacking everything eternal, staking claim on land and sea just as the Pope had said it could, just as the Pope had said it should.

Glory and God are borne in the wind with little more than words. But Gold lies much heavier, and beasts of burden take a toll on all the profit gains. The natives of the New World cannot be impressed upon to meekly bear weight on their backs in the name of Europa's empires. They resist subjugation, unwilling to submit. They are felled by the plagues that the iron-clad indifferently carry in their lungs, in their blood, in their seed. The Empire Terror crushes them, and Death comes rushing in beside. And so, the prowling beast turns its plundering eye toward Africa to see if it can find there men and women made of sterner stuff and of such mettle that they, however much abused, will not stop for Death.

Those that they find by whatever misfortune befalls the unhappy soul, they seize and bind and carry off to barter, brand, and brutalize; some they hunt in raiding parties endowed by merchants and kings and queens; some they trap at the rivers, or in the fields, or in the markets; others still — betrayed by kith and kin and sold for flattery — they purchase for copper rings and blown-glass beads and other trinkets. Even so, they cannot hold in bondage everyone for whom Life, even cast off in the briny depths of the open sea, is not too high a price to pay for natural liberty. But such a will to dignity does little to deter the purpose of Europa's agents to invade, search out, capture, vanquish, and reduce to perpetual slavery the souls from all around the world whom they tear from hearth and home.

The royal houses and the merchant companies confer to normalize and globalize the horrors of their fortunes. But the silent spaces in Alex's History books remain thickly impenetrable to poetry's truth. All that he can see are the words and the dates, but none of the tragedies — of shattered lives and scattered dreams veiled and buried underneath all the empty spaces in the lines of those History books. Nor can he hear, in the names and titles, the clanging clash of colonizers slipping past Memory's glare. The histories that Alex reads are fairy tales where Empires strike a dulcet tone, and all the natives strain like infant birds awaiting love and guidance from imperial masters weaned at Europa's bosom.

When the second Tudor king broke away from Rome and formed his own religion, cathedrals all across his land became Anglican churches. Henry's daughter, Elizabeth, stayed true to the

Tudor spirit and resisted continental ties, rejecting all pretenders for her hand, preferring glory. Perhaps it was because she was herself a pirate deep at heart that she raided Dutch flotillas, Spanish fleets, and Portuguese armadas. Her most devoted plunderer, a slaver by the name of Drake, struck fear in the heart of every child born in New-World bondage. He elbowed England's way into a piece of Empire profit, mugging ships and caravels, and waylaying merchants at sea wherever he could find them. Although Drake could not claim California for his Good Queen Bess, England finally found a foothold in the trans-Atlantic world when James Charles Stuart took the crown and sat the throne. Holland, Spain and Portugal were getting much too much of the plundered silver and gold and blood from worlds both Old and New. At some point, all their monarchs and their merchant fleets decided that it cost too much to keep the English pirates all at bay, or scramble in the open sea to stay out of their way. As long as English privateers kept robbing every sailing ship, profit gains would suffer, and the fledgling empires could not stand. So England joined the spreading league of colonizing nations to carve up America, and carve up Asia, and finally, in a scrambling dash, to carve up slices of Africa, too.

Running hot with Portugal, Spain, and Holland all over the world, setting up their colonies and taxing them all to revolt, the English clutch their pearls in shock and disbelief when France — in their newfound faith in liberty, equality, and brotherhood — supports colonial rebels. England joins in, by the by, where France and Holland planted flags in India for their cotton, silk, indigo, rice, opium, tea, sugar, and spice.

So naturally, England is present when that most redoubtable Otto Eduard Leopold, Prince of Bismarck, Duke of Lauenburg, Chancellor of the North German Confederation and Minister

President of Prussia convenes a conference in Berlin to sort out the most potent ways that the children of Europa will use to crush the backbone of Africa.

For thirteen weeks and fourteen days, fifteen nations gather 'round — Germany, Austria-Hungary, Belgium, France, Italy, Spain, Portugal, Netherlands, Sweden, Norway, Denmark, Russia, the Ottoman Empire, along with the United States — to carve up the African continent for themselves, unbeknownst to their prey.

They will obliterate all the kingdoms, dukedoms, counties, principalities, and dominions in Africa, appropriating to themselves and to their future heirs all the rivers of diamonds and rubber and gold that flow through the heart of the land. They will convert African goods and possessions to their own use and profit to cobble together Empires to rival Caesar's Rome, and maybe even the Kingdom of God!

Now that they have smashed and burned the handlooms in India, and now that they have crushed and torn the thumbs of all the weavers, there is plenty of cotton milled in the world to weave into breathable cloth in England's very own new mechanized industrial looms. So under the equatorial sun with their palanquins and parasols, careful not to burn too much, ready to carry off all the Gold, for Glory, and, of course for God, too!

But what of the natives? somebody asks. Oh, they will love some civilization! We are, after all, saving their souls by extirpating their heathen ways and showing them to the light of our Lord. They won't understand, someone objects. No, but we will bring them words of salvation whether they like it or not, and yes, they will worship us.

Why let such a paradise go to waste, go unexploited, undevastated, especially when there is wealth to accrue, cathedrals and churches to polish and paint, palaces to build, and jeweled tiaras to craft for Queens and Princesses alike. Eden was never meant to remain untouched by the grabbing hand of man. He must ravage and squeeze it and bleed it and turn all its life into mortar and stone – monuments to dead sailors and kings, thus is the will of the Lord our God. *Invade, search out, capture, vanquish, and subdue* all the souls of the world. *Reduce their persons to slavery and take all their kingdoms* and smash them to dust, show them the living hell on Earth and teach them to pray for our mercy and the salvation that comes with paying with blood for the greater glory of God, and faith in the Universal Church, or just an international bank. It would be a shame, and surely impious, to let all that paradise go to waste.

Resistance? Rebellion? Restitution? What is to be done when the locals object? That their Lakes and Mountains and Grasslands are sacred, and must not be destroyed? What should be done to silence their protest, but keep the riches flowing north, along the Nile, if you like? France has a brilliant idea. Take everything you can, entail the rest, and then leave and never look back. While the African nations west and north struggle to get their bearings in the world that we made for ourselves, make sure that we are siphoning away all the life and wealth that we entailed. It was always too hot down there for civilization anyway. Britain wants to do the same, but those pearls demand clutching, and one cannot actually *appear* to be stealing. Give them membership in the exclusive club of Empire states. Ah, they'll like that! France sees this and thinks, Zut! I should have thought of that! Well, at least I have entailed all their wealth and made them believe that they must all speak ineffable français… Now Portugal thinks, "ah, yes, we, too, gave them our tongue…" And Belgium… Well Belgium has cut a deep, raw, gaping wound right in the heart of the land, murdering, and mutilating, and mangling whomever they can, because if they cannot dominate the locals of the land in perpetuity like the Pope said they could, like the Pope said they should, they will crush them all and leave them for dead, silencing all their tongues.

Sons of Italia — *brava gente!* — make their entrance into the game, Abyssinia their singular aim. How better to raise the old glory of Rome than to conquer the land of the Queen of Sheba, the land of the children of Solomon? But the warring sons of Italia cannot make Abyssinia submit. So, instead, they engage in chattel trade with the fathers of daughters, of babies not yet maidens, and these children the sons of Italia confine to their harems for service both carnal and menial, gifting and trading these girls as they please, because after all that is how it is done. Caesar and Marc Anthony both took pleasure in Queen Cleopatra's bed; these sons of Italia the infant daughters of Abyssinia instead.

The Dutch, for their part, strive to prove that thinkers of the Enlightenment — who claimed and argued that all the sons and daughters of Europa were natural conquerors born — were right to so argue and claim. Damned they will be if anyone is going to make them budge from where they have squatted. There is just too much gold, and far too many diamonds, and as yet unimaginable riches to leave behind just like that. Let the French entail. Let the British clutch at their pearls. Let the Belgians savage the people and bleed the land to despair. Let the sons of Italia defiling children imagine dominion in Aksum whence they looted the stele of the ancient King Ezana. The Dutch will just try a little of this, and a little of that, enough to shove all the indigenous Africans into misery and keep paradise all to themselves and their offspring.

In all of the centuries it takes Europa to finally live out Charlemagne's dream, Britain has risen to global dominion, enjoying the privilege to simply exploit, to snap its fingers and bring all to heel, to be worshiped and lauded just because. Victoria, the first Hanoverian Queen, has claimed the savanna and nearby valleys and highlands for her own, naming the Great Lake at its heart, without deigning to ask the Spirit of the Lake that watches over the peoples and all the creatures that live in the lands surrounding. Victoria's children and their children, too, cousins who sit on thrones across all Europa, vent their rage and greed and fear on everyone in sight, waging wars that draw in the world and leave millions slaughtered and starving and torn. The most recent Queen who wears the crown of England, of Saxe-Coburg and Gotha stock, along with all her heir and brood, goes by the name of Windsor, her first just like the pirate Queen's. She looks decorously on as her ancestors' measureless realm fractures and crumbles, conceding to natives of African nations and Asian lands, and even across all the Oceans and all the Seas, that yes, they, too, are people and no, the Empire will not strike again; it will only ensure — with their consent, of course — that they stay underfoot believing the myth of belonging; to a common cause and to a common wealth, perhaps, where the custom of four o'clock tea seals their proud complicity.

But all that Alex learns from his father's history books is the ritual acclamation for the conqueror's campaign. What he does not hear, and what he does not see — in the quiet, empty spaces twixt the letters and the lines — is the wretchedness and woe that the conqueror begets in every corner of creation, all in the name of God, in the name of Glory, and — if only truth be told — in the name of Gold.

Book VIII. Snow

Anna Adongo flies her children across the ocean to America where they will see snow for the first time. • The children start a new adventure at Union Saints Academy. • Maya continues her reveries about Gweno, the hen and Ongowo, the hawk. • Maya sneaks out of the dormitory at night and discovers a mermaid fishpond. • How Esther became a mother to all of her siblings in the Old World and the New.

Canto Fifty

On the second day after bringing her four children to America in the greatest adventure of their lives, and settling them all in her apartment in Boston, and enrolling them in the local schools, Anna left to attend to important business. She admonished them to avoid talking to strangers and to let no one into the house; to be on time for the school bus and to switch the television off at eight o'clock; to buy the weekend newspaper and to cut coupons from the grocery store advertisements. She filled the refrigerator with frozen vegetables and chicken wings and drumsticks, and the cupboard with canned beans and cereal, instant rice, instant potatoes, and bottles of Allspice. She told the children to take turns preparing meals and cleaning up the house. She would be away for a while, she said. She was away for two months.

Maya began to vomit uncontrollably after three nights in Boston. She had an aversion to the food that left her unable to keep anything down. At first, no one took her seriously when she complained that the milk was salty and tasted of brine, and the food had no flavor at all. She had always been a finicky eater, and Esther imagined that after a while she would forget to grumble once she got used to the new place. But every attempt to feed Maya only made her regurgitate more violently. On the fourth day her skin became cold and clammy, even as her temperature continued to climb. She did not go to school that day, nor for several weeks following. Esther was fourteen years old, and she did not know what to do.

In four weeks, Maya went from being a plump child with a still and fierce energy, to becoming little more than an exhausted collection of bones loosely held together in her skin. Still, the child could not stop her body from trying to eject the contents of a long since empty stomach. Her throat ached within from the corrosive bile that surged upward unbidden, and without from the strain of convulsive heaving. The muscles of her abdomen were torn and sore from ceaselessly contracting, and yet they continued to close more tightly around her small ribs. The bones, grown brittle from slow starvation, gave out one day, cracking under the pressure. No longer able to bear the pain and fatigue of her rebelling body, Maya shunned everything but water. Her ordinarily inquisitive face, by turns pensive and curious, became ashen and drawn with pain, gray around the mouth and profoundly somber where her eyes sank deep into their sockets. Those once sprightly eyes that seemed to devour everything they fell upon now became listless and lethargic. She repeatedly asked that the curtains be drawn because the streetlamps outside were too loud. Esther feared that her sister might die. She also worried about what she would tell her mother if that happened. She was fourteen years old and she did not know what to do.

Perhaps Anna expected her to look after everyone just as she had when the children went to Union Saints. Esther, after all, was much older by three years now, a newly and proudly affirmed teenager. But the important difference was not the children's age. Rather, it was that in boarding school at Union Saints Academy, house matrons, and teachers, and coaches, and guards, and groundskeepers all saw to the care and safety of each of the children, including the two hundred others their age, just as they might have in a village in the middle of Paradise. At Union Saints there was a school nurse who tended to the children when they fell ill, so even if no one knew what to do, at least the nurse could be called. The nurse could even admit ailing children to the infirmary when they required special treatment, or just close monitoring for illnesses of greater consequence. At Union Saints, the children could go outside and play, they could have meals with their friends, and classes too, and they could get up to all kinds of mischief together – even Hehra, the quietest one of them all, who never seemed to get anywhere on time and disappeared for ages into story books.

Hehra was only six years old when all of the children entered the Union Saints Academy boarding school in the Rift Valley highlands. Maya was eight, Esther eleven, and David all of thirteen. Anna had just returned home following a five-week absence that began shortly after the previous school term ended, leaving her mother and her sisters to look after everyone. Ma Ruth spent those five weeks wringing her hands over being left at her age to provide for the minute and endless needs of such small children. David fretted with bated breath for a fortnight, and then he became a fountain of tears that did not abate until Anna returned. Ma Ruth's nerves were frayed, and she could often be heard delivering increasingly strident instructions to the twins, Sara and Rachel, to keep the house in order. After Anna, they were her eldest girls, even though they were still quite young themselves, both preparing for their O-levels in secondary school. Sara was more gregarious than Rachel who, in her gravity, was the more responsible of the two. Rachel, in fact, did not take kindly to Anna's frequent desertions, nor to the burden it placed on them despite Sara's optimism that Anna would always return. Mamma Akoth, now at ninety-five Rains, spent all her time with the children playing in the garden, often regaling them with stories and legends, and especially teaching Esther who had been born to remember the songs of Becoming. Hehra never left Esther's side, so naturally she absorbed all the stories as well, learning, as time went by, to mimic the melodies that Mamma Akoth sang to them.

The Short Rains were about to begin. Ma Ruth decided to take the children together with Mamma Akoth from Nairobi across the country to her house on the Bay to spend the Christmas holidays. Hehra worried about leaving Bruno alone in Nairobi and so she made the houseboy promise that he would take special care of the cat. She bid a forlorn goodbye to both Bruno and Serena when they left for the train station. She had yet to develop an intuition for finality. Coco, the German shepherd that guarded the grounds, followed the car all the way down the lane, barking ferociously at the rolling tires, frantic over something Simba, his mate, could not really fathom. Simba followed only part of the way, abandoning the chase and sending the children off with a few hesitant barks. Her little pup, Coco the Second, and her even more sedate brother, Kendo Nagasaki, stayed behind with her, excited and perplexed, but ultimately unconvinced of Coco's immoderate passion.

Hehra was by then old enough to start Primary One the following year and, partly because of Esther's accounts, was thrilled to be finally ready to enroll in the same school with her older siblings once the holiday was over. Esther liked to play teacher, reminding Hehra that Primary School was completely different from anything else she had ever known. Everyone wore uniforms and did homework after school, Esther said. There was no nap time or story time, although, once she got to Primary Three, they also had a History class which was like story time, only different, because the stories were only about people and events that had been turned into stone monuments. There wouldn't be any stories like the ones Mamma Akoth always sang to them of Spirits, and chickens, and hawks, and lions gazing at elephants playing in mud, but that was okay because when they got back home, they could ask Mamma Akoth to sing to them again. Hehra took it all in, learning to read over Esther's shoulder, or on her lap, or lying next to her in the library playroom, gradually venturing beyond the picture books of Hindu gods and demons all by herself. Sad though she was to leave Bruno behind when Ma Ruth took them all to Nam Lolwe, at least she had Primary One to look forward to once the school term resumed.

When Anna reappeared at the tail end of the Short Rains after five weeks away, Hehra was thrilled because she imagined that now they would all go back to Nairobi, back to Bruno, best of all, and also back to Serena, and back to Coco and Coco the Second and Kendo Nagasaki and Simba. But her joy was short-lived. Anna announced, even as she unpacked the trinkets she had brought back as gifts, that her children were going to boarding school. They would attend Union Saints Academy, a school set in the edge of the Rift Valley in the fertile hills of a farming town.

The school had been founded to serve English colonizers and their families when the British Crown declared East African lands a protectorate of the Empire. As far as news could travel beyond hidden horizons, all lakes, mountains, and grasslands became dominion of His Majesty, and all who dwelt therein subjects of the Crown, bidden conform to the new law of the land in the name of the King. Many years after this land and all its peoples declared their independence from the British colonizers, the school came to serve Cabinet Ministers and other such luminaries of means and offered a boarding school for their children from the primary school First Elementary to secondary school Form Four. No other place, Anna declared, would do for the children of a Modern Woman of quality, taste, and grace.

Making preparations to attend Union Saints Academy introduced the first unequivocal note of exotic adventure into the children's lives, and all of them, from David to Hehra, gave no thought to saying goodbye to the homes of their infancy. At Anna's behest, Rachel took the children shopping for their new school uniforms, armed with a list of the provisions that the school required. Under her sister's supervision Rachel measured each excited child for three sets of uniforms: dresses and shirts of blue gingham, dark gray short trousers, gray pullovers and cardigans with matching socks, navy blue blazers, striped ties, indigo exercise shorts and t-shirts, black leather shoes with laces and white canvas athletic runners, rubber sandals, petticoats, swimming pool bathing suits. The list also said that the children had to bring with them suitcases, bath towels, face towels, shoe polish, shoe brushes, soap, toothpaste, toothbrushes, combs, shampoo, lotion, pencils, colors, rubber erasers, fountain pens, ink, writing tablets, envelopes, stamps, blotting paper, rulers, compass sets, …

When everything on the list sent from Union Saints Academy had been purchased, checked off, name-tagged, packed and repacked, Anna and Ma Ruth boarded the overnight train with the children and made their way across the country through the Rift Valley. From there Anna hired a large car to the farming town, and they reached Union Saints at noon without much ceremony. After settling the children in their respective dormitories – Victoria House for the girls and Albert House for the boys – Anna, her mother Ma Ruth, and the children all had tea with the Headmaster, Father Singleton, and his wife Gloria.

~~~~~~~~~~~~~~~~~~~~~~~~~~

Canto Fifty-one

The Union Saints Academy was set on a hill surrounded by towering eucalyptus groves and massive jacaranda trees, its paved lanes lined with luxuriant bottlebrush willows. Beyond the school grounds, there were more hills where local farmers cultivated pineapples, and maize, and beans, and tea. The farming town was a distance away through the surrounding forest and ordinarily accessible only by private automobile. As evening approached, Gloria Singleton, the headmaster's wife, invited Ma Ruth and Anna Adongo to stay the night, and both accepted happily, Ma Ruth, enchanted to be hosted by an Englishman and his wife, Anna, mildly excited and enormously flattered that he should lavish so much attention on her. The next morning, they returned to Nakuru for their train back, admonishing the children to listen to their teachers and to be good. The Headmaster told them to expect weekly letters as the children would write home every Friday.

A singular point of pride for the school was that everyone had to speak English, whether in class or on the playground. Esther was amused to hear the language everywhere and all the time, even away from the classroom. At first it felt a bit forced to have to say even ordinary everyday things in English. And it was not enough to just use the language; it had to be a certain kind of English: *May I have some tea, please*, not *Give me the tea*; or *May I be excused, sir*, and not *Can I to go to the toilet*, or worse yet, *I want to go to the loo*, or – God forbid – *I need to wee-wee*. They had to remember to always use the correct combination of object pronouns together with prepositions when saying *me, us, him, her, them, whom* as in *two-by-four—whom*.

Maya was also hugely diverted to find that they were known as the 'Ocholas.' Suddenly theirs was the name that belonged to their father, a name to which they had never paid much attention, and which they had only ever seen on their birth certificates.

Because they arrived to start school one week after the term had already begun, their late arrival piqued the interest of the other children considerably. Word quickly spread that Anna and Ma Ruth had been guests of the Headmaster that first evening, and this information made the new arrivals all the more welcome a curiosity. The three girls were in the same dormitory in Victoria House, which stood at the opposite end of the grounds from Albert House for the boys.

In both cases the House Matrons introduced them to their dormitory Prefects, who in turn led them around the corridors of the expansive house with instructions on timetables, responsibilities, and etiquette. Some children followed the newcomer siblings going through their tour, talking away and asking questions, wanting to know why they had arrived so late in the term, wanting to know where they lived, where they came from. Had they been abroad, was their father a diplomat, would they be staying long…?

Surrounded so by the other children, Esther drew Hehra close, her arm across her baby sister's shoulder, as they followed the Prefect who guided them through the corridors of the House. Mamma Akoth had taught her to watch over all her siblings, yet, like Joseph for Benjamin, she minded Hehra with a pronouncedly grave sense of responsibility, fearful lest any harm should come to her baby sister. Only Hehra could inspire the heavenly clear-water cooing laugh that Esther had once heard spring from their mother, and in her still-young life, Esther imagined that her baby sister perhaps had a divine gift for inspiring joy, a gift none of her other siblings shared, a gift no one else in the family seemed to possess. Walking through the corridors of their new House at Union Saints Academy guided by the Prefect and surrounded by a sea of other girls, Esther felt Hehra's other hand on her belly, clutching her pullover, clinging to her. Esther's heart, still only eleven years old at that point, and yet ascetically solitary, swelled to shield her sister from all threat of harm, enveloping her in precocious maternal shelter, all burden of duty vanished.

That heightened sense of guardianship awakened Esther to the myth of Love in a way she had never conceived of it before; this chimera everyone seemed to know about and speak of, write and sing about; this unknowable way of being that melded the best of the self to another; this ineffable myth so powerful that it rivaled the wind's phantom force and moved not in the matter of the world, but in its very soul. As if a match had been unexpectedly struck for the first time in a room perpetually dark, Esther thought, when attending to Hehra, that she glimpsed 'things' that she had not even known were there.

And so, Esther held Hehra close as they followed the Prefects through the increasingly crowded corridors. She was tall for her age and could see above the heads of most of the other girls around her. She wrapped both arms around Hehra, holding her even closer. Hehra buried her face in Esther's waist as they walked along, emerging only when she had grown used to the closeness of the crowd, the strange language, the cascading questions. Esther smiled politely and answered some of the other children's queries. No, they had not been abroad; no, their father was a doctor; yes, the stylish lady was their mother; no, the other one was their grandmother; yes, really; no their father was not at the Headmaster's house; no, they lived in Nairobi, in the hills; yes they had a garden; yes two cats and four dogs, one of them still a puppy… Maya was mute. Although she felt neither fearful nor especially timid, she was unused to so many new voices. Her face registered curiosity that mirrored that of the faces around them. She too was amused to hear everyone speak in English here in the dormitory. She wondered how the classroom would be. She stared at everyone in tacit contemplation, the fleeting thought of what Alex would say brushing her mind as the questions continued to tumble over their ears. Hehra turned her head into Esther's waist time and again, hiding repeatedly from the unrelenting assault of their curious peers.

They were first shown their beds in one of the four long dormitories. Esther would sleep between Hehra and Maya, and she would make sure that they both made their beds and folded their counterpanes down properly. Beside each bed there was a small wooden locker where they could keep their clothes and books. Each locker had to always be neat because sometimes there were surprise inspections. Demerits were given for untidy lockers and untidy beds. All their toiletry needs went into a different locker in the bathroom along with their socks and shoes and waterproof gumboots. Only rubber sandals could be worn indoors.

When the Matron woke them up in the morning, everyone had to make their beds, wash their faces, and carry their socks and shoes to the rack outside, and then line up in the veranda by class level and height, and wait for the dining room doors to open. Breakfast consisted of buttered bread and tea or porridge, and they learned to recite Grace at the start of every meal. There were eight long tables, each presided over by a Primary Eight Prefect and her junior assistant. The Prefects saw to it that everyone was adequately served, and that the smaller children, in particular, finished all their food. No one could rise from the table until every plate was clean, and every cup or glass drained. After breakfast and lunch, they all tidied up and made their way to class across the lane and through the gardens.

After finishing supper, the children gathered in the dormitory Common Room to see off the day with homework or leisure. Esther read to Hehra from a large anthology of folk stories, trying to distract her from missing Bruno. Maya lay on the floor next to them, absorbed in the large mural decorating the wall, drawn into the stylized tableau of an English foxhunting party where black and white foxhounds darted alongside horses in full gallop, the smartly dressed riders sporting scarlet coats and black top hats.

Just behind the tree line, beyond the horizon of the busily noisy foxhounds, Maya thought she saw unfold the drama of the story Esther was reading to Hehra. It was a story she knew well, because Alex recounted it time and again. There, just out of sight in the Common Room mural, a large, beautiful chicken surrounded by hatchlings was scratching and picking at the ground, scattering roots and soil with her legs, and turning her head now and again to eye the sky warily, cluck, cluck, clucking away. The chicken worried the passive soil with an urgency that nobody understood. Nobody, that is, except the hawk who circled above, ready to pounce at any moment to carry off hatchlings.

Canto Fifty-two

On the second night at Union Saints, after Anna and Ma Ruth had departed, Esther sat on her bed between her sisters, asking them how their day had been. The newness of Union Saints absorbed all their attention as they took in the faces and voices around them. Maya would soon notice the swallow's nests in the eaves of Victoria House, and Hehra would one day discover that she liked to draw and play the piano. For the time being, all Hehra could say was that the House was enormous.

Maya, for her part, had wandered off alone while returning from the Union Saints dairy farm with her sisters. In her wanderings she had discovered a fishpond near the Headmaster's office. There was a fountain above it that drip-dripped into the stone basin below where dark gray tadpoles with wriggly tails, large bright orange fish with iridescent sparkly scales, and small shimmering silvery guppies all darted about in the splashing water. And behind the Headmaster's office in the middle of the Junior Primary block stood a clump of loquat trees, and all the classrooms had large, glass windows that went from the ceiling to the floor. Thinking of the darting guppies and wriggling tadpoles, Maya resolved to show Alex the fishpond in the morning.

Little Hehra's discovery was a large open terrace on the roof of the House just above the ground level terrace that led to the garden behind the House. No one was supposed to go up there, but children did anyway, to play jump rope and to do handstands, especially when the terrace downstairs was crowded. While Hehra chatted away, Esther undressed her and helped her put on her nightgown. Maya sat quietly on her bed, watching the flannel envelop her sister for a while, waiting for Hehra's head to reappear, Hehra's hands to reappear, her fingers snaking their way through the sleeves of the light green, flowered garment. The nightdress was new. At home no one had ever paid any attention to their sleeping clothes. Here at Union Saints, the other girls had all kinds

— from scotch plaid flannel pajama separates, to closed-toed overalls, to flowing nightgowns. Some of the children even walked around in slippers and combed cotton robes.

Maya suddenly had the urge to go and find Alex. At that moment, Hehra also remembered, with piercing nostalgia, that she had left Bruno at home. It was nearly two months since she had left her cat in Nairobi, nearly two months since she had seen her. She asked Esther if they could go and get her. No, Esther explained, they would go home when the school term ended, and then they could see Bruno. But she wanted to see Bruno now, Hehra said. Cats did not go to school, Esther told her firmly, they just had to wait until people returned. But Bruno did not even know how long the school term was, Hehra pressed. Esther was at a loss. She may not have been able to answer for Bruno's sense of time, but her sisters had to finish changing and washing up so that later they could be tucked in quickly when the Matron called lights out. Everyone else was in the Common Room.

On their second night at Union Saints, they were allowed to remain in the dormitory a little bit longer after supper to get settled properly and get accustomed to doing things. They would have to shine their shoes and brush their teeth and wash their faces before joining the other girls in the Common Room. They would have to pay close attention as they all recited Grace before jumping into bed for the night. Esther helped Hehra down from the bed and led her and Maya to the bathroom. After they finished brushing their teeth and washing their faces, they made their way to the Common Room for the rest of the evening long before bedtime was announced.

Hehra wanted to hear the rest of the story about the chicken and the hawk and the magic needle that came between them. Esther obliged happily, pulling down the volume of traditional folk stories from the Common Room library bookshelf. Maya found her spot behind them, facing the foxhunt mural and slowly, ever so slowly, she let her mind drift into the drama only she could see beyond the mural's tree line.

Gweno had resigned herself to marrying the rooster. If she was going to spend her life looking for a needle she feared she would never find, she might as well take the mate that no one else would have, especially since it was her fault that he was stuck wearing her gown. After a while of married ennui, she finally hatched some chicks and they became the center of her attention. By now she was so used to scratching the ground that when she finally took her babies outside, she started doing it without thinking and the little ones naturally followed suit. She had nearly forgotten Ongowo's last words, half believing that he had only spoken in frustration, but when she saw her hatchlings imitating her, she told them to watch for a magic needle and to tell her if any of them happened to find it.

One day a shadow passed over the ground near where Gweno sat with her brood. She recognized her old friend and went out to greet him. Ongowo however, was not paying a social call. He had spent a long time isolated from everyone because he did not want to hear about the big party in the sky, about what he had missed. He did not want to face the frustrated avian flocks that crowded to his workshop. At first, when the birds had come to him to have their finery removed, he had asked them to return later, hoping to buy time to find his magic needle. It quickly became apparent that he could not help them, and many who had formerly sworn devotion to him suddenly became hostile. They were forced to walk around in all-too splendid attire, even when running quotidian chores, and they were not at all pleased. They thought that Ongowo was playing a trick on them and they shunned him for it. To this day, all the birds who had gone to Ongowo for a party dress still have on their festive attire. So you can understand that Ongowo's life became very difficult, and he grew quite sad and bitter. His troubled mind found some comfort in the once careless idea of raising one of Gweno's chicks as his own, and he gradually became convinced that it was the only way he would ever have any company, anyone to love. So he swooped down to where the little chickens were and in a single swift motion lifted one neatly off the ground and flew away.

Gweno was stunned. And at first, she could not move. Then she tried to follow him, but she had spent so much time scratching and pecking away at the ground that she could no longer take to the sky. Her body had grown round, and squat, and her wings lacked the strength to lift her up. When Akoth told her grandson Gabriel this story, and then later her great-grandchildren as well, she said that the hen was forced to learn how to drink water looking up at the sky, just so that the swooping hawk would not catch her off guard again. And all of her children, and theirs after them, inherited their matriarch's habit and plight, forever scratching the ground for the magic needle they could never hope to find.

Canto Fifty-three

Long after lights out on the second day at Union Saints, Maya left Victoria House to go see Alex, too impatient to wait for the morning. The front door was locked, and the Matron had taken the key. The two Matrons who looked after the day to day affairs of Victoria House lived in small cottages that stood apart a brief distance away, and for a moment Maya wished she could somehow reach them and ask them to let her out of the House. Perhaps she could just knock on Mrs. Fonseca's door, she thought. The House Mistress's apartment abutted the House at the far end of the long corridor that led away from the main door. The Prefect who had shown them around the House had said that although she was very strict, Mrs. Fonseca was also much revered by the girls of Victoria House. Surely, as long as Maya asked politely, the House Mistress would let her out?

Maya walked along the dark, quiet corridor and found the small, gray door that the Prefect had pointed to during the tour. At first, she knocked gently, careful not to startle Mrs. Fonseca. She knocked again more firmly when there was no response. She knocked for a little while longer, getting a little bit louder with time, before she decided that either Mrs. Fonseca was a very sound sleeper who could not hear her, or who, God forbid, would suddenly wake up and become very annoyed to find a child she did not yet know at her door in the middle of the night. How silly! Maya thought, shaking herself alert. What on earth was she thinking?

She began to feel trapped, and unaccountably imagined falling asleep in the dark corridor and being attacked by wild river horses while she slept. She could have simply returned to her bed in the dormitory at the end of the corridor. Instead exit became imperative. The terrace! Why had she not thought of that before? Everyone was asleep and the corridors were completely silent and now, thwarted in her attempt to wake Mrs. Fonseca, yet relieved in her defeat, she was suddenly apprehensive about drawing any attention to herself. With tacit and tentative steps, she sneaked back halfway down the hallway to find the Common Room. Slowly she pushed open the heavy door, afraid that it might creak or suddenly bang against something on the other side. As soon as there was enough room for her to pass through, she pressed against the door frame closely and entered the Common Room, careful not to turn on any lights. The empty Common Room, with the century-old grand piano on one end, and paintings of foxhunts and steeple chases hanging on the walls, now looked enormous in the saturating silence of the night. Along the far side of the room, half a dozen French windows looked out onto the terrace and the garden beyond. Making her way across the floor, Maya stumbled over a loose wooden tile and stopped, terrified that someone would discover her. For an interminable while, she stood still in the middle of the expansive room, trembling in her core, willing her pulse to settle down, wishing herself already outside. Finally, she moved again. She reached the French window at the center and turned the cold metal handle. It gave way! The door swung open and, in the next instant, Maya had traversed the terrace and was rounding the corner at the edge of the garden, intent on getting to Albert House.

The moon shone large and round in the sky, a translucent lantern gleaming over the eucalyptus trees, and the jacaranda canopy, and the bottlebrush willows that swayed serenely in the languorous, yet somehow sprightly wind that fluttered through the avenues of Union Saints Academy. To Maya's eyes the trees seemed to be dancing to the sound of the glimmering moon and she was glad for their company. When she rounded the building she had left, she discovered that she did not know which way to go. She had not actually been with MaAnna and Ma Ruth to settle the boys in Albert House on the other side of the school grounds, past three other Houses, and near the gate. She could have just followed the winding avenue that curved around in a wide arc all the way to the entrance of the school, but she decided to make her journey short by cutting through the junior block behind the Headmaster's office. It had not yet occurred to her that she did not know how she might enter Albert House once she arrived there, nor did she know in which dormitory she might find her brother. Esther would have already thought of all these things and postponed her visit until she knew where exactly she was going. But unlike Esther, Maya thought only in the moment.

Entering the courtyard of the junior block, Maya tripped on something soft, and round, and firm on the ground. The grass was littered with loquats that glowed a pale yellow by the light of the moon. Before she could pick one up, she imagined she saw someone, or something, dart behind one of the loquat trees on the other side of the courtyard. Suddenly her body was shaking again, but this time she did not just stand still. She quietly ducked into the shadowy veranda of the classrooms and continued to move through the block, intent on getting to Alex.

"Nyangi, Nyangi," came a sharp, cautious whisper, "is that you?"

"Alex!" Maya whispered back, relief saturating her. He must have had the same idea at the very same time. "Alex, it's me!"

Alex emerged from the shadow of a large loquat tree and grinned at his sister.

"Someone's going to get into a lot of trouble," he said, still whispering, but now more playfully. He was wearing pajamas that matched her nightgown, and all his pockets were bulging with what looked like round pebbles.

"Look," he said. "I was on my way to see you when I found these loquats lying around, so I got you some!" He kept grinning and Maya could not help laughing gleefully.

"Someone's going to get into a lot of trouble," she mimicked reaching for the fruit he offered her.

"I also found a pond full of fish and tadpoles. The plants in it look like little round rafts. Come and see." He handed her the loquats he was holding and placed his hand at the base of her head, just above her neck.

Maya let him guide her, her heart singing as they neared the pond, and then skipping merrily along when she heard the two-tiered fountain in the middle drip-dripping into the water below. At the center of the fountain a meager stream trickled out of a small, round clay pot that rested on the right shoulder of a stone woman whose back leaned against a rough-hewn column. From her waist down, the woman became a fish, her tail dipping into the basin of the fountain's upper tier. At the bottom of the basin her luxuriously carved fin rose teasingly out of the water, then curved back under the surface just at the tip. While her right arm curled upward around the clay pot on her shoulder as if to hold the pot steady, the other arm came across her breast, and her upturned palm held the vessel from below. Maya imagined that serene face bending to look down at the iridescent orange fish with sparkly skin tintinnabulating in the moonlight, chiming with the tiny sparkles of the small shimmering silvery guppies that clinked in the splashing water.

"Ooo!" she cooed, enchanted by the siren, and the fish, and the water lilies dancing on the sparkling moon wavelets. She had never heard watery moonlight before. "Oooo!"

They sat on the paved ground beside the shallow water and rested their elbows on the stone edge of the basin that made up the lower tier of the fishpond. Alex slowly and laboriously took all the loquats out of his pockets and started peeling them, pulling the skin off the ripe orange fruit. He gave some to Maya and ate some, plopping the smooth brown pits into the pond to her delight.

"How about the pot?" Maya asked. "Can you get it into the pot?" The mouth of the pot was no wider than a teacup.

"Of course. Watch this," replied Alex taking aim. He tried two loquat stones, and both of them missed.

"Ha ha! 'Of course'," his sister parroted.

"I'll get it next time." He peeled another loquat and sucked the two smooth stones out of the succulent flesh of the fruit. He took aim again and sent a seed flying.

"Inside the pot, not on her face!" Maya said, chortling with glee.

"Quiet, I need to concentrate." This time the missile struck the mermaid just over her belly on her left elbow.

"This is how you do it," Maya announced, picking up one of the loquat seeds accumulating on her lap. She straightened to stand on her knees and blew on the seed. She launched it and it went so wide that it did not even strike the column behind the mermaid.

"Oh, is that how you do it?" Alex sing-songed at Maya, gloating just a little bit.

"OK, OK, OK. The first person who gets one in the pot wins," Maya said, carefully aiming her second seed.

Loquat seeds went flying at the quiet siren who remained intent on the small fish below. Some struck the mermaid's mouth, some her eyes and forehead, her collarbones her chest, the fingers that cradled the round pot. Some glanced off her elbows and wrists. Others rolled down her tail to settle at her curved fin. She made no noise.

Maya told Alex about Victoria House as they absently sent loquat seeds flying at the mermaid. She described the terrace just behind the Common Room and the garden beyond. There was a large, dark brown grand piano decorated with carvings of vines and leaves in the Common Room. Hibiscus bushes and beanpoles, and something that looked like gourds were strewn all over the small garden.

He told her that near Albert House a hedge of gooseberry bushes stretched along a narrow road near the track field that led up to a small black gate that was chained shut. He had gone out there with David to play football with some of the boys in Albert House just before supper, and someone said that there was a monastery on the other side of the locked gate.

"A monastery!" repeated Maya, full of wonder. "What kind of monastery?"

"Some nuns live there. They wear only black, with white headbands, but nobody ever sees them. No, actually, sometimes they go into town to escort visiting missionaries who are traveling through the Rift Valley. They walk all the way from the farming town through the road in the forest!"

"Do you think we could visit?" she asked, suddenly excited by the idea of living in a monastery.

Alex laughed, imagining little Maya bombarding the laconic nuns with questions. She had once reported to him that Mrs. Da Silva, way back in Kindergarten, had told her, rather tightly, that she asked too many questions. If the worshipful but inquisitive child had so tested the pious Mrs. Da Silva's patience, Alex could only imagine how much more inspired and testing she would be in the presence of real nuns.

"They call us 'The Ocholas' here," she said after a brief silence, tossing another seed into the fountain. "That's funny, isn't it?"

"Gabriel would be very happy, I think," Alex said.

"I don't see why MaAnna said that we are called Ochola if Gabriel is such a bad man. Doesn't it make us bad too?"

"Maybe it doesn't matter whether he is a bad man. We have to have his name because he is our father."

"I don't want his name. I want yours."

"I already gave you a name," Alex replied.

It no longer mattered that the reason his first word became Maya's name was because he did not know how to properly say what he intended to say. He had simply wanted to echo the gentle *"Opolo, this is your sister"* that Mamma Akoth had said to him. When he replied, "mara," — *mine* in the tongue of his great-grandmother — he meant it with all the pride and happiness of his phantom heart. The sound that Mamma Akoth heard instead became his sister's name.

"Not that one," Maya said emphatically. "Not *Maya*. I mean like the one Esther inherited because she was born after you and David. *You* are my father, not Gabriel. So, my surname could just be 'Okello', or maybe even 'Opolo', like you!"

Surname. She tested the weight of the word in the moonlight, feeling its newness in their strictly English universe. Alex fixed his gaze on Maya's face, surprised by joy to hear how his heart's best treasure saw him. *Anyango mara*, he thought silently, this child truly *was* his.

They were quiet for a while, and then they both burst out in reeling mirth, not unlike their father's unguarded laugh, their eyes brimming with glee as they followed the logical path of Maya's thoughts.

"Can you imagine Esther being called, 'Esther Akello Okello'," Alex said, giggling, "instead of 'Esther Akello Ochola'?"

"What about David" Maya asked, "and Hehra? Their names don't sound so funny."

"Opiyo Ochola, that's not so bad. Akoth Ochola – that sounds okay, too."

"Oh, but that's the best one! Rain and Born after the Father's Death," Maya mused. "That's exactly what happened! It's perfect!" Her excitement made her sound incoherent.

"Happened to who?" Alex asked.

"Happened *to whom,*" his sister corrected.

"What?"

"*To whom*... happened *to whom!*"

"Oh." But Alex did not understand. "What's wrong with you? What do you mean?"

"*To whom!*" Maya repeated, now gesturing with both hands, holding two fingers up on the right, and four fingers up on the left. "*Two by four whom!* Weren't you paying attention?"

"I don't understand what you're talking about!" Alex gnashed at her, his patience thinned by confusion.

"When you ask a question you only say 'who' unless there's a *to* or a *by* or a *for* in front of the 'who' you are asking about. They told us all of this during the tour when we were learning about all the rules of the school. Weren't you listening, Alex?"

"I wasn't there, Nyangi," he said. Then he mimicked her, "*two by four whom...*"

"Yes. So, *to whom*... get it?"

"Yes, yes, I get it." Alex said, regaining his equanimity. "So, that is exactly what happened *to whooom?*"

"Huh?" Now it was Maya's turn for confusion.

"Argh! Never mind!" said Alex, finishing the rest of a half-eaten loquat.

Maya sighed.

"The moon sounds beautiful," she murmured happily.

She had finished all her loquats, so she tossed all her seeds at the silent mermaid. The point of the game was long forgotten by the time the last seed bounced against the siren's left ear. At the base of her fin a cluster of loquat seeds floated in the upper tier of the fountain bouncing off each other in the tiny wavelets of the basin. Only one seed rolled about in the water at the mouth of the mermaid's pot. Maya shifted and leaned further against the stone basin and laid her cheek against her arm, listening to the moonlight dancing in the pond. Alex came around behind Maya and curled up beside her. Slowly, Maya fell asleep by the water, the weight of her body evanescing into dream.

The moonlight was sunlight and the pond was gone, transformed into the Great Lake beneath Maya's raft. She was sitting with her legs tucked beneath her on the floating vessel, just like she sat with Alex in their father's library, the sudden grown-up size of her body disorienting yet again. She was far away from the edge of the water, once again adrift, peering at her great-great-grandfather on the shore. Akoth sat beside her, looking out onto the bank where the parade was growing more distant. Although she could see the drifting procession, she could not see her father as Maya could.

"Mamma Akoth, he knows my name!" Maya said with an urgent whisper.

Akoth stopped singing. "Who?" she asked.

"Olóo. He knows my name," Maya said again, turning to her great-grandmother.

"How do you know, my child? How do you know he knows your name?"

"He's standing on the shore, calling me. There's a woman with him. I don't think she can see me. She looks just like him, just like you, just like Esther." Tugging at the edge of Maya's mind was a question that seemed out of place and strange. Where did Alex go? He was just here, next to her. She was quite sure they had fallen asleep as children at the mermaid fountain pond, lulled by the glimmering moonlight beams that played on the water that splashed from above. And even though she wanted to ask Mamma Akoth, who was now sitting next to her, the pull of the question relaxed a little. Tugging more insistently was the other immediate concern: *How does he know my name?*

Akoth, sitting beside Maya on the raft, herself weightless and immaterial, peered in the direction that Maya was looking, trying to see what her great-granddaughter saw. They were apparently in the presence of both her long departed father, and also her grandmother Nyanaam. But she could not see them, not like Maya could. If they were not in the world outside Time with her, and Anyango could see and talk to them, then… how?

"How?" she asked. "How can he call you?"

"I don't know. And the woman, she looks exactly like Esther. She's older, though. But not really by much. And she's next to him, but I don't think she can see me."

Suddenly Akoth understands. She thinks she knows why she cannot see what Maya sees. She realizes that she is witnessing Maya living a waking dream. The man and the woman – Olóo and Nyanaam — are still in the world of Time like Maya.

"Go, Anyango," Akoth says to Maya. "Go to them. Go to them, now."

A cluster of loquat seeds floats in the upper tier of the fountain, bouncing in the tiny wavelets, held inside the basin by an ornate ring of carved stone shells. The night is bright from the light of the moon. The air is clear, growing more limpid as it gently cools down over the grounds. Morning is still far away. Dew still has some time to gather on the hair and the skin of the sleeping child by the mermaid fountain under the moon.

Canto Fifty-four

Maya was not in her bed when the Matron came to wake everybody up.

"Girls! Get up girls!" the Matron called, "Rise and shine!" She rapped against the door and moved on to the next dormitory once she saw some of the girls stirring.

Esther woke up facing the side where Maya's bed lay. She imagined that her sister must have already gone to the bathroom, so she thought nothing of simply turning to wake Hehra up and prepare her.

Hehra sprang out of bed overflowing with excitement. It was their first day of classes and they would have morning assembly right after breakfast. They started their daily routine, stripping their beds down and making them up again. As they left to go to the bathroom, Esther noticed that Maya had not yet returned. Her bed was still unmade. Esther hastily pulled the bedcovers up to order and went with Hehra, making a note to remind Maya to tidy her bed first thing in the morning before doing anything else.

But Maya was not in the bathroom either and she was not in any of the tubs or the showers. Girls of all ages, from six to fourteen, were milling about in the hallways and in the bathroom.

Esther hesitated for a moment before approaching the Matron who had come to wake them up.

"Excuse me Miss Mugo, I cannot find my sister Maya."

Miss Mugo looked at her for a moment.

"Did you wake her up?" she asked.

"No, Miss Mugo, she was already out of bed when I woke up. I thought she had come to get ready in the bathroom, but I have looked for her and I cannot find her."

"Is she queuing up for the dining room?" Miss Mugo was slightly irritated. Nothing ever went as smoothly as it should.

"No, Miss Mugo. She did not make her bed this morning."

Esther wondered at the Matron's questions, how she could imagine any of them useful. She had thought that perhaps the Matron would be able to tell her where she could find her sister. It was clear now that Miss Mugo would be of little help.

Miss Mugo saw the other House Matron, Mrs. Kitur, approaching them.

"Eunice," she called. "This child cannot find her sister." She was now speaking in Kiswahili and not in English. She looked at her colleague helplessly, hoping that the older woman would know what to do. It crossed Miss Mugo's mind that if Mrs. Fonseca, the House Mistress, or Father Singleton, the Headmaster, heard that a child was missing, they – no, she – would be in serious trouble.

Mrs. Kitur, for her part, had three very small children of her own, so she no longer got excited about the unaccountability of the young. Children were rambunctious, impulsive, and imprudent. But despite all this, God favored them above all other creatures. She tried to reassure Miss Mugo, who she could see was beginning to panic a little. She asked Esther if her sister was sick in anyway, if perhaps she had gone to see the nurse early in the morning.

Esther said that she did not know. "She was fine last night before lights out."

"Don't worry so much." Mrs. Kitur repeated. "Sometimes girls get lost because they don't know their way around. But tell me, was she homesick? Did she seem homesick, or did she say she was homesick?"

"Maya does not get homesick," Esther said.

"What do you mean, is she OK?" Mrs. Kitur asked, absently intrigued by Esther's categorical answer.

"She is always happy, I mean, she does not get sad," as Esther said it, she realized that it was true. "I mean, she can get very serious or very annoyed, but she cannot, I mean does not get sad."

The more she spoke, the more she knew it sounded confusing. She was simply trying to make it clear that there was something about her sister that ruled out 'homesickness' as a motive for her disappearance – her absence, that is.

"OK, so maybe she went to see the nurse," Mrs. Kitur said, letting Esther out of an uncomfortable spot. "I will send a Prefect to go and look for her."

The Prefects at Union Saints were all appointed from the Upper classes by the Headmaster and they were responsible for helping younger students learn the rules of the school and keep them. Some of them took on roles as older siblings to the very youngest children who needed close guidance. Where several children were of the same family, the older siblings, without having to be Prefects, sometimes were assigned charge of their own younger brothers or sisters. Every child in Primary One had an Upper school mentor, and even some in Primary Two or Three who still needed help remained under the care of an Upper schooler until they found their feet. The beginning of each school term was easily the most difficult time for the youngest students, especially that moment when they had to bid their parents and other family goodbye.

With the power bestowed upon each Upper-class mentor by the school Headmaster and by their ward's parents, these Upper-class students gained tremendous power. Besides their everyday obligation to guide the younger children, they also enjoyed the privilege of holding the purse strings of the only currency that really mattered at the school: the treasury of sweets and treats that parents bequeathed their children as a parting gift. Some students started the term with a bounty of fancy cookies and candy and all kinds of goodies that were not of the sort available in the school's dining room kitchen. The ones with the richest endowment sometimes arrived with entire suitcases full of the most coveted sweet treats. Others had only just a little bit, and others still nothing at all. Whatever students brought with them was kept under lock and key, and withdrawals were only allowed on Saturday mornings for weekend enjoyment. Therein resided the power of the Prefects assigned wealthy charges.

Everyone, from the richly endowed to the completely destitute, all looked forward to this weekly allowance of sweets and treats. When the time came to open the treasury and draw out treats for their wards, the Upper-class guardians made certain to withdraw generously for themselves and their friends. Control over the bounty and access to it afforded these guardians the privilege of deference from others near them as everyone flocked around the storage room with urgent intensity to lobby for the favor of a morsel of "even just a crumb." In this respect Unions Saints mirrored the world of Empire. The more the Prefect mentors enjoyed of the younger children's treats, the tighter their power to impose their dictates on their wards became, ensuring that the young ones always bent to their will. Some of the very youngest ones had to learn to petition their prefect-guardians for their own treats, often reduced to begging, too, for "even just a crumb." Anna's intuition to send her children to a place that would train them to become the future leaders of the world was more prescient than she probably understood. For what better training to inhabit roles of power than to rehearse and to perfect the drama of exploitation?

In every corner of the world, *protectorates* and *colonies,* both the current and the late, all let the Prefect nations siphon off their natural wealth to build themselves inscrutable thrones with all the stolen bounty. Nobody wonders if it is a joke that all the most richly endowed by Nature have to beg for scraps to feed their children day to day. Nobody wonders if it is a joke that all the desperate destitute learn to never question the magnanimous benevolence of missionary nations who have turned them into beggars for the bounty of the land bequeathed to them by Heaven's grace. Nobody wonders if it is a joke that local native Prefects make the most effective agents of the Empire's control.

~~~~~~~~~~~~~~~~~~~~~~

Canto Fifty-five

The groundskeeper at Union Saints found a child sleeping by the fishpond at dawn and carried her to the Headmaster's cottage. When he arrived, Gloria, the Headmaster's wife, was in the kitchen near the window that overlooked the garden path in front of the house, smoking her morning cigarette. When she saw the groundskeeper approach carrying a child, she thought immediately that something unforgivable had happened.

"Luke! Luke! Come quickly! Oh, dear!" Cigarette forgotten, she jumped to the door and sped down the garden path to meet the groundskeeper.

"Muzeh' Abdul, what is the matter?" Her inability to say 'Mzee' properly endeared her to the small, wizened groundskeeper.

"Madame, I found this child sleeping in the garden," he told her, bowing slightly.

"Is something the matter with her?" She did not have her glasses on yet and could only just make out the shape of the child who had not stirred once in all the commotion.

Her husband came bounding down the lane, his body heavy, and his eyes still swollen from interrupted slumber.

"What is the matter?" He asked. His voice was a deep baritone that dipped into an even lower register in the wake of sleep.

"Muzeh Abdul said he found this child sleeping in the garden. Where in the garden?" she asked, turning back to the groundskeeper. "In which garden?"

"Madame, she was sleeping by the pond in front of the main office, in front of your office, sir." Mzee Abdul now turned to the Headmaster and bowed to him.

Father Singleton looked at the sleeping child, wishing for a moment that he too could sleep so soundly. He recognized her as one of his, but for the moment he could not quite place her.

"Luke, what are we going to do?" his wife asked, slightly less agitated now that her husband stood by her side, his bulk reassuring, his voice comforting.

Father Singleton then recognized the sleeping girl. She was one of the children that Anna Adongo, the smartly dressed young woman who had been their guest over the weekend, had just placed in their care.

"Dear, she's one of our new ones. Her mother and grandmother were just here." He turned now to the groundskeeper, "Muzeh, please bring her inside."

He led Mzee Abdul through the house to a small bedroom next to his wife's study. Inside there was a cot made up with flannel sheets, soft blankets, and an embroidered counterpane. He pulled back the covers and nodded to Mzee Abdul to lay the child inside. As Mzee Abdul put her down, she did not move, nor shift, nor stretch the way sleeping children were wont to do when they were laid in bed. Father Singleton sent up a silent prayer that the child was not unconscious but just in a very deep sleep. He pulled the covers over her, touching her cold skin and realizing that she must have been outside all night. There was dew in her hair between the braids, and the beads that hung from each braid were icy to the touch.

Luke Singleton asked his wife to stay with the child, and then he addressed the groundskeeper again, "Muzeh, please show me where you found her."

"Yes sir," said the old man, and they set out for the junior block.

When they arrived at the fountain, Mzee Abdul pointed to the side of the fishpond.

"Sir. I found the child there."

'There' was littered with already browning loquat peels and shiny seeds. Some partially masticated fruit, along with the white membrane that separated the umber seeds from the edible orange flesh was loosely discarded at the base of the fishpond. A clutter of ovoid loquat seeds floated in the upper basin of the fountain around the mermaid statue, and some rolled around in the lower basin. It looked as if the child, he still could not remember her name, had spent the night in an age-old school tradition of raiding the loquat trees and dunking loquat seeds. Word traveled fast, Luke Singleton thought, the side of his mouth rising in a reluctant smile. Mzee Abdul cleaned the pond every morning, so the little girl must have been quite busy since there was an impressive number of loquat seeds floating in the upper tier.

Father Singleton had been caring for children long enough to guess the motions of their young hearts. He could imagine a child going to remarkable lengths in the name of a small infraction like leaving the dormitory after lights out. The motives were always the same: raiding the loquat trees under the cover of darkness, and in the case of the older children — the ones in the throes of adolescent fervor — moonlit trysts with the impossibly idealized object of their affection. It was not unusual for the younger children to suddenly become too frightened to return to the dormitory in the dark, especially once the loquat raid and subsequent feast were over. Sometimes a matron, or a teacher, who lived near the junior block would receive a hesitant knock on their door from a suddenly squeamish child too overcome by fear of the dark to retrace his steps, or to cover her tracks. It always amazed Luke Singleton that a child could brave pitch darkness on setting out, and then remain paralyzed at the prospect of the journey back. All the same, this was the first time a child had been found asleep outside and effectively *in flagrante delicto*. Perhaps this child was a sleepwalker. The Matron would have to keep a careful eye on her.

In the two years that came and went with the children of Anna Adongo in his care, Luke Singleton remained perplexed about what ailed the middle girl. She did indeed seem like a sleepwalker, for they found her in odd places often. And she was a day dreamer, always distracted in class, her mind wandering off in the middle of a lesson. Yet her marks were excellent, even though she never completed her homework. She finished exams so quickly, it was as if she already knew the answers before the questions were even asked. So Father Singleton did not know what to do or what to recommend. What if he made her change her ways and her marks fell as a result? But what would become of her if the school never tried to teach her how to behave like every other child? He asked for advice, but nobody seemed to know what to do with the girl. So they left her alone in her own little world, a world where she seemed content and complete.

Father Singleton did not have to worry for long, because Ms. Anna Adongo, as she preferred to be called, took her children out of Union Saints Academy in the middle of their third year. They were leaving everything behind and going to America. All of their school friends envied the Ocholas. Going to America! What an adventure!

Canto Fifty-six

During those two months that Anna was away when they first got to Boston, the children settled into school. Maya attended classes for three days, and then had to stay home for four weeks because she became too sickly and weakened to go outside. Alex sometimes stayed with her and read to her all day long from David's books and from Esther's books. Sometimes, when Esther came back to find her sister awake and serene, she would describe their day at school, while Alex chimed in about the curious habits of the natives, making it sound as if he was reporting on an exploratory expedition.

They were incurious people, Americans. They didn't really inquire about where the 'Ocholas' came from, not like the children at Union Saints Academy had done. Funnily, though, instead of asking if they had cats and dogs, they asked if they had gorillas and giraffes in their yard. In America, a garden compound was called a 'yard' even if it measured more than a meter, Alex glossed. The idea that wild animals of the savanna would even want to go near people amused Alex and Esther both, and made Esther rather wonder about anyone who could imagine such a thing.

In the morning, the report continued, everyone rushed straight to their classroom at school – their 'home' rooms. They did not line up and go to assembly like they had at Union Saints. Nobody wore school uniforms. Everyone was dressed as if they were going to a Saturday end-of-term party. They even wore jeans and sneakers to class — that's what they called rubber shoes, Alex added helpfully — and they wore jewelry and watches. There were no fields and there were no hills, and in the neglected tennis court, paved and painted green, tufts of grass poked through the cracks in the tarmac and the seams of the net poles. Instead of hedges and wrought iron gates, the school was surrounded by wire fences, like the kind used for chicken coops at the Union Saints farm.

Besides not wearing school uniforms, American children spoke like adults. They talked about adult things and seemed to have very little interest in schoolwork. The teachers, though, were even more curious. They encouraged the students to call them by their first names, talked to them as if they were age-mates, and dressed as if they too were going to visit friends on a Saturday afternoon.

Esther liked French, Mathematics and Computer Science, all of which had the distinct virtue of being (mostly) free of local vernacular. She was miserable in the English and History classes, both too mysteriously provincial to grasp. They would have to reconsider the assumption that Americans spoke the English language, Alex quipped cheekily. The Geography teacher who hailed from Texas was densely incomprehensible. Esther had to continually ask someone to translate what the teacher had just said.

And it wasn't just the sound, the words even looked different. Esther was confused, and a little appalled, to get back compositions that she had carefully copied out in her best handwriting disfigured with red ink abridging 'humour' and 'colour' and 'neighbour' and 'honour', switching the letters in 'centre' around, and questioning her use of grammar – as if saying *'if I was'* were the same as saying *'if I were'*. It didn't help that every day, upon the giant poster billboards on the bus route to school, in television, and magazines, and newspapers as well, they saw many familiar words that looked somewhat strange, and which only whispered their provenance when spoken out loud. 'Nite' was altered 'night', 'lite' a lighter 'light'. And yet despite this general trend, 'mite' remained the opposite of 'might'. In school, students simply announced, 'I have to pee,' and left the room. Those who were somewhat polite just said 'O please, can I go?' — the answer to which surely only they and God, and no one else, could know.

One day, at the start of October, Maya asked Esther whether Christopher Columbus was Spanish or Portuguese. When Esther told her that she thought that maybe he was Italian, Maya stopped for a moment, confused, as if trying to reshape an idea she had been forming while waiting to confirm this last piece of information.

"Are you sure? Are you sure he wasn't Portuguese?" She asked, tired and curious.

"Mmm-hm. He was a sailor from Italy, but Isabel and Ferdinand sent him here from Spain in the Niña, the Pinta, and the Santa

Maria," Esther said. "But I don't think he went alone" she added. "There were probably a lot of Portuguese sailors with him."

"So the Portuguese are *not* the "Greatest Explorers in History"?" Maya asked.

"It doesn't matter," Alex interjected quickly. "Columbus only stumbled on America. Vasco da Gama and Bartolomeu Dias set out to find India by sea, and they did actually find India."

While Alex grumbled beside her, Hehra sat on the bed at Maya's feet, bouncing up and down chanting playfully, "In fourteen hundred ninety-two, Columbus sailed the ocean blue…"

She liked the sing-song rhyme. She especially liked the sound of the names of the three ships: nursery rhyme names that tasted like butterscotch sweets.

"Niña," she said, and waited two beats. "Pinta," she added, waiting again before finishing finally, "Santa Maria, Santa Maria, Santa Maria…" She let her voice fade out as if in echo, drumming out the rhythm on her lap and bouncing on the edge of the bed.

"Next week is Columbus Day and we don't have school on Monday," Esther informed them over Hehra's drumming.

"Can we go outside?" Maya asked, looking up at Esther.

"Yes, we can go to the playground behind us."

"Santa Maria, Santa Maria, Santa Maria, Santa Maria…" Hehra chanted, swaying her head and body from side to side.

It was the first time since Hehra had started going to a school — in her mind Kindergarten did not count — that she attended a day school. She had at first been a little bit disappointed that she would not finish her last term of Primary Three with her friends at Union Saints and move to the senior block for Primary Four. The transition from junior block to senior block was the first major milestone at Union Saints Academy, and Father Singleton hosted a huge party for the finishing Primary Threes at the end of the year to celebrate. But they had left for America at the beginning of September, one week into the third term, so Hehra would not be there for the party. Nor would Esther be there for the Primary Eight end-of-year festivities. Theirs was an even bigger party that lasted into the wee hours of the night and made up for all the compulsory nine o'clock lights-out they had heeded. But Esther did not seem to mind, so Hehra took her cue from her.

More than missing the junior Primary's final celebration, Hehra missed returning to Victoria House where she lived with all her friends as well as her sisters. It seemed strange to her to have to return to their own flat at the end of the day. But since Anna was away, the little apartment they lived in felt somewhat like a dormitory anyway, albeit a small one with no other children, but also no Matrons or House Mistress.

They spent the weekend before Columbus Day indoors, because it was too cold to go outside. The television weathermen were agog and aghast. Not before anyone could remember had the temperature been so low on Columbus Day weekend. The cold front was expected to pass over Boston quickly, though, and leave "a balmy Indian Summer" in its wake.

Anna's children did not yet have coats and gloves and other such winter clothes. Such attire at Union Saints, or in Kisumu or Nairobi would have been utterly superfluous and they had not yet learned to need them to face the arctic weather of North America. When Monday came, they tumbled out of the apartment, intent on spending their free day playing. A Monday without obligation was easily worth ten Saturdays together and could not in good conscience be wasted indoors. Esther made sure that everyone piled on sweaters and socks to keep warm, and raincoats and gumboots to keep out the cutting wind. Maya was in a tee-shirt she had been wearing for several days. Since her stomach no longer contained anything, she had been able to keep this one tee-shirt clean for a while. Her temperature was still high, and she did not want to put on layers of clothes, complaining that it would just make her hotter. Esther ignored her protests and dressed her in even more layers of shirts and pullovers than anybody else. By the time they were properly dressed they all felt too hot, Maya in particular, and even Esther wondered if she was overdoing it a little. They made their way to the playground in the middle of their apartment complex, expecting to find other children there, but instead found it deserted.

The chill was not as unforgiving as it had been over the weekend, and the sun shone quietly, almost hesitantly, through the morning cold. Maya took her raincoat off as she wobbled beside her sisters, grumbling that little streams of sweat tickled as they ran down her back. She then took off her first sweater and then her second and third sweater, eager to feel the cooling air against her skin. Finally, she had on nothing but her tee-shirt with the three pairs of trousers that Esther had made her put on – one corduroy, one denim, and one linen – and her gumboots. Maya's skin glistened from sweat and Esther thought that perhaps the fever had worsened.

Quite unexpectedly, small, feather-like icicles appeared in the air, languidly tumbling down from the sky. One by one, and then by twos, and then by half-dozens or so, flat, icicle flakes drifted downward. All the children squealed with delight to see the first snow.

"Snow! That's snow! It's snowing!" cried David, leaping in the air and pointing to the sky. Nothing they had ever seen or heard about snow could have prepared them for this weightless, untouchable thing that now fell so lightly from the heavens.

Maya stuck out her tongue as she did whenever it rained, willing the drifting flakes to settle on her mouth. But they fell erratically, cooling her heated skin where they touched down with featherweight pinpoint precision. Icy kisses landed on her eyelids, and some on her cheeks, others yet on her outstretched arms, making her flesh tingle as they vanished into the heat of her skin.

"Maya, here. Put your sweater on." Esther said to her, lifting Maya's outstretched arms and trying to thread them through the discarded sweater.

Maya paid no attention, her face turned upward to receive the falling crystals. Esther managed to get both her sister's arms into the sleeves of the pullover, but then had some trouble getting Maya's upturned head into the garment. She finally just covered Maya's head as if with a cowl for a moment before finally letting it poke through the pullover neck.

Esther looked at her sister's emerging face in amazement. It was shining again as it normally did. The listlessness that had rendered Maya's eyes unrecognizable had now vanished. The cheekbones that so mercilessly poked through her emaciated face now made her look a little bit less skeletal, and a little bit more like Mamma Akoth. Her skin, which an instant earlier had been gray and clammy, now shone taut, rapture emanating from every pore. Maya grew more elated watching the snow fall. Worried for an instant, Esther touched her sister's forehead. Instead of the febrile heat that she had come to expect, she felt only radiant coolness, nothing out of the ordinary. She decided not to dress Maya in her other sweaters, hopeful that the cool air was responsible for the clear improvement. All the children hurried back inside when suddenly hail began to fall, small and harsh and hard as if furtively swept out of heaven. The ice balls clattered against the pavement, against windows and doors, against car bonnets.

By the following day, Maya was in excellent spirits, eating heartily and playing around the apartment and with her siblings wherever Alex was. But for her marked thinness and deeply sunken eyes, now radiant with curious energy, no one would have ever guessed that anything had been amiss.

Book IX. Hehra

Where Maya steps out of Time and begins to learn how to follow the path of the Dream Walker. • In the trauma of giving birth, Hehra's fracturing psyche collects itself around the fantastic memory of a childhood stage production. • Olóo teaches Maya how the drought of memory has devastated the peoples of the Great Lake • When an elephant births a new calf, all the cows of the herd gather in a circle around until the calf can stand on its own. • Maya Anyango sings the naming invocation and the Song of Becoming that tells of the Wandering Walker of Dreams who forged the compass in an age before history. • Hehra's twins receive their names and inherit an ageless legacy.

Canto Fifty-seven

"Anyango, bih ka'e," Olóo called again. "Nam Lolwe will carry you."

The loquat seeds and mermaid fountain now long forgotten, Maya stood up on the raft and then, unquestioning, she stepped off onto the glinting, shimmering water of the Lake. Was it faith or fatigue? She could not say. She took one step, and then another, and then she walked toward Olóo. The thousand sun rays bouncing off the surface held her aloft, their immaterial photons seemingly forgetting that they could bear no weight. Everything was luminous and charged, a gentle tint of blue. The woman standing next to Olóo now seemed more clearly seated. Olóo himself was also seated, watching Maya come closer with every step.

"Anyango, this is my mother," he said, without taking his eyes off Maya.

"Where are we?" Maya asked.

"We are in my mother's hut."

"I was on the Lake with my great-grandmother," Maya said, sitting down cross-legged on the floor in the middle of the hut.

"I know. Akoth," he said. "My youngest child."

Maya's eyes widened, and then she broke out in laughter, her mirth glimmering through the room, making Olóo grin gleefully.

"Hmm…," she mused quietly. "My great-grandmother was once a child, too."

"And soon she will be born," Olóo said. "Very soon, I think."

The gaping stare of Maya's delighted surprise made him laugh again.

If only Alex could see this, Maya thought, with a tugging twinge of nostalgia.

"When? When will she be born? When? Can I see?" she asked.

"I don't know," he said. "Soon. Can you see when I am not here?"

Suddenly Maya remembered all the stories Akoth recounted about the day Olóo died, and her heart sank.

"But…" she started, and then she stopped, words refusing her thoughts.

Olóo kept his eyes on her, the luminous blue air brightening as his smile grew.

"But. I just. I just…" She felt disoriented again. The waking dream was going to pass. The dream was going to pass! The dream was …!

Without considering whether or not she could even touch him, or if she should even try, Maya reached out impulsively with both hands and clasped Olóo's forearms. The contact of their skin sent a violent jolt crashing through both of them. Olóo responded reflexively, gripping her forearms and gritting his teeth to bear the force of the quake, his eyes shut tight in pain.

"You will be fine," Olóo muttered, the words a whisper through the shock that was now making him tremble uncontrollably. "Stay close, don't worry."

Maya, too, reeling from the impact of this contact across Time, braced herself and let the violence pass.

"Why now?" she asked. "Why did it have to be now? Can we go back? Let's go back to yesterday, or even the day before. Please." Her voice broke in a sob.

"We are already yesterday," her twice-great-grandfather said, still holding her forearms tightly. "I remember still the cold flakes in the wind that pricked my burning flesh in a waking dream that I was too young to understand. You were in a place where ice fell from the sky like on the Mountain of God's Repose beyond the Great Valley. And you could not eat, and it broke your bones. We are already yesterday. And we are always tomorrow."

"We are always tomorrow," Maya echoed slowly, getting drawn into his gaze. A small memory of the first time she ever tasted snowflakes peeked through the folds of her mind, reminding her of a Monday spent playing outside in Boston with her siblings in the cold. Like so many other forgotten troubles, she did not recall the illness itself that ended with that snowfall, nor fourteen-year-old Esther's stifled panic that she did not know what to do to help her ailing sister.

"We are already yesterday," Olóo's voice was the sound of hope.

"We are always tomorrow," Maya echoes him again, her words pacing slowly.

"Before the song begins, we hope the melody will be..." Olóo nods gently to her.

"Before the song begins, we hope the melody will be..." Maya says after him.

"And once the song begins, the melody becomes," Olóo's voice is hypnotic.

"And once the song begins, the melody becomes," Maya mimics his tone.

"The melody is always there, hoping to be sung..." his voice modulating more clearly into song.

"And once the song begins, the melody becomes," Maya now concludes.

Olóo nods approvingly, and then continues on, "Once the melody becomes, the singer, too, becomes."

"And as the melody continues, so the singer too," says Maya.

"A Hope that has become a song, now becomes a Memory," Olóo proceeds.

"Memory is the song that once upon a time was Hope," Maya recapitulates.

"Memory is the song that once upon a time was Hope," Olóo now echoes Maya.

"We are already yesterday," she says, finally understanding.

"We are always tomorrow." Their voices have now melded and together grow silent.

Maya feels much calmer, appeased, yet awakened. Oh, how like Akoth Olóo sounds! Now a memory emerges of a ship afloat in the still, misty waters of the Atlantic, holding a bearing south and slightly east, but not too much. *Starboard!* the pilot cries. *Obrigado Frei João.* Why had she told Alex in the tub that the monk was called the *Son of the Mountain Lions?* But then another ship draws near, another time, returning now the other way, destined to deliver the same Frei João to the flames of The Inquisition.

Olóo, gripping Maya's forearms more tightly, looks into her eyes and speaks in a voice that will brook no dissent.

"There! Go. Anyango, go. Go now. Go now!"

Maya can feel all the lightning in the room pass through her body in tune with Olóo's command. *Go where?* His grip on her arms seems to hold her together, his gaze the anchor that is keeping every cell in its place.

"Go!" He says again, his grip tightening even more.

The ship! *The ship!* Maya thinks, pulling together the thought. *Go to the ship!*

Holding Olóo's gaze with her own, Maya begins to feel the tension ease inside her as her mind turns to the ship afloat in the dead of night in the Atlantic. She discovers Frei João de Sousa, he of the foggy caravel and the bright cross of the pilot's compass, *obrigado Frei João*. There is a gash on his head. It is no longer bleeding, but the bruise has turned a mangled, violent purple. *Who did this to you, Frei João? Where is your shepherd?* Maya relaxes even more, the lightning in her body filling up the small wooden room, the cabin. *Frei João!* Maya calls, startling him awake. *Miserere mei!* he mutters breathlessly. *Quick, get up! Let us go!* she calls to him. He jumps up from his slumber, and the chains binding his ankles and wrists slide off soundlessly. He wraps a cloak around his shoulder and rushes out behind her, tripping over something hard on the floor by the cabin door. Reflexively, he stoops to pick up the something, folding it into the sleeve of his cassock.

Maya is already descending into the lower decks when he catches up. She enters the cargo hold, and there she sees people — women, children, men — bound in chains and packed as if in wooden crates. The blue lightning surging through her crackles and hisses. As she passes by each captive soul, the shackles binding them hand and foot slide off, making no sound. Maya reaches the end of the cargo hold. *Is there anyone else?* she asks. *No*, heads shake. The captive souls are all together in this cargo hold. *Go!* Maya declares. And so it comes to pass that sixty-three souls who ran afoul of other men's preference for trinkets over justice slip the sentence of bondage.

Maya suddenly finds herself sitting in front of Olóo once again, holding the gaze of his luminous eyes. Her body has not moved, it is still all there, and yet the memory — of wading through the brackish waters of a mangrove swamp shielded by the night; of laboring with bated dread, climbing deeper inland, letting the forest swallow their tracks, emerging at last, in the mountainous heights into a forest glade where friends await and offer refuge, asking only the story of whence they came and of their lives — that memory is present.

"They called him *Tejo of the Lioness Mountains*," Maya says, smiling to herself, remembering her childhood folly.

Olóo nods, understanding. "You have done well, Anyango," he says, "you have done well, my child. Theirs is a quiet life, up on that Lioness Mountain. Some leave for a while, but soon they return when they have had their fill of the valley."

Yea, the valley of the shadow of death... death in iron and stone...

"I remember them all," Maya tells Olóo. "I remember as if I was actually there!"

"You did well, my child," is all he says in response. A veil lifts a little. Olóo traces the shapes of his own unborn daughter's face in the visage before him. Maya's sense that she is looking at Alex strengthens with every breath. If only he could see this.

"Where is Alex?" she asks, after a fleeting hesitation. There is nothing she wants to know more keenly. "Where is Opolo?" That is the name Mamma Akoth prefers, so maybe...

"You can find him," Olóo responds. "You will find him."

"I have looked for him everywhere... I don't know where else to look." Maya says, her voice catching. "I think... I think... he disapp... I lost him in Lisbon. Twelve years. I have looked everywhere. Where is he?" *How can I find him if I don't know where he is?*

"Do you have the instrument that Tejo of the Lioness Mountains gave you?" Olóo asks quietly.

"No. Wait... what? No... I don't know." A lingering gossamer veil of sleep is suddenly making it difficult to speak. Their arms are still entwined, each clasping the other. Is that where the compass came from? She is sure it was on the raft. But was it? It felt heavy. It vanished. It fell? "I... don't know," she repeats, convinced... convincing herself.

"Go and get it, Anyango," Olóo tells her.

Maya hesitates. If she goes back to the raft, will she be able to come back here? She really does not know how to cross in and out of waking dreams. They just happen, and then she has to sort herself out. *I don't know how to go back there...*

"I don't know how to go where I want to go..." she might as well confess. "It just happens. I don't know how to control this... these... I don't know how to find my way..."

"You do know how to find your way, Anyango. You did it just a moment ago," Olóo says, urging her to notice. "And you did very well, my child."

"But I don't know how I did it." Why won't he believe her? Once upon a time, maybe, someone could have taught her. But now, professionals would just prescribe pills or injections or confinement. What a gentle word, "confinement."

"Anyango, listen. You do know how. Listen." Olóo's touch and grip on her forearms is still feather light.

Maya holds her peace for a moment, trying to remember what she did before. He said *Go!* So she went... she went... to the ship... The ship. That was the last thought on her mind. *The ship.*

"I thought about the ship," she says, her eyes growing wider.

"Yes," he replies.

"But it took me there to another time." And she had thought of the Holy Office of the Inquisition. How could she remember something that she had never known? "When I was there before, the ship was sailing south. We walked on the deck in the fog. But just a moment ago, the ship was sailing north at another time. Frei João was in chains."

"Yes."

"But he wasn't in chains before."

"No."

"I don't understand. I don't know how to go back to the…"

"Listen." Olóo says. "The melody is always there, hoping to be sung…"

Maya repeats automatically, "The melody is always there, hoping to be sung…"

"And once the song begins, the melody becomes," Olóo urges. *Yes!*

"Yes," Maya affirms, "once the melody becomes, the singer too becomes."

"Yes," he says.

The melody becomes. Maya thinks, *yes. The melody becomes…*

Maya lets herself relax again. She thinks not of Now or Then or Later. She thinks only of the compass. The compass on the raft on the glimmering Nam Lolwe… the compass, she is sure, on the floor in the wooden room… in the admiral's cabin… in the mangrove thicket… in the swamp, in the hill… climbing up the mountain forest… keeping to a bearing … a bearing away from *the valley of the shadow of death* in iron and stone… *I will fear no evil…* the compass in a glade, in the clearing…

The compass dancing, drawing. *Surely goodness and mercy shall follow me…*

"They call him Tejo of the Lioness Mountains," Maya says, quietly.

"Yes." Olóo answers, his gaze growing keener, more luminous.

I shall dwell in the house of the Lord forever, Maya's ears echo…

He lives in the Mountain of God's Repose. No. Not that one. He lives in the mountain. He lives in the Lioness Mountains. He lives in the House of the Lord in the glade at the heart of the Lioness Mountains…

Maya's gaze is fixed on Olóo's, and his gaze is fixed on hers.

He seems to be saying something. *Hello.* Perhaps. *Say hello…?* Olóo's grip now tightens, and then tightens some more.

Go! he says, clearly, she can see, but she cannot hear. *Go now, Anyango. Go!*

Once again, lightning courses through Maya. She cannot look away from Olóo's eyes lest she vanish, atomized into photons immaterial. Her heart no longer beats. It trills.

Hello.

"Hello," Maya now hears her own voice again. She is in the doorway of a hut at the edge of a clearing in the forest that looks… *I have been here before.* Is it evening? No, it is dawn. No, it is evening. The light of the sun is fading, the sky browning all around. The sound of birds beckoning one another to repose resounds in the stilled wind of the air. The hut, reed-thatched and round, stands just behind a few other round, reed-thatched huts that gird a wide-open area where small children play around a group of women at work on the ground. *I have been here before. This is the House of the Lord. This is where Goodness and Mercy follow…*

A thin, brown, sinewy man, hollow eyes deep, stands before her, hair dressed in clay and nut oil and bound in reeds. He is old. Much older than she remembers. Yet it is him, *Frei João.* She speaks his name, "Tejo…"

The old man looks around to find standing before him the twice-great-granddaughter of his brother of waking dreams. She is exactly the same as she was a lifetime ago, clad in shimmering blue lightning, eyes deep and luminous, expectant, knowing. She has not aged a day, it seems. And yet when he first beheld her in his most callow youth, she was but a baby, barely four years old, it seemed, and happy, curious. They walked the deck of the São Raphael together, singing his favorite psalms. But when he, bound in shackles, saw her again in the Admiral's cabin, only three years had passed, yet she was a woman, fully grown, eyes as deep and luminous and sad as those he now beholds.

"Bem vinda" he mutters absently, marveling, his fingers playing with the beads of a rosary partially wound around his wrist.

Maya draws closer and their hearts embrace overflowing, old friends who have not seen each other in an age.

Tejo of the Lioness Mountains tells her of how his life and those of all the souls she spirited from the Admiral's ship have fared in the mountain village. She can see his children and the mothers of his children, and then among the youngest, even some of his grandchildren. The village has grown over the years, spreading deep into the forest, but they stay up in the mountain and as far away from the Portuguese who still stop in the coast and carry off those unhappy souls betrayed by kin and countrymen and sold for trinkets and flattery.

Maya speaks of her twice-great-grandfather, and his Song of Becoming. Tejo of the Lioness Mountains smiles when she says that even as they stand together, Olóo awaits the birth of his youngest daughter, Maya's great-grandmother. He can see, he tells her, that one day, she, too, will await the birth of a child who will learn from her, as she is learning from Olóo. Maya, now, can see what he sees, and so she tells him that the children she awaits are his descendants, those of them who find their way to the Lake at the eye of the Nile. Upon hearing this news, the old man approaches the doorway close to where she is standing. He reaches into a basket hanging from the door beneath which Maya appeared. He draws out from it a large, flattened, cylinder that never has left his side.

His face is radiant with joy, his body becalmed and at peace as he holds the ornate disk before her. He asks her if she remembers. Maya nods, tears stinging her eyes, recognition glowing in their depth. She remembers the compass. She wonders, *Don't I have this already?* Where, o where is Alex? She knows, and yet she still does not know. *How do I have this already?*

Give this to my kin, Tejo of the Lioness Mountains says, the compass aglow in his hands. *May it always keep my children and their children true, away from death and bondage, away from rage and boundless hunger, and from the blood and bile that putrefies the hearts of all the kings and captains of the land where I was born.*

He is gone in an instant, and Maya is once again looking into the glowing light of Olóo's eyes. Hovering in the air between their clasped forearms, the compass does not seem quite tangible. And yet the needle on the turntable whirls into a blur, undone by the lightning flowing around the two Dream Walkers.

Olóo's grip on Maya's arms grows a little more gentle without letting go. Maya notices that, for once, she is not disoriented.

A long moment passes, and the air grows more dim as Maya draws herself deeper into the moment in the middle of her thrice-great-grandmother's hut.

Olóo takes in the sight of her noticing for herself that she no longer feels lost.

"You did very well, my child," he says. "When you return, you must do something that I could not do. You must make it rain, Anyango. Ensure that the children do not lose their way."

Maya nods, wondering.

"A serpent ship comes," Olóo begins.

"No," Maya interjects quietly, "it is just a train."

"A serpent ship comes," he continues, "from the sea with the rising sun, and it tears through the land, burrowing the mountains and the hills, toppling the homes of every creature great and small in its way."

323

Maya is chastened. Listening. She knows this story well. Mamma Akoth has often told it. Esther, too, has told it. Even Hehra has been drawing pictures and making sculptures of the Myth of the Iron Serpent. Maya knows this story well, and yet, as Olóo's retelling turns into a song, she holds her tongue to hear him sing it now to her for the first time.

"A serpent ship comes," he sings, his voice a lamentation, "and the water runs bitter where it passes, and the rain burns through stone. Small ships follow, and their keepers feed them water and blood drawn straight out of the veins of the land. Now the air hangs bitter, too, and rain burns through flesh. Men work very hard to conjure more poisons from the blood and the bone and the stone that hold the roots of the land intact. If Lolwe, the Spirit of the Lake, abandons its poisoned home, no fishing boat will ever be safe, nor fisherman fill his nets and his baskets, if Lolwe flees in fear. Do you know that even fish will drown if they swallow so much poison? The serpent ships tear the land. The serpent tears at Time."

Slowly, understanding illuminates Maya's mind. "Just a train" is apparently not simply "just a train." It is a cascade of derangement cutting through the natural rhythm of ordinary life. But we are already tomorrow.

"We are already tomorrow," she says, once her great-grandfather's voice falls silent. "What must I do? What can I do?"

"Keep the children close," Olóo says. "Teach them. Walk with them so that they are not lost in the Valley of the Shadow of Death."

"But I don't know how," Maya says, feeling the lightness of her own futility.

"Use this instrument," Olóo directs her, "forged by the Wandering Walker of Dreams who walked the world of Time in an age long before I was born. One day, in a dream at dawn, she saw the monsoon winds carry the ship that brought Tejo of the Lioness Mountains from the land of his birth all the way to the bed of his death. The Wandering Walker's heart was deep, her thinking luminous and wise. And so, to guide all those who lose their way, she carved a map into the brass sheet of this instrument and made its needle from the iron veins of the land beneath our feet."

"It doesn't work" Maya says. "I tried, but I can't make it work properly. Compasses are supposed to point North, but no matter which way I turn, it only points straight at me."

"Yes, I know, my child. It comes from the veins of the land beneath our feet."

Olóo really is too much like Akoth, because now he sounds even more enigmatic.

"I don't understand," Maya confesses. "How do I find my way if the compass will not show me where to look? I just want to know which way to go."

"Yes, I know. I know, my child. Open your eyes and listen."

He loosens his hold on Maya's forearms and pulls his own hands away from her searching grip, unleashing all of the storm that together they have been holding at bay. Maya, pulled into Time once again, is suddenly knocked backward. She strikes her head against a stone wall, confused, distressed, unprepared for the dream to break so abruptly. In his mother's hut Olóo, too, chases his breath for a moment, his sudden fall backward softened when his mother's arms catch him and then hold his head on her lap.

Outside, thunder shakes the earth, and lightning cuts through the darkened sky. Furious winds fling the falling rain hard against the walls of the hut, beating wildly upon the roof thatch. Insulated within, Nyanaam holds her son's glowing head, willing the trance to pass, and for her son to return to her once again. But intuition tells her that Olóo has finished his own Song of Becoming. Now, another voice will come to sing the songs that await to be sung.

~~~~~~~~~~~~~~~~~~

Canto Fifty-eight

Maya stumbled and then steadied herself, the hard column behind her letting her lean on its cold, unyielding might, her head smarting where she had slammed it against the stone. Her mind, still drawing back into Time, pulled her into the cathedral, weaving together threads of history drawn from her waking dream. She peered across the aisle at Vasco da Gama's richly dressed figure, and suddenly she was suppressing the monstrous wave of nausea that assailed her. By everybody's measure he had earned the honor of resting in peace in Santa Maria de Belém. It was apparently a meaningless detail that he simply took where he could not purchase, charm, or persuade. Surely, it no longer mattered that, to prove his might and that of his God, Vasco da Gama had taken all of the merchant cargo from a ship of pilgrims, and bound up in the holds all the babies, and the mothers, and the fathers, and the brides, and the grooms, and all the crew traveling home from Mecca, and then burned them all to ashes when he set their ship ablaze in his righteous conflagration. The wailing screams that rang in Maya's ear had long ago died into silence. The stench of burning flesh and blood and peat and straw and wood had by now dissipated in the air of the world and could no longer really choke her. She made herself draw in deeper breaths, quelling her revulsion. For now, she would just be a tourist. She would admire the enormous soaring columns that reached up into the vaults of the church and spread their fingers to fortify the great cathedral's petrified skeleton. She would marvel at the finely carved ashen stone that gave Santa Maria de Belém its bone-dry starkness from without. She would celebrate the golden light filtering through the glass rosette to warmly glow inside the church.

"Here we have two of the most remarkable figures of the Portuguese renaissance, both dreamers and explorers in their own way…" the German tour guide was saying, assured that her flock was securely positioned around the poet Camões.

We. How vast! A river whose beginning touched its end for eternity, indeed. The German tour guide offered the history of Portugal and all its past glory as the story of humanity. The gaping wink carved into the poet's perpetual stone head made Maya uneasy. Was the misery of History just some private joke to him?

"For want of an eye…" she sighed, looking at the petrified poet, her voice subdued, as if divulging a violent and sensitive secret whose very weight weakened and bent her will.

"How can you say that?" Alex said to her, suddenly loud, irritated, and perhaps a little hurt by his sister's clear dismissal of a figure he so revered. "Everyone saw a lot of action back then!" he cried, "and many of them made painful sacrifices."

Maya was startled to hear her brother's voice once again. Of course, she was not thirty here, she was only eighteen again! They were once again in Lisbon, the air unmistakable, soaked in musty fetor. They were finally visiting the tomb of Vasco da Gama, along with his laudator Camões. Alex had not vanished yet, not yet, and yet she held the memory of the heartbreak of a dozen years, losing him and then searching, searching for his Spirit in vain.

She took in the sight and sound of him now, her heart brimming with — she knew not what. She wanted to tell him that he was right, even if only because she had missed him so. She wanted to say she was sorry! Why had she wasted so much time grieving when she could always find him here? Find him anywhere in Time? She wanted to say, *Oh, what did she know anyway?* Eighteen was still but the age of a child. He had tried so very hard to draw her out, in everything they did, to get her to let herself enjoy the petrified greatness surrounding her. How could he know that it was not just the memory of a dozen years, but of dozens of generations that kept her from playing along?

Maya thought that at least she could concede that no one, it seems, could really escape "the action." Every story Alex told her about his most beloved poets recounted how they were always induced to sing by wars. Sometimes it was a war of hope, a war of faith, a war of love – all myths that, like the wind, no one had ever seen, their presence betrayed only by how they moved the tides of the hearts of men. Sometimes the war remained within the single man's breast, wreaking havoc only on his mind, or only on his soul. But sometimes war spilled out onto the land, and the air, and the sea. Then just the soul was not enough, it wanted tithes of flesh and stone. When clarions sounded their call to serve the needs of empire, what man did not answer and offer whatever was able and whole of his body — his hands, his legs, his bowels, his eyes — in faithful sacrifice. What prince did not send his subjects hence to hold the walls of his realm? And were poets not also just men? Why else would they shoulder the burden of singing of war, of rage, of loss, of doubt, and painting it all as glory? Nothing new could come of war, it seemed, except the songs of poets.

And oh, how different from infantry soldiers war-singing poets can be! Theirs is the province of words, of song. They wield such instruments as untangle Despair and Hope in the muddled minds of men and lend their thwarted souls a voice. For although words bear no corporeal weight and leave nothing to the touch, these insubstantial specters cut more keenly than the most cunning blades, invoke whole worlds to haunt the dreams of mortals, and ignite rage in the meekest of breasts. However, it was the sword, and not the word that had blinded the eye of Camões, and crippled the hand of Cervantes. Yet together, these Iberian cousins, and others of their ilk, by the sheer power of their quills could draw the mind of the world, Old and New, to a singular notion of Beauty and Truth. For even those who raged against the ravaging conqueror conceded the beauty and truth of his Arts. From the Realms of Dawn's Abode, through the Land of the Fifth Sun, Humanity rose in applause at the might of the pen, even at the heart of the Lands of the Nile.

What song might Camões have sung, had he not let his silences cover the true thrust of the wars his hero waged against all the children of God? What greater life sublime might Europa have found for herself had she stayed the sadistic hands of her blunt butchering sons, her blithe, blighting daughters? What friends and kin might she have made had she not let them terrorize the world? She sent them out, invoking the names of God, and Gold, and Glory in galleons, and carracks, and man-o-wars, and when they arrived in distant shores, some did so by design, riding the back of the monsoon winds, sailing currents tried and true. Others washed ashore by chance, riddled with scurvy and dying of thirst, expelled by the deep salt sea. And with them they brought their serpent machines and turned men into moles that made poison of the blood of the land. *Trailblazers!* Alex loved to say. Yes, trailblazers leaving nothing but ash in the wake of their conflagration.

Perhaps it had always been Olóo – and not Mamma Akoth – bending her ear to show her behind the veils of History's public face. Mamma Akoth was fond of saying that her father had seen and felt the pain of the world much too deeply. The stories Nyanaam told about him were warnings, quite unlike the triumphant myths that Alex so loved to share. Maya looked up at her brother smiling, clearing the ghosts from her mind. Seeing the shadow lift from her eyes as she returned to him, Alex slowly relaxed and stood quietly for a while. He was by now used to the ebb and flow of Maya's musings, and ordinarily he let her drift off alone, hopeful that she would return quickly. But every once in a while, like this time, it frustrated him that he could not go with her where she went when she left him.

The murmur of shuffling feet and hushed conversation rustled just beneath the punctuated voice of the German tour guide who, long forgotten by Maya, but intent in her charge, led her flock around the poet's tomb and then across the aisle toward the illuminated Admiral. Maya pressed even closer to the stone wall near the poet, eager to avoid getting swept up in the whirling current of Germans, her ear closing to the tour guide's voice shepherding the group away. A new other gaggle, clad in identical caps, armed with cameras and folding maps, entered the cathedral trailing just behind an English guide. Once the aisle was clear to pass, Alex and Maya left the church.

Canto Fifty-nine

"Do you know where you are?"

Hehra opened her eyes when she felt a hand on her forehead.

Pots and pans!

"Mrs. Akoth, do you know where you are?"

No! I'm not Mrs. Akoth. Ogot, my husband's name is Ogot. She no longer had the strength to speak. She did not want them to confuse her with someone else. *I am not…*

"Mrs. Akoth, you are in the hospital. You were brought here because you went into labor. Your doctor's office in Kisumu has been trying to reach your husband and we will keep trying."

The voice was gentle, but firm, telling her things she only wished could actually come to pass. Hehra wanted to laugh. She could not talk quite yet, and she could barely see even though her eyes were finally open again. And she was thirsty. *Water.*

"Water. Please."

Somebody heard her. Or at least understood. She felt a cup touch her lips and then cool, tasteless liquid flowed into her mouth – just enough for her to swallow. She would not die of thirst. She opened her mouth again, and the cup touched her lips again. How could such fatigue be? She could not even raise her head; she was so tired. And the twins were still inside her womb. She wondered whether they were as tired. She guessed they were even more enfeebled by their labor to come into the world. Her body clenched in agony just as she was sipping some more water and she did not notice the water gush from her nose. Someone held a towel to her face and wiped her forehead and told her she was almost there. The boys were almost there.

Push.

Breathe.

Haraka haraka haina baraka.

Pole pole ndiyo mwendo.

Was that Mamma Akoth?

"Mamma Akoth!" Hehra panted. "Akoth!"

"Yes, you can do it, dear. Don't give up now. You can do it."

The voice again. Firm and gentle – a professional voice. A Texan voice? Her geography teacher from middle school in Massachusetts, the rectangle state with a curly cue. What was a Texan woman doing teaching geography in Massachusetts? For one very small moment, Hehra thought of something other than the pain that pulled at her body. "That's right, madame. Just breathe into it. Just let them come, yer doin' good."

And now she no longer recognized the voice. It changed to become a parody of her Texan Geography teacher. A welcome trick. No, a Japanese voice? The boys would be here any minute, and Hehra wanted Esther and Maya and Solomon more than anything.

Pots and pans! Maya—Esther—Esther.... Where are we? Hehra did not care.

"Please call my sister," she said to the professional Texan Japanese voice. No, a Kikuyu voice? "Maya Anyango. She lives with me. Please call her, tell her where I am."

"Is she authorized to make medical decisions for you?" the voice asked.

Thou shalt not make unto thee any graven image, or any likeness of any thing that is in heaven above, or that is in the earth beneath, or that is in the water under the earth. Thou shalt not bow down thyself to them, nor serve them: for I the LORD thy God am a jealous God, visiting the iniquity of the fathers upon the children unto the third and fourth generation of them that hate me; And shewing mercy unto thousands of them that love me, and keep my Commandments.

"Is your sister authorized to make medical decisions for you?" the voice asked again, patience persistent in its professional folds.

Hehra did not understand immediately. She would later. Now it sounded like a rote question to her. "Yes. Yes. Please call my sister. Call my mother-in-law."

What *was* a Texan doing teaching Kikuyu geography in Massachusetts Japan?

Honor thy father and thy mother that thy days may be long upon the land which the Lord thy God giveth thee.

How could she keep that Commandment so often repeated by Mrs. Da Silva, Mrs. Fonseca, Mrs. Kitur, Father Singleton, that Commandment that continued to loom so large in her life? Hehra was filled with dread. Did God exonerate the father and the mother from honoring their children? If she honored her mother and let herself accept becoming like her, would this be the end of the life she desired? If instead she refused to be like her mother, would she be breaking God's law and dishonoring her parent? Would her days be short upon the land, the world into which the eye of Heaven had caused her to rain? O, how God, the God of Mrs. Da Silva, the God of Father Singleton, was unjust! Or was God just so inscrutable? In her long memory Hehra could find none of her kin that had so hated Him that He should visit such iniquity upon them. Unless their affliction, though not of their own doing, so offended Him that He purposely let them languish in ignorance of what so many others seemed to know, seemed born knowing, but that she had only just discovered. Hehra sobbed for the first time since her labor began. She wanted Esther. And Maya who still said 'inquinity.' Hehra laughed.

Inquinity! The clangor of a dozen metal pots and pans falling and tumbling ring loud in her ear. *Mother Mary, help me!* Terror seized her in fits, pierced her twisted rapture, urged her to stop her twins from emerging, to shelter them as one with her in body, to bless them and keep them holy, to repudiate the bonds of inherited pain, the habit of hopelessly scratching for lost needles that could never be found. But she had no choice, even if they were taking their time to finally arrive. Had they been girls, even just one girl, they might have come into the world of Time more quickly, impatient to discover the river of Now. Where boys were languid, happy to sleep and be carried everywhere and always kept safe, girls arrived with exclamation, ready to share and declare and proclaim the truths that Heaven whispered to babies while paving their way to the world of Time. Girls might have already made their appearance, ready to make Hehra coo, and hum, and laugh under her breath with infinite joy, like Esther said her mother had done when she brought baby Hehra from Sierra Leone.

<hr />

Canto Sixty

"Pots and pans, pots and pans, who will buy my pots and pans?" The stage instructions are clear, but I cannot deliver my lines without giggling. "Pots and pans, pots and..." The sing-song phrase dissolves into peals of laughter.

"If you can't say a simple line, you'd best just step down, young lady!" The drama teacher is decidedly not amused.

"Pots and pans." Not so bad.

"Pots and pans!" Better.

"Who will buy my pots..." Impossible to continue.

Nine-year-olds on stage are a spectacle to behold. At no other time will you find us so unencumbered by our condition as actors. A few years younger, and we are still too dependent — on parents, on guardians, on siblings, on teachers. Our tongues are weak and our minds still unformed; liquid wax absorbing all, fixing nothing, perhaps. A few years older and the wax has cooled, slowly setting permanent molds. Awareness of being an autonomous self weighs on the consciousness ever so slightly, every word uttered meaning exposure to measure and to judgment. Babies, though weak, are not so weak for they cannot speak for themselves and know neither forgiveness nor blame. With age come strength and choice and shame; the voice grows sharp, *J'accuse...! J'accuse...!*

The sacred age? Seven to eleven. Both prime numbers, separated by the distance of a perfect square, in the middle of which lies the perfect square, although some might argue that a century is the perfect square. I am inclined to favor the square of a prime, of Trinity, whatever you will. To me they are magical numbers all. It is a fleeting time, full of the charm of a world whose every part is sound; whose every face a friend; and every foe yet unknown. And this nine-year-old world knows the sound of the merrily sonorous voice of God Nyasaye that sings all into Becoming.

Who indeed will buy my pots and pans? If anyone needs pots, surely, they know to come here for them. And should they need pans, same reason applies. Why the need for so much commotion when everyone knows that for pots and pans the place to go is the market? Then I might quietly sit by my pots and simply wait for the passing buyer. I might play silently with my pans or warm my feet by the fire. I might hum a tune, or blow upon a whistle, toss a marble, or maybe more. And then I might look up when called upon and offer some advice when asked. Then I might say, perhaps what you need are not in fact a pot or a pan, but rather a plate and a bowl, a cup and a gourd. Might we not, instead of crying, sing? Or simply say hello? For surely if someone comes to market for pots and pans, he should know where to find them without needing to be told.

But that is not how the story goes. The play calls for a noisy place with vendors shouting high and low, trying to outdo each other with their mighty, mighty cries. Here we have some fresh laid eggs! Over there some honeycombs! Just beyond a mound of charcoal blocks, the rows of maize and beans! Kids, lambs, roosters, tortoises! Alligator, catfish, cured Nile Perch! Cotton, wool (?), and piles of rice! Pepper, onions, mangoes and spice! Every sound and every smell that ears can catch and noses tell fills the air through and through. Or so we make believe.

Agnes Day, the best of us all, knows to twist and turn her nose, shake her head and haggle, and haggle, all to save some of her coins of silver and of gold. Agnes Day is a charm to behold. She is living beauty, full of joy, but not the kind that is worn for show like a garment offered and traded for love. She moves without art and speaks plainly, unknowing how all she does moves the unquiet soul. For that reason alone, she is the best among us. At nine years of age she is the perfect age and we all love her beauty.

Is that all you'll give me auntie, she asks, pained that her children will eat less today. Her children? What children? She is only nine! Her son (who is seven) rubs his tummy and echoes the words of his make-believe mummy, *is that all you'll give us, auntie?* Nehema, Sophia, Fredrick, and Ibrahim play the part of bartering villagers and so have all been transformed. Nobody wants my pots and pans, no one will buy my pots and pans.

So why should I cry out for pots and pans which nobody cares for and nobody wants? When they will want them, when they will need them, surely, surely, they'll know where to go, for it is to me that they'll have to come because before me laid out in rows, dangling from hooks and piled up behind are dozens and dozens of pots and pans. I wonder, as I offer my lines: How did I get all these pots and pans to the market all by myself today? And must I return with all of them home, and must I return with them here again? What if I sell every pan here today, what will become of my part in the play? Perhaps I shall have to ask for them back: Will anyone sell me their pots and pans?

The teacher is not amused, I see. But has he thought of the trouble I see? Where did he get all these pots and pans? True there are none, only fictions of crockery. Still, his mockery stings when my only job is to sell all my pots and hopefully also all of my pans. Pots and pans, pots and pans, who will buy my pots and pans?

"If you cannot play a simple part, please remove yourself from my heart, my stage!"

'My stage' he says. His stage, his heart. But am I not the one on stage, and does that not make this stage my own, even more so than his? The costumes are his, the props are his, even the make-believe pots are his, and pans which clang in their make-believe clutter as they make-believe fall to the ground are all his. Agnes, clutching her hungry boy, makes her way around the make-believe mess.

"Pick them up!" the action stops. The teacher has seen, as Agnes had seen, the pots in a pile on the floor. I look to him, and look to her, and wonder, could it really be so?

"Pick them up. Yes, just like that. Agnes, that was very well done."

Agnes smiles, the world is sound. I try to chase a straying pan that rolled too far from my stall.

"Where are you going? What are you doing?"

"I'm trying to pick up the ones that rolled and rolled too far from my stall."

"You're reaching too far. There's nothing there. Don't just make things up! Somebody...!"

337

Don't just make things up? I look at all my glistening pans and listen to all the clatter they make. You cannot just make things up, he says, you have to follow the script, he says. I do not recall any talk of pots crashing about and have no memory of pans rolling away. But Agnes acted as if they had crashed, and so I acted as if they had rolled, but it would seem that only so much may be made-believe on somebody else's stage.

"OK. Pots and pans..."

"You don't have to say it all the time. Once or twice is enough."

And now it is I who am not amused. This world makes no sense at all to me. First you invent, and then you do not. Suddenly hungry children abound. Well, actually, only one hungry child. There is a market where there is none, and bartering villagers where there are none. Agnes moves and therefore makes the make-believe world, as only Agnes may do.

I look at my pots, and I look at my pans. Now they are silent, now they are mute. Agnes Day, the Mother of God, leads her boy through the marketplace. She has saved him from Herod and now he will grow and grow in strength and wisdom. One day soon she will lose him, only to find him in his Father's house, advanced in strength and wisdom and age and grace with God and men. She will scold him for worrying his mother, and he will remind her that all is well in the House of the Lord forever.

I look at the slowly retreating figure of Agnes Day and wonder, does she know? Does she know that her precious boy will someday hang from a tree for the salvation of man, as they say? For now she has saved him from tumbling pots, and he is fairly safe from falling pans. But that will mean nothing when he is conscripted to give up his life simply because he can.

Mother Mary, come to me!

Canto Sixty-one

Hehra woke up, if waking up it could be called, from the fevered dream of clanging pots to find both her sisters in the armchairs near her hospital bed. Esther was asleep with a large, colorful book splayed across her lap, while Maya had curled up in a bundle in the low armchair at the foot of the bed. Gone were the crushing pangs of labor, the pressing weight of undelivered twins. All that remained was a bloated swell and an unfamiliar numbness.

"Where are they," she said, not even as if asking a question. Her voice was frail and thin.

Esther shot up in her chair and jumped to Hehra's side. Maya wheeled around the bed and came to stand slightly behind her older sister next to Hehra.

"Welcome back, mamma!" Esther said gently, placing the palm of one hand on Hehra's forehead and the other one on her cheek. "Welcome back, my dear."

"Esther, where are they?" This time it was a question. "Are they okay? Are they alright?"

"Yes, my dear, they are wonderful."

"Where are they?"

"They are with grandma now. She's in love with them."

"She's here?"

"Yes. In the NICU, with Uncle Aaron."

"Is MaAnna here?"

"Yes, she went to the gift shop, and then I think to the cafeteria. You were asleep for a while, my dear."

Hehra relaxed into her pillow, her eyes heavily beckoning sleep.

"Where are they? Can I see them? Can I see them? Can I see them, please?"

"Yes, yes, dear," Esther replied quickly. "As soon as you feel up to it, the nurse can help us take you to see them."

"Hehra?" Maya interjected.

Hehra turned to look at her in reply.

"Hehra, how do you feel?"

Hehra nodded her head feebly. "I am fine," she said, "but I can't feel my tummy at all. I don't think I can feel my legs."

She tried to waggle her body, but only her upper torso moved.

"It's okay," Esther told her. "The doctor said not to worry if you woke up and you couldn't feel anything down below your waist. They numbed everything for the Cesarean, but you'll start to have feeling again soon."

"Why did they do a C-section? I was doing everything right."

"The labor went too long and when you got too tired, she was worried that you were becoming delirious, that your blood pressure was getting too low. We had to consent to the operation to help you and the boys along safely."

Esther was choosing her words carefully, selecting only the lightest ones. She was glad that MaAnna was still somewhere away. Dramatic, emotionally fraught accounts of how close to death Hehra and the twins had come could wait until much, much later.

"Where are they? Can I see them." Hehra was exhausted, unable to hold a coherent thought, except for those of the babies.

"Hehra, they are beautiful," Maya said to her.

Hearing that, Hehra closed her eyes again and let herself drop into sleep.

Esther sat down on the armchair closest to Hehra's pillow and took up the discarded storybook. She opened it to a page somewhere in the middle and started reading to Hehra a story of how the People came out of the Nile. She read slowly and quietly, sometimes lost as if to herself. She would stop every once in a while to look at Hehra sleeping, and then she would resume reading again.

Maya listened, smiling. This story, too, she knew it well. Of how they came leading their livestock, with their children ahead and their elders behind. Drifting off just enough to leave the world of Time, she turned her will to the west, calling to a Spirit from far away, unsure whether what she was trying to do would actually work.

Hehra woke up again after a few hours. This time MaAnna was waiting and she showered her daughter with kisses, praising God for his bountiful mercy in seeing her baby and her grandbabies through the ordeal of their lives. Hehra was deeply humbled and grateful to see her mother. How could she have thought ill of her? God's grace was indeed bountiful. MaAnna proudly showed Hehra the army of pink pastel animal toys she had brought with her from the gift shop. She cooed and hummed and kissed her child and told her that she had done wonderfully well. The boys were beautiful beyond measure, and healthy, and robust, and loud, and strong.

The pain was beginning to make itself felt everywhere below Hehra's waist. On her back, where the needle had pierced her spine, she felt a focused soreness. Down at the bottom of her belly the soreness was more broadly spread, but it thrummed to the beat of her pulse where the incised flesh had been sewn back together again. Both aches made her move gingerly, forcing her to shift her body with bated breath, especially when the nurse finally came to take her to see her newborn babies.

The trip to the NICU was the longest Hehra had ever taken. The corridors were long, the corners far too sharp, the wheelchair painfully slow. The lights illuminating the halls made them seem longer and even more vacant. By the time Esther rolled to the door of the room where her two babies slept in adjacent hospital cribs, Hehra was ready to jump up and run, but her surgical wound constrained her. Before they could let her into the room, the nurse explained to Hehra, she had to wash her hands and face and then put on a tissue gown, all of which protracted the eternity that still kept her from meeting her two babies. Finally, her hands and face washed and dried, her tissue gown properly laced, the nurse rolled Hehra into the room to meet her twin boys. Thankfully, the hospital cribs were just low enough for her to reach in without having to stand from the wheelchair. Before the nurse laid one baby on her left arm and another baby on her right, Hehra moved to the high-backed armchair that stood by the nurse's white board. Both of her babies smelled wonderful, the smell of joy distilled into nothing else but joy.

Everyone who accompanied her was asked to stay outside the room. Anna stood next to Rebecca, both of them silently bonding as grandmothers. Esther stood beside Maya, her arm wrapped around her sister's shoulder. Next to them, Mamma Akoth, too, stood outside the room, unseen by all but Maya. Aaron and Jonathan would soon be back, and no one had spoken to Gabriel yet. Ma Ruth was away in Homa Bay and she would come up to the city in a few days. David had long ago vanished without telling anyone where he had gone.

"When an elephant births a new calf," Mamma Akoth said to Maya, "all of the cows of the herd gather in a circle around until the calf can stand on its own."

Maya smiled and looked at her kin – her youngest sister inside the room holding her newborn twins, and outside the door two grandmothers, two aunts, and the Spirit of their matriarch. Yes, *when an elephant births a new calf, all of the cows of the herd gather in a circle around until the calf can stand on its own.*

After waiting outside for a while, the grandmothers left to get some rest and promised to come back soon. The nurse then said that since there were only three of them left there together, the aunties could also go inside, as long as they washed up and put on the paper hospital gowns. And so, for a few minutes all three sisters gathered around Hehra's boys. None of them wanted to leave that room, Maya, apparently, least of all. But soon Hehra insisted, echoing the nurse, that the babies also needed to rest. Together they all returned to Hehra's room, a journey somehow much shorter than the one they had taken to see the twins. Hehra's heart was full of everything she had ever known to feel.

"Sol," she said under her breath, as Esther wheeled her along back to her room, "our children are doing wonderfully well."

Canto Sixty-two

The sun was departing and the settling dusk delivered the twins of their first day's toil in the world of Time. Esther got to work making phone calls to inform family and friends everywhere that mother and sons were flourishing. Maya helped her for a while and then went to the hospital courtyard to see if she could catch a glimpse of the painted sky. It was a large, open garden, the courtyard, crisscrossed with footpaths between facing wings. Benches adorned with name plaques standing on the grass near the paths beckoned Maya's tired legs. What a wonderful evening, she thought, today is my first day as 'auntie.' There were no patients out in the hospital courtyard, just a few doctors and nurses, some in pairs, and some alone, and only one small group of four by the surprisingly baroque fountain near the middle of the garden. Maya approached them, attracted by the fountain, and then she walked a little bit more around. Anyone watching her might have noticed that she was listening to the water as she circled. The fountain was laid out in two scallop shell tiers, a mermaid holding a round clay pot seated upon the upper tier. From the downturned pot she held, water trickled and splashed into the basin where she sat, and then spilled over the rim to the tier below. The sound of the sparse cascade under the lamplit night of the hospital garden called to Maya, inviting her into the water, but the small group of doctors standing near the fountain kept her at bay, forcing her instead to take the bench directly opposite the fountain. No sooner was she seated than she heard a familiar voice next to her. Maya sat up straight.

No. This was a joyful day. This was a joyful evening. *I don't want this dream. Not today! I don't have the energy to fall ill again…*

"Anyango, listen," the voice of Olóo.

She could not ignore him now that he had spoken up in the world of Time.

"Baba!" she said, opening her eyes and turning to him. "How are you here? I lost you in Lisbon, a long time ago. And then I lost Alex in the stone sea. How are you here?"

"You are not dreaming, my child," Olóo said.

Sitting on the bench with Olóo, Maya saw Mamma Akoth, and next to her, Alex as well.

"Alex!" she cried, "where have you been? Where did you go?"

"Do you really not know where he has been?" Olóo asked, as both Alex and Mamma Akoth nodded gently.

Maya shook her head. There was still so much she did not understand, not just about her waking dreams, but also about the persistent presence of Spirits beside her, unseen by all others.

"At least tell me," she said to Olóo, "why you are here now. You died long before I was born, and yet I never saw you except in my dream on the day that you died."

"Yes, but I am always with you. Every day, from the day you were born. Daily."

"Yes, I know, but those were just echoes," Maya complained. "I didn't even know it was you until it was too late."

"Anyango, it was never too late. We are always yesterday."

"And we are already tomorrow," she said automatically.

"Yes. Before the song begins, we know the melody will be." Olóo intoned.

"And once the song begins, the memory starts to become," she responded reflexively, surprising herself.

"Yes!" sang Olóo, Akoth, and Alex all together.

"So… I see you now in Time because," Maya said, trying to work it out for herself, "… because until the day we sat together in the hut with Mamma Nyanaam, the melody was still becoming, and the song had not yet ended…"

"Yes!" Olóo intoned again.

"…so, as long as I could hear it, even if only as echoes, then you stayed outside Time for me until the day I knew you had died."

All three, Olóo, Akoth, and Alex, nodded quietly.

"But Alex…" Maya began.

"Did not live a day, my child," said Olóo. "He has no memory of Time."

"I have no memory in Time," Alex echoed helpfully.

"But where did you go?" Maya insisted, refusing to let her twice-great-grandfather and her Mamma Akoth allow her to forget how bereft of her brother she had felt for so many years since their trip to Lisbon. "I looked everywhere for you, but you had simply vanished."

"Anyango, my child," Akoth offered, "Opolo has only really lived outside Time. He cannot tell you everything you need to understand how and why he was gone from you for so long…"

"But he lived with *me*!" she cried, indignant, impatient to know whatever it was they were taking so long to say.

"But today is a joyful day. This is a joyful night," Olóo said, echoing her earlier resistance.

"Tell me!" Maya insisted, frustrated that he could see her mind and still withhold.

Akoth looked on calmly, very much just like her father. Sitting beside her, Alex echoed her gaze and so, for a moment, Maya thought that perhaps if he truly did not know where he had been for all those years, perhaps neither one of the other two knew. And then Olóo began, speaking slowly, taking his time with the cadence of a song that sounded like Mamma Akoth's liquid chant:

Anyango, my child, listen to this memory, listen to this song. We came to the world of Time through the River that flows against the wind. We followed the waters to the eye of the River and there the Great Lake gave us a home. Lolwe, the Spirit who dwells in the Lake, offered us water and fish and fruit, taught us to sail to the Great Lake islands, to use elephant dung for our huts, and lake shore rushes and reeds for thatch. We met our neighbors from other places. Some became friends and some did not. With friends we rejoiced in weddings and births; but with those others, every fruit of the earth was a cause for war. Yet when it rained, the blessing of Heaven bestowed on us all the same bounty. In every village across the land, whether we thought we were friends or not, Lolwe, the Spirit who tends the Lake, sent all the children to play in the puddles and cover their faces with mud when it rained. And so it was, for as long as we knew, the children of friends and those of not friends all grew up playing in puddles and mud when it rained.

But then one day, not long ago, a man who was made of drought sent his spirit forth to the heart of the land of the River the flows against the wind. This man made of drought had never known the taste of rain in all his life. Some said that when he first tasted the rain that fell in the heart of the land's Great Lake — rain rich with memory and rich with song, rain that filled the earth with life — when the man made of drought tasted rain more rich than he knew to taste, he gorged himself and glutted himself because his hunger knew no depth. This man made of drought who knew only thirst was named by his father for courage and strength; Leopold they called him. But the only courage that drought knows is terror, the only strength in wreaking death.

This is a man who was raised to be king, and kings who believe they are gods, do they know the slippery, slimy clot of the coppery tang of blood? Do they know the acrid stench of bile regurgitated in fear? Perhaps. Perhaps they have a taste for it and when they cannot have it themselves, they make their subjects live their dream. The taste of the bile and the blood mixed together, it was an acquired taste, bitter, yet somehow imperative for the palate of terror and drought.

Hunger is natural and easily sated with nuts and roots and milk and fish and bitter greens and fruit. But a starving man with a taste for blood must never be called to a banquet. Instead he should have only coconut milk for days until he is strong. And then he may stomach some mash of bananas and, maybe, some bitter greens for good measure. All of this must be served with generous portions of water, but sparingly drunk; the danger of killing a starving man is keenest when he does not know how to swallow his food in natural measure like infants who learn at the teat of their mothers. The man made of drought was just such a man, starving and famished wherever he went, gorging and glutting whatever he saw. His arid soul had no memories to share. It bound and cut and sucked all the marrow of all the land and poisoned the air, and his kin came following fast behind, cutting and binding and carrying off the children of the land. Can you still hear the panting pain of the phantom limbs they severed?

347

To ensure that their sickness was not just their own, they tortured and maimed every man they could find, slashed at the women and gutted the children so terror and horror replaced the sun. When villagers rose every morning to greet the day, they found terror and horror above. These burned ever hotter the older the day, and dried every fountain of memory and song, leaving the people with one lamentation: "What can be said of the blood of a land where we who feed cry parched tears, and common joy is not even brief?"

By command of the man who was made of drought, all the people were pressed into service to bleed the trees and dig at the earth for copper and gold and diamond crystals wherever they were. The venomous mixture of blood and bile — blood from the torture and bile from the terror — it poisoned the land that was their womb and made it their grave wherever they stood. Their cries, like muted, bleating goats, could find no solace for broken hearts from which their own Spirits had fled in fright.

Lolwe, the Spirit who nurtures the Lake, no longer called children to play in the rain, for it no longer rained anymore. Everything dried up and everything died, and even Nam Lolwe shrank at the pain of the blood and the bile of the terrorized land. Time in the world of Time went on and the children who did not play in the rain grew up unknowingly made of drought. They did as the king with the bottomless hunger had done, and killed every man in sight, slashing the women and gutting the children and brewing more venom from rubber and gold. All these souls bereft of rain who suffer a biting inherited greed knew well that the well where they drank was envenomed, and yet they glutted themselves to the last. With pangas and axes they set out to slash their own women and gut their own children, as if they had never developed a memory of playing with friends in the mud and the rain. The rivers ran red with bilious rage and poison seeped into the land, and everything dried up and everything died in this land bereft of rain.

Lolwe, the Spirit who watches the Lake, and sees that the memories of the land flow into the rivers, and up to the sky, and come back as rain to enrich every *life, was crippled by those of this very land who killed and slashed and gutted their kin. For memories carry the souls of the people who lived in the world of Time for a while. They call us to you who are still in this life and let us watch over the life of the land. But when the land is choked in poison that turns all the waters the color of blood, the Spirit who watches the Lake cannot see, nor hear, nor feel, nor care. A land bereft of rain in this way will always languish in drought.*

The first to be lost to the life of the land are the children whose souls have not lived long enough to find an anchor in Time of their own without depending upon Lolwe. When all memory turns into vapor and then is carried away by the wind, but there is no rain to return it to rivers, or lakes, or soil, or mountains, the languishing souls, bereft of rain, become like that Spirit of drought that mangles and maims and chokes and starves and kills every creature because it has nothing to share.

Do you still wonder how Opolo was lost to you for so many years in Time? For one hundred days at the heart of the Lake, the soul of that foul and ravenous king passed over this land demanding a tribute in slaughter, and men of this land to the south of the Lake decided to answer the call. Lolwe, the Spirit who watches the Lake, could not console the anguish they sowed, and so for a while kept all rain at bay lest rivers or lakes, or soil, or mountains, or even the children who play in the rain, be glutted with memory of horror and pain. Without Lolwe carrying his Spirit in rain, letting him hold with your Spirit in Time, your brother Opolo, he vanished from Time. Because he had finished his Song of Becoming that first day the sun set upon his life, Opolo was carried away in the wind of drought at the end of those one hundred days.

But it is you, my child, who carried his memory in sorrow and pain in a place where dreams are safe to remain. It is you, my child, who anchored his Spirit and kept it from drifting away from your heart. You my child, begotten of dreams, summoned your young brother's quickening soul, and you my child, Walker of Dreams, kept him aware with your Song of Becoming — a song that you sang in the voice of Akoth of the light of the Sun and the memory of Rain.

Now you, Anyango, must take care to see that your children can play in the rain. You, Anyango, must see that if ever they lose their way in the desert forgetting, that you bring them rain to replenish their strength, and anchor their roots in the memory of Time. You, Anyango, you must make it rain!

"Yes, Anyango you must make it rain," Akoth said, echoing her father's words.

"Thank you, Nyangi, for making it rain," Alex said, his phantom heart beaming.

And then they all held their peace.

Canto Sixty-three

Maya came in from the garden, utterly at a loss for words. Everything Olóo had said by the fountain made her rejoice and made her wonder. Had she really drawn Alex to her even before she was born? Had she bid his phantom Spirit await her advent with a song of Becoming from beyond the world of Time? And had she summoned him back from oblivion by simply willing it so? If only she had known that she could draw him back to her with a song of will, she could have spared herself more than a decade of listless sorrow.

But there was no point in self-recrimination now. Alex had returned! That is all that mattered. That, and the enigmatic directive that she make it rain. How was she going to make it rain? How had she made it rain, exactly? And what of the beautiful babies for whom she had waited, unable to help as they and Hehra struggled and strove just to come into the world of Time. Once more, her thoughts turned to the west, to the monk who was surely since long gone from the world of Time like her twice-great-grandfather, Olóo.

She entered Hehra's room and found Esther asleep on the chair at the foot of the bed. This time, Hehra was still awake, tired, slowly thumbing through the book that Esther had brought to read.

"You're back," she said. "How was the garden?"

"It is beautiful," Maya replied. "There is a mermaid fountain just like the one at Union Saints." She giggled, and Hehra chuckled a little bit with her, the memory of childhood's happiness warming both of them.

"Maya," Hehra started, "I want to name the boys the way that Mamma Akoth and Ma Ruth named us when we were born."

Maya's face lit up even more. "Yes! I'll help. What do you need?"

"When Ma Ruth arrives tomorrow and everyone is here, will you sing the Song of Becoming for the invocation? I think you and Esther are the only ones who really know how."

Maya looked at her little sister for a moment. Tears welled up in her eyes, stinging and suddenly making her sob.

"Oh sweetie! I am so sorry!" Hehra said to her gently. "I really didn't think you would mind."

"Me? Are you sure?" Maya responded, overwhelmed, feeling silly and clearly misunderstood. "No, I mean, do you really want me to sing the invocation to name your beautiful boys?"

"Yes, you." Hehra said, smiling.

"Oh Hehra, that is the greatest honor of my life," Maya replied, sobbing and sniffing loudly, her words coming out in fitful gulps. "I can't believe it. You want me to call for the names of your children."

"Shh. It's okay, baby. Don't cry. Maya, don't cry." Hehra sounded so much like Esther just then that both of them stop for a moment, and then burst out in tearful laughter.

"Ow!" Hehra gasped, wincing and clutching her belly where the stitches held her together. "Oh, don't make me laugh. I can't. Oh…"

"I'm so sorry!" Maya blurted, trying to catch her breath, her hands darting out to hold Hehra's belly. "I'm just so happy."

The two sisters sat in silence a while looking at each other, Maya's hands over Hehra's on top of Hehra's tender belly.

"What about Esther?" Maya asked. Tradition always called for the elder members in the family to preside over rites of birth, and naming, and marriage, and even death. "She's the elder auntie, and she knows all the songs, too, maybe even better than I do. She learned them all from Mamma Akoth. Did you ask her?"

"No, I didn't. I had not even thought about the naming until she mentioned it when you were outside," Hehra replied. "She told me to think about asking you to sing for the babies. She said you should do it — that she thought you were right for it."

Again, Maya was at a loss for words. She suddenly felt the memory of snow on her fevered skin; of Esther holding her sweaters and coats, looking at her smiling in a playground in Boston; of Esther holding a cup of cold water to her lips; of Esther holding Hehra close, following the tour guide at Union Saints; of Esther holding her close at Hehra's naming invocation; of Esther naming Rosie and singing a Song of Becoming with Mamma Akoth to help the kitten bloom in grace and wisdom and strength despite Maya's resistance; of Esther holding David, even while he raged. A moment passed in silence and Maya resolved to honor both her sisters in this rite.

"Do you have names for them already?" she asked.

"No, not yet," Hehra said, hesitantly. "Sol and I never talked about this. We never had the chance."

Maya retreated a little, Hehra's unspoken distress radiating throughout the room. And then she came closer again and put both her hands on Hehra's warming cheeks.

"It's okay," she said gently.

"I wanted to ask Auntie Rebecca, you know," Hehra continued quietly, making an effort to keep her voice even, "if maybe she had some ideas, but I think it's okay if we wait and see what happens at the ceremony."

Maya reached into her satchel and pulled out a box. She handed it to Hehra. "I didn't go to the gift shop, but I brought something for the boys."

Hehra took the box and opened it slowly to remove a round, heavy object shaped like a giant pocket watch, almost the size of a desktop clock. A light spread over her face. She looked up at Maya to see the same light glowing in her sister's eyes.

"Where did you get this?" she asked, her voice hushed in wonder. "It's beautiful!"

The tiny leaf patterns on the pendant and bow disappeared into a smooth spherical knob attached to the edge of the case. The case itself was made of pierced engraved brass and tortoiseshell, inlaid with mother of pearl leaves and berries. At the center was a circle, delicately woven into the intricate curves.

"Open it," Maya said.

"Where did you get it?" Hehra repeated, holding the case in both hands. "What is it?"

She could not guess what the jeweled vessel contained. It was too big to be a pocket watch; her palms only just covered it completely. Maybe it was a small clock. Mamma Akoth did always like to say that the day a child was born was the day they began their journey in the world of Time. Maya folded her hands together and waited, contentment spreading through her. Hehra pressed the knob, and the case clicked open. She stayed a beat, staring at the thick, flattened cylinder inside, captivated, unable to speak. The mirrored lid of the jeweled case reflected the radiating arrows of the compass rose within.

Finally, she said softly, still gazing at it, "Ah, Maya Anyango, thank you."

The sisters remained silent for a while. In that moment all was well with the world. The needle hovered tremulously, pointing toward Hehra's heart.

~ ❋ ~

It took seven days to finally arrange the naming ceremony for the boys. First, the babies were released from the NICU, the doctors impressed with their robust recovery after such a trying labor of birth. It helped that they were both born at term, and neither had suffered injury during delivery. They settled with their mother in their grandparents' home in Got Ramogi, in the land of the clan of JokOwiny, a short distance from the Great Nam Ataro, on the western lake shore of its tiny sister, Lake Saré, where Aaron and Rebecca were married.

After the naming invocation, Jonathan would return to London, visiting every once in a while, he said, because the twins deserved to know their cool uncle. Esther and Maya moved in with Hehra to help Rebecca run the house, and the new grandmother was over the moon with joy to finally have women at home to balance out all the men.

Hehra's body still hurt a week on, her sutures tight and her pelvis sore. Laughing was out of the question for her, and it did not help that Maya had taken to calling the babies "The One" and "The Wonder." She did so indifferently, it seemed, or perhaps depending on which of the two was fussier or more serene at any given moment. Hehra could not even sneeze or cough without wincing in pain, and the belly binder wrapped around her middle did little to help whenever an outburst occurred. She still needed help getting into and out of the shower, or just traveling to relieve herself. Esther was always on hand to assist.

Whenever it came time to feed the boys, the ordeal that Hehra's body had suffered just made that experience more painful than she could ever have imagined. Among the bigger surprises of childbirth was just how much milk her body was making. The left-side breast was much more robust, so it quickly became a favorite when either twin was especially hungry. Whenever she gave them the right-side breast, their gummy jaws would clamp down like pincers and pull with such force that Hehra was grateful that at least "The One" and "The Wonder" still had no incisors. Even with all the growing pains, both of her babies still smelled wonderful, a smell subtle like joy that made her heart sing, a smell that sent the aunties and grandmothers into transports of pure delight.

The day of the naming invocation finally arrived. All of the living elders were there – Ma Ruth, Grandmothers Rebecca and Anna, and Grandfather Gabriel as well. Esther had called Gabriel and told him that his first grandchildren wanted to meet him. Anatole Basile Tejo, too, flew in from Paris at Maya's invitation, accompanied by his wife Marie. He stood next to Gabriel, as he had before, present to welcome the younger doctor's grandchildren born of the marriage that he himself had helped shape so many years ago.

Of Hehra's living siblings, only Esther and Maya were present. Alex, too, joined them all, standing together with Olóo and Mamma Akoth, all three accompanying Hehra at the head of the newborn children's crib. No one could see the three Spirits but Maya, nor did she know if they would choose to speak for the boys once she started the rite of naming.

Maya stood at the foot of the crib where the boys lay, on the opposite end facing Olóo, and Akoth, and Hehra. Hehra was seated, her hands caressing the heads and the shoulders of the twins, both of whom seemed quite content despite the crowd arrayed around them. Maya saw that Hehra had put the ornate compass on a shelf at the foot of the crib. She smiled to herself and then looked first at Alex and called him by his name.

"Opolo, here are the sons of your sister," she said. Alex, too, smiled and nodded, remaining silent. His phantom eyes were full of joy.

"Mamma Akoth, here are your grandson's grandsons," Maya continued. Akoth also smiled, keeping her peace.

"Olóo," Maya said, "father of us all, here are your daughter's great-grandsons."

"I remember when their mother was born," Olóo spoke up, audible only to Maya, "we did not know her when she arrived."

Maya waited, expectant. Hopeful. Would he elect to speak for the twins?

"I know of her now," Olóo continued, "I know of her father, and his father before him." His gaze did not stray from the babies, but Maya's head turned to look up at the elders gathered in the room for the ceremony of naming. Her eyes came to rest on the downward-turned face of Anatole Basile Tejo who stood beside her own father. "And his father and mother and father before," Olóo continued on, "and all of their line for twenty-two lifetimes of birth into Time and passage beyond."

Maya looked at the twins again, and then she also looked at her sister. Hehra was still caressing their heads and seemed not to notice the length of the silence since Maya's call to Olóo.

"I knew him well. He was my kin," Olóo was saying. "Tejo of the Lioness Mountains, a brother of my waking dreams."

"A man of the Word of God," Akoth said.

"A man of faith, a man of joy," Olóo continued.

"A man of the *Psalms,* and songs, and miracles."

"A man not born to our ways."

"A man who walked through the Valley of the Shadow of Death fearing no evil."

"A man who knew freedom from bondage in iron and in stone."

"A man of the cross. A man of the compass. A man of true compassion."

The voices of Olóo and Akoth interwove in counterpoint, overlapping in song. It took Maya a moment to understand that they were inviting her to continue her prayer.

"Tejo of the Lioness Mountains," she said aloud, "Frei João, hear my call."

All of the elders gathered around shifted and made a small sound together. None of them recognized the two names that Maya had just pronounced. None of them, that is, except Anatole Basile Tejo who grew very still next to Marie, daring himself not to stir, not to look at Anna Adongo who seemed not to have heard what Maya had just said. Among those assembled, he was the only one who looked up startled, surprised to hear a name that he only knew belonged to the mythical past of his family lore.

Standing next to her husband, Marie sensed his sudden stillness and reached out for him, her first instinct to make sure that he was alright. Her eyes still trained on the young new mother caressing the heads of her newborn twins, Marie's own hand was moving to hold her husband's when suddenly it stopped. Hehra's hand was curved just so, the shape of the hand of Marie's youngest son, the shape of the hand of her last grandchild. It was the shape of the hand of her husband who stood frozen by her side. Thirty years it had been since Anatole Basile returned to Sherbro Island to dedicate the hospital fund in his mother's name, and a library in his father's memory. Thirty years had come and gone and even though it had been his dream, the first he had ever shared with her, he had said nothing of it when he returned. All he had said when she told him that Anna Adongo had come looking for him was that by the time Marie's letter arrived in Bonthe, the young lady had found him.

"Here are the sons of your children's sons," Maya was saying, "Tejo of the Lioness Mountains." With bated breath, she waited, hoping that the song she was hearing was the Song of Becoming that she was supposed to sing. Esther would know, wouldn't she?

Maya's eyes turned to look for Esther, searching but briefly before they caught sight of her older sister who had always been a mother to them all — the Union Saints Ocholas — the storyteller of their lives. Esther would know, indeed, and she did not look worried at all. So Maya let herself relax, and then waited to see if her call would be answered.

It was true that Frei João de Sousa was not of their land and he had not been born to their ways. Even as Tejo of the Lioness Mountains, though father to lines that branched forth from the glade at the heart of the mountains where he had found the House of the Lord, the erstwhile monk had never stepped foot in the lands of the Lake at the eye of the Great River Nile. Maya had tried to reach his Spirit on the night when the twins were born. She still remembered the day on the mountain clearing when he told her that she would await the birth of children who would learn from her. She also remembered well the promise she made to pass the compass he gave her to his descendants when the time came. She knew that all this would come to pass, but still it held the thrill of discovery. What she did not know was whether he had heard her call into the world outside Time to his Spirit on behalf of the newborn twins, and on behalf of Hehra. But she need not have worried. His voice, clear as a song, filled the silence of the room when he finally spoke.

"Do you have the instrument I gave you?" Tejo of the Lioness Mountains said, his voice the sound of peace. He looked just like she remembered him, browned, and bent, and wiry, with bright, deep-set eyes, his fingers still playing with phantom rosary beads.

"Yes, but I gave it to Hehra," Maya replied only to his hearing, "your children's daughter, and now, mother to both of the boys whom we gather to name today."

"Then you have done just as I asked," continued Tejo of the Lioness Mountains. "May it always keep them true, away from death and the bondage of iron and stone, away from rage and boundless hunger, and from the whips and swords of the land of my birth."

"Who may I call to name them?" Maya asked, speaking aloud once again so that everyone present might hear. All who were gathered wondered too, because the surprise of calling a stranger who bore the name of Gabriel's mentor had left them all a little bewildered.

Both Tejo and Olóo spoke to Maya's hearing at once. "Call on their father," they said, "he will name the sons of his children's mother." And then they both fell silent.

Maya looked at Hehra and held her peace for a moment. Finally, she spoke again, her eyes fixed on her baby sister, holding close the gaze that was also now fixed upon hers. Hehra seemed to know that the moment had come when the one voice whose silence she felt most keenly would speak, yet she would not even hear it.

"Ogot," Maya said slowly and clearly, her voice even more a song than it had ever been before, "Ogot, here before you are the sons of your children's mother."

Hehra kept her composure, yet tears hot and sharp still pricked her searching eyes. She tried to deepen her silence to that place where she might maybe hear that most wanted voice. Holding Maya in her eyes she began to see that whatever her sister was hearing now remained only silence to everyone else who was gathered around.

"Anyango Maya," the voice of the Spirit of Solomon Ogot, soft, yet also clear as song, spoke first before his form appeared to Maya's eyes. "These are the sons of my children's mother." And then he stood before her.

"These are the sons of your children's mother," Maya echoed reflexively. The song that was hoping to be sung had now sounded its opening strains.

Solomon spoke the names he had chosen for his and Hehra's sons: both would carry their father's own, following the current custom; they each would also bear the story of their mother's father. Theirs would be the rising Sun, and the beating heart of the blessed land, and the kingdom of the Seas that covers all the Earth. As he spoke, Maya reached down for the compass. Holding it up in both her hands, she closed her eyes listening, just as she had listened to Olóo. And so the voices of Olóo and Solomon Ogot and Tejo of the Lioness Mountains all rose up in Maya's heart to sing the Song of Becoming for The One and The Wonder.

"These are the songs where we come from, these are the songs we become," she began. "In Sierra Leone, where Hehra was born, there lived a man a long time ago. This man traveled across the world from Portugal to India and stopped along the way for a short while in Mombasa. After he started his journey back, his legend grew across the seas. He was known as a miracle worker, a man of faith and wisdom, a man of great compassion, a man who inspired admiration across the seas of half the world."

All who were gathered listened closely and quietly to the song that Maya was singing. After the silences when they could not hear the exchanges between her and the Spirits, they welcomed the liquid timbre of the voices that played with Maya's own. The Song of Becoming that Maya sang welcomed the twins into kinship with Tejo of the Lioness Mountains and the clan of JokOmolo whence their mother's twinning heritage had laid the path for their coming. Maya continued by invoking the Dream Walkers of JokOlóo, saving the place of honor for JokOwiny, the children's father's people, the first to emerge from the River Nile to settle the shores of Nam Lolwe.

"This old man came to live in Sierra Leone and did not return to Portugal. When he had lived a long, long life he welcomed a sister of his waking dreams who lived in the land of Nam Ataro. To this sister he entrusted an instrument that drew its truth from the heart of the Earth. For in time immemorial, long before Iberians took to the sea, a Wandering Walker of Dreams, who lived near the turbulent cape at the end of the Great Land of the Nile, told her mother of troubling dreams that plagued her, asleep or awake."

"One day, she said, men carrying war to lands across the seas of the world, the name of God on their lips, the cold and ice of their native lands held hard in their hearts, these men would come rounding the cape, seeking the way to salvation by foisting dominion on all of the peoples in all of the lands in all the world. They would believe that they had to *invade, capture, vanquish and subdue,* and reduce every person to bondage and take from their heart and their home every hope, and only that way would their kingdom come."

"But the Wandering Walker, believing that she could save all the lands from the pillaging sailors who boasted the mandate of pontiffs and kings in the name of God and Gold, set out to find a sign in her visions to send through the ages intact in Time. It could not need breath but had to be able to give all the guidance that guidance could give. And so, the Wandering Walker walked many moons to the very end of the world, to the Cape where the Needles all pointed North, and the pulse of the land hammered true. There, she entered the caverns that opened to sea, and deep from the heart of the Earth, from its veins, drew out a morsel of iron and copper and zinc, and then returned to the open air above. And when she emerged, she found that all the sentinels of the sea had gathered in those ocean waters to help guide her hand."

"As far as the eye could see, countless dolphins played in the sea, speeding and jumping and spiraling over and under a pod of whales around the cape, surfacing every so often to blow out air from their giant lungs, turning and twirling and flipping their tails, holding close to the seashore caves. The Wandering Walker soon set to work and mixed the ores that she had drawn from the veins of the Earth. She told her mother in later days that the heat from the breath of the circling whales made the metals soft to her touch. She shaped the plate and shaped the needle and used the spine of sea urchins to carve the stories of wind and sea and whales and sails on the shining brass. And then she molded and sharpened the iron pointer whose pulse was true to the pulse of the Earth, and this she placed on the carved brass plate, and made this compass you now behold. It would always direct the traveler's way, showing the searching wanderer where to seek the path to salvation."

Maya's song of invocation now drew to a close: "These are the songs where we come from, these are the songs we become."

Both the babies had fallen asleep, lulled by the touch of their mother's hand. Maya placed the compass in the crib between the two infants, and then she lifted her voice to finally speak their names.

"Anatole Tejo Ochïeng Ogot," Maya said to the babies, "and Basile Tejo Otïeno Ogot, this is your mother, Hehra Akoth. Receive the names of your fathers from the guardian Spirits of Solomon Ogot, and Tejo of the Lioness Mountains."

Hehra, and all who were present, took in the names that Maya pronounced. Nobody noticed the look that washed over Anna Adongo's face. Nobody noticed the arrested hand that Marie Madeleine Clémence d'Harcourt-Lévêque withdrew, denying her husband her touch. Nobody noticed the effort it took Anatole Basile Tejo to keep his head from sinking, nor his heart from rising.

The room began to resonate as one by one by one by one the voices of the Spirits rose to echo the children's Song of Becoming. The iron needle on the compass rose hovered between the babies, first pointing at the heart of The Wonder, and then at the head of The One, then pointing at the head of The Wonder, and then at the heart of The One.

Atho tinda!

~~~~~~~~~~~~

"Adong' adong', arom gi bawo maka nera."

Acknowledgments

Afterword

Dear Reader, when I first set pen to paper to write the story of *Rain*, I took it for granted that the completed text would take the form of a novel. However, I never nurtured aspirations of becoming a novelist, or a writer of any kind really; the uncomplicated joy of reading to my heart's content was always enough for me, and the treasure trove of written matter around me gloriously abundant. I started composing *Rain* for the simple reason that I wanted to commit to written record the voices of storytellers of yore who could breathe song into lives and worlds with seamless ease. I wrote as one transcribing the words of a song once upon a time beloved, but now fading in waning memory. The song I heard and tried to write down was itself a meditation on History examined through the lens of Oral Tradition. I found, in listening to this meditation, repeated invitations to unwind from quotidian tensions, to attend more closely to the beauty of the moment with deeper reverence. The turns my pen took as if by intuition traced a journey through living memory unbound from the shackles of time, and I finally understood that the book I was writing was just the kind of song I had heard growing up.

Like many songs, the voice that sings and holds the principal melody in *Rain* is joined by other voices, sometimes in harmony and consonance, sometimes in contrapuntal play, and sometimes in jarring dissonance. This principal voice, I realized quickly, was that of my own great-grandmother, Rebecca Apiyo Nyonditi Nyariba Atiga ng'ute bor Nyodongo, the matriarch whom we all simply called "Ruba." Ruba's name, all by itself, already told the story of her own journey through life from birth, to marriage and motherhood, to maturity: she bore the name of the first of twins (Apiyo), the daughter of Onditi (Nyonditi), born of the River (Nyariba), a graceful pearl (Atiga ng'ute bor), and descendant of Odongo (Nyodongo). Even her Christian name, Rebecca, bore witness to the matriarch she eventually became. Throughout my childhood, Ruba breathed life into the memory of generations through song. She sang histories and poetry, allegories, and parables, and her songs recounted stories of creation, of heroes, of retribution, of justice. Her voice closely guided my quill and continues to resound in my ear still.

I cannot say whether any single notion or event can account for the growing prominence of Ruba's voice in my imagination as I grew up and grew older. But I remember, for example, how when I applied for graduate school, it was her voice that echoed through the Statement of Purpose I submitted. The admissions committee later told me that it was that voice that inspired them to invite me to the program of my choice. *Rain* is a testament to the continued guiding strength of that voice.

And each of the multitude voices and stories flowing into *Rain* is a vital tributary to a dynamic polyphony that explores and illuminates the conflict between sanitized histories of colonialist aggression and the unvarnished accounts of their savagery. It will not surprise readers familiar with the voice of Dante Alighieri's *Commedia* that the Great Poet's most important animating influence in *Rain* is the way it emboldens this story to draw back the veil of recorded History and bear witness, with an unflinching and conscientious gaze, to the brutality of the agents of colonial dominion — figures celebrated for the Age of Discovery whose incursions wreaked unconscionable horrors on peoples around the world for Coin in the name of Church and Crown and set the precedent for presumptuous appropriations like the Scramble for Africa centuries later. The poetic voice of Dante *artifex* also permeates the comprehensive structure of *Rain*, from its general architecture to the network of internal memory manifest in the story's narrative refrains, as well as the musical rhythm and flow of the storyteller's language. The most dulcet tones of Dante's voice resonate deeply in the contemplative strains of *Rain* devoted to singing the unspoiled beauty of Nature in the bounty of Africa's expansive savanna grasslands, gleaming equatorial mountain glaciers, opulent Rift Valley, cascading waters and wending rivers, and shimmering Great Lakes.

Other familiar voices that resonate throughout *Rain* — thanks to Ruba's uncomplicated faith, and thanks to the instruction of teachers from earliest childhood — include Bible verses that saturate the popular imagination of the world of the story's protagonists. Many of these verses are quoted in the text from a number of different translations of the Old and New Testament. The four Bible voices in *Rain* include:

- The *Vulgate Latin Bible* translated by St. Jerome.
- A Portuguese translation of the Gospels and Epistles of the New Testament published in Porto in 1497 based on an earlier Spanish translation of the Bible by Gonçalo Garcia de Santa Maria: Guilherme Parisiense, *Evangelhos e Epístolas com suas Exposições em Romance*, translated to Portuguese by Rodrigo Álvares. Although Martin Luther's translation of the Bible to the German language enjoys greater renown for making the Scripture more readily accessible in the vernacular, it is all the more fascinating to see in the evidence of these Spanish and Portuguese translations that Luther was not the first, but rather part of a practice that extended over several decades, if not centuries, before his German

translations appeared. The significance of this Portuguese voice in *Rain* resides in the fact that it serves as witness to the availability of Scripture to the literate speakers of the language from at least the middle of the 15th Century when Pope Nicolas V issued the Papal Bulls *Dum Diversas* and *Romanus Pontifex*, both of which figure significantly in the polyphony of *Rain*.

- The third Biblical voice with deep resonance in *Rain* includes the English translation commissioned by James Charles Stuart, King of Great Britain and Ireland, published in 1611 — less than a century after the first translation of the New Testament into English by William Tyndale appeared in 1526. The influence of the *Authorized King James Version* extends beyond the liturgy of the Protestant Church and into the linguistic timbre and rhythm of literature for the centuries that followed its publication, integrating seamlessly into English-speakers conception of Scripture and the voice of God.

- The forth Biblical voice in *Rain* rises from its more recent translation into the Luo language, *Muma Maler*, published by the Bible Society of Kenya and the Bible Society of Tanzania in 1976. Like other translations in local languages of East Africa and beyond, this translation is a testament to the evangelical vigor and success of the Christian missionaries that served as the velvet glove over the iron fist of the colonial enterprise.

Less nuanced and unabashedly ruthless are the voices of Popes in Rome who mandated brutal aggression against Peoples across the world in the name of God and the Catholic Church for the glory and legitimacy of the Crowns of Portugal and Spain in the 15th Century.

Several readers of *Rain* have noticed the obtrusive violence of these voices in contrast to the story's natural flow. Their incursion takes the form of the ritualistic refrain of passages from a series of Papal Bulls issued by Pope Nicolas V (1447-1455) and Pope Alexander VI (1492-1502) authorizing and encouraging the Portuguese and the Spanish monarchs to encroach upon and take for themselves the riches of the Peoples in those parts of the world from which the Iberian agents of colonial dominion wanted to wrest profit.

- The Papal Bull *Dum Diversas* — issued to Dom Afonso, King of Portugal, on 18 June 1452 — emboldened the crown's already robust maritime ambition to map a trade route to India to further press their efforts with the zeal of Crusaders. In authorizing Afonso V of Portugal to reduce any "Saracens and pagans and any other unbelievers" to perpetual slavery, Pope Nicolas V established the legal and moral authority for the campaign of terror that European slavers and colonialists unleashed, unchecked, upon the Peoples of the world that they subsequently assailed.

- On 8 January 1454, Pope Nicolas V's Bull, *Romanus Pontifex,* reaffirmed the Catholic Church's mandate to lay claim on the homes and resources of the Peoples that the agents of the Portuguese Crown beset, repeating the call to exploit and enslave their persons wherever they lived. With this reiteration of the tenets of the previous Bull *Dum Diversas,* *Romanus Pontifex* extended the presumption to dominion over the lands of others to the Catholic nations of Europe during the Age of Discovery.

- Before the century's end, on 4 May 1493, Pope Alexander VI again affirmed the aforementioned mandates in the Papal Bull *Inter Caetera,* making sure to state that Christian nations were exempt from being subjected to dominion by other Christian nations.

Awakening to the brutality hidden behind the veil of bowdlerized History also draws attention to the silences of those poets who wielded their craft in service to glorifying agents of colonial aggression and whitewashing the campaigns of terror and obliteration that these putative heroes carried out around the world. *Rain* owes a debt of gratitude to those chroniclers among Vasco da Gama's contemporaries and travel companions, like João Figueira, who recorded accounts of da Gama's three voyages around the coast of Africa to India and back. Among the historians of the early 1500s who wrote and published details about the ships and crew of Vasco da Gama's voyages, timelines and related documents, the most revealing voices in *Rain* include those of:

- Gaspar Corrêa's *Lendas da Índia (*1550-1566), available in English translation as *The Three Voyages of Vasco da Gama, and His Viceroyalty, from the Lendas Da India of G. Correa. Accompanied by Original Documents.* Translated by Henry E. J. Stanley. London, 1869.

- Renowned historian João de Barros, author of *Décadas de Asia* (1552), and sourced through *Da Asia de João de Barros e de Diogo de Couto*, vol. 2. Regia Officina Typografica, 1777.

- The highly regarded and widely translated historian Fernão Lopez de Castaneda, author of *História do descobrimento e conquista da Índia pelos portugueses* (1551), which is available in English translation in *The First Booke of the Historie of the Discouerie and Conquest of the East Indias, Enterprised by the Portingales, in their Daungerous Nauigations, in the Time Of King Don Iohn, The Second of that Name*, translated by Nicholas Lichefield (1582).

- Alvaro Velho and João de Sá, *A Journal of the First Voyage of Vasco da Gama, 1497-1499*, translated by E. G. Ravenstein.

Together, the voices of these chroniclers and historians — whose works drew upon first-hand accounts and contemporary documents pertinent to Vasco da Gama's voyages — add an illuminating note to the willful silences of paradoxically panegyric myth-making in the face of empirical accounts. And few examples of this willful myth-making are as roundly celebrated as *Os Lusíadas*, the epic poem immortalizing Vasco da Gama as the greatest son of Portugal, written by Luís Vaz de Camões.

Despite the acrid taste of History's reality, the song of *Rain* is sustained by the resilience of deeply rooted cultural traditions that persist to this day, even if only in the fading echoes of forgotten songs.

And so, I invite you, kind reader, to listen with a benevolent ear and an open heart to the poetic meditation on History that resounds through the voice of Oral Tradition, and to discern the truth born of allegory in *Rain – A Song for All and None*.

~~~~~~

A Moment of Gratitude

I want to start by thanking my indefatigable mother, Beldina Auma, for her unwavering support of *Rain*. They say a mother's pride has no measure, and my own mother embodies this so thoroughly that it continually opens my eyes to new wonders.

My sister Grace Ajode Jibril — who best exemplifies her very name — and my brother-in-law, Yisa Jibril, two dedicated patrons of the arts who contributed enormously to making this volume possible, have my everlasting gratitude for letting me find the peace of mind to finish *Rain* in the shelter of their beautiful home and the company of their brilliant, beloved children, Aminatu and Saidu. Nor would I have resolved to complete this work after so many years of hiatus and distraction had my sister Tania Magoon not been the clear voice of purpose who never tired of spurring me on to make it *Rain*. For my family, especially my siblings, I offer the completion of this work as my heartfelt song of gratitude.

The family to which each of us is born has the potential to become all the richer for all the other families that we discover along the way. I owe an incalculable and irresolvable debt to Dorothy Kim, a fellow scholar of Medieval Literature who became for me, as she has for countless others, a guardian angel of agency. My heart overflows every time I think of the natural insouciance with which Dorothy enabled me to stand on my strengths. Thank you, with all my heart. I also wish to express my deepest gratitude to Mary Rambaran-Olm, who — I am certain — came into the world express to inspire and embolden every soul to embrace the unvarnished truth and speak without fear in the name of Justice.

When an elephant births a new calf, all of the cows of the herd gather in a circle around until the calf can stand on its own. I thank you, my sister, Tegla Kibor, for being first reader of *Rain* to ask those sincere and important questions about our understanding of the meaning of our histories. I thank you, my sister, Margarethe Matere Green, for listening, immersed, to every phrase and every word of *Rain*, and then coming back impatient for more! I thank you, my sister, Cecilia Rague-Kaisha, for listening and reading, patient and sober, to everything the story has to offer. I thank you, my sister, Caroline Rono, for so many beautiful stories of everyday life in that place where we all come together. I thank you, my brother, Andrew Muge, a man with no tolerance for nonsense who will always keep us all on our toes. I thank you, my brother, Rodney Enane, who, by *fiat*, made it imperative that I finish writing *Rain*. I thank you, my brother, Leonard Khafafa, a man of faith and Letters who extols the virtues and decries the vices that rise up in our land. To you, my brothers and sisters, I offer my humble, lifelong gratitude.

I offer sincere gratitude to my 언니 in Letters and Spirit, Yvonne Adhiambo Owuor: yours is a place of honor graced in the light of beauty and truth together with all the poets who illuminate the way for us who follow the paths that you all have mapped before us.

Thank you every one.

—Adoyo, *Rain.* MMXX

~~~~~~~~~~~~~

The Story

Rain tells the story of the Dream Walker Maya, an empathic clairvoyant who experiences history through the eyes of other Dream Walkers across time.

Born into a world that no longer has a place for her kind, Maya strives to find her bearings as she is swept up in the thousand-year saga of the devastatingly insidious legacies of colonizing empires that continue to ravage her home. Under the guidance of ancestral Spirits, the young Dream Walker braves uncharted waters where she discovers illuminating truths concealed behind the veil of History's public myths.

Maya's quest unites her across the centuries with ancestral Dream Walkers who will teach her to understand the power of her gifts, and Maya learns to fulfill her destiny as a visionary steward of both the Past and the Future in an ever-changing world.

A poetic meditation on History through the echoes of Oral Tradition, *Rain* recalls the song of storytellers born on the shores of the Great Lake Nam Lolwe at the eye of the Nile in the heart of East Africa.

Key words: speculative historical fiction; visionary; metaphysical; folklore; mythology; African Literature; Luo; Great Lake; Nam Lolwe; Rift Valley; East Africa; River Nile; Mombasa; Age of Discovery; colonial empires; Dante; Commedia

The Storyteller

ADOYO is a storyteller, musician and artist who finds happiness when drawing, playing the piano, and listening to stories.

Born and raised in Kenya, Adoyo attended Hill School in Eldoret (Rift Valley) and Alliance Girls High School in Kikuyu (Central Province). Her education in music composition and literary scholarship continued as an undergraduate at the University of California, Davis where she studied Music and Italian Literature. She then completed a Masters and a PhD in Romance Languages and Literatures at Harvard University in Massachusetts.

Adoyo teaches Medieval literature of the Romance Languages and lectures on Dante's poetics. Her next book, *Dante Decrypted : The Order of All Things*, is a work of literary scholarship based on her doctoral dissertation about Dante Alighieri's musical design for the textual architecture of his masterpiece, the *Commedia*.

Contact the author via email

adoyo@zamanichronicles.org

CPSIA information can be obtained
at www.ICGtesting.com
Printed in the USA
LVHW032219240222
711932LV00004B/715